David L. McDaniel

The Warrior's Bane

War for the Quarterstar Shards

Book One

Black Rose Writing | Texas

ISBN: 978-1-68433-114-7
PUBLISHED BY BLACK ROSE WRITING
www.blackrosewriting.com

Printed in the United States of America
Suggested Retail Price (SRP) $20.95

The Warrior's Bane is printed in Andalus

To my wife and family for putting up with my occasional disconnect from the real world. I thank my children for reminding me that the story is what is most important. I thank my mom for reading to me at a young age, catching my creativity on fire, and for teaching me that no story is good unless your villain is an active part of the story. The better the villain, the better the story. I miss you mom and I hope Fyaa is a witch you would've loved. For Eve Hall for believing in me.

magic within him to scare away the adults when they came bringing their crude weapons, taunts and fear.

"Oh wise one!" one of the boys shouted in reverence. Of all the children, only this boy had been at every meeting. The old man suspected that this boy was in charge of deciding who would be allowed to see him and who would not.

"I have a new group to hear your tale," the boy announced as he bowed in reverence. "Please tell us of the Kronn Man."

"You know the rules then," the old man said as he stooped to take a seat on his rock. The boy heard his aged bones creak, and the old man grimaced in pain as he sat.

"We must recite the seasons of old," the boy announced.

The boy looked at his four companions and nodded and they then began to recite in unison an ancient poem.

"The age of the Quarterstar contained five seasons:

Trilea, the season of growth: where new life begins aplenty.

Flamespan, the season of heat: time of festivals and life.

Doreal, the season of harvest: time to reap the season's bounty.

Ethinar, the season of frost: if one is not prepared, it is a time of strife.

And the Markenhirth Grimshaed, the necessary season of frozen darkness."

When they said the word darkness, they all made deep grim sounds with their voices.

"Then it begins anew by bringing in the New Trilea: where all are full of happiness," they finished.

"Very good!" the old man said as he clapped, and he began to weave his tale with vivid animation as he spoke by moving his arms about as if he were not an old man, but a young man in his twenties.

With a voice no longer frail, but strong and full of clarity, he began to tell his tale:

"Dark storm clouds tumbled over each other as they raced across the sky and caused the wind to sway wildly the leafless and dormant Sippling Tree. The small willowy tree began to whip its skinny branches like spidery appendages making a web as the power held within its roots harnessed the magic of the realm and therefore was the magical center of Wrae-Kronn.

It controlled the flow of magic as it sat alone atop a large snowy cluster of granite rocks. The tree looked as if it had been embedded into the rock purposely without any soil, to make it impossible for it to survive, let alone grow. Yet somehow, survive and grow it did. In fact, it thrived as it protruded from the frozen mountain face and reached up into a lightless dark sky.

This tree grew in spite of its natural conditions and it controlled the seasons of the world through its magical roots that were like living veins within the rock below it. At this place, below the tree, a river began its journey. This river, for most of the year, began its journey here and, churning with white foamy water, rushed out from the lowest point of the rocky mountain face. However, for fourteen days during the Markenhirth Grimshaed, the river froze over and remained frozen and crystalline.

The tree had grown here since the beginning of time. Some say a man sprouted from this tree, a soulless man, not only looking for his soul, but for his very being. This same man, some believed to be known as the god of the humans while others believed him actually to be Kronn himself, the keeper of the realm. However, if he truly were Kronn, how could someone so powerful lose his being, for wouldn't he be more powerful than the elven gods who created this world?

He had wandered the realm like an empty soul. He wandered the realm regardless of the season, naked and hairless, a man with pale white skin and dark eyes searching for something, something no one else ever knew, but could only guess.

He wandered the land for many years. He even returned to the tree and tried many times to destroy it, but to no avail. No one knew why he tried to destroy the tree. It was a crucial element to the five seasons of the land. Many believed that he tried to do so because without the tree, the realm would die. Others believed that he himself was the reason for the fifth season, the Markenhirth Grimshaed, the season that only lasted fourteen days, fourteen days when all of Wrae-Kronn became a frozen wasteland that sent the tree into hibernation.

Then one day, many, many years ago, the man merely disappeared and left the land and the tree to do what came naturally.

For many, many years thereafter, all the seasons completed their cycle naturally, but one day the Sippling Tree went into its hibernation period and did not awake for an extended time, fifteen days, not fourteen. The wraith-like agents of the frozen underworld, called grimshadows, roamed the land during that time and took advantage of the weakness of the Sippling Tree. They celebrated their brief freedom by ravaging the land and taking back what was once theirs.

Twenty-nine days after the Sippling Tree went into its dormant stage, it came back to life and summoned the grimshadows to return to their frozen wasteland. When all the grimshadows had returned, the Sippling Tree closed the opening at the Markenhirth Mountains and allowed the warming temperatures of Wrae-Kronn to intercede with their natural processes.

However, the damage to the magic within the land had already been done on that fifteenth day."

The old man paused from his tale to make sure his audience was still with him. The four new children looked upon him with wide eyes of wonder, not only because of the words of the tale, but from the manner in which he told it. The fifth boy, whom had heard the tale many times, only smiled at his peers, as if to say, "Did I not tell you it would be more than what you expected?"

Satisfied with the reaction of his audience, the old man began anew.

"The Markenhirth extension caused a few events to materialize which were not only prophesied, but which all feared would soon come to pass and show themselves as a signature of troubled times to come. The first and most notable of these events was the temporary opening of the Aaestfallia Keep, as the humans had renamed the Time Keep, a stone tower that when in the hands of the elves was a magical gate they used as a door to other worlds or other ages within the Known Lands."

The old man stopped talking again. He looked to the sky for a time and the children looked to the sky as well, but saw nothing. He looked out of the corner of his eye, waited for the right moment, and then looked directly at them again.

"You will learn about all of that in good time," the old man said baiting them, "but first you must learn about how the realm was invaded and terrorized by a wicked fire loving sorceress."

The children gasped, "A Fire Sorceress?"
And he knew they were hooked…

Markenhirth

Year 0889 Ten days into the Markenhirth extension

A single, thirty-foot stone tower stood in front of a massive snowdrift amidst the icy and frozen landscape. Massive pine trees stood around it as if they were frozen giants with long white cloaks guarding it from escaping its domain. The limbs of the pine trees wilted from the heavy snow and weighed them down, making them look as if they were beginning to tire from their age-old sentry duty.

A large ice wall surrounded the outer perimeter of the tower and exposed it in the center of ice-hardened rocky ground that was completely void of snow. The frozen rocky dirt remained exposed as if it had been constantly swept clean to keep any snow from collecting there. A simple outer stone wall also surrounded the tower to keep others from accidentally wandering too close.

For years men guarded the tower, but they did nothing to keep the snow off it. No snow ever touched it. Somehow the wind always blew the snow in different directions, never touching the tower or the soil around it. Plain and simple, without windows or battlements, the tower was made only of dark gray stones stacked one on top of one another and rising as a circular structure that reached thirty feet in height.

The elves called it the Aaestfallia Keep, but the humans just called it the Time Keep because it was nothing more than a portal with unknown magical properties. The only entrance was a solid stone door that had been sealed shut by the elves many years earlier when they left their northern homeland to build a new kingdom on the western reaches of Wrae-Kronn at Lake Quarterstar. The elves had removed the Triestones, the magical element of the Keep, rendering it a dormant shell of a magical portal. The humans made a promise to the elves to keep it closed in order to protect them from the possibility of the magic somehow activating without the Triestones.

It seemed conceivable to them that the magic could be reactivated by an outside source.

***

"Garge? Where are you, Garge?" Detch called out as he walked noisily towards the Time Keep where his fellow warrior was standing guard.

As Garge heard his relief approaching, his feet crunching on the frozen snow, he looked up and saw Detch's head was slumped down to keep his hood over his face in an attempt to keep the snow flurries from stinging his skin. He looked up into the crisp frozen air once, only to verify his location, and saw Garge standing in front of the tower waiting eagerly to be relieved of his position.

"I hate guarding this ancient artifact," Garge said to Detch when he was close enough to speak. Detch shook his head.

"At least we're not fighting off the dragons like they are down in the Moonshaed Kingdom. For that matter if the Markenhirth Grimshaed doesn't go away soon, the grimshadows are all going to get us any way, so I guess we might as well be fighting the dragons. Either way we die fighting."

Garge's eyes widened a little, but then he closed them tightly for the cold air had burned his eyes as he did so.

"Bring them on!" he said. "That is the kind of excitement I want. Dragons, grimshadows, I don't care. I want to live as a warrior and die like a hero!"

Detch offered the ceremonious salute, but Garge was too cold for drill and ceremony. He simply gave Detch a half hearted smile before he headed back to the guard shack to report to the Guard of Arms, warm up in his bunk and then wait for his turn for guard duty again. It gave him great relief that he had three more shifts of four hours apiece before he would be required again to stand in the cold and hope no Grimshadows would have confronted him during his guard duty.

Garge approached a small stone building that extended out of the ground. The small door on top was only a wooden latch that allowed entrance to their guard shack, a tower that descended underground below it.

He knocked on the small wooden door and waited only a few seconds to hear a voice from inside.

"Who knocks?"

"Private Garge," Garge said in an impatient, but professional tone, before he gave the password. "Broken Axe."

"Enter," the voice said from behind the door.

Garge bent down, opened the door, and squatted without touching his knees to the ice hardened ground. He turned around and backed his way inside to climb down the wooden rope to the center of the room. The room was only a small circle, big enough for two people to sit comfortably, but Sergeant Tremm sat at the far end of the room at the table next to the fire. A massive iron door loomed ominously next to Sergeant Tremm's desk. It would only be used in case of an attack, or in an emergency, when all of the warriors would exit through it and go up a steep flight of stairs to defend their tower. All of Tremm's clothes and belongings cluttered the area, including his weapon and his shield, which hung on the iron door. Garge had to walk around everything and be careful not to step on anything in order to reach the trap door at the center of the room.

"Welcome back, Garge," Sergeant Tremm said pleasantly.

"Thanks. I'm going to get some sleep."

Sergeant Tremm watched Garge climb down into the lower room where he and his three other guard mates slept. He would give Garge a few minutes to get himself settled in and then he would go down there, make a check on the fire and see that Garge had secured all of his weapons and personal belongings. If he caught one soldier without their sword tucked neatly in their scabbard by their side, they would all have hell to pay. He liked being kind to his men, but he did not tolerate sloppiness.

Meanwhile, Detch stood his watch next to the keep and felt the frigid cold biting at his face. He looked at the tower with disgust. He, like Garge, hated this type of duty. He wasn't the greatest, nor the most motivated soldier there was, but he did like to be useful with his time, and this was not one of the things that he considered useful. Plus, he hated the cold.

Detch looked up toward the sky and made sure there were no grimshadows flying or scurrying about. So far it seemed it would be a calm day. Or was it nighttime? It was not easy to tell with any degree of certainty when it was day or night during the season of the Markenhirth Grimshaed. Regardless, he took a torch off the mantle on the wall and carried it with him as he walked the perimeter, not only so that he could see, but because it also made him feel a little more secure holding the light and heat source near his face.

Detch looked back down at the cold hard snow and hoped that the rumors about the Markenhirth Grimshaed never ending were not true. They better be false, he thought as he shivered from the cold harsh wind. He turned around and began to retrace his path around the Time Keep. The wind had begun to pick up and he wanted to walk around to the other side of the Keep to keep out of its frozen grip. He looked down and saw his sword and scabbard dangling at his side.

"What a joke," he said to himself, realizing that if something were to happen, he couldn't defend himself. He had so many layers of clothes underneath his oversized parka that he had nowhere near enough flexibility to even begin to think about drawing his sword, much less fight with it.

He was still deep in frustrated thought when he heard a loud crackling noise coming from within the Time Keep. It sounded as if there were a raging campfire crackling within, but he knew that to be impossible. The Time Keep was made from stone, and it was far too cold.

He knew something was amiss and he backed away from the tower just before a flash of bright light along with a deafening explosion came from within the tower. Chunks of stone flew into the sky and scattered back down into the snow as they dropped to the ground with dull thuds and disappeared into the snowdrifts.

In an instant, it was dark again.

Detch stumbled blindly to the front of the Time Keep to see what had happened. When he rounded the side, he saw a woman lying face down in the snow. She had no clothes on, and her skin looked to be slightly on fire, as if all the little hairs on her body each contained a single flame.

Slowly he walked towards her with his torch in front of him and looked at her body. Even in shadowy torchlight he was able to see dark blood dripping from her head into the snow.

Before he could reach her, he heard the crackling noise again. Knowing that something else was coming, he backed off safely behind the first pillar at the gate of the outside wall. He saw Sergeant Tremm followed by Garge and two of his other platoon members running across the snow toward him from their guard shack. They had their swords drawn and their shields on their arms, but held down by their sides and were running toward him as fast as their bulky parkas would allow.

Detch yelled and tried to warn them that something was coming, but his voice was drowned out by the loud pop from within Time Keep. Sergeant Tremm and his men fell to their knees and squinted their eyes from the bright light and felt ringing pain in their ears from the thunderous noise.

Detch was the first to see them coming out of the tower. Men with wings, huge men, and twice the size of the average person. Three in total. They had no clothes, and their muscles were perfectly defined and bulging beneath their skin. Their wings were on fire as they flew towards Sergeant Tremm and his men.

He saw the first one land on top of Sergeant Tremm's shoulders and unhinge its mouth to an unreal enormous size. With incredible speed, the huge man covered the sergeant's whole head with his mouth and ripped it off with his long sharp teeth. The beast spit out the severed head and curled back his lips to reveal his fanged smile. Teeth extended from his mouth as far as the length of a dagger and spread apart in such large gaps that even when his mouth was closed, fire could still be seen from behind, highlighting them with a ghostly red glow.

Detch's mates did not have a chance to run. The three naked winged men attacked the guards as if butchering the humans was their sole purpose for invading their realm. The creatures shredded their bodies into pieces from head to toe. They did not eat their kill, but they laughed as they wildly threw the bloody flesh and bones into the snow.

Detch managed to escape unnoticed and watched the gruesome attack from behind one of the nearby pine trees.

When there was nothing left of any of the bodies to tear apart, the creatures stopped and scanned the area. They saw blood and body parts littered across the hard, icy snow and they seemed content until they saw the woman lying in the snow, unconscious. They screamed so loudly then that Detch had to hold his ears with the excruciating pain of their noise.

Without delay they took to the sky and flew off to the south. Detch watched as their wings, now fully aflame, lit up the dark sky and left a dark trail of smoke as they flew away.

Detch approached the woman in the snow, hoping to sort out exactly what had happened. These birds of fire were worse than any grimshaed demon he had ever encountered. Some grimshadows were easily killed, but it was the numbers of them only that many feared. For some, even ten in number was not an impossible task. But these things were vicious, far more vicious than anything he had ever seen. He couldn't imagine killing even one of these creatures.

As he stood over the woman's body, she began to stir. He kneeled down and out of curiosity touched her red hair. To his surprise, he found that her hair was indeed on fire. Tiny little flames flickered from the ends of her hair and shot out sparks into the air. He jumped back, startled, and stood in confusion and awe as he watched the woman sit up and then rise to her feet.

"Where am I?" she muttered curiously.

"Uh,..Wrae-Kronn," he answered, unsure if it was right even to speak to her. He thought of running, but curiosity had gotten the best of him.

"I think you hit your head."

"I don't care what you think. What am I doing here?" she spat.

"Behind you is the Time Keep. The magic within it is supposed to be dead, but somehow you came through it." He paused and looked into her cold black eyes and began to think about the flaming men and the slaughtering that had just occurred. "There were...these monsters, with wings of fire, do you...have anything to do with them?"

Her eyes brightened and changed from black to orange.

"Monsters?" she asked, looking even more confused. Then, as if a revelation had occurred to her, she asked "How many and where are they now?"

When he hesitated, she grabbed his parka and lifted him up off the ground. Detch shook his head as he saw that his parka had begun to catch on fire, set by her touch.

"South . . . they went . . . south. Who… what are you?"

"I am called Fyaa. Where are they going?"

Detch felt his parka begin to burn the skin about his neck.

"Help me...I'm on fire."

"I don't care. I want to find my friends, and they are not monsters. Why did you call them monsters?"

"Because they were three flaming beasts who killed my friends. Look around you."

She did and noticed the blood that had painted the snow red.

She shook her head, confused, and then angry, and she threw Detch to the ground. He hit the hard snow and all of the air from his last breath instantly left his lungs. He rolled over in the fetal position and tried to fill his lungs. As he gasped, he could feel his chest begin to catch on fire. When his breath had returned, he rolled in the snow in an attempt to put out his burning parka. "I don't know what happened," the woman said. "We have been here before, and did not change, but I will find out and Wrae-Kronn will burn before I leave!"

Fyaa looked to the man on the snow and watched him peel off his burning parka as he began rolling in the snow. She shook her head in worthless pity, and waited for him to stop. After he shed his parka and stopped squirming in the snow, she walked over to him and bent down. Detch looked at her naked breasts as she bent over.

"Are you cold, love?" She smiled and looking down at him, cocking her head to the side as an empathic lover might.

Detch only nodded.

"Here. let me warm you up.,"

Fyaa took both of her hands and placed them on his face. Her hands were uncannily warm, and the warmth felt comforting and refreshing. She rubbed his cheeks slightly for a few seconds before her hands burst into flame. She held his face tight and kissed him as he squirmed in fear. Her hands began to melt the skin off of his face.

When he screamed, she let go and stood up. He put his face in the snow to stop the burning, but when it still hurt just as badly, he rolled over and covered his burned face with handfuls of the cold white ice.

He finally opened his eyes to see what further fate might befall him, but he saw that she had already taken to the sky, just as the sun began to rise, and had headed south looking for her three partners.

Detch watched her go. His face hurt and he could feel the skin oozing off his chin. He knew he would be scarred for life, but somehow he was thankful to be alive. For once, the cold and the snow felt good.

Chapter 1

Year 1231

The sun burned down on Alaezdar as he walked behind the ox and plow to turn the rich, dark, powdery soil. Sweat beaded off his forehead as the plow worked the soft soil so common to this fertile Valeland area. The dust rose behind the plow, and it had an almost sweet smell to it as it mixed with the stale hot air.

As he plowed, he looked around at the other fields surrounding him. Farmers worked their fields as well, tending to them, reworking the soil, plowing, weeding, or harvesting their final crop. Some of them had livestock that grazed the open lands to the east. Some had smaller herds of stock in fenced areas. The land was dotted with ranches and farms in the fertile valley west of the jagged Vixtaevus Mountains that jutted up along the horizon.

Though he had been there almost a full year now, the villagers still considered him only a stranger who lived amongst them. Just about a year earlier, during the last Doreal, he had wandered from the outlying forest into the open vastness of the vale. He was exhausted from his traveling and hungry from eating only what he had found or tried to hunt. His face was dirty and his hands were sore. His long brown hair had been knotted up on his head, but now it fell over his face and covered his eyes. His head hung low as he walked and his back hurt, not because he was weak, but because he had been pushing his once fit body of twenty-five years to the limits with little to no sleep.

Even though he walked slowly, tired and near the point of exhaustion, he was thankful for some things, like the fact that he no longer smelled himself because he had grown so accustomed to his own stench. He didn't even look up as he exited the forest grove and came into the opening of the vale.

The day he had arrived, the oak, birch and alder trees were beginning to turn red and yellow with the changing of the season. A light breeze was blowing from the south and caused some of the leaves to give up their hold upon the limbs that had spent the last six months of their lives providing shade and beauty to the quiet village.

Alaezdar breathed in the crisp, dewy smell along with the pungent aroma of the farm animals which came with the breeze. He knew then that he wanted to stay, and that here he would welcome the change of smell which accompanied the change of the scenery.

He lumbered along with his overstuffed backpack concealing most of his sword. The only part exposed was the hilt that stuck out over his shoulder. His bow was slung over his other shoulder and his quiver dangled on the bottom of his backpack. His sword and scabbard were tucked underneath in a way that prevented any quick use if he ran into any trouble, but he was exhausted and had been for many days now. If he had been attacked, or needed quick use of his sword, he had been ready to forgo his life if it meant he had needed any quick action.

He carried everything he owned in his pack. He had left his home in Daevanwood in a hurry and barely had had time to take anything but the essentials to keep him alive while he traveled. He had been on his own for a little more than thirty days when Tharntarius, the leader and founder of the village, saw him slumping in. Old but strong, Tharn worked the largest ranch in Valewood and among many other things commanded the security fence on the more dangerous eastern side.

Tharn stopped feeding his chickens and watched the stranger walk along the edge of his fence line. Alaezdar said nothing as he walked past him, but Tharn, not the type to passively watch a stranger walk into his village, stopped him and asked him where he was headed. Alaezdar ignored him at first and kept walking, but when Tharn grabbed his arm and spun him around, Alaezdar stopped and stared emotionlessly at the man who began asking him questions.

"I am hungry," is all that he said in answer to Tharn's barrage of questions.

"Come with me, young man," Tharn said and he headed back to his ranch house. Alaezdar followed him. For his advanced age, Tharn had a quick step and he still had some silvery stubble-hair on the sides of his head above his ears, but he was bald on top. His frame was large, but not overweight, and he was still strong, mostly due to his rigid work ethic of rising early and working late

Tharn fed Alaezdar a simple sandwich back at his modest ranch home, but Alaezdar still did not talk. He remained quiet as a rock, which was his nature, and "Rock" was also his name when he had been with the Rager's House of Renegades.

Many in the realm know of that guild, and many feared, but respected its members. Those who were outside of the guild only know its members as "blade," and addressed them only as "blade." Only the members within the guild knew their guild names, such as Alaezdar's name, Rock Blade, or his friend's name, Shadow Blade.

Alaezdar had decided to leave the guild under undesirable circumstances, circumstances that, in fact, had forced a death hunt upon his head for he had killed one of his own guild members in a mission gone wrong.

Tharn finally persuaded Alaezdar to talk enough for him to understand that he needed food and shelter. Tharn wanted to let him know this was a safe place for him, so he offered him a job to work on his ranch. At first Alaezdar was put up in the bunkhouse with ten men who were tasked to cleaning out the horse stables and mucking out the cow stalls. It did not take long for Tharn to see that Alaezdar had an excellent work ethic and was flawlessly diligent at his tasks.

As good as he was, he made Tharn even more curious. He seemed out of place for a common drifter. It seemed odd to Tharn that he knew how to care for a horse, knew how to trim the hooves and knew how to care for their teeth. He even knew how to care for the cows, sheep and chickens with very little instruction. Tharn put him up to a level of more advanced work, even passing up some workers he had had on the ranch for years. He even moved Alaezdar into one of his few single room villas on the ranch.

After Alaezdar had lived at Valewood for a year, he had learned firsthand what it was like to be a rancher, caring not only for the livestock, but also learning the dynamics of running a farm for a complete cycle. He had impressed Tharn, but in the end this was exactly the quiet life he had sought out. That fall he and Tharn had harvested the last of the honeydew melons that grew there and he now tilled the land in preparation for the next crop.

The last batch of melons he had picked, boxed and loaded into crates and had them ready in the wagon to sell at the village harvest market. Tharn had put Alaezdar in charge of this harvesting operation with many workers working for him. It actually surprised Alaezdar just how rewarding this type of work was. Tharn's farming operation was not the type of work he had ever done. Sure, he had done simple farming and ranch chores before, when he was a child living at home, but those were just simple chores to provide for a single family. What he learned in a short time was that there on Tharn's farm, they provided for not only the village, but they also sold produce at the large market for thousands of people in the northern kingdoms.

Valewood lived and thrived as one community comprised mostly of farmers, livestock hands and blacksmiths. The woman folk cared for the children, did the cooking, sewing and weaving, and gathered food from the available trade markets within the community. Every person -- man or woman -- in the Valewood area took part in the effort to make Valewood a strong community.

During that first year, Alaezdar had tried to stay anonymous, but living in a town where everyone knew each other made anonymity a daunting and nearly impossible task. Soon, even though he had tried to avoid friendly contact, by a natural process of time he still made friends as he worked by their side. His new friends, in their early conversations, were eager to tell him how the best parts of farming were starting with un-worked soil and raw seeds and watching the plants grow and flourish to bear fruits and vegetables and finally harvesting the crop and taking it to market to watch the profits grow from the year's hard work.

They said sometimes, unbelievably, the best part was working the crops from sunrise to sunset until it was time to harvest the crop. It had something to do with the hard labor and the pride of a hard day's work and never having to worry about not falling asleep quickly enough. When the last crop was harvested and the 5th of Doreal celebration began, the whole village came together and was ready to celebrate their hard work. During the festival their crops and creations were sold at market and the excess was then stored for the Ethinar.

As Alaezdar tilled the land one afternoon, he stopped and wiped the sweat off his forehead. He watched as Aaelie walked towards her house in the distance, coming with her mother from the Sippling River and both carrying the village's daily wash. Although her mother was middle aged and just beginning to show some gray streaks in her hair, Aaelie was still strong and beautiful. She had the beauty of her mother and was slender and strong. Her long brown hair was tied in a tight braid and hung down to the middle of her back. Alaezdar watched her long legs keep pace with her mother as she trailed behind.

Their daily routine was to wash the clothes in the cold Sippling River and bring them back to their home to dry, fold and then deliver to the owners. Taking advantage of this service was something most villagers did, and they paid well for it. Even the other women in the village took advantage of the service and used the extra time for a break or to get some extra chores finished before night fell, especially during the shortened daylight hours that were coming.

Aaelie and her mother reached their home and set the clothes down. Her mother immediately began hanging up the clothes on the line while Aaelie walked on towards the house. When she reached the step, she noticed Alaezdar watching and she waved towards him and smiled demurely. Alaezdar smiled and waved back. He took a deep breath, a little embarrassed, and urged the ox to go forward once again.

He thought of her as he worked. She was younger than he was by at least five years, and he thought her too young to be flirting with, or so he told himself. She was beyond her teen years, but she still had some maturing to do, as far as he was concerned.

His life before his quiet and peaceful escape to Valewood had caused him to grow up quickly. In his earlier days, as a mercenary, he had experienced many harsh things in life and had seen worse. He felt too mature now to be fawning over a young girl like Aaelie, but that still did not keep him from being attracted to her charm and a youthful outlook that made her so pleasant to be around. He had made up his mind early, however, that he would keep a safe distance from her. A task much easier said than done, for he did find her attractive and her personality magnetic, but for everyone's sake, he had to keep her at arms length.

She had just gone inside her house when he saw movement behind the trees near her home. Straining to look, he only saw shadows as something darted from tree to tree. He unhooked himself from the ox and, shading his eyes from the sun, walked towards her house. He was beginning to think that he was just seeing things when he saw it again. Still he saw nothing more than shadows, but now he knew that he had indeed seen something.

The guild? They couldn't have found him, could they? He shook his head in disbelief as he broke into a run and jumped over the wooden fence that surrounded the field.

He had reached Aaelie's front porch when the first arrow whizzed passed his head and sank into the column holding up the low roof of her porch.

"Aaelie!" he yelled. "Don't leave your house! Stay inside!"

He charged into the tree line where the arrow had come from, but he did not immediately see anything. He quickly scanned the area again, but still saw nothing. Fearing the worst, he looked back at Aaelie's house and saw her and her mother standing on the porch, watching him run frantically back and forth through the woods.

He was about to give up looking when he saw three figures come around the house and grab Aaelie and her mother with knives pressed to their throats. People from the village had begun to gather and gawk at what was going on, and Alaezdar yelled for everyone to get back inside their homes and hide. As he ran towards Aaelie, he waved his arms at the crowd to get their attention, but none of them moved. They stood watching, transfixed on the men who were holding the two women.

"They are here for me!" he yelled as he ran, but as soon as he yelled, a hail of arrows from the woods behind him fell into the growing crowd and killed villagers as the arrows hit their marks.

"Let them go! I will come peacefully!" he begged, running faster now, but the faster he ran, the slower time began to move for him. Arrows screamed through the air and each found a villager. Still the gathered crowd stood, helpless, merely watching the events unfold around them.

"Run, you fools!" he screamed at his friends. He was now out of breath as he neared Aaelie. The villagers now began to run, but they seemed not to be running from the arrows, but rather to get away from him. What is wrong with them, he thought. How could they be so ignorant of the danger? These men are killing them wantonly and the attackers don't care if they are women or children.

He was about to jump onto her porch when someone came from his left side, tackled him and took him down, knocking the wind out of him. He felt his ribs crushing under the weight of the man who then threw himself on top of him.

"Alaezdar!" the attacker yelled at him after he had rolled off, grabbed Alaezdar's tunic and lifted his head up off the ground. "Snap out of it!"

Alaezdar opened his eyes and saw Tharn, his opened palm ready to slap him.

"Wait!" Alaezdar said and broke free from Tharn's grip and rolled away. "What is going on?"

Alaezdar looked around him and saw no massacred villagers. Instead the villagers were untouched and were milling around him shaking their heads with wide eyes, as if he had lost his mind.

Maybe I have, he thought.

He looked over his shoulder and saw that Aaelie's mother was holding her as if shielding her. Aaelie had concern in her eyes, but her mother looked at him as if he had committed a heinous crime.

"What happened?" Alaezdar asked.

"Are you ok now?" Tharn asked. "We don't know what happened. You just snapped and were screaming and waving your arms and running towards Aaelie.

"I'm fine," he said.

Tharn gently helped him up, brushed off his pants and tunic and then walked away, hoping no one would say anything more.

"I'm sorry, Tharn," he said meekly.

Alaezdar walked back to the ox and plow, trying to remember the vision he'd had, but already the details were fading. Confused, he went back to work. He wished no one had noticed what happened, but he knew he had achieved what he wanted the least, attention.

Chapter 2

The village center of Valewood bustled with its busy townsfolk preparing for the harvest reaping and the upcoming celebration. The cloudy day did not discourage the villagers, but motivated them to work faster for they welcomed the coming of the cool temperatures in contrast to the recent months of the hot Flamespan days.

In just a few short days the representatives of the northern kingdoms would come to bid for the best price for their yearly supply of goods. Down the two main streets of crowded businesses, the villagers were cleaning their shops and tending to the locals who brought in supplies for their booths. Inns especially were busy, cleaning up, painting and sprucing up their facilities in hopes of attracting the richest of the representatives to their inn alone.

Carpenters hammered noisily as they built a stage for the performances to be held near the fountain at the end of the lane. The fountain –– merely a miniature replica of the wheelhouse that brought the water from the Sippling River into the duct system for all the farms of Valewood –– had no water in it at the moment. The workers had painstakingly painted the fountain to restore its glossy look and bring about its majestic presence as the focal point to the whole town, just as it had always been.

Rivlok watched the painters briefly before he hefted a bag of feed onto the back of an old spotted gelding.

"Thank you, Rivlok," Marlie said as the strong teenager finished tying down the old woman's load of feed onto the horse.

24

"My pleasure, Marlie." Rivlok checked the straps one final time before handing the reins over to the old woman. "Are you sure you don't want me to walk you home?"

"No, I am quite alright. Thank you, sweetie."

Rivlok smiled, turned from Marlie and continued his stroll down the center street of Valewood. He held no real job, but he kept himself busy all day long. He would rather roam around and help others as he saw fit. A village hero, as he liked to think of himself. He was young and energetic, but did not work well with a crew in the fields or as an apprentice to the blacksmith, although he had done it all. The fact that he did not have a single purpose in the village did not bother him, though, because he enjoyed his freedom to do whatever he wanted.

Most villagers did not care that he didn't have a job, although he did get harassed time and again from some of the older men in the village who tended to believe in their own old work ethic, but Rivlok didn't care. He was well liked by the people who knew him well. His biggest disappointment to others, and to himself for that matter, was that since he was such a quick learner, he usually just got bored after he mastered what was taught, and he felt the urge to move on to something else.

Some took this as cockiness, but he didn't see himself as cocky, just better, that's all.

As he walked down the center of the street, he saw Rankin, the village blacksmith, talking to a young teen named Kunther. He was holding a new sword that Rankin had been working on for him. Rankin laughed as Kunther did a few swings with the sword and ran off into the middle of the street, moving towards Rivlok. Not looking where he ran, Kunther swung the sword carelessly in front of him.

Rivlok jumped in front of him and grabbed the arm that held the sword.

"Where are you going in such a hurry, Kunth?"

Kunther looked up, startled.

"I am going to see if Kord has my scabbard ready. Like my new sword?" Kunther said, displaying his blade proudly.

"Yeah, it's nice, but be careful where you swing that thing."

Kunther gave Rivlok a glance that told Rivlok that he didn't care too much for his advice, and then he continued off to find Kord.

Rivlok continued walking and his thoughts began to drift off to Aaelie. Out of all the girls in the village, he found that he spent most of his time with her. She was sweet, soft-spoken, gentle, and pretty. The prettiest he had ever seen in Valewood. He smiled to himself and figured he had done enough for today. He decided to pay her a visit.

Still deep in thought about her, he didn't realize that he had walked all the way out of the village and onto the country road that led to her home. He saw her outside with her mother and quickened his pace, but he also noticed Alaezdar plowing Tharn's field across from her home.

Alaezdar saw Rivlok as well, and made no acknowledgement, but he stopped to watch. Rivlok stopped to talk to Aaelie's mother while she hung up the clothes on the line. Alaezdar could not tell what they were saying, but he watched as they both went inside. After a few moments Rivlok came out holding Aaelie's hand and leading her towards the southern side of the vale near the river and into the forest.

Rivlok turned and saw that Alaezdar had stopped his ox and was watching them as they began to run. Rivlok smiled, boasting, and waved to him as they ran towards the forest. Aaelie followed, still holding Rivlok's hand, but she blew a kiss to Alaezdar with her free hand and finished with a loving wave and smile as the two of them disappeared into the woods.

Alaezdar laughed to himself. He still felt awkward after the incident that he'd just experienced, but he waved back just the same. Aaelie did not see his return wave, but he smiled at her. It was just like her to be so forgiving and to be flirting with him while she held another man's hand.

When he first came to Valewood, it was Aaelie who had first embraced him in friendship. She took him by the hand, keeping him close, and introduced him to what seemed to Alaezdar to be everybody in the village. Rivlok seemed to hate every minute of it and he made certain that he was never a few feet away during Aaelie's introductions.

Alaezdar rested on his plow, still deep in thought, when Tharn walked up behind him.

"Alaezdar, you don't have to work. After this little incident, I think you need a break. Why don't you come inside?"

Alaezdar said nothing, but unhitched the ox from the harness. He followed Tharn back to his cottage, feeling a bit apprehensive, though, as he walked past the ox and patted it's head.

"Where did you say you were from, Alaezdar?" Tharn asked as he reached the steps of his large ranch house. He knew he had asked before, but he now thought the question needed further probing to confirm some of his suspicions after this morning's incident.

"I was raised in the village of Hyronael, where my father raised me, until I left home."

"So your father was a farmer?"

"No, my father is a mage. You probably have heard of him. He is well known as Valvektor-Sor," Alaezdar answered unenthusiastically, almost with caustic bitterness, as he spit the words into the air.

Tharn let the door close while looking quizzically at Alaezdar.

"I have heard of him, though I haven't heard of him since I was in the service of King Toron II for the Kingdom of Triel. Is your father still alive?"

"I am afraid so."

"Come on into the kitchen," Tharn said and he motioned Alaezdar to follow.

Alaezdar walked straight into the dining area and sat down at the table where a sandwich and fresh strawberries were already neatly assembled at one setting.

Tharn reached the table, sat down looked intently over at his young friend.

"Now I wouldn't have figured you to be the son of a great mage. In fact, I would have laid down my life that you were simply the son of a lifelong farmer."

"Sorry to disappoint you," Alaezdar said and took a bite out of his sandwich.

"No. You misunderstand, I am far from disappointed. You see I knew Valvektor-Sor. Though it was many years ago, and long before I retired and created this settlement, I served with him on a mission. I was serving the Kingdom of Triel upon the Kingship Swordfist. Now, I will have you know I was not a sailor, but a soldier in charge of the detachment of warriors on the mission. Valvektor-Sor at the time was the king's advisor and the king sent him as his proxy. He and I were both younger then, though it really wasn't that long ago, it seems," Tharn paused and smiled. "Though I would guess it was before you were even born."

"My father wasn't much of a father. He wasn't around long enough to tell me tales of his great magic."

It was true that Alaezdar hadn't seen much of his father until just before reaching manhood. He did indeed love to hear his tales when he was younger, and when his mother was still alive, but he began to despise the tales later on because they were the reason behind his father's absence and became a source of great jealousy for him. When his Mother died at the hands of a rogue wizard that meant to punish Valvektor-Sor for some mal deed that he suffered at his hands, Alaezdar was sent away to live with his aunt and uncle for safety.

Growing up with his cousins wasn't all that bad though. It gave him an outlet of normalcy for they were a normal family, not born to any magical abilities. It did not take long for him to take notice of the talk from his cousins who were running off to the human kingdoms to be soldiers or off to Daevanwood to join the great mercenary guilds. He remembered that when his cousin Dreg left to join the fighting force of the Moonshaed Kingdom, Alaezdar was thirteen. His father had moved him to his cousins' and he had known Dreg for three years before he left for his enlistment.

Alaezdar told Tharn that it was with this family that he had lived for four years, until Valvektor-Sor came home with the goal to teach him to be his apprentice. By this time, Alaezdar had seen three of his cousins leave for duty as swordsmen. They had come back at least a dozen times between them and they told stories of great adventures which, unlike his father's tales, stuck in Alaezdar's heart and soul. Thus began his yearning to be a swordsman and nothing else.

After Alaezdar had finished, he and Tharn sat quietly looking at the walls for many moments before Tharn broke the silence. "Why didn't you follow the magic, Alaezdar?"

"Somehow I knew you were going to ask that. The truth is, I don't get along with my father. He is a cruel man to what little family he has, or had."

"How was he cruel?"

"He tried to force his magic skills upon me in the name of saving the Known Lands. I refused his teachings and eventually he ended up beating me to try to force his will upon me. It really came down to not only my refusal to learn the art, but my refusal to believe that we needed to be strong in magic to save the realm or that we were part of the elven prophecies. To be honest with you, I don't believe any of it."

"I don't believe I agree with you. I think the magic in this realm can be used to prevent horrible things from happening. Things that are supposed to be locked down, events like the Time Keep opening up and spitting out strange beings such as that evil flaming witch, Fyaa. I find it odd that magic is weakening when it seems that magic could possibly be the only thing to rid this land of the likes of her."

"Possibly, but with the right weapons and with brave men we could defeat her without magic. Magic is too dangerous a weapon to have around for it can also be used against the forces of good."

The two sat in silence a few minutes. Alaezdar just wanted to leave, but Tharn had something to prove to the young man in front of him. He could tell Alaezdar was getting frustrated with the conversation, but he had to push it a little further.

"How can you ignore the prophecies?"

Alaezdar shook his head, incredulous, and spoke slowly and sarcastically. "Because they are elven?"

"That is where you are mistaken. Yes, they are elven preached and studied, but they are based on the return of the first human king, Dar Drannon."

Alaezdar shook his head in frustration. "This is the part that kills me. Why would elves depend on the return of a human to advance their cause? That makes absolutely no sense to me. Besides, when it all comes down to it, they are just elves. It makes no difference to me."

"Why are you so against the elves?"

"You're not serious, are you?" Alaezdar raked his fingers hard through the hair on the top of his head. "Because they are a dying race. They had their time here in this realm, but they lost it because they fought against each other and lost their advantage against humans. Now they preach the returning of the human king to pry themselves back into power by using the fear of this prophecy against us."

Tharn laughed. "So, you do know about the prophecies and the elven religion."

"More than I care to know."

"So you know about Val Eahea, Raezoures, Val Elves, Sor Elves, and the Sorae, but do you know about the role of the Aginsorae in the prophecy?"

"I have heard about it."

"Shall I entertain you with my spin on the prophecy, one that you may not have heard about?"

"Tharn, talk all you want, but if you are looking for a debate on this issue from me, you aren't going to get one. I have spent my whole life listening about this from my father and then dealing with the political fallout amongst the kingdoms while…well, let's just say, I know more than I care to admit right now."

"Follow me to the porch. I know you aren't interested, but I want to show you something."

Tharn left the kitchen and Alaezdar followed him.

As soon as Tharn walked through the door, he pointed to the northeast. "Many miles beyond the river and north of the Goblin Tribes forest is the fortress of the first human king, Dar Drannon. It may seem like just an old abandoned fortress to you, but it is much more than that. Think about it. This fortress was built in the face of a cliff during a time before humans sprouted upon this land. Where did he come from and how did he build the fortress?"

"There are so many tales explaining this legend, but it is just that, a legend."

"I don't think so, young man, and you would be wise to take heed as you have more at stake than you may know. We all do, in fact."

Dar Drannon is not from this land. Many believe he is the spawn of the Markenhirth while others claim that he arrived with the elves and is elven in god-like form. Some even claim that he arrived to destroy the land. However, the three gods, Val Eahea, Raezoures and the dwarf god Har Ron battled him in his natural form, but they could not defeat him using their magic for he had magic of his own that counteracted and twisted all of their spells of Wrae magic. A star fell upon the land and pierced his heart just as he was about to destroy the three gods. That star separated into four shards and fell in four different places upon the land. Hence, the Quarterstar Shards. The star wounded him severely, but did not kill him. He was not found again in the same form as they had last seen him. Now this is where the tale changes to what I believe. He is not a spawn of Markenhirth, but he is part of it. He is not completely elven, but he is elven. He will return, but not as everyone predicts. All the prophecies predict his return for different reasons. I believe all the prophecies to be accurate, but they all have different outcomes to suit their needs. I also believe there is a power struggle to force each prophecy to come true."

"You aren't telling me anything new, Tharn."

Tharn faced Alaezdar and smiled. "Here is the twist. Dar Drannon is already here. He is in human form, but he doesn't know who he is yet and he has not been awakened."

"You're right. I have not heard that one. You know what? I think I need to get back to work."

"No, I think we have done enough for the day." Tharn ran his hand over his nearly baldhead. "Let's pick up our tools, put away the animals and call it a day."

As they walked to the field, Tharn continued to talk again about his days in the service of Triel. Alaezdar listened with interest to tale after tale throughout the rest of the afternoon. They broke their conversation only once, to bring the ox in from the sun, and Tharn talked the whole time, following Alaezdar while he brought the animal in.

Afterward they came back in, sat comfortably inside and shared tales, thoughts and ideals from magic, elves, kings and kingdoms. When they had exhausted their topics, Tharn excused Alaezdar and went to bed.

Alaezdar meanwhile went back to his small cottage thinking about their conversations. He was glad that he could have an encouraging and stimulating conversation with an ex soldier without divulging the fact that he was once a member of the Rager's House of Renegades.

In fact, Tharn had never even asked where Alaezdar had gotten all of his experience. He was so wrapped up in his own tales that the thought might never have crossed his mind. Later, he might see the correlation, and might even confront Alaezdar about it, but that would be a conversation to dodge another day.

Alaezdar thought that maybe it would even be safe to tell Tharn. He would most likely understand, but it would jeopardize his safety within this village, as well as the safety of the villagers, if the members of the Rager's

House of Renegades found him here.

Still deep in thought, Alaezdar walked through the front door of his cottage. The cottage was a small, three-room villa only big enough for sleeping and cooking. There was a small closet-sized extension for a bathing area. His bed was against the far wall. He went to it, sat down, put his elbows on his knees, rested his head on his hands, and covered his eyes with his fingers.

He sat there for a few minutes before reaching under the bed and pulling out his sword, still in its scabbard. It was a common bastard sword covered with an elaborate scabbard and it had been there untouched since he had arrived at Valewood. He had hoped that he would not need the use of this it ever again. He read the inscription on the scabbard. "Loyalty, honor, trust in the House. No mercy to others."

He turned the scabbard over and looked at the other side. It had an inscription that was similar, but it read "To Honor, to Death: Rock Blade."

The hilt of the sword was the only part of the sword showing. The handle was wrapped with pounded dragon hide from stolen baby dragon eggs that had been taken from their lairs within the Dragon Cross Peaks many years ago, when the dragons were in their hibernation period. The pommel had a platinum red stone, still shiny and new, buffed to appear transparent. Implanted on the butt of the pommel was the simple inscription, "RB."

Alaezdar missed his friends, Shadow Blade, Half Blade, Stolie. He even got along with Talon Blade, even though he was Red Blade's closest friend. Now Talon Blade would want Alaezdar dead, and he would stop at nothing to see that end come to fruition.

"I will not allow my friends to die because of my actions," Alaezdar vowed to himself. "I will lie to obtain a better outcome. I will protect my friends and this village." He paused. "But hopefully I won't have to."

Alaezdar had loved the Rager's House of Renegades mercenary guild, but he knew that he had to leave. When he killed Red Blade, he had no choice. It was at that terrible moment, during a mission when they were inside the castle of their worst enemy, Reiker-Kol, that he had realized that being a soldier of fortune was not what he had long sought to be.

He did love fighting for the good causes, where it was clear that it was a struggle of good against bad, but more often than not it was not always as clear as black and white. In the end, the members of the Rager's House of Blade were dispatched to the highest bidder, whoever that might be.

Sometimes the members were at the mercy of those in charge, such as when eight members, including Alaezdar, went to hold Reiker-Kol's children hostage and wait for Reiker-Kol to come to the rescue, at which time they would expediently assassinate him. Reiker-Kol never showed up. Instead, he sent a message back to inform his guards that some members of the Rager's House of Renegades would be there and they were to seal all entrances and exits, search out the intruders and kill them.

When Red Blade realized that the mission was going to turn into a failure, he killed one of the children in a rage of fury and in cold blood. While Shadow Blade and Half Blade watched, Alaezdar, then known as Rock Blade, cut Red Blade down. Afterward Alaezdar ran from the castle, but Shadow Blade, Alaezdar's close friend, tackled him, but then let him go before the others could find him. Shadow Blade told him to hide and never to return, lest he be killed.

Sitting on the edge of his bed, Alaezdar touched the hilt of the sword lightly and then placed it back under the bed. He sat motionless for many moments.

Finally he decided to go into town for a while.

Chapter 3

"I love our spot," Rivlok said to Aaelie as he watched the slow ripple of the Sippling River churn past him and continue its journey to the Val-Ron Sea. It would only be a short walk now through the forest and past the water wheelhouses along the river to get to their favorite place, past the noise of the creaking wheelhouse wood that dipped water out of the river and into the troughs that led to the sloughs carrying the water to the crops.

They always had to get permission from either Tharn or the Captain of the Guard -- usually Morlonn the Hunter -- and today had been no different. They called him Morlonn the Hunter because it is what he did when he wasn't on the gate. He hunted for his family and for many other families in the village as well.

Today he was on the gate and when he was on the gate, they didn't have much problem getting through, but Tharn often would not let them pass. They knew that Morlonn would be there today and that they wouldn't have a problem. However, they still had to get past him.

They came to the wooden outer perimeter that Tharn had built to protect the villagers from the occasional brave, usually young goblins who occasionally raided the village looking for notoriety within their tribe. After Tharn had built the wall for protection, no raids ever happened. He had built it wide enough to have guards walk on it and he also built lookout towers every couple hundred feet and one tower big enough to house a guard tower and headquarters. Kunther often guarded at the small gate below while

Morlonn paced the top of the wall.

Rivlok and Aaelie smiled at Kunther, who was there today, and they all waited a few minutes for Morlonn to return. They watched him walk towards them and when they saw him, they waved.

"Hey, let us through!" they shouted so that he could hear them from below.

Morlonn stood on top of the fence with his hands on his hips. When he was on watch, he wore his leather armor and his metal shin and elbow protectors and had his shield slung on his back. His sword hung loosely about his waist. He was in his early twenties, kept in great shape and his athletic build showed it. He had dark brown eyes and short brown hair that he kept cut close to keep it out of his eyes at all times.

"Where are you going?" he yelled down.

"Just to the river for a spell," Rivlok answered.

Seeing his friends, Morlonn changed his tough stance and softened his tone. He liked to play tough at first, as he loved being Captain of the Guard, but his friends always made him break down the façade.

"Why don't you two come up here for a bit. I have something to show you," Morlonn yelled down to them and then asked Kunther to show them up.

Within a few minutes, Kunther had opened the door that allowed them inside the gate. It led to a narrow hallway only wide enough for two people to walk side by side. The three of them walked to the end of the hall and into an empty anteroom that had a caged gate on top of its ceiling. Morlonn stood on top of it smiling.

"Kunther and I just made this. Tharn told me all about it. He calls it a murder room. If anyone ever gets in, we can lock them in this room with that sliding door behind you…now, Kunth," he said as a wall from the ceiling came slamming down, trapping them in the room.

"Now we can do many things. We can stab them with spears, shoot arrows in through here or even pour hot oil onto them from above. Tharn said that all the fortresses do this."

Rivlok grinned from ear to ear with excitement, but Aaelie just shook her head. "Morlonn, you really shouldn't spend so much time out here," she said.

"I know," he said, but was unconvinced. "Come on up. That's not really what I want to show you."

He jumped down out of sight and quickly came into the room by opening a door that could not be seen from the inside, where Rivlok and Aaelie were. They jumped, clearly startled.

"This is another improvement I made," he said, laughing to see the surprised looks on their faces. "But still not what I want to show you. Come on up."

They followed Kunther up the steps to the top of the gate and to one of the towers where the floor was wider. Morlonn had parts scattered around of what looked to be an old, rusty, broken catapult. The base was put together and there were no wheels were on it yet, but the axles had been inserted into the base. The throwing arm lay next to it, but it did not have its launching mechanism connected.

"Tharn gave this to me at last year's festival, but I didn't break it out until last week. I am going to use it for the dance. I will give everyone a nice fire-show and use this to launch the fire."

"With that piece of junk?" Aaelie frowned, unimpressed.

"I can help you fix that!" Rivlok said at the same time.

Morlonn smiled proudly. "No, thanks. I know you could probably build a better one from scratch, but I want to put this one together myself and add a few neat features to it that will launch the projectiles so high that they will burn out long before they hit the ground...so I don't catch the whole forest on fire."

"What are you going to use?" asked Rivlok.

"A lot of flammable items, like straw, sticks and bit of my own invention of oil and cow manure mix."

"Oh, yuck," Aaelie said and shook her head. "So cow dung is going to be falling on us at the festival. Be sure to warn me when you start shooting that thing."

"No, don't worry about that. Look, follow me over here," Morlonn said and motioned them to follow. He could hardly contain his excitement.

Morlonn took them to the northern corner of the gate and showed them a small cliff ledge above the water tanks.

"See that ledge over there? I'm going to set the catapult up over there and shoot it over the fountain square, landing just over Drostin's ranch over there. It is somewhat poetic in the sense that that is where I will be getting my manure from to start with and then giving it right back. I will probably be scaring enough dung out of the cows in one night to supply all the dung I need for next year!" he said, laughing.

"Too much enthusiasm," Aaelie said smiling.

"Thanks, Aaelie," Morlonn said.

He realized that they were getting bored with his catapult. He sorely wanted to get back to work on it anyways, but he didn't want to send them off so soon. He really did like both of them. They had been friends since they were very young. Rivlok and he had often played swordfighter together when they were kids, and a lot of times their pretend battles turned into real fights because Rivlok was so competitive and high strung.

So as not to make them feel like he was sending the couple away, Morlonn started a subject that would certainly cause them enough awkwardness that they would want to leave.

"So, Aaelie, what are you doing for the dance?"

"Same as usual, skipping it," she answered.

"Why? Isn't this guy taking you?" he asked and punched Rivlok in the shoulder.

"Oh, I am sure he would like that," Aaelie said, "but no, the dance is soo boring."

"Then go with me. We'll have fun," Morlonn said with a huge grin.

Aaelie blushed, but Rivlok flushed.

"I am sure we would," she said. "Actually, I might go, but I don't think I will go with any one person. Why don't we all go together?"

"Let's do that," Morlonn said. He smiled and looked to Rivlok, who did not like the turn in the conversation. "Hey, Rivlok, it's time for the boar hunt again tomorrow. Are you going?"

"Yeah, I suppose," Rivlok said, turning away and looking towards the Sippling River. "Same time, same place as last year?"

"As always," he answered.

Morlonn walked them back to the stairs and Rivlok and Aaelie left the gate and headed out towards the river.

"Don't be long, you two!" Morlonn yelled down. "It will be dark soon and I don't want to have to look for you."

They ignored Morlonn. Kunther opened the final gate at the bottom for them and they ran down the trail leading to the river and followed it downstream for about a mile before they came to their spot. They had to walk that far just to escape the wheelhouse sounds and to get away from the noise and the hustle and bustle of the village and even to get far enough away from the sounds of cows, goats and chickens. Their spot was absolutely silent and so secluded that it gave the couple the illusion that no civilization or people were even close.

When they reached the grassy bank where had spent so many hours, they sat and watched the river flow by for a few minutes, enjoying the tranquility, before Rivlok spoke.

"Remember when we were little? I kissed you for the first time near that tree downstream," he said pointing to a massive, spotted white alder tree just a few feet off the river's edge.

"Yes, I do," Aaelie said laughing. "I remember. I also remember how gross it was and that I ran away."

"Gross? You didn't seem to think it was gross when I chased you down and tickled you until you kissed me again."

"That was because you wouldn't stop unless I did."

"Then why did you keep kissing me even after I stopped."

"Oh, Rivlok," Aaelie said blushing. "It wasn't like that."

"No?"

"We've been friends a long time, Rivlok."

"Long time?" Rivlok repeated, not sure if she was being tender or just putting him off and discrediting what he thought was love and passion as friendship. "That's just it, Aaelie. We have known each other a long time. How old were we when we met?"

"Well, we were both born here, but I think we were five or six when we first met at one of the festivals.

"That's over ten years ago."

"Long time," Aaelie repeated.

"Aaelie," Rivlok said and turned his body to look at her, holding up his weight with his left hand on the grass behind him. "Don't you agree that during that time we have become more than friends?"

Aaelie smiled and blushed again, but did not look up from the river.

"Yes, Rivlok, I do love you…. sometimes like a brother, sometimes like a lover, and sometimes like my best friend. I will always love you one way or another."

"I, uh…" Rivlok hesitated, but changed his tact. "How do you feel about me now?"

"Does that matter right now? I mean, I am here with you, am I not? We have known each other for so long, we are comfortable around each other, we have fun together, and we share everything together. What more could you want?"

"You. Unconditionally," he said. He touched her chin and made him face her.

"That isn't for anyone to have," she responded. "You know, it is amazing," she said in a voice a little louder than the soft tones they had been speaking in an attempt to change the subject. "We have been here all our lives, and then comes someone like Alaezdar -- who knows nothing about us -- and yet he quickly becomes part of our lives."

Rivlok nodded quickly and turned around to face the river.

"Alaezdar? I don't trust him either."

"No, that's not what I meant. I like it…him. He fascinates me. He has seen a part of the world we haven't, and he adds change to our ever dull community life."

"Aaelie, don't fall for him. I think he knows even more than he says. I think he is either dangerous or is in danger himself. Either way, I think he will just bring you…us…trouble."

"Rivlok, that's the best part," she said and turned to him for the first time since they had sat down on the soft grass. "He brings a newness, and change, and possibly adventure."

"Don't do this, Aaelie. I love you. I don't want to see you hurt."

"Rivlok," she said, blushing and smiling, "you're so sweet. It's not like that."

"Do you love me?" he blurted out in his growing frustration.

Her smile faded slightly.

"Yes, Rivlok. We just went over this, remember? I want to be more than your friend, more than like your brother, even more than best friends. You know I love you with all my heart. I want to be with you always."

Aaelie leaned over and gave him and a quick kiss on the lips.

"Right now we are more than friends, and that is the best I have to offer right now."

Rivlok slid closer to her and took her in his arms. He let her gently settle down into the grass and lie on her back and then he half rolled over next to her and rested his head on his hand.

"Don't hurt me, Aaelie. I don't want to hear any more talk about Alaezdar, okay?"

"Okay"

Rivlok took her into his arms and lay with her by the river, holding her as tight as he could. His heart pounded and his mind raced with thoughts about how to win her heart completely. Aaelie lay next to him and looked over his shoulder up at the sky, her mind wandering.

Later, they talked and talked, even as the sun set and the towering pine trees cast dark shadows on their conversation. Rivlok began to wonder if Morlonn would really come looking for them. They were still deep into a conversation when they heard noise on the other side of the Sippling River.

"What is that?" Aaelie asked, apprehension evident in her voice. "Do you think it is Morlonn?"

"No. Why would he be on the other side of the river? Though, I am curious to find out. Want to come?" he said and he stood up and offered her his hand.

"Well, I am not staying here in the dark alone," she said and took his hand and let him lift her up.

"Come on. We'll cross at the bridge."

They ran as quickly as they could in the dark. Even though they knew their way around, though, they still had to go cautiously to be quiet and not run into anything in the darkness. Within a few minutes they were at the only bridge that crossed the Sippling River and connected Valewood with the dense forest that eventually rolled into the Goblin Tribes Forest a few miles east.

They hid for a second under the bridge abutment, but they could not see much in the darkness. Finally they heard a wagon led by a team of horses coming toward them, fast. Then, on the other side of the bridge, Tharn and the village smithy came out of a thicket of trees holding torches.

Rivlok could now make out the wagon as one that he had seen before parked outside of the armory. It was a covered wooden wagon with no windows. Rivlok had never seen what was inside of it. He had just assumed that it was metals for making swords and shields that the smithy crafted for Tharn to sell to the Kingdom of Triel, but that whole operation had always seemed suspicious to him.

When they came close, Tharn raised his torch and signaled the wagon to halt. The driver pulled up hard and fast on the reigns. He usually was not stopped on this side of the river.

"I need you to unload quickly and go back tonight," Tharn said loudly.

The driver gave the reins to his partner and stepped off the wagon, his already short temper surfacing at Tharn's command. "You can't be serious?"

Aaelie recognized the voice of her uncle, Corben.

"I am very serious," Ambassador Krostos will be here soon, and he will want double his normal allotment of iron, so I don't care how tired you are, there are two of you to team drive back."

"It isn't a matter of being tired. There is a lot of activity at the mine recently."

"What activity?"

"Goblins, of course. They hacked poor Horbel to death while he was at the outhouse. They just destroyed the outhouse and left. I don't know why other than that they just were bored, I guess...I hope. Something is brewing out there. I can just feel it."

"What do you mean?"

"I don't know for sure. There just seems to be a lot more movement closer to us than there used to be. The men are suspecting that there's going to be a tribal war between clans, and if there is, I don't want to be caught in the middle."

"Fine. I will send you a few more of Morlonn's guard for extra security."

"Thank you, I suppose," Corben said, but shook his head in doubt.

"Now, get that thing unloaded so Rankin can get to work prepping the iron."

Corben hopped back onto the wagon without another word and left.

Rivlok and Aaelie could hear Tharn walking across the bridge and saw him begin walking back to Valewood.

Chapter 4

Alaezdar awoke before dawn the next day for he had a lot of work to do before the festival, the day after next. He loved rising early, but he was not always the first one up. Many of the villagers rose an hour or so before the sunrise. Their early activity did not discourage him, but rather made him feel at home.

It wasn't just the fact that he rose, ready to work, and loved it, it was that sometimes the crisp morning air invigorated him and gave him enough charge to last all day. Today was a day like that. The pre-dawn sky was clear and he felt the dew on the ground underneath his boots as he walked. The air had its country-fresh smell, too, and that meant the manure smelled sweet today and not as rancid and rotten as on some damp mornings.

He worked hard most of the day. He tended to the cattle and the other farm animals first and then worked on repairing the fence lines that were deteriorating from age. Tharn hadn't asked him to fix them. He just had noticed that they needed repair and figured that Tharn wasn't in shape to repair them by himself any time soon.

After fixing most of the simple things he'd had his eye on, which only required quick maintenance repair, he worked his way over to the wheelhouses at the river. It was still mid morning and he was feeling in a good mood as the sun was weaving in and out behind the clouds in the sky and the shadows shielded him from the increasing heat of the day. He felt the temperature change frequently and he liked that. It added a feeling of uniqueness and quality to his day.

When the village had first been created, its inhabitants, led by Tharn, had constructed ten wheelhouses and five large water tanks that were filled by them. Tharn had engineered and constructed the wheelhouses with a handful of family and friends. He had found the area after he had retired from the Trielian Guard and had decided he would become a rancher and farmer and could make a good living doing so. He thought such a fertile valley near the Sippling River would be the perfect place to begin.

First, he had engineered a simple system to store and then distribute the water from the river to the valley to use for drinking and for the watering of the crops. Afterward he had constructed the water tanks and then the wheelhouses to transfer the water into the tanks that sat on the highest point outside of the village. The concept was also simple, but he had to construct the wheel large enough to transfer the water from the river up to the top of the hill.

The river filled long tubes on the wheel which then dumped out into a trough on top of the hill to fill three very large tanks. The tanks had wooden ducts coming from them that carried the water down to the village through an elaborate slough pattern that funneled the water to each farm and crop bed. Twice daily the water was released from the tanks to run down through the sloughs to water the crops. Each owner could control the flow of the water into his crop with a valve at the top of its entry point.

Alaezdar worked straight through the rest of the morning and into the early afternoon with only a short lunch break. He fed the grazing oxen, greased the wheels on the pump houses, fixed a broken latch on one of the locks, and re-nailed some handrails on a few of the water tanks. He was just finishing the handrails when Tharn came up behind him.

"Alaezdar! My goodness, you are hard to find sometimes."

"Just working hard for you," he said without looking up or stopping his work.

"That's what I mean. You work so fast I can hardly keep up with you."

Tharn watched him finish up before continuing.

"Alaezdar, can you stop for a minute and let me talk to you?"

Alaezdar stopped, wiped the sweat off his forehead, and looked at his boss.

"I have been giving this some thought lately, and I think I want to start a new tournament for the kids in the village. Nothing big, but I think it would be fun to start a sword fighting tournament with wooden swords. I think the kids would really get a kick out of this."

"I suppose."

"I want you to run it," Tharn said and gave him a quick wink.

Alaezdar tried to look unimpressed. He wanted to cover up his anger.

"Why me?"

"Well, I am not going to beat around the bush anymore, my young friend. You have been a mystery of sorts around here, but you don't have to deny it from me anymore. I mean…that I know that you are a swordsman of sorts."

Alaezdar's lips went tight in frustration and he took a few seconds before responding.

"What made you come to this conclusion?"

Tharn laughed legitimately, but with a slight sense of condescension.

"Come on. Do you really think I am so blind? If you remember, when you first wandered into our village -- worn out and beat up like a stray hound -- you had a sword on your back."

"That doesn't mean anything. Every man who has any sense knows not to travel without protection. Just because I carry a sword doesn't mean I know how to use it."

"Come on, Alaezdar, I have been a swordsman for the Trielian Guard myself, and I think I can spot a fellow swordsman when I see one, if not a fellow warrior."

"Tharn, really, I don't know what you are talking about."

"Alaezdar, really…you insult me. Your scabbard is not a standard scabbard for a plain sword as protection against the common brigand. Your scabbard is very elegant and a source of pride that only a warrior would take the time to make and own. In fact, I would say it is a scabbard that holds the sword whose owner is a professional swordsman for hire."

"I have to get back to work, if you don't mind," was the best Alaezdar could muster.

"Don't worry, my friend. Your secret is safe with me. Others suspect, as well, but they won't put it together as well as I have," Tharn said proudly.

"You don't understand, Tharn."

Alaezdar took a step toward Tharn with his fists clenched.

Tharn took a few steps back, surprised that he had invoked such anger with his young friend.

"I am on the run!" Alaezdar shouted through clenched teeth. "But I want to stay here! If I am discovered, I will be forced to leave. If you know my past so well as you claim, then I am actually endangering you by being here, and I should leave."

"Alaezdar, it's okay," Tharn said and put his hand on his shoulder. "We are safe here. I have built a wall that would make any commander of any outpost fortress proud. It will protect us from anyone who might do us any harm and I have trained men along this wall to hold anyone off and keep those we don't want in, out."

"You mean, Morlonn, Kunther and a handful of other inexperienced men barely old enough to be called men? Besides, I found my way in without anyone stopping me."

"Because I let you in."

Alaezdar looked incredulous. "You knew I was coming?

Tharn laughed.

"No, goodness no, but I saw you before you saw me. That is why you came through the gate unopposed. Besides, to be honest, you came in from the civilized side of the gate. We don't have a lot of need for extra protection on that side."

Alaezdar shook his head. He began to think of where he should go next. He honestly could not stay there any longer. He liked it there, but he knew he would be endangering everyone if he stayed.

"I can't stay. I have to go," he concluded. He felt defeated.

"No, Alaezdar. You can't leave. I won't let you leave."

"You have to. You are not safe as long as I am here."

"Let me worry about that. I am the ruler, so to speak, of this village. Even though I really don't consider myself the ruler, in essence that is what I am. I am the leader here and I am responsible for everyone's life here, including yours, and I am determined that you stay. Also, I am now not asking you to teach the kids how to use their wooden swords, I am telling you."

"Why me? You said you have enough people working the wall who can teach them the same things I can."

"No, they can't. You are correct about their experience. Sure, they can teach them some, but they won't be able to teach them like you can."

"I am not going to make them killers. It really isn't that hard to teach basic foot stance, blocks and attacks. Anyone can do it."

"I don't care, Alaezdar. You will do it," he said with a warm smile.

Alaezdar shook his head. Oddly, Tharn's smile made him feel at ease, but he was still angry and anxious about being found out by Tharn. At least he didn't insist on knowing which guild he had belonged to. If he had known that it was the same guild that accepted any mission as long as the price was right, he didn't think he would be still standing there being asked to teach kids how to use wooden swords.

"I will do it," Alaezdar acquiesced.

"Fine. I will get a group of interested young boys together either today or tomorrow and you can start directly."

Alaezdar nodded.

"Now, get back to work," Tharn said slapping Alaezdar on his shoulder.

Alaezdar did just that, but only after Tharn had walked completely out of his sight.

***

By mid afternoon Alaezdar had stopped and gone into the village center to pick up a few items he needed to make more repairs. The people were bustling along the dirty fairway and preparing for the upcoming festival. Many people -- mostly the dignitaries from the two most powerful human kingdoms in the north -- would be arriving soon and bringing with them their gold and silver. For most of the villagers their purchases could be enough to get them by for the rest of the year.

Alaezdar looked to the sky and felt the warmth of the early Doreal sun and he took pause for the moment to appreciate his place in this village. The village, even though he liked it, still wasn't the perfect place for him, though. He found it unnerving that everyone knew each other so well, but he admitted to himself that he was beginning to get used to it. The people cared about each other even though, of course, there were some family rivalries, and he found that interesting.

As he walked, he saw men and women packing their horses in front of the shops, with supplies for their ranches, or by the booths that the villagers were beginning to build by the fountain square at the end of the row. Kids were running through the streets with careless abandonment, and why not, he thought. What did they have to care about, what fears filled their souls? Nothing but boredom, Alaezdar concluded. Sometimes boredom was his biggest fear. He smiled in spite of himself. Yes, fear of boredom. And how do you cure that, he thought. Work, that's how.

"Alaezdar! Hey, look at this!" a blond haired ten year old boy in muddy clothes with a dirty face yelled as he ran towards him swinging a stick like a sword. "I found this by the river yesterday. Look! It has a hilt like a real sword," he said and ran up to him, out of breath, thrusting the stick in his face for him to inspect.

Alaezdar took the stick from the boy's hands and smiled.

"Well, Rowlf, you might be able to smack a few squirrels with this stick, but I don't think you would be able to hurt anything else."

"I know, but look at the blade. It looks like a real sword…well, a wooden one, if you want," he admitted and kept shaking his head, attempting to keep the fantasy alive.

"I see," Alaezdar said and took the sword and inspected it more closely, running his finger over the bladed area. It did, he admitted to himself, look like a blade in a crude sort of way. It was flat and beveled on the edges, somewhat. He turned it over, ran his finger over the other side of the blade and pretended to cut himself.

"Ouch!" he mocked and put his finger in his mouth. "You'd better take this back. I don't want to hurt myself."

"Can I come with you, Alaezdar?" the boy pleaded.

"If you want, but you will be bored."

"Nah, I won't. I promise!"

"Suit yourself. Follow, but stay out of my way."

Alaezdar walked through town and Rowlf followed, but he did very little to stay out of the way. He pestered Alaezdar with questions on everything he did and about everything he touched. Once Alaezdar smiled at Rowlf and then ran around the corner to lose him, but Rowlf quickly found him, pointed his stick sword at Alaezdar's belly and mimicked a highwayman.

"Give me your money pouch, old man!" he shouted with a big smile, as if he had just bagged the biggest deer in history.

Alaezdar smiled back, ruffled Rowlf's hair and went back to walking through the village, but the boy continued to follow, smiling and swinging his stick-sword as they went along. Alaezdar stopped a few times to order more items for the festival. Walking by a tack store, he had remembered that a couple of Tharn's horses needed some new blankets and stirrups. Rowlf didn't notice that he had stopped and kept on walking ahead, skipping along, living in his own fantasy.

When Alaezdar had finished, he smiled, thinking that Rowlf had gotten bored and wandered off, but then he heard a crowd of kids' voices a little farther down the street. He looked over and saw that Rowlf was down on the ground being kicked by a group of boys. One of them, a blond haired large boy with a bit of a belly, was breaking Rowlf's stick sword over his knee. He threw it down on top of Rowlf and then spit on him. The other boys laughed and walked away, slapping the big kid on the back as they left. Alaezdar ran to Rowlf and knelt next to him.

"Jor again?"

"Yes, he doesn't like me. He told me I was too young to be playing with a stick like a sword."

"Well, maybe you are."

Alaezdar laughed a little as he grabbed Rowlf's hand and helped him up.

"But I like playing swordsman. What is so wrong with that?"

"Nothing, I guess. Just don't play with real swords."

"Really? That is a stupid thing to say," he groaned.

Alaezdar smiled, tousled Rowlf's hair again and pushed him in the chest a little so that he had to step back. "If you really want to learn how to use a sword, I will teach you in a day or two."

"Really? You are going to teach me? Yeah, you and a few others."

Rowlf smiled looked at his broken stick and grimaced. With his dirty, tear-stained face he looked up at Alaezdar and said. "But I don't have a sword anymore."

Shaking his head, Alaezdar stuck his toe underneath one of the broken pieces of his stick sword and kicked it in the air towards Rowlf.

"That wasn't a sword anyways. It was a stick. Get outta here. I will take care of the sword for you!"

Rowlf jumped away from the stick and watched it hit the ground.

"Yes!" he shouted as he turned and ran away.

Alaezdar watched him leave. He liked Rowlf. He liked his eagerness to learn. It reminded him of himself at that age and how he wanted to learn so much from his older cousins and how he had begged them to teach him. Look where that had gotten him now, he laughed to himself. Nothing and nowhere. But that did not matter now. He wasn't entirely happy with his life so far, but living here at Valewood gave him just enough purpose to survive and just enough distraction to forget about what he was running from.

As he walked down the street and passed the bakery, he could smell the yeasty smell of fresh sourdough. He smiled again, enjoying his new home. The baker's son smiled at him and waved. Alaezdar nodded and kept walking. He passed two more shops when he saw Morlonn at the armory picking up arrowheads that he had specially made just for him. They were arrowheads formed from the fire hardened black rock from the Dragon Cross Mountains.

Morlonn waved to get his attention when he walked by.

"Alaezdar!" Morlonn called and slapped him on the shoulder as he approached.

"Morlonn, the Hunter. How are you?" he asked.

"I am well," Morlonn said with a big smile, genuinely happy to see him. "Tharn has asked me to assemble a bore hunting party for the Fifth of Doreal celebration. I'd like you to come."

"I'd like to come, but I don't have much experience with a bow," Alaezdar lied. Even though his primary weapon was a sword, the members of Rager's House of Renegades had to be proficient in many weapons. Half Blade, a half elf, had taught him how to use the bow with the expertise of an elf, just as Half Blade had learned it from his elven father.

"That's okay. It's not so much for the hunt, but for the company. We will be camping out that evening and coming back in the morning to set up some of the final booths for the celebration.

"Who is coming so far?"

"Tharn is going, but you are the first that I have asked. I'd like to see Rivlok and Kunther come along as well."

"Sounds great. I think I would like that."

"Good. Meet me at my place an hour before sunrise."

"I'll be there." Alaezdar said as he and Morlonn continued walking back to the village center.

As they approached the center plaza, a group of villagers were listening to a man wearing a long black robe. They stood around him in a circle, some listening intently to his words, others mocking him as he spoke.

"Who is that?" Alaezdar asked Morlonn..

"Oh that...He's nothing. It's just Gartan the Dark, from the Watchers Guild," he said mockingly, as if the name had meant something powerful and important. "He shows up a few times a year, but he always shows up a few days before the festival. Tharn invited him once, and since then he always shows up."

"The Watchers Guild, you say?" Alaezdar asked, feigning both interest and ignorance by asking the question, even though he knew the answer. He knew the Watchers Guild very well In fact, they had been useful in many of their missions while he was with Rager's House of Renegades, who had kept close communication with the Watchers Guilds for their knowledge of the land, and its prophecy. His commander, Carsti Balron, had many times used the guild's knowledge of the local geography for inside information before he dispatched his men on dangerous missions.

No one knew how they knew what they knew. It was especially puzzling how they were able to communicate amongst their members because no matter who you talked to, they knew everything that was going on around the land, even if there was a hundred miles separation from the next guild member. As a group they were quite harmless. All they did was watch and report what they saw and even though it had been reported that their guild was very large, no one ever saw more than one member at a time.

"Oh, they claim to know the land as well as the dying races of elves and dwarves," Morlonn said, "but unlike the elves and dwarves, who feel the land, they spread the word through many of their traveling outposts, I don't believe that, but I don't know how they do it either. I just think they're freaks."

"Have you ever really spoken to one without ridiculing him?"

Morlonn laughed.

"No. Are you serious?" he said and looked at Alaezdar as if he were a crazy fool for even asking.

"Yes, I am serious. How are you to learn the land without listening to what others have to say?"

Morlonn shook his head quickly as if to shake a fly out of his hair and said, "You are serious."

Alaezdar realized that he might be treading a bit too far and he changed his tactic.

"No. I just have never seen such a thing this one and I am curious as to what he has to say. It just seems fascinating to me. What is this one saying now?"

"Who cares?"

"It might prove interesting. Come on, just for a little while," Alaezdar pleaded.

"Oh, come on, Alaezdar. We've got so much to do, we don't have time for this. He really isn't that interesting, I promise," Morlonn said, but Alaezdar was already turning in the direction of Gartan. "Alright, fine. We can spare a few minutes since you're new here, but only for a few minutes...no more," he said and followed behind him.

Gartan the Dark stood on the top step of a five-step base that circled the freshly painted center stone fountain with a group of villagers gathered about him. He had dark clothes covered over by a rough, wrinkled and dusty black cloak that matched his dark hair and pointed goatee.

"I tell you again the true words of gloom, my friends. I know not the exact village, but it could be yours. I cannot stay and join your celebration this year, for I am off to see another village to spread the dark word. Take heed and please spread this word amongst your friends, for I am Gartan the Dark, from the Watchers Guild."

Gartan the Dark then pulled his hood over his head, stepped down from the fountain and slowly walked towards the outskirts of the village.

"Let's talk to him," Alaezdar suggested to Morlonn and he began to walk towards Gartan the Dark.

"Why? I told you he is a freak," Morlonn whined.

"Do you know this one in particular?"

"Everyone in the village knows him," Morlonn said with a smirk. "He has been here many times before today. The people find him interesting and listen to him, but only to mock his so called truths."

"So you're saying that nothing he has said has ever come true."

"No, not really. Some of what he says has come true, but anyone can predict some of the things he has prophesied. Most are purely coincidental. He also tells us of events that happen all around Wrae-Kronn. Like what battles are waging in the human kingdoms or how the magic in the land is not dying, but is at conflict with a foreign magic. Whatever that means. He claims to communicate such things from the other guild members who are scattered throughout the known lands. It's all a fraud though."

"I suppose," Alaezdar agreed.

He wanted to tell Morlonn everything he knew about the Watchers Guild, but chose not to in fear that it would prompt more questions, questions he would not want to answer. The Watchers Guild's powers mostly came from their founding fathers. In the early days, the days of the dragons, they went by the name of the Dragon Watchers guild. Their leader at the time, Dragos Gartan, helped the dragons leave the realm of Wrae-Kronn and return to their homeland through the Aaestfallia Keep. For his help the dragons gave him, and whomever else he chose, the gift of foresight. The dragons did this as a thank you and requested only that Dragos Gartan change the name of the guild. They therefore became the Watchers Guild instead of the Dragon Watchers Guild.

With the power of foresight given to them by the dragons, they saw the great demise that was infecting the land of Wrae-Kronn and they dedicated their lives to spreading the ominous word so that the people could prepare themselves for the dark days ahead. To do this they spread throughout the land and communicated to each other by channeling Kronn, the land's magic. Alaezdar had become acquainted with the Watchers Guild and eventually had become very familiar with Gartan the Hooded One, who was in charge of the area surrounding Daevanwood.

"Gartan, the Dark!" Alaezdar yelled to the man.

Gartan turned around. His overly large cloak covered his head and revealed only his face below his forehead. His cloak was dirty and black. Now that Gartan was closer, Alaezdar noticed that what he had thought from a distance were wrinkles were actually vertical and horizontal red stripes that still looked like blood seeping through someone who had just been swiped numerous times by a dragon or by some large creature with vicious talons.

Gartan the Dark stopped and looked at him.

"What message do you bring, Gartan the Dark?" Alaezdar asked after he had stepped in front of him. Morlonn followed and he sighed and rolled his eyes.

"You did not hear?" Gartan asked with a tone of arrogance and condescension.

"No. I beg of your patience to repeat."

Gartan the Dark stared into Alaezdar's eyes quizzically, but then with a sense of slight familiarity.

"No…it can't be…not you. You look…have we met before?"

Alaezdar froze. Gartan the Dark could not possibly recognize him. The only member of their guild to know Alaezdar had been Gartan the Hooded One.

"No, I am new to this area," Alaezdar responded.

"Maybe so, but your eyes bring a strange familiarity to me. I see trouble ahead for you..." He paused to allow Alaezdar to introduce himself by his name. While he waited, Alaezdar noticed that Gartan stared at him in a strange way, as if he could not decide if he was looking at a man or a god.

"Alaezdar," he said finally, filling in the silence.

"Yes, Alaezdar," Gartan the Dark said and removed his hood to show his shoulder length black hair. He was middle-aged, but he showed no signs of aging. He had a youthful look, yet his face held the wisdom of many years. His eyes were dark and colorless. His skin was a darkened bronze with the appearance of someone who rarely saw the indoors. Even though he was cloaked and hooded, it seemed that the sun always found a way to every part of his skin. Over his left eye he had a tattoo of a dragon, facing left, with its wings tucked in tightly. Its tail hung downwards and went around the outside of his eye and then across the top of his cheek, curling underneath his eye.

"I know you now," he said in a sense of understanding. "I told Tharn you would be coming here."

"Oh, come on!" Morlonn protested, a bit too loudly.

"You bring trouble. Dark trouble for many years to come." Gartan again ignored Morlonn's outburst. "I also see confliction and division, though I do see a great victory in the end, but in that victory I also see great darkness, separation, division and bitter cold…dark, solid cold." He paused to reflect, as if he were putting together scattered puzzle pieces in his mind. "Odd…your place upon this realm is important. It is strange, for I do not see pictures of the future beyond that when I look upon you, only dark feelings that end in complete…nothingness. Not death, mind you. Just…nothing."

"Is this what you were telling the villagers?" Morlonn interjected.

"No, it is not," Gartan the Dark said as he came out of his deep state of concentration. "I bring troubled news for your village…"

"Oh? What's new?" Morlonn interrupted in a tone of complete boredom.

Gartan the Dark ignored Morlonn and continued.

"Beware the human kingdoms of the north, and beware of the trouble brewing from the east. I see many problems for these villages here. The Kingdoms of the north are in the beginning phase of a massive turmoil and a tribe of Goblins from the Markenhirth Forest is ready to attack a village in the Valelands. The 89th Bloody Fang Goblin Tribe has called upon their god to help them in their annual battle against the 21st Death Ogre tribe. They request their god's assistance in this battle, but in exchange, he will demand a human sacrifice. I know of nowhere else where they can get a human sacrifice other than within these villages so close to the Goblin Tribes Forest. So I ask you, where do you think they will come? I do not know whom they will take, nor do I know what village they will strike. Nevertheless, it will be soon, and it will happen. Watch for the purple sunset. So, please take heed and protect yourselves from these evil beasts. I must go to spread the word to the other villages."

Gartan the Dark looked at Alaezdar and Morlonn sympathetically, turned abruptly and walked away in a great hurry to leave Alaezdar's presence.

"Now if that isn't the best story I have heard yet," Morlonn said and snickered.

"I think we should protect ourselves," Alaezdar said and stared at Morlonn seriously.

"You've lost it, Alaezdar. Ah, never mind. You're new here. After you hear a few more of these dark tales of false prophecy, you'll catch on."

Alaezdar grabbed Morlonn's arm as he turned to walk away and stared hard into his eyes. "He speaks the truth, Morlonn. Don't ask me how I know, but I know! We should be worried."

"It can't be true. Ever since we built the wall, the Goblin Tribes have never crossed the Sippling River, and they never will. For the most part, they are like snakes…they are more afraid of us than we are of them. Where are you from, anyway? Everyone knows that."

"I was raised in Hyronael. I know it is far removed from the Goblin Tribes, but I know that the Goblin Tribes cannot be trusted or expected to stay in any one place forever, and though they don't like to leave their area, they are not afraid of us."

"Alaezdar, my friend, do not worry. Tomorrow we hunt, the day after that we fest for three days, and the Goblin tribes will not bother us."

Morlonn finished in such a determined voice that Alaezdar knew he could not convince his friend of the possible danger ahead, and he reluctantly let the matter drop. He knew that continuing the conversation could possible trigger in Morlonn a suspicion that Alaezdar was more than he claimed to be.

Alaezdar knew that he had already said more than he wanted to by telling Morlonn where he had lived and his knowledge of the tribes. The only way to convince Morlonn of the truth would be to divulge his credentials and show how he knew what he knew. All he could do now was hope the Goblin Tribes did not attack Valewood, but if they did, he would have to do his best to defend the village.

Chapter 5

The boar came out from behind a cluster of overgrown ferns shrouded by white pine trees. Something had spooked him and he came charging out of the brush at full speed snorting and squealing. Alaezdar lifted his bow, aimed and released.

The arrow hit the boar in the chest behind his left leg. He fell to the ground with no more than a short squeal.

"I got him!" he yelled, happy with his shot.

"Not even close, my friend," Morlonn said from behind Alaezdar, startling him as he spoke. "Your shot was high and wide."

"Sorry, Morlonn the Hunter," Alaezdar said, smiling as he mocked him by emphasizing the words *the Hunter.* "I saw him first, fired, and got him, plain and simple. And fact."

"Come with me, my friend, and I will prove to you whose shot was the deadly one."

They walked to the dead boar and stood over its hairy body. He was a stout boar and would provide plenty of pork for the feast.

"My arrows," Morlonn said and began staring at Alaezdar with his best *I got you* look. He withdrew the arrow with a tug, wiped the blood off the arrowhead, and showed Alaezdar the black diamond tip. Alaezdar looked at the arrow blankly and said nothing as his friend wiped down the whole arrow and returned it to its quiver.

"Maybe next time. Let's find the others so we can clean and pack the boar.

Then we can start the drinking."

Alaezdar, Morlonn, Rivlok, Tharn and Kunther all gathered shortly thereafter, cleaned the boar and set up their camp in a small clearing surrounded by the thick forest trees. They built a fire, more for light, than for heat because the early Doreal evenings were often warm and dry. They sat down around the fire as Morlonn broke out one of the many flasks they'd brought of ale and mead.

"Do you always celebrate the kill of the boar by spending the night in the woods drinking?" Alaezdar asked.

Morlonn laughed, but Tharn answered before anyone else.

"These boys like to drink. All they need is an excuse. Morlonn here works hard for us, so we let him hunt the boar and take us for an adventure in these woods. No one knows the outlying area better than he does."

"I find solace in the woods," Morlonn admitted. "I love to hunt, but I love being alone out here. But even more, I love being out here with friends drinking!" he said as he took the first swig from the bag of mead and passed it to Alaezdar.

After an hour of small conversation, they sat quietly for a few moments, watching the smoke drift into the sky from their crackling fire.

Morlonn broke their silence. "So, Alaezdar, during your travels you said you have seen the Watchers Guild, but have you seen any elves?" he asked, not really probing him for information, but more giving him a sarcastic ribbing.

"I have seen them a few times," he admitted, lying about the frequency. Not only had he seen elves, but also during his time with the Rager's he had both fought with and killed elves many times. He feared they would ask more probing questions, so he decided to give them some information that would defer them from asking more.

"Did you know that there are different types of elves?"

Their silence on the matter told him he was about to keep them interested long enough to give them something new and keep the placated from asking him anything else for a while.

"There are the Val elves and the Sor Elves. The Val Elves are aggressive and have very little magic ability, usually Wrae magic, but the Sor Elves are pure elves who live peacefully and have learned how to use the magic from the land, called Kronn."

"You mean there really is magic in the land?" Kunther asked, showing great interest.

"Very much so. In fact, it is much more complicated than just the ability to use magic because it gets into their religion, their gods and their belief system. As far as the magic is concerned, my father, a wizard, can control both types of magic, I am told. He supposedly can master both Wrae and Kronn, and as far as I know, he is the only human who can control both. Many Sor elves can control both, but not very well, and no Val Elves are known to be able to use Kronn. However, the use of Kronn is dwindling, as magic in the realm overall seems to be fading."

"Do the elves ever fight each other with opposing magic? Kunther asked. "I mean, I have heard that there is magic, but I didn't really believe it, and I had no idea there were different kinds."

"No, not that I know of. The elves have long since joined and have almost blended. Long ago the Val Elves lived just on the other side of the Goblin Ridge Mountains, but the goblins chased them away and they found a home up north with the Sor Elves, where they found a way to live in harmony, blending their differences. But during the Human–Elf war, the elves moved to Lake Quarterstar where both tribes live together. Though sometimes I hear they have internal struggles, because the Sor elves are pure and expect their leaders to be pure of elven heart, but the Val Elves just want to advance their cause. It is actually even more complicated than that, because they actually have two different gods that they worship, but they have learned to accept each other's theological differences. Mostly, they now work together to preserve their magic, but even they know it is weakening. They believe that the extended Markenhirth periods have everything to do with the weakening of the magic."

"How do you know so much, Alaezdar?" Kunther asked, wide-eyed with fascination.

Alaezdar swallowed hard. He had begun to speak too much, but it felt good to explain what he knew about the realm. He was surprised that these people knew so little, except maybe for Tharn, and he was obviously purposely silent during Alaezdar's explanation.

"My father beat all that history into me at a young age. There is no way I could forget any of it."

"Did he teach you any tricks, Alaezdar?" Kunther asked and looked at him as if he were an overachieving schoolboy.

Alaezdar smiled genuinely and told the truth.

"Oh, yeah, lots of times, but I was horrible at it, and I fought him around every corner. The last thing I wanted was to be known as a freak going around the realm using magic at all those freak shows. I did not want people thinking of me of as a man who is laughed at like your friend Gartan the Dark. So, for my disobedience he beat me when I refused, and I gladly accepted the trade off."

"You got beat, did you?" Rivlok finally spoke up after taking a swig of the mead and passing it to Tharn.

"At least every day that I refused my lessons."

"Did he pound you with a fireball or something?" he asked and smirking to himself.

"No, he would never do that. He had too much respect for the magic. If he is one thing, he is loyal to the land and the magic that produces it."

"Then magic comes from the land?" Morlonn asked.

"Kronn does, but Wrae is mostly a learned talent. He could do both. It was pretty amazing what he could do by using both simultaneously. Morlonn, my father would like you. You find the solstice in the woods. He might even be able to teach you simple magic, like how to work the plants, herbs and even the stones from the land to do almost anything from healing to making weapons to calling animals. As much as I hated it, it *was* fascinating to watch him do what he did. When I saw him, that is."

"You told us that your father left you. Now I think I know why I would too if I were him," Rivlok said, smiling.

Alaezdar looked at Rivlok and saw his cocky smile in the firelight. He knew his type. It annoyed him, but he didn't let it show.

"Yeah, once he realized that I would not be his apprentice, he left to do his business in the Northern Kingdoms. He had thought to take me, but when I showed absolutely no interest, he just left and had me live with my cousins."

"I don't think I would've turned away the chance to learn the magic of the land," Kunther mused.

"Yeah, well, maybe sometimes I do regret it somewhat, but when I think long and hard about it, no, not really."

"Morlonn, we need another flask," Rivlok said. He needed to change the subject. He was getting tired of all of the attention Alaezdar was getting.

As dusk gave way to nightfall, so too did their soberness and the five men laughed and chided each other as the night wore on. Morlonn teased Alaezdar off and on throughout the evening about his missed shot. Alaezdar took it well, but wished he could have something on Morlonn to come back with. Instead, he turned to Rivlok for some gossip and revelation.

"So where did you and Aaelie go yesterday?" Alaezdar asked. He knew he would hit a nerve.

"To the woods. You saw us," Rivlok said and took a swig from the leather bag. "And it is no concern to you what Aaelie and I do, or where we go,"

"I was just curious. I thought maybe there was something special by the river that I didn't know about."

"Well, there is something special by the river, and it's for Aaelie and me to share, so it would be wise for you to butt out."

"Sorry," Alaezdar said, not surprised by the attack.

"Alaezdar," Tharn began. "Rivlok and Aaelie have been together ever since they were little kids, and our young friend here always gets a little protective when it comes to his girlfriend Aaelie."

"I think she has some feelings that are changing," Kunther added coming into the conversation for the first time after waking up from a drunken stupor.

"He's alive!" Morlonn announced loudly.

The others looked at the just awakened Kunther and laughed.

"Go back to sleep, you fool," Morlonn said.

"No," Kunther insisted. "Aaelie asked me the other day if Alaezdar was fond of her."

The others looked at Kunther in surprise, and then watched him as he got up and ran to the trees to vomit.

"That's all changing, though, back to the way it's supposed to be," Rivlok defended himself. "Aaelie loves *me* and no one else."

Rivlok then stood up and went to the trees to relieve himself both physically and of the stress of the conversation.

"Don't worry about him, Alaezdar," Morlonn said, looking into the fire as it crackled before him. "Aaelie and Rivlok have been close almost all their lives, just as Tharn had said, but they have been through some rough times together, as well. I think they are beginning to grow apart and their relationship has changed to almost sibling-like."

"I understand. I am a bit fond of Aaelie, but I don't want to disrupt their relationship."

"Relationship?" Morlonn quizzed. "Their relationship has been off and on ever since that foul wizard Torz came here."

"Torz?" Alaezdar said almost too loudly and with too much excitement from the shock of hearing such a familiar name. Alaezdar caught himself and looked around, but the others were just drunk enough not to have noticed his surprise.

"Yeah, a few years ago," Morlonn said, "he and his followers came to Valewood and bullied a few villagers out of their homes. They were rude, but surprisingly did no harm to anyone or their property. They just wanted a place to sleep. Tharn knew Torz, I think. Anyhow, Tharn was able to convince him to leave us alone somehow, because the next morning they left and he hasn't been back since. The real problem, though, came later that evening when a mercenary group came chasing after the wizards. They called themselves the Rager's Swords, I think..."

"The Rager's House of Renegades," Alaezdar interjected without hesitation.

Morlonn looked up at Alaezdar, shocked by the quick correction.

"Yeah," he said, and then continued. "Anyway, one of the men grabbed Aaelie and attempted to take her for his own, but Aaelie's father stepped in and attacked the man with his sword. Aaelie broke free during the attack and ran to find Rivlok. Rivlok came running, but stopped short when he saw the two men locked in combat. Aaelie yelled for him to do something, and Rivlok hesitated, although he did finally take his knife and run toward the two men. Ironically, all he did was distract Aaelie's father long enough for the mercenary to cut him down. Aaelie was irate and blamed Rivlok for her father's death. Rivlok contends that even if he hadn't jumped in, and had stayed out of the fight, Aaelie's father would still be dead."

Morlonn stopped and stared back into the fire before he continued. "So you can see why they are having problems. It took Aaelie a while to let go of her anger toward Rivlok. Not just for letting her father die, but later for not avenging his death. Rivlok often has to defend himself against Aaelie's attacks, but worse yet, he condemns himself for being part of her father's death. I think they have worked through a lot of their problems of late, though."

"I believe they both still hurt deeply, though," Tharn added. "Whenever they fight, Aaelie brings it up to wound his heart..."

"And she does it quite a bit, and she doesn't care where they are. Public places aren't off limits when she fights," Morlonn added.

Alaezdar nodded. He understood, and he laid back and looked into the stars above him. The others saw him move and slowly began to ready themselves for the night, as well, while Rivlok stood just outside the reaches of the firelight. He had been listening to the whole conversation and he stared blankly at Alaezdar with clenched fists.

David L. McDaniel

Chapter 6

Once a year, during the transition from the end of the hot season of Flamespan to the coming of the Doreal and the harvest season, the small village community of Valewood became a center of excitement and bustling energy. The fields, once full of the diligent labor that would determine the success or failure of the whole year, became silent and were left alone to stand while the village shifted their efforts from the fields to the construction of the annual harvest festival.

Throughout the village, bright colored tents and tall banners surrounded the main center. The banners displayed the markings of all of the kingdoms of Wrae-Kronn in order to welcome all the representatives from those kingdoms who would arrive in the splendor and grace of their home kingdoms. Also in attendance were the surrounding Valeland communities that had spent the whole year producing crops for all of Wrae-Kronn. They all migrated to Valewood, as it was now the center of importance in all the Valeland communities. The representatives from all the kingdoms partook in the Fifth of Doreal celebration in the Valeland communities and bargained for the best prices for the newly harvested crops and anything in the market was available for its best price, too, through the beginning of the next year. The Valelanders competed amongst other villages to get the business from all the other kingdoms.

The crop owners ran each tent and displayed the fruits of their hard work. Some tents had not just food, but other wares created in the Valelands,

63

such as glass blown items and handcrafted clothing made with intricate detail by the wives and children of the farmers. There were even tents displaying weapons created by the local sword and bow maker's guilds.

The villagers catered to the guests with free samples of their products as they tried to obtain the visitors' permanent business, and those representatives took advantage of their catering by promising the merchants to purchase their product, but they often remarked that they must first keep an open mind to other markets. In exchange, the representatives brought down items that many of the Valelanders enjoyed, such as the black arrowheads that Morlonn used.

After having just dropped off their boar at the butcher to be prepped for the festival, Alaezdar and Morlonn walked through the village to find Tharn and help him finish with the final preparations to his tent. His honeydew melons were all displayed and ready for testing by the Trielian and Battleworth representatives.

The morning air still had a slight chill to it, but the sun had already risen above the Goblin Ridge Mountains, or the Waerymyn Crags, their original name given to them by the ancient elves who once had lived there. The elves had long since left after the Goblin tribes had overrun the area many years earlier. With the sun now cresting the jagged peaks, warmth filled the valleys and chased off the evening chill as the early morning dew evaporated.

Villagers were busy and had been for many hours. Alaezdar thought it was nice not to have a pressing purpose right at that minute, and he was enjoying watching the other villagers work. Morlonn tapped his elbow with his and pointed to the bakery with his chin.

"Smell that?" he asked.

Alaezdar could indeed smell the fresh baked treats that were just being put out onto the shelves outside of Baker Cutch's booth. The smell of fresh baked goods mixed with the morning sun and added an air of freshness and excitement to the morning, a true sign, Aldaezar thought, that a festival was right around the corner.

"Good morning, Master Cutch!" Morlonn said, but before the baker could respond, the whole village radiated with a loud blowing of horns from less than a mile away. Everyone in the streets began to scatter to safety, either inside their tents or into one of the permanent establishments along the street.

"I truly hate this part," Morlonn muttered. "Come on. We need to get out of the way."

Within minutes soldiers in full armor charged in on horseback, led by a man in armor who was more distinct, cleaner, and shinier than all the others. He led the charge with his sword drawn. Those that followed also had their swords drawn and their shields raised as they charged into the village's two main streets. The streets opened at a Y at the western end and the soldiers split the difference and covered both avenues with horse and warrior.

They wore square, dark blue helms with sharp black rectangular blades on the top, back and sides. Most had swords, but some had bows and were firing arrows into the sides of the shops. Some arrows were lit, but the warriors only fired the flaming ones into the dirt directly in front of them. The horses were also armored and had the blue and black colors of Triel on their overcoats with the emblem of a peak from the Stoneridge Mountains and on a black-over-blue shield on their hindquarters, a lightning bolt splitting the mountain.

The warriors on horseback blazed through the streets and were gone, but right behind them were the foot soldiers charging in with shields up and swords drawn. They came in screaming their battle cry, and behind them were the horn blowers playing the battle charge and making a noise much louder and chaotic, although their ranks had a hint of strategic organization.

The horse and foot warriors circled the village in this fashion three times before elegantly dressed pages marched in carrying the Trielian blue and black banners. Behind them a chariot pulled by four white mares appeared and stopped at the end of the street just before the fountain. Slowly the people began to come out of their safe hiding places and crowd about the fountain where the chariot came to a halt.

"Does Triel do this every year?" Alaezdar asked as they began walking to the fountain.

"Unfortunately, yes. They seem to feel the need to display their dominance over our village. In a way, they do own us remotely. Tharn, a Treilian warrior once, has given Triel the feeling that we owe allegiance to them, even though we are independent. I think they also do this so that they will have better deals than any Battleworth representative."

Alaezdar and Morlonn arrived at the fountain just as a well dressed, fat bald man stepped out of the carriage. He had four warriors on each side of him and a fifth warrior stood directly in front of the large man, facing him. His armor was different from the others, shinier and the colors darker and deeper. It appeared as if his armor had never seen any combat, but he had the air and composure that he was indeed a warrior who had been in many battles or had led many more.

Once the fat dignitary stepped out of the carriage, the warrior said a few words and stepped aside. He looked in front of him and saw Tharn bending to one knee, his head bowed low.

"Stand, my friend and equal!" he said, laughing. "You do not need to kneel. We are here on a visit to your lovely village."

"This village belongs to Triel and King Toron!" Tharn said humbly.

"Oh, Tharn, you and I both know better than that! You may swear allegiance to the King, but Triel does not own this land…not yet, at least," he added quietly with a wink.

"Rise, my friend," he said and placed his hand on Tharn's head. "Show me to my quarters. Same place as always?"

"Yes, the finest inn in all of the Valelands. The Honeydew Inn. I have cleared it of all its customers for your stay so that you will be most comfortable."

"You really are a dear friend, Tharn."

"Will your soldiers be bivouacking outside of the village as always?"

"No, my friend. Not this year. I have reason to keep them close this year, so they will be sleeping wherever they want. If they find a suitable home, they will take it. If not, they will sleep in the streets or on the floors of some of your other great establishments."

"But Ambassador Krostos, I don't understand."

"I don't expect you to, but you will now follow me. I want you to meet someone."

The ambassador motioned to his warrior in the shiny, deep blue and black armor to come over.

"This is Warrior Azrull, my most trusted warrior for protection. He even offers me sage advice, and he tells me that I am foolish to allow myself to trust you so dearly."

"But we go back a long ways, Krostos. Surely, you don't think that I would allow any harm to come to you?" Tharn protested.

"Of course not. I have assured him that you are harmless now. You were once a great warrior, but now you are just an aged veteran. However, warrior Azrull has told me some things about our king and these lands that bring me pause. He is worried about the Battleworth Kingdom building up forces along the mountains near our border. He does not trust the Battleworth ambassador because of this, but do not worry, it is only politics and all will be well in the end. Trust me."

Before Tharn could answer, Warrior Azrull stepped in and guided the ambassador down the road towards the inn while giving orders to his troops to mount up, secure the area and prepare to set up encampment.

Tharn started to walk with them when Warrior Azrull turned to Tharn and put his hand in his face. Tharn saw nothing but the iron gauntlet in his face as the warrior spoke.

"You will come no further, old man. Your time here is numbered, as I will be making a few changes very soon that you will not like."

"Take you helm off while you speak to me!" Tharn yelled at him and he knocked his hand out off his face.

Warrior Azrull grabbed Tharn's arm and pushed the old man's face down to the ground in one swift motion. As he held Tharn down, he hissed in his ear through clenched teeth.

"You will kneel to me, old man. You have no grounds to make any demand of me, ancient one, from the old days that no longer exist. This is not your typical visit. This time we have secured and taken over your town. Whether we leave as a unit or if I decide to leave a small garrison post here to keep you in line will depend upon your hospitality over the next few days. If your allegiance truly is with Triel, then we will have no problems here. Understand?"

Alaezdar and Morlonn saw what was going on, but could not hear what was being said. The minute that Tharn was pushed to the ground, Morlonn stepped forward to intervene, but Alaezdar grabbed his arm.

"No, not yet. Not now."

"He can't do that to him," Morlonn said in anger.

"Trust me, I believe he can. It will only get worse if you step in."

Then, as quickly as it happened, Warrior Azrull turned Tharn loose, spun around and he and Ambassador Krostos left Tharn, still on his knees in the road. They weren't more than ten steps away, when Morlonn ran to Tharn and lifted him back onto his feet.

"Are you okay?" Morlonn asked.

"Fine. I have been expecting that this day would soon come. Don't worry about me, just get on the wall and bring as many young men to it as you can. Get Kunther up there as well. Alaezdar, I think it is time you set up that tournament for the kids. Make sure they are old enough to carry a real sword if need be."

"Do you think there may be a fight?" Alaezdar asked, astonished, knowing that a fight with seasoned troops would be suicide.

"No, I don't, but I do want to give the impression that we aren't to be bullied around. In the meantime, I will send word to my superior about this. That isn't going to change things directly, but it might help make things a little smoother for next year."

"I will start right away," Alaezdar said.

Tharn looked around and noticed that the crowd that had arrived to watch the annual spectacle of the arrival of the Trielian forces was now gawking at him in fear.

"Do not worry, friends," Tharn began. "Our friends from Triel mean no harm to us. I just misspoke to the Ambassador and his overanxious guard took offense to it. Ambassador Krostos is our friend and he will straighten out his overzealous body guard."

"Now go," Tharn whispered to Morlonn.

Chapter 7

By mid-afternoon Tharn, Morlonn, Kunther and Alaezdar were on top of the gate overlooking the Sippling River.

"What are you doing with this piece of junk?" Tharn asked, looking at the scattered parts of Morlonn's Catapult. Bolts lay scattered on the deck next to the base of a small wheel-less catapult. Stretched bowstring twine lay balled up next to the arm of the catapult which was also disassembled.

"A project for the last night of the festival," Morlonn answered, almost embarrassed after this morning's event.

Tharn shook his head. "Never mind. I am sure that I really don't want to know. Alaezdar, I have about fifteen teenagers headed over here for your tutelage. I am going to have you show them the ropes and then Morlonn will put them on the gate for a tour to show them where to be in case of an attack and where to post, just so that we look strong. Kunther, you will be with Alaezdar and assist him. Morlonn, tonight you and I are going to meet at the smithy to send off for another load of metal before Ambassador Krostos can figure out that we have come up short with his load."

Tharn looked down from the tower toward the village side and saw his group of kids walking up to the gate.

"There you go, Alaezdar," Tharn said and pointed them out. "Head on down to the river and give them some techniques and explain the rules of the tournament that they think they are training for."

"Are we still going to have the tournament after what happened this morning?" Alaezdar asked.

"Even more so than before. Let me get this straight. I am not expecting anything bad to happen. Ambassador Krostos is my friend from a long time ago and I trust him. However, I do not trust this Warrior Azrull. I do not know him and I have never heard of him. I know nothing about him. So, because of this, and because I am an ancient one from the old days, I know how quickly things can go sour and I am just taking precautions to assure that our festival does not turn out to be an ugly one."

"You won't get any argument from me," Alaezdar said. He respected Tharn's thought process and initiative in the situation.

Alaezdar and Kunther ran down the steps and off to meet the kids. Tharn had made a dozen wooden swords and had them placed in a barrel by the small iron gate that led from outside the village to an open grove next to the Sippling River.

Alaezdar liked this part of the river. It had a sharp bend in it and white water rushed by and ran directly into one of Tharn's wheelhouses, which picked up the water and started its journey up the hill. The scrub pines, oak and alder trees in the lower valley lined the grove and kept the hot sun from burning the soft grass there at the neck of the river.

"Everyone grab a sword. You too, Kunth, but stand next to me," he said once they were all assembled and the young boys were staring at him with eager eyes.

They all did as commanded, and he had them line up in by height from tallest to smallest. He was pleased that most of the kids were the same age and surprisingly close to the same height.

"This is going to be a ton of fun for you guys. You will compete in a tournament during the festival in front of the whole village and, even more impressive, you will be competing in front of all the warriors you saw ride into our village today. Any questions before we begin?"

A stocky, dark haired boy about twelve raised his hand.

"What is your name?' Alaezdar asked him.

"Jor"

"Hi, Jor. What is your question?"

"My dad says you are dangerous and I shouldn't be here, but I like you and I don't think you are dangerous," he said with as much arrogance and cockiness he could spit out.

Alaezdar just shook his head.

"Well, I am glad you don't think I am dangerous, but I have a secret for you…come here," Alaezdar motioned with one finger for him to approach and when he was just within arm's reach, he grabbed the back of his shirt and turned him around so that he faced the group of boys.

"See this boy here?" he said, releasing the back of Jor's shirt and walking around to his left side. "He is a big strong boy, is he not?" he asked, facing all of the boys.

The boys nodded in unison. A few of the boys that were part of Jor's group smirked. They thought that Alaezdar might be about to prop up their leader.

"He is strong. In fact, he might win this tournament by beating all of you, so maybe we should just end it all now and go home…"

"Noo!" they all moaned in unison.

"Really? Fine. We will train, but first I would like to get something out in the open. Kunther, throw me a wooden sword."

Kunther picked up one of the wooden swords, threw it to him and Alaezdar caught it by the blade. He handed it hilt first to Jor.

As soon as Jor took it, Alaezdar withdrew his own sword from his scabbard. It was a borrowed sword and scabbard from Rankin's shop and rusty flakes fell onto the ground as he withdrew it. Alaezdar looked at it and smiled briefly. He realized he shouldn't have been surprised at the condition of the sword. I love it here, he thought to himself.

He took a single step forward and pointed and held the tip of the sword inches away from the bridge of the boy's nose.

"Defend yourself, Jor!" he yelled.

Jor raised his sword timidly.

Alaezdar took his sword and smacked the wooden sword out of Jor's hand. As it fell onto the soft grass, Jor grabbed his wrist and looked as if he were about to cry.

Alaezdar sheathed his sword.

"Does this look like a fair fight to you?

All of the boys shook their heads.

"No. Of course it is not a fair fight." He pointed to Rowlf. "Come here."

Rowlf lowered his head and stepped forward, stopping a few feet in front of Alaezdar.

"What I want to know," he said, grabbing Rowlf by the shoulders and turning him so that he faced Jor, "is who thinks this would be a fair fight? The big Jor versus the young and scrawny Rowlf."

All the boys were silent except for of Jor's friends, who began snickering again.

"Rowlf is not only small, he is also touched in the head!" one of them shouted.

All of the boys began to laugh.

"Enough!" Alaezdar put his hand on Rowlf's head and tussled his hair. "Go back to the group."

Rowlf ran back to the group and hid behind some of the taller boys. Alaezdar grabbed Jor by the back of the shirt again and turned his back to him, withdrew his sword and smacked him on the back with the flat of the sword.

"Ouch!" Jor screamed and he went to his knees.

Tears began to form in his eyes as Alaezdar grabbed him and picked him up to face the group again. He stood behind Jor and replaced his sword in its scabbard. He leaned towards Jor and whispered in his ears loud enough for everyone to hear.

"I have a message for you and your dad. If you touch Rowlf again, you *and* your dad are going to find out just how dangerous I am. You should listen to your dad more. Now, go home!" he said.

He kicked Jor in the butt as he ran away.

The other kids laughed, and Alaezdar grabbed Kunther's sword and smacked the two blades together. "Enough!" he yelled.

"I am about sick and tired of you and your families not trusting me. Everyone have a seat."

Every kid sat down. They were listening now with all of their eyes and their ears wide open.

"I know I am kind of a mystery to you all, but I really am not as dangerous as you think. I have seen many things in my short life and have done many things, many of which I will never tell. But I will give you a little bit about myself."

He looked at the kids and remembered what it was like when he had been about their age. He remembered his fascination letting his two cousins teach him how to use a wooden sword. He respected those two boys and they had treated him as if they were brothers. Even though they had never met him until his father had dropped him off to live with his aunt and uncle, they agreed to take care of him after the wizard Torz had killed his mom.

"My father is a very well known and powerful wizard in this realm," he began. "You may have heard of him. He is called Valvector-Sor."

He waited to see their reaction, but no one seemed to recognize the name.

"However, he is one of very few people, now and ever, to be able to use Wrae magic and Kronn magic together. Does anyone know about those two types of magic?"

A few kids raised their hands timidly as if to say that they had heard of it, but they did not look as if they wanted to be asked to explain what they knew.

"I figured as much. Wrae magic, according to my father, is elven magic that can be resourced from the air and is a manmade magic that anyone can learn to use, but the elves are masters at it, especially the Val elves who worship Val Eahea. Kronn is a native magic and can be resourced through the land. Those that can use Kronn feel it coursing through their soul from the ground up. The Sor Elves are masters of Kronn, which is really quite impressive because it is a foreign magic to elves. Is every one lost yet?"

One of the kids raised their hands and blurted out, "So..." He paused. "Elves are real?"

Alaezdar laughed and ran his fingers through his hair.

"Maybe we should just start with the training."

Another boy immediately stood up and blurted out, "But wait. You really haven't told us anything about yourself."

"Fair enough. I was born in Hyronael, a small village north of the two Daevan Kingdoms where half elves live...Oh, but you guys probably have never heard of half elves. Anyhow, after my mother was killed, my aunt and uncle raised me. My cousins, who were older than I was, grew up and went off in search of adventure in the human kingdoms of the north to become great warriors. As far as I know, one of them could be one of these soldiers from Triel. Everything I learned, I learned from them, and now I will teach you what they have taught me.

Alaezdar instructed them to jump up and proceeded to teach them some simple basics of sword fighting, beginning with the proper stance and balance. He then taught them how to attack and to defend and how to do it using techniques such as the thrust, the swing and the parry. They practiced for about two hours until he thought they had done enough.

When he tried to end their practice, they whined and complained so loudly that they talked him into practicing for another hour.

It felt good for him to be around young teenagers again. It gave him a solace and a feeling of redemption after the terrible fate of the kids on the mission that had caused him to leave the Rager's House of Renegades. It was nice to see these boys smile, laugh and have fun. When Tharn asked him to do this sword tournament, he was reluctant to do so, but now he was looking forward to it. It might even raise his standing with some of the suspicious villagers who thought him so dangerous. Yes, this was a sword fighting skill he was teaching them and that could exacerbate their fears that he was dangerous, but if they saw him interacting with the kids, they might see a different side of him than they had when he was hidden away on Tharn's ranch.

Not that he was seeking acceptance with the village, because when it came down to it, he really was just in hiding. It would be nice to be rid of the idea that he was dangerous, though. If he could erase that misconception, he would really be embedded in the community and therefore truly hidden in the village and harder to spot if any outsiders came looking for him.

He and the boys practiced for another hour before he finally told them that they were doing exceptionally well and learning at an advanced pace, but it was time to quit for the day.

***

Later that night Tharn and Morlonn stood outside the smithy's shop. Torches flickered in a light breeze near the building and they could hear Rankin pounding metal on his anvil. They stood talking quietly and waiting for some of the Trielian warriors to settle down for the night.

A handful of them still mingled in the streets. They had long since lost their full battle armor, and instead had changed into their lighter, black leather armor over blue silk tunics. They also had replaced their combat ready bastard swords with a lighter short sword. Tharn wasn't sure if this was because they felt unthreatened or because they wanted the smaller sword for closer combat and the need for quick stabbing. Either way, it made Tharn uneasy.

Earlier, Tharn and Morlonn had broken up a fight at the tavern two doors down from the smithy. Three soldiers had taken the barkeep's wench, dragged her outside into the streets and started to lift her dress. Morlonn wasted no time in getting to the three and tackled the one that was at her feet.

Tharn had been impressed at how quickly Morlonn had reached her. With two quick strides, Morlonn aggressively tackled the soldier before the other soldier, being trained in such circumstances, immediately went to the aid of his comrade and was about to stab Morlonn in the back with his short sword. Tharn then came up behind him, grabbed his sword hand with his own right hand, and had his dagger to his throat with his left.

"Listen, now," Tharn growled.

He looked to the third soldier, who was now holding the wench. Not wanting to lose his advantage, the soldier backed away two steps so that he could see Morlonn and the third soldier. Morlonn was still struggling with the soldier he had tackled, but he soon ended up on top of him with his dagger at his throat.

"You boys are wrong," the soldier holding the barmaid began. "This is our town now, and one word from me to Ambassador Krostos and I am sure you will be sent to the dungeons, or worse yet." He gave the two a dark grin, "I will even volunteer to remain here and be a rancher and I will own you as a slave and work you to your bones until you die. Your choice."

At first, no one moved, but when Tharn placed his dagger deep enough into the throat of the soldier he was holding, the soldier stood on his toes and stiffened.

"Let her go," Tharn commanded again, "Morlonn, let him up."

The other soldier released his grip on the wench. She started to walk away, sobbing, but she took the time to spit at the soldier's feet before she ran back into the tavern.

Tharn still held his man at knifepoint. "Drop your sword," he said.

When the soldier dropped his sword, Tharn walked over and stepped on it, and then pushed the man away.

"Warrior Azrull is not going to like this, old man!" he spat as he helped up the soldier who Morlonn had knocked to the ground. The three of them walked away.

"Why do they have to call me, old man?" Tharn mused. "In my day they wouldn't have stood a chance."

"What are you talking about, Tharn? They didn't stand a chance today. You showed them who was boss tonight."

"No, I think we are going to have some repercussions from this Azrull. We had better get ready for a bumpy road. Friend of Triel or not, I think we are in for trouble."

Darkness now covered Valewood like an ominous foreboding and the torchlight in the streets brought shadows that flickered in the warm evening breeze. Tharn and Morlonn heard Rankin pounding mightily on his anvil in his smithy while they waited even longer for the night to settle down. The soldiers continued to mingle as if on watch, waiting for something else to happen.

After Tharn had chased away the three deviant soldiers, they were still present, but it seemed no one would come to confront Tharn or Morlonn. Warrior Azrull either was pre-occupied or did not care, and Tharn doubted the latter. What did concern him was that he did not know what Azrull was preoccupied with. Was it the molesting of one of his villagers or the planning of a bigger demise for the village. Tharn was not happy with either prospect.

"I don't think we can wait any longer," he whispered to Morlonn.

"I think you're right. How do you think we can get the caravan out without anyone noticing?" he asked.

"I don't know," Tharn admitted as he walked inside the smithy.

Rankin saw Tharn and immediately put down his hammer and stopped working on the blade. Inside, Jord worked on some leather breastplates and five other men sat in the back of the room, either sleeping or leaning against the wall quietly and talking amongst themselves. Tharn motioned to one of the men to stand and join them and he jumped right up and approached.

"Coben, are you and your men ready to go back?" Tharn asked.

"No, we are not," he responded with anger, but with a hint of fear on his face.

Tharn turned to Rankin. "How much raw Goblin-Touched Ore did you get on the last trip?"

"Not enough to fill the Ambassadors quota he gave us."

"How much are we short?"

"It looks like another two loads, but I think I have enough junk ore lying around, I could mix it in to get us close."

Tharn shook his head.

"Ambassador Krostos isn't the most observant of men," he said, "and you might be able to sneak it past him, but I don't know about this Warrior Azrull. He may know the difference. I don't want to take a chance of causing more problems than we already have. If we can get one more shipment back here before the festival ends, I think I can make that work. If I can keep Warrior Azrull away from the Ambassador, I think I can convince him that that it is enough," Tharn turned and looked to the caravan leader again. "You will go back."

"But Tharn, the goblins are raiding. There is no guarantee that we still have a mine to work in to get your quota. I'll go back if we can take some of these Trielian soldiers with us."

"No, that is out of the question. The King has mandated that if we want to keep our autonomy here, we are not to use -- or even request -- the king's soldiers to help us with anything. The fact that we used them to dig our sloughs years ago was a special favor that he made clear would never happen again."

"Then what are we supposed to do if the mine is overrun by goblins?"

"Kill them," he said caustically.

"We will die! I can't believe you are asking this of us, all for a kingdom that doesn't belong here, supplying them with this nasty poisonous metal!"

"This kingdom is going to protect us if other kingdoms decide to invade the realm, and King Toron assures us that a war is coming. And when this war breaks out, what side do you want to be on?"

"Neither," he said.

"That is foolish! You will end up dead and ignorant if that is what you believe. You will take your men and head back to the mine. Go cautiously and quietly or storm the mine. Either way we need this ore to survive another year. I can talk favor after being a little bit short, but not as short as we are now. If I could go with you, I would, but it is more important that I stay. I will send you a rider to act as a scout and give you an ample supply of arrows and shields, but nothing more. Or you can refuse, and I will send you and your families away from this village, never to return."

"Look at these men," Corben said and pointed to his men as they sat and leaned against the far wall in the shadows. "Look at their eyes, and look at them good, because you have just condemned them to death. We will go, not because we believe in your cause, but because we do not want to be exiled from our home. Believe it or not, Tharn, we love what we have here, and I may not agree with you, but we *will* die for it."

Tharn extended a hand of friendship, but Corben only looked at it at and shook his head and tightened his jaw.

"Offer me that hand when I return, if I return. Let's go men. We're going back!"

Corben and his men loaded up their carriage with the necessary supplies. They were quiet in the night and they snuffed out the torches on the back side of the shop where the carriage and team were parked. Tharn made sure that they had the extra gear he had promised, and when they were loaded, he climbed up to the top of the carriage where the team leader and Corben sat ready to go.

In the dark Tharn could barely see Corben's face, but he could tell he was not happy. He had known Coben for many years and knew him to be one of the bravest men, even braver than some of the soldiers he had served with. He knew the fear within him about not returning was great, and the prospect of him not returning was more probable than not.

"Bring this load back with all of your men," Tharn said. "I will send a scout for you in the morning. He will know how to find you, if you stay to your normal path."

"Send someone good, and not a young boy."

"I will. We'll see you soon."

"I don't think so," Corben said.

He motioned to the team leader to move. The horses responded to the quiet command and they slowly rolled away into the night and headed for the gate out of Valewood and into the Goblin Tribes Forest.

Chapter 8

Alaezdar and Kunther stood in the center of the round pen, just south of Tharn's main horse stable. Tharn had built it in the middle of a cluster of oak trees so that it provided some shade and respite from the hot Flamespan sun when he was training his young fillies or his unbroken studs and mares.

A crowd of over fifty villagers and guests, including some Trielian soldiers, crowded around the pen and watched as Alaezdar assembled his group of teenagers, all armed with shields, elbow guards, shin guards and helms that the smithy had lying around and had never used. He had even custom made a few to fit some of the teens. Most of the boys stood quietly inside the pen while a few fidgeted, eager to get started.

Alaezdar turned a full circle and looked around at the spectators. Most of them he had seen before, and although he may not have spoken to them, he knew their faces. Some of those he had spoken to did not always have kind words for him, so it impressed him that they were there. He could feel the festival atmosphere about the place and he could smell the food cooking on the grills. It was nearing lunchtime on the first day of the festival.

"Today is the first round of the tournament for these boys," he said to the crowd. "We will start with a free-for-all fight that these young men have been working so hard on lately. Kunther and I have been giving them some tips on how to fight with their wooden swords. Your Kunther here is an accomplished apprentice. He learns quickly and your young boys have responded well to Kunther's teachings,"

Kunther smiled at the crowd after hearing Alaezdar's accolades and his chest puffed out a bit.

"Kunther, get these young warriors ready!" Alaezdar commanded and Kunther withdrew the sword that Rankin had made -- which he had promptly named Straight Edge -- and yelled to the boys to get in the pen and line up beside him. Alaezdar continued his introduction.

"The rules to this part of the tournament are simple. They will fight until only one is standing victorious. This is their showmanship of what they have learned in just a short time. Then we will move onto one-on-one combat, matching the boys evenly, until we reach the final two, and then we will have them fight on the final evening of our festival. We will crown the winner at the Fountain Dance."

Kunther had the boys spread out with their backs to the round pen wall, and he and Alaezdar walked outside of the pen and gave the signal for the boys to go at it. They all charged to the center while the crowd shouted encouragement. The boys immediately responded to the cheers and they went at it with great enthusiasm as their excitement and adrenaline kicked in. They all went on the attack, and their wooden swords clacked when they hit each shield and sword. They blocked and sparred and displayed both their offensive maneuvers and defensive maneuvers simultaneously. Even Rowlf fought well. He defeated one kid before two of Jor's friends teamed up on him and took him out. All the boys fought as they had been taught and they fought fairly. When they were hit in the kill zone, they fell to the ground and waited for the match to end.

Alaezdar felt pride that he could teach these skills to the boys and that they could learn so quickly. It almost made him yearn to be back with his guild, until he remembered the blood, the gore, the politics within the guild, and the politics of the realm that had made him sick and regretful that he was even part of it. He loved this simple farming life and felt a bit resentful that Tharn would even ask him to do this.

That thought brought about his concern again for how Tharn had suspected that he was so knowledgeable about his swordsmanship.

Alaezdar did miss his friend Shadow Blade. Shadow Blade had saved his hide more than once. His friend had very much lived up to his name as he never liked to be in the spotlight or at the front of a mission, yet he was always a critical component to the success of every mission in which he was involved.

Alaezdar thought of the last time he saw him, and it saddened him. Shadow Blade had found him alone to tell him that even though he was his friend, the next time he saw him, he would kill him. That was his mandate with the guild, now that Alaezdar had just exiled himself.

Alaezdar wondered, if it came down to it, if that time came, could he kill Shadow Blade in combat? It might come to that, he feared, just because he would have to defend himself. He would not want to, and he also wondered how far Shadow Blade would go to kill him. He knew Shadow Blade would have no problem fulfilling his mandate. His loyalty was one of his strongest points, but Alaezdar knew he would be conflicted with his loyalty to the guild and his loyalty to his friend.

The crowd's sudden cheer brought him out of his thoughts. The last boy had been victorious. The other boys stood up as Alaezdar came to the center of the pen and congratulated them all before the crowd. The boys rushed out of the round pen as a hurried, but organized team and grabbed a half dozen of Tharn's scarecrows and went back and placed them in random spots around the inside of the pen.

"Ladies and gentlemen," Alaezdar announced, "I have a nice surprise for you all. While our boys are resting, we have a little spectacle to show you involving one of your very own. Boys, release the pig!"

Five younger boys came into the pen, one of them carrying a small pot bellied pig. He let the little animal go and as soon as the pig was on the ground, it began to run around squealing and all the boys started to chase it. The pig tried to escape through the pen, but small boards had been placed around the outer edge to stop him. The crowd laughed as a few boys dove for the pig, but missed and landed in the soft sand.

Then, without any warning, Morlonn jumped into the pen from one of the oak tree limbs overhanging the pen. With his bow in hand, he reached into his quiver, nocked an arrow and released. He hit one of scarecrows in the chest. The boys kept chasing the pig, oblivious to Morlonn, who went to the next scarecrow, nocked another arrow and fired hitting another scarecrow in the forehead.

The boys now ran randomly around Morlonn as he rolled on the ground, nocking another arrow and firing from one knee. His arrow flew above one of the boys' heads and hit the scarecrow in the chest again.

The crowd screamed in terror and began yelling curses at Alaezdar for Morlonn to stop before he hurt one of the boys, but Morlonn continued. He fired another arrow that landed directly in front of the pig, and the pig changed directions one more time. Morlonn then ran to the edge of the pen, climbed to the top and did a back flip off the top rung while he nocked another arrow and fired at another scarecrow. He hit it in its head right where the nose would be.

He fired off three more arrows in succession, hitting each scarecrow in the same spot where the first arrows had landed. Then he stood up and fired a series of arrows, so quick in succession that his hands were a blur as they went from quiver to bow. He fired inches in front of the pig's path, each time forcing the pig to change directions, until it ran into one of the boy's hands.

The kids cheered and now even the crowd cheered.

Alaezdar wasn't sure if it was from relief that the spectacle was over or if it was from their pure excitement watching the spectacle. Maybe a little of both, he figured. Two adults, obviously parents of one of the boys, were still yelling curses at Alaezdar and Morlonn, but Morlonn took a sweeping bow, spinning around while doing so to incorporate everyone who had surrounded the round pen.

Alaezdar went over and raised Morlonn's hand as if he had just won a tournament.

"Ladies and Gentlemen, this is your village hero. Morlonn! At no time, I promise you, was your child in any danger…as Morlonn has just proven to you!"

The two parents grabbed their children and left the round pen. One of them, a heavy-set woman, was still yelling curses until her husband finished whisking her away.

Alaezdar smiled deviously. He knew he would never hear the end of it, but he could not help himself. He knew the kids were in no danger, but not having kids himself, he figured he would never understand a parental perspective. He had once known how to use that powerful emotion to gain advantage, though, because he had witnessed it when his leader, Commander Carsti Balron, had sent them on that final mission of kidnapping the children of his nemesis Reiker-Kol. Now Alaezdar was witness to that love bond again, but was still calloused to his reaction because he knew that the skills of Morlonn were beyond any he had seen in his life. He had felt this would be the best way to display those skills, by using other peoples' kids for an emotional effect. For the most part it had worked.

"Now it is time for the tournament to continue," he called out to the remaining crowd.

Two boys came out on cue and Alaezdar gave them a brief instruction on the rules and let the boys fight. They sparred for a few minutes before one was victorious, and another two came out and fought. They did this for about an hour before they worked their way down to a final fight between the two boys who were undefeated.

That ended the tournament for now, and Alaezdar sent the crowd away after assuring them of a *safe* final fight on the evening of the dance. As everyone left, Alaezdar went to Morlonn, clapped him on the back and smiled.

"Are you okay with your new and eternal criticism?" he asked, referring to the angry parents who had left early.

Morlonn smiled.

"Oh, yes. I know them very well. They have never liked our family, anyway. There has been a feud between us going on from when I was very little. I used to shoot at her brother with my arrows all the time. My dad beat the snot out of me for that, but I kept teasing him."

"I am surprised you are still alive," Alaezdar chided him, laughing.

"Yeah, I think my dad's belt might have been the only thing that would've stopped me."

"Well, I need to get back to Tharn and see if he needs help at his booth," Alaezdar said. He smiled at his friend, pleased with both of their efforts.

"I'll walk with you for a bit," Morlonn said.

As they walked back to the village center and down through a row of booths, they began to smell the air clouding the area with the smoky smell of the burning wood in the cooking pits. Pork, beef and chicken would soon be thrown on the grills in preparation for the feast. The smoke lingered heavily in the air just above their heads and they both smiled to themselves and enjoyed the smell.

They were both feeling festive when they saw Tharn's booth and, without saying a word, Morlonn parted and left Alaezdar to Tharn.

When Alaezdar had approached, he noticed that Tharn was talking to Ambassador Krostos, now dressed in his dark blue and black garb that signified he was from the Kingdom of Triel. They were standing in front of Tharn's booth, full of the ripened honeydew melons that were known throughout the realm for their juicy sweetness, but as Krostos talked with Tharn, the ambassador did not seem too interested in his melons.

Alaezdar heard the pitch of the ambassador's voice increasing and he saw Krostos grab a melon, smash it to the table and point his finger in Tharn's face.

Alaezdar ran over to the booth, but when he got there, Krostos seemed slightly calmer although he was still red in the face.

"Tharn! Sorry I am late," Alaezdar said. "I wanted to be here to relieve you earlier, but I just returned from the tournament."

Krostos turned to Alaezdar, barely acknowledging him, and then faced Tharn again.

"You are running out of time!" Krostos said. "I need an answer from you soon, little man."

He emphasized the word "little," for Tharn, well past late middle age, was no longer as muscular as he had been in his prime and he was now getting paunchy around the middle, and other places. Tharn took the word "little" to heart.

Krostos shook his head, pointed at Tharn's face with his finger one final time, turned and walked away.

"What was that about?" Alaezdar asked.

Tharn exhaled and ran his round hands over his bald top.

"Oh, nothing really, I guess. We have been friends for such a long time, but sometimes he gets like that and then apologizes later…after a few meads."

"Are you sure that is the extent of it? I have already seen enough of these Trielian friends of yours to make me nervous. Triel is a powerful kingdom with a powerful influence among the other kingdoms, Tharn," Alaezdar began, trying to be careful not to sound too educated about the nature of kingdoms and power. "What could he possibly want with a vale man merchant other than his merchandise?"

Tharn looked at Alaezdar unemotionally through his wizened eyes. The leathery wrinkles on his face barely moved as he spoke.

"Free merchandise," he lied.

"What do you mean?" Alaezdar asked. "He wants you to give him your harvest?"

"He threatened to take the vale and steal the food from our crops every year if I did not give him this year's entire melon crop."

"Tharn," Alaezdar spoke quietly. "Take a break, a walk, or whatever you need. I'll take over for a while."

Tharn took a towel and wiped his brow.

"All right. I think I will. I'll be back in a few hours. Sure you got it?"

"Go! Relax for a change."

Tharn, confident in Alaezdar's ability to run the booth, gave a few brief instructions and left.

Alaezdar had seen enough of Triel through the years to know something was brewing in the realm, and whatever it was, it must now be seeping into the Valelands. He could not imagine why this area would be so important to have a Trielian ambassador struggling so for power over an area they could just take by force.

After a few minutes, Morlonn returned with a grilled beef and onion sandwich.

"Hey, have you seen Aaelie?" Alaezdar asked him as he handed him the sandwich.

"No, I haven't seen her since the morning feast. She was with Rivlok last I saw her."

"Oh, just as well, I guess," he said gazing blankly in the distance and taking a bite of his sandwich.

"Hey, I'm going to go. You seem to have your hands full here at this booth," Morlonn said, half laughing, half insulted. He walked off to join in some of the other festivities.

Alaezdar worked the booth for a few hours, dealing with the customers and all the ambassadors of the many kingdoms of Wrae-Kronn, but his mind was wandering. He couldn't stop thinking about where Aaelie might be and what she was doing. Was she with Rivlok or was she with her mother?

He thought again about what was going on with Triel. There were so many representatives there from all the Northern Kingdoms. They had all begun to arrive, rolling in uncelebrated, nothing at all like the Trielian entrance. The inns and pubs were bursting with coin and carnage, all of it flowing full and fast. The Trielian soldiers were both the biggest violators and the biggest destroyers of the peace.

It seemed to Alaezdar that they had quite an elaborate rotation for who was on guard and who was on free time. They seemed to be treating their time there as an actual duty station, much as if they had actually overrun the village and were now in charge. If a fight broke out, whether it was between two kingdoms such as Battleworth and Triel, or even Triel on Triel, the soldiers on guard were diligent in breaking the skirmish up and reprimanding their own if necessary. They were rough on the other kingdoms' representatives, but none of the other kingdoms arrived with such a full-blown aggressive military force as Triel had.

Alaezdar was dealing with an ambassador from the province of Korlond in the Kingdom of Battleworth when he finally saw Aaelie out of the corner of his eye. She had actually seen him first and was walking toward him with a brisk walk. Seeing her apparent determination to meet him, though, Alaezdar decided not to attract her attention, but continued to work with his customer.

"Alaezdar!" Aaelie called to him after she had reached a short shouting distance.

He ignored her as he gave the Korlond ambassador some melons and a note of intent to sell.

"Alaezdar!" she yelled again, her left hand waving over her head, frustrated that he was ignoring her.

Alaezdar finished with the ambassador, and then quickly switched his gaze to Aaelie just in time to see her change direction and walk away. She was moving her arms quickly back and forth to exaggerate the speed at which she walked.

She was just about out of Alaezdar's sight when he heard and saw Rivlok call after her. She either did not hear him or ignored him, too, because she continued to walk on. Rivlok called her again, and Alaezdar smiled because she kept on walking even after Rivlok had caught up to her. He tried to slow her walk down so they could talk, but still she would not do either.

After the two of them had gone out of sight around the corner of one of the booths, Alaezdar saw Tharn walking back with Krostos. As Aaelie passed quickly by them, Krostos turned his head, grabbed Tharn by his shoulder, turned, and pointed at Aaelie as she walked by. This seemed to make Tharn angry, and he pushed Krostos in the chest and caused him to stumble back three steps before he caught his balance.

"You are beginning to test our friendship, Tharn!" Alaezdar heard Krostos yell, but he could not hear the response. Though heated, Tharn's grisly voice did not carry like Krostos'.

"The day may come when you will regret those words, old friend," Krostso continued loudly. "Triel is just in the infancy of its power, and if you don't get on board, you will be eaten alive. In fact, I will make sure that you and this tiny community are the first to go!"

Krostos then turned away and stormed down road, but he kept looking left and right as he walked as if he were looking for something or someone.

Tharn shook his head and looked over at Alaezdar and started to walk toward him, but he changed his mind and walked the other way and disappeared out of sight.

Chapter 9

"That should do it," Tharn exhaled as he tied down the final strap, securing the tarp of his booth. "All we have to do is tear it down tomorrow," he joked.

Alaezdar stood up and wiped the dust off his knees. They both looked at the booth for a moment. They had taken everything out of it, including the last of the honeydew melons, loaded them onto a cart, and taken them to the food tent where the dance would be starting in a few hours.

Alaezdar swatted at a gnat flying near his face and noticed the sun dipping below the mountains, leaving a purple orange sky. For a few seconds he continued to gaze at the sun going down behind the mountains as he wiped the sweat from his brow.

"It is still hot," he said, almost unconsciously. Tharn just grunted in agreement.

Alaezdar stood there thinking of Aaelie and what she was doing. He didn't like admitting it to himself, but he could not wait to see her that night. He even wondered what she would be wearing on such a hot evening. The clouds in the sky were orange from the sunset, but a strange black tint was changing the sky to purple. He thought how beautiful a sunset it was, even though it was very odd. He remembered Gartan the Dark saying something about a purple sunset, and that thought caused him a brief pause and a sense of foreboding as the darkness overcame him.

"What do you say we go back, get cleaned up and get ready for the evening festivities?" Tharn asked. He looked at Alaezdar staring blankly to the sunset. "Are you alright?"

"Yeah, sure. I think it is time we got out of here," he said as he walked away from the booth.

They had not quite left the main street when they saw the Ambassador and Azrull coming towards them. Ambassador Krostos had a wrinkled and worried brow, and Warrior Azrull had his sword in his right hand. He was in full combat gear, except that he was without his helm. He looked angry and his pace was as brisk as a dog coming in for an attack.

Tharn sensed there was a problem and he put his hand on Alaezdar's shoulder.

"Do not say anything. In fact, you can keep going. They won't bother you."

"No, I'd rather stay, if you don't mind."

"Suit yourself. Just keep your mouth shut," he said and he turned to Alaezdar to make sure that he understood.

Alaezdar nodded.

"Tharn!" Ambassador Krostos shouted. "I have something to tell you."

Tharn and Alaezdar stopped walking and waited for the men to approach.

"Move away!" Azrull said and he pointed his sword at Alaezdar's chest.

Alaezdar looked at Tharn and Tharn just nodded, so he sidestepped a few feet away.

"Stay there and do not move or I will remove your head from your shoulders, rancher." Azrull said and moved the tip of his sword from Alaezdar to Tharn.

"What is wrong?" Tharn asked as he bowed his head before the ambassador.

I have just been to the storage shed to load up our supplies and your shipment is very much lacking from our agreement."

Tharn nodded slowly. He knew this conversation would be coming.

"We have been having problems with the goblin tribes on the other side of the river," he said.

"That is not my problem. What is my problem, though, is that the King is going to be very disappointed in this shipment and I am going to have to try either to defend you or disregard you and let someone else take over the procurement of the ore, which would mean soldiers taking over this village of yours. Now, is that what you want?"

"No, it is not," he admitted.

"Too bad. It is going to happen regardless!" Azrull said.

Krostos looked at Azrull and smiled at him.

"Please, Azrull. Tharn is my friend. I do not want to jeopardize that friendship. However, you, my friend," he said turning back to Tharn, "are putting me in a bad spot, and I do not like having to cover for you."

"We are doing the best we can with what we have. I do not want or need soldiers milling about our village. However, it would be nice to have a small -- and I mean small -- detachment at the mine."

"I am sorry, Tharn, but the king has trusted you to do with what you have. If he sends in troops, it will be in full scale."

"Then I do not know what to tell you," Tharn admitted.

"Well, it just so happens that I have come up with a solution that will help us both. Azrull, please escort Tharn's man to his cabin so that Tharn and I can talk."

"I do not need to be escorted," Alaezdar objected.

"No, I suppose you don't. This is your home. Just the same, Azrull, follow him home."

Alaezdar looked at Tharn, but Tharn said nothing and only nodded to let Alaezdar know that he would be okay. Azrull took the flat of his sword and put it to Alaezdar's back and nudged him away, smiling as he did so. Alaezdar turned and faced Azrull and put his fist in front of his face.

Azrull, instantly enraged by the defiance, kicked him between the legs and dropped him to the ground. Alaezdar curled up in agony.

"Stop!" Tharn shouted. "That is not necessary!"

"I agree," Krostos added. "Let him be, Azrull."

Azrull sheathed his sword and offered Alaezdar a hand up, but he just shook his head, crawled away from Azrull and slowly rose back up to his feet. He started to say something, but Tharn spoke over him.

"Go home, Alaezdar. Tonight we will have a pleasant time at the dance."

Alaezdar turned and walked away. As Azrull started to follow, Tharn put a hand on his shoulder.

"Leave him be. He is not going to hurt you. Besides, what can he do? He has no weapon."

Azrull started to respond, but Krostos stopped him. "He will be fine, Azrull. Let him go. I need you here near me anyhow."

"What offer do you have for me, Krostos?" Tharn quickly asked, wanting to get this day behind him.

Krostos pulled him aside, out of hearing range of Azrull, who was still pacing back and forth in anger as he watched Alaezdar walk off.

"The king will listen to me," Krostos told Tharn. "If I tell him your shipment will be double the next time to make up for this season's shortcomings, he will believe me. However, you really need to come up with that, or else I will be the one who is in trouble. Now, there is only one person in the world who I can trust will do as I ask, and that would be you. I know this governorship of the village hasn't been exactly perfect, but you have been doing an outstanding job with the illusion that this place really is just here for the benefit of producing outstanding crops for the northern kingdoms while you are excavating and shipping out the iron ore from the mines to produce Goblin Touched steel for us. It really is beautiful, my friend, how the two of us founded this place thirty years ago and came up with the idea that we would sell this toxic steel to make swords for our kingdom under the guise of a peaceful farming community. Now, we are just about done, but when we have just about reached our ultimate goal, you are coming up short. To be honest, it seems to me that you have lost sight of our mission."

"In a way, I have lost sight," Tharn admitted. "I still want to remain here, but I am not so concerned with the Goblin Touched Steel as I once was. But since I am still loyal to the king, I will do what I can. What more can I say to you?"

"Give me a hostage," Krostos said. "I will take one of your beautiful women to be one of my servants -- and you do have many -- but I do have my eye on one in particular. Do this and when you double your quota next year, I will return her to her home, if she wishes."

"I can't allow that," Tharn said, shaking his head.

"Then I will order soldiers to maintain a post here to make sure you obtain your quota, and they will be here within a few weeks. Is that really what you want?"

"No, of course not."

"Then what do you say?"

"Who do you have in mind?"

Krostos smiled. "Remember that sweet young girl I pointed out to you yesterday?"

"Aaelie?"

"Yes…Aaelie, she is a sweet girl. I like her. She will do fine for me at Triel."

Tharn put his hands to his face and rubbed them up and down.

"This can't happen," he muttered underneath his hands. "How do you expect me to just turn her over to you and have her understand what is going on?"

"Quite honestly, Tharn, that isn't my problem. That is why you rule this village. You are the one who needs to take care of such matters. Just turn her over to me tonight near the end of the dance and I will make sure that she is well taken care of and returned safely next year, if you reach your quota."

"Why is this quota so important now? Before, it was merely a loose goal to obtain with no retribution for falling short, and now you show up as if it has always been standard that I follow through with the quota. Why the change?"

Azrull now stepped in between the two.

"Not for your concern," he said. "The Ambassador needs to get ready for tonight. I suggest you do the same. Have the girl ready so that we can leave directly after the dance. I will finish loading up the ore and I'll have all of my soldiers out of here before sunrise and you will have nothing to worry about until next year's quota."

"Just have her ready, Tharn," Krostos said and Azrull led him away.

***

Dusk arrived and villagers crowded at the fountain square where the musicians were setting up to perform on an elaborately decorated stage above the tiles that workers had painstakingly laid down to create a marbled dancing area. Lanterns were placed in multicolored tents and were glowing with their brilliant colors as they surrounded the perimeter of the main pavilion in the center of the village. Large poles with flags of all the kingdoms swayed gently in the breeze in another circle within the perimeter which marked the dancing area. Just outside of that was a large ceremonial bonfire pit.

A group of near adult boys dumped seasoned firewood into the pit on top of the dry kindling, and then lit the fire. They joked and chided each other and were giddy with the excitement of the lighting and the festive mood of the evening. All of the booths, every tree and every bush had a lantern placed near or upon it, so that Valewood was alive with brilliance on the evening festival.

The villagers were beginning to wander in groups towards the center of the village. Conversations took on hush but excited tones as the final day and final evening of the festival was near its end. Tomorrow there would be no more representatives, no more working the booths, no more harvesting. Only a full day's rest was on the agenda for the next morning. The harpists, flutists, and drummers on the stage began to play their enchanting melodies. Initially no one responded, just continued in their conversations, but soon they did begin to sway and respond to the music. Alaezdar stood within the outline of the trees and watched his fellow villagers finally begin to take partners and dance to the Vale folk songs. They formed small circles and held hands and sang, spun in circles and clapped their hands to the music. As he watched, he could faintly hear the rippling waters of the Sippling River in the distance.

He thought about Aaelie, and wished she were with him, but was also glad that she wasn't. He wanted to belong to this community, but also knew that he could not. He knew that he would eventually leave because Rager's House of Renegades would soon be closing in on this new home of his. It would only be a matter of months before men like Talon Blade, Scar Blade and Torn Blade would be on his trail and closing in like a fox on a wounded rabbit that had stayed out in the open to protect its young, still in their hole.

He knew that if he became too attached to these people, a wounded rabbit is what he would have to become in order to save these villagers. He would have to expose himself at the cost of his own life to save these people from a problem that was not theirs.

He worried that familiarity and time would eventually cause him to let his guard down, and that concerned him greatly. Alaezdar looked behind him and saw only the darkness of the forest. One dancing group then gave a short shout from in front of him and Alaezdar came out of his thought and turned away from the darkness of the forest.

Might as well have fun tonight, he said to himself, and he walked towards the circle. Rager's House of Renegades would not be here on this night. He supposed the Goblin Tribes could cross this river, but everything seemed so peaceful on the other side of the river. This thought alone did cause him some hesitation, but Gartan the Dark had admitted that he did not know if Valewood was the village that would be attacked, only that the attack would be on the night of the purple sunset. He walked back to the village and as soon as he got to the circle, he saw Morlonn, Rivlok, Aaelie and Kunther and a few others their age. Kunther saw Alaezdar first, raised his hand excitedly and beckoned him to join them.

"Alaezdar!" Kunther, obviously feeling the effect of a few ales already, clapped him on the shoulder as he approached. "That was so much fun today at the sword fighting tournament. Thank you for letting me be involved."

"No problem. It was actually Tharn's idea. You should thank him."

"I will," he said. "You know what is great about being in that tournament? I have had a lot of attention from older girls in the village who normally wouldn't talk to me... even if I was milking their cows for them."

"Oh, really?" Alaezdar said.

"That is all he has been talking about all evening," Morlonn added. "Glad you came out, Alaezdar. What took you so long?"

"Always one more thing to do when you work for Tharn. You know how it goes," he said and looked at Aaelie, but she would not return his gaze.

"Yeah, actually I do," Morlonn said. "In fact, I have one of them to attend to right now. I am going over to the fence and get ready for the fire show."

He clasped Alaezdar on the shoulder, winked and ran off.

"I am so bored," Rivlok said as he stared out over the crowd. "This is the only excitement we get out of this tiny little rat hole."

"Why do you talk like that?" Kunther asked. "I hate it when you get like this, Rivlok."

"Don't worry about him, Kunth. He gets this way every now and then," Aaelie said and looked at Alaezdar, but dropped her smile. She then turned from him and looked out at the dancers.

She won't even look at me, Alaezdar thought to himself, and this made him want her even more. He knew it was a game, but in the faint light, her long wavy brown hair, tied tightly in braided circles into a bun like a crown,

David L. McDaniel

made her more beautiful than he had ever seen her. Her neck and shoulders were exposed. Her dress showed her cleavage and fit her tightly at the waist, but loosely down to her legs.

He was certain that he had not seen a more beautiful woman. He continued to stare at her and looked away only once and saw that Rivlok was staring at him resentfully. When their eyes met, Rivlok took Aaelie by the waist, spun her around and forced her into the crowd who were dancing removing her from Alaezdar's eyes.

Alaezdar watched them dance for a few minutes until the song ended. The musicians paused and smiled at each other and announced that they would begin playing again after a few rounds of ale. Alaezdar chatted with Kunther and then looked at Aaelie. Catching her gaze, he watched as she frowned at him, spun around, and walked away.

He didn't like her reaction and feeling the need to talk to her, he decided to start towards her, but he had only gotten a few steps when Tharn, who had just arrived, grabbed his shoulder and caused him to stop in his tracks.

Alaezdar turned and shook his hand off his shoulder, but saw that Tharn was giving him a concerned look, as a parent might look while stopping a child from playing in the fire. Alaezdar understood and he nodded, but he turned around again and chased after Aaelie regardless of his friend's wordless gesture.

"Aaelie! Wait. Will you stop this time?"

"What is wrong with you?" she snapped without turning around and quickened her pace.

"What do you mean?" he asked and ran in front of her and stopped her by putting his hands on her shoulders. He tried to look into her eyes, but there were too many dark shadows from the torchlight and he could not see her face clearly enough to gauge why she was reacting so.

"You didn't want to talk to me today when I called for you," she said.

"I was busy!" he protested.

"Well, if you're too busy for me, then too bad. I know other people who aren't too busy."

Alaezdar shook his head and began to smile. She looked at him, but could not contain herself any longer and she too laughed.

"You're too serious, Alaezdar. Come on," she said and grabbed his hand

95

and began to lead him away from the dance, but Tharn approached and stopped them.

"Alaezdar, I need to talk to Aaelie. Alone."

"So do I!" Rivlok said as he stormed up in between the three of them.

"You don't understand," Tharn said. "This is important, and I don't think Aaelie wants to hear what I have to tell her with you two here."

"Well, whatever it is, you are just going to have to include me in," Rivlok said and put his hands on his hips.

Tharn sighed. It might be best if they knew, he figured, because maybe they would be mad enough to do something that he himself was too afraid to do. Young men full of passion often did the wrong things, thinking with egos before thinking clearly. He had been like that once, long ago. Most of the time, he had made poor decisions, but he was beginning to think he was making poor decisions of late anyhow.

"Aaelie, Rivlok, Alaezdar," he started after taking a deep breath. "Ambassador Krostos wants to take Aaelie with him to the kingdom of Triel where she can learn to be a servant to him and the king."

"What? That can't happen!" Rivlok said.

Aaelie covered her face.

"Why?" she asked, her eyes beginning to tear. "I won't go. You can't make me!"

"Unfortunately," Tharn said. "Ambassador Krostos *can* make you. There is no one to stop him. You have no father, your mother is an old lady…"

"You can stop him!" Rivlok protested. "You are in charge here. You make all the decisions. Just tell him no. Please, Tharn, don't let this happen."

"It just isn't that simple. Look. Here he comes now. Just talk to him, Aaelie, dance with him for a few dances. You'll find that he is a kind, strong man of power. You can benefit from his graciousness."

"No! I can't, and I won't!" she screamed at Tharn and hit him in the chest before she ran away towards the woods.

Rivlok saw the Ambassador coming and ran towards him with his knife pulled out. Alaezdar chased after Aaelie.

"No, Rivlok!" Tharn yelled.

Warrior Azrull, who walked beside the Ambassador, glared at Rivlok. Azrull was dressed in formal attire and had no combat gear on with the exception of his sword, strapped to his side. When he saw Rivlok coming at him, he withdrew his sword and stood in front of the Ambassador.

"Don't come any closer, kid!" he yelled.

Rivlok, seeing that he had no chance, stopped in front of Azrull, just out of reach of his sword, and began yelling at the Ambassador. "You will not take her from her home, I promise you that!" he yelled and waved his knife in the air.

"Calm down, young man," Krostos said. "I will take good care of her."

"No, you won't because she is not leaving"

"Put down the knife, boy," Azrull said, looking around and noticing a crowd had formed. It seemed that every villager was there at that moment to witness what was going on. Many were beginning to mumble and some even tried to get Tharn's attention by asking him what was going on.

"I will not," Rivlok yelled. "You are going to have to kill me if you want Aaelie!"

"I will do that, and it looks as if I will have to do it in front of everyone you know."

"You do that and you are going to have to deal with all of us!" someone shouted from the crowd.

Hearing the crowd getting anxious, Azrull lifted his sword a little higher, backed up and put his left hand gently on the Ambassador's chest pushing him back slightly.

"Let's go, boy," Azrull said and raised his sword, taunting Rivlok to come at him.

Rivlok grimaced, raised his knife and took a few steps forward just as there was a loud, snapping hiss and a booming crack above them all. The crowd looked up and saw one of Morlonn's fire rocks flying through the air above them. It exploded when it hit the empty cow field on the other side of the square.

Some of the villagers ran away in fear while some oohed and aahed the spectacle.

That was enough distraction for Rivlok to charge after Azrull and try to plunge his knife into the warrior's chest after catching him slightly off guard. Azrull's experience in combat saved his life as he turned slightly from the knife to cause Rivlok to miss his mark. Rivlok still managed to slam into Azrull and they both fell to the ground.

Tharn, still quick and strong for his age, grabbed Rivlok and pulled him off Azrull before he could regain his composure and strike again.

"Run! Now!" Tharn yelled and he kicked Azrull in the ribs and then ran off behind the fleeing Rivlok.

***

Alaezdar chased after Aaelie and finally caught up with her at the edge of the forest. She said nothing, but grabbed his hand and led him deeper into the forest towards the river. They ran away from the people, the sounds, the torches. They ran deep into the dark, but Aaelie ran knowing her way in dark as if it was light. She led him past the eastern gate to the river, and they crossed it, they saw Morlonn fidgeting with his catapult, but he didn't even raise his head to stop them. She led Alaezdar past the gate and clear from the trees and now the harvest moon was shining on them and reflecting off the river as well.

"I love this river, you know?" she said quietly and watched the water faintly reflecting the moon's light as it rippled in between the rocks. She spoke as if nothing had just happened at the dance.

Alaezdar faced Aaelie and could now see her clearly in the moonlight.

"Are you ok?" he asked as he pulled her close him.

"Oh, you mean the possibility of being shipped off like a hand maiden to a place I have never been? What do you think? Of course, I am not alright, but I feel a little better now that you are here."

"This is a dangerous realm right now. There are things going on that are not going to end well."

"I don't care, Alaezdar. I am tired of being here in this dull village. I might go with the Ambassador just for a change in scenery."

"What about Rivlok?"

"What about him? He is just a boy. Oh, don't get me wrong, I do love Rivlok, but not like he loves me. I will hate to leave him, but I am so tired of this village, of Tharn and of everything else here. I have no future here. Rivlok has no future here. Believe me, I have no desire to go away with a fat old bald man, but if it gets me out of here…"

"You don't want that…"

"What do you know what I want?" she interrupted. "I want you, silly I want you to take me away from here. You know this realm. Take me away and show me the world."

"I can't do that. I want to stay here, more than you know. I would like nothing more than to stay here with you. You said that you like the river. Well, in many ways you are like this river. It is untamed. It is strong. It is beautiful. It is so free and full of life, and you can still be all that here."

Aaelie watched Alaezdar as he spoke and smiled.

"Are you trying to seduce me, Alaezdar?"

Alaezdar thought for a moment and realized she might be right. He was. But was he ready? Even he wasn't sure of what he wanted.

"I don't know. I just like what I see, and I think you should stay here."

"Then what about the Ambassador? You can't just tell him that you said I have to stay here."

"No, you're right. I have to come up with something."

"I know you will. Stay here with me for a while and we won't have to worry about the Ambassador, Tharn or Rivlok until morning."

"Then, what about Rivlok?"

Aaelie turned away from Alaezdar and walked into the river and toward a large rock protruding from the water.

"I told you already about Rivlok. I love him," she paused and looked into the river, "and I don't want to hurt him. I also don't want to be without him, but I can't stay here any longer and I want to be with you."

She turned and sat down on the grassy bank at the edge the river, put her arms on her knees, her chin in her hands, and was silent.

"I really don't know what to do right now. With you, Rivlok or the Ambassador," Alaezdar admitted.

Aaelie turned her head and looked up at him standing behind her.

"Love me. Love me more, and love me more than he does. Solve my problems for me."

She took her hands and began playing with the river's currents. Alaezdar stood transfixed. He wanted to take her and make love to her, right then, but he knew that he should not. If he wanted to continue with his reformation, with this new beginning, if he wanted it to work, he could not, must not. He and Rivlok were not exactly friends, but he had learned to respect his feelings.

Another side of Alaezdar told him what he also knew. His story at Valewood was nearing an end. Maybe this whole episode with the Ambassador was just the earliest sign of that. That would mean that he would be leaving, so what harm would befall him if he betrayed Rivlok's feelings and used Aaelie…and then left her to her own fate with the Ambassador.

"Aaelie," he said.

"Alaezdar," she returned, almost mockingly.

When he heard her voice, he knew he could not forsake her. He knew he could not create another problem just to save his own skin. He would find another way.

"Come to me and take me away from here," Aaelie said and she stood up, took his hand and led him ankle deep into the cold water.

She put her cool wet hand on Alaezdar's left cheek, and he grabbed her hand and stared into her eyes. With his other hand, he reached behind her neck, drew her close to his body, and kissed her. Aaelie gave herself to him freely and held him tightly. They kissed, feeling each other's warmth and passion, and for the first few minutes, it felt right to Alaezdar until he realized again that he was leading her -- and himself -- down a road that would not have a good end.

He abruptly broke away.

"I'm sorry, Aaelie, but Rivlok..." he lied. Any excuse to break away, he thought.

"What do you mean, 'but Rivlok'?"

"We cannot do this. It is not my place to come here and take you from him. We need to figure this out. With his help. He loves you dearly and together we can find a way."

Aaelie smiled a hurt, confused smile, but soon she turned to anger.

"What do you mean, this is not your place? You are here. You are the man I want. I don't want Rivlok. He is more like a brother to me now. In time he will understand."

"No, Aaelie. I am sorry. I cannot."

"But..." she began, hurt again. Tears welled up in her eyes. Stepping back, she looked at Alaezdar, his face firm in front of her. "I needed you, and you built me up, drew me into you. I have been watching you and hoping for this, and now it has finally happened and just that quickly, you let me down? What kind of evil are you?"

Aaelie turned and ran down along the river and deeper into the woods. Alaezdar stood motionless and wondered what the next few minutes might have evolved into, if only he would have allowed himself to do what in his heart he really wanted to do.

"I am a swordsman," he finally whispered to himself. "What code do I follow?"

He knew he followed no code as a swordsman anymore. He knew that he did not want to continue as a swordsman, either, and that was actually why he'd ended up in this little hidden away farming community. Now his deeper feelings were confusing him. Feelings of neglect, of broken pride, were now mixed with love and somehow had become entwined with code and honor.

He looked at the river, thinking of Aaelie, for many minutes afterward, but soon he concluded he must leave. He would walk away now and leave everything behind -- his sword and his gear. He would take nothing with him. He would truly be a homeless wanderer until he found another village. No more sword or past to cling to him like a curse.

Yes, he would walk away and start over once again.

He had only taken a few steps back along the river when he heard screams coming from the village and it was not the same type of screaming that came from dancing. It was a screaming that he was all too familiar with, from fear and death.

Chapter 10

Morlonn had just finished firing off the last shot from his catapult. He smiled as he watched it sail over the area where his friends and villagers were dancing. Red and blue sparks trailed off the ball like a shooting star streaking through the sky and then it smoldered out as it hit the ground on the far side of the town square, exactly as he had planned.

Morlonn clapped his hands and bent over to secure the small catapult when the fence next to him shook violently. He looked a few hundred yards down the fence line toward where the shaking had come from and saw that the small gate there had erupted into flames and fallen to the ground. What he saw next terrified him.

Gronts.

Not that he had never seen them before -- because he had many times -- but he had never in his life seen so many at one time. There must have been more than twenty of them and they ran straight through the gate and over the top of the shattered, burning wood pieces of the gate as if they weren't even on fire.

Terrified, he headed off toward an underground room to find a defensive position. While he ran, he thought how ironic it was that they had built this fence for protection against such an attack, but since it was the final evening of the festival, he was the only one on the fence and he was shooting their only real weapon into the crowd of partiers, not at a real enemy.

He jumped down into the murder room and waited a few minutes for the attack to come, but he quickly realized that he was again all alone. The gronts had charged through the gate unopposed and were not stopping to look for him or for anyone else to kill. They were on a mission, and the gate offered little to slow them down.

How had that happened, Morlonn wondered. Why did they even have that fence if it offered no protection during the time that they most needed it?

He sensed a need to get to the village, and quickly, and he then exited the gate and ran toward the village.

***

The last dance of the night had just begun. The crowd had just finished witnessing Morlonn's red and blue shooting star. They had all looked to the sky and clapped and then turned to the musicians as they began to play a soft ballad. A young man and his younger sister sang the soft and enchanting song, an ancient elven tune about the return of their god Val-Eahea, and the villagers gathered in front of the stage and watched. The flickering torch lights around them gave a mystic effect to the ballad.

Tharn watched his villagers enjoying the evening. Everyone had finally calmed down and resumed the evening's festivities and, Tharn hoped, they were no longer thinking about the confrontation they had just seen. Of course, the night had not quite gone as planned for him, but in terms of the whole festival, it was quite a success, apparently, as far as the majority of the villagers were concerned.

Most of them had no idea of the internal politics that were happening. At least Tharn could hold onto that little victory. He knew he was eventually going to have to deal further with Krostos and Azrull, but that would be another day. He was resolute that he was going to enjoy the rest of the evening, watch his people enjoy themselves, and take his satisfaction in that. He was happy the evening was now winding down to a calm and quiet conclusion.

The two singers were finishing the final song and as the man raised his voice slightly to bring in the close of his song, his face froze in fear. Without another sound, he raised his hands up to the top of his shoulders and fell forward, exposing six arrows in his back.

The man's sister screamed and fell to her knees by her brother while the other musicians jumped off the stage and ran into the shocked and paralyzed, feeble crowd. When the creatures came out of the woods firing their arrows, the people were released from their initial fear and could gather up enough courage to realize that their lives were in danger and that they should run for their lives.

A handful of gronts jumped onto the stage and fired arrows into the crowd. Many villagers ran to safety, but those too slow in recovering from their shock discovered the penalty for that slow recovery. The gronts stood on the stage and picked off nearly a dozen paralyzed villagers before they had even thought of running for their lives. The gronts then loosed more arrows into the fleeing crowd and took out a few more villagers before they had no more targets left to shoot at.

They jumped off the stage and joined in pursuit. There were ten gronts on the stage, each about five foot in height and two hundred pounds of solid, iron-like stout and rounded muscle. Most of their mass was in their trunk-like legs, although their upper torsos were muscular, but thin. Their monstrous faces were smooth and hairless under their bald heads. They had only small holes in the sides of their heads for ears. Their grotesque, pale-milk faces showed no fear.

Their jaws were wide from chin to cheek and held their crowded teeth. Aside from the over- and under-bearing teeth, or fangs, their mouths had a dozen more teeth, like humans, but these gave them a grotesquely wide shape to their jaws. Their noses were small, but the nostrils were wide at the base and the bridge disappeared into their head before it reached between their eyes.

On the backs of their heads they had various animal tails sewn into their skin by the base of the tails. Some gronts had more than others did because they had been sewn on as tribal rites of passage or as trophies for individual accomplishments. They wore no armor, but their skin was so hard that any weapons made by humans did little damage to their thick hide on first contact. They only wore skins of forest animals which now reeked from rotting death, but those had been added purposely to cause fear to anyone they fought and attacked.

Once they had expended all their arrows, they drew their short swords as they jumped off the stage, and they ran into the heart of the village and they chased down more village prey, who they then caught and sliced away at, especially the unfortunately slow at the rear of the fleeing pack.

After each victorious kill, the gronts stopped in their tracks and screamed, and then the others screamed in return as if to acknowledge their clan's progress. This caused a cacophonous noise throughout the village, from both the victorious, bloodthirsty screams of the gronts and the wailing of the terrorized, fleeing villagers. Once the gronts had reached the height of their blood lust attacks, they ran to the area of the village where the booths were and, in their own separate rampages, destroyed every one of the festival booths.

Back at the stage a robed man had appeared.

He wore a simple dark green cloak and he had his hood over his head, but he removed it to better survey the destruction. He stood there on the stage for several minutes and surveyed the damage and death caused by his gronts. He enjoyed the sight. It wasn't pretty, nor was it glorious, but it was productive, and for that he was satisfied. He enjoyed watching his plans be executed as he had anticipated, especially when he was using as his instrument these unpredictable and almost uncontrollable gronts.

Torz, his mentor, had warned him about using such creatures, but had also told him that if he could succeed in using them, he would be nearly unstoppable because of the destructive havoc they could wreak in such a short time. Torz's pronouncement had been a challenge Ra-Corsh could not shy away from.

He stood there for several minutes absorbing the whole scene to determine what to do next. Without a word he jumped off the stage and walked quickly towards the center of the village and as soon as his feet had hit the dirt, a flaming woman with wings of solid fire flew to him from the woods behind the stage. A human woman in tight chainmail with nothing but flesh underneath showing her tight figure, she hovered above him and her chain mail glowed orange as the small hairs on her body were lit with fire. Her wings were like a bird's wings, but were engulfed in an aggressive flame that left a trail of smoke behind her when she flew.

She landed directly in front of Ra-Corsh and as she did so, the wings on her back disappeared, but small wisps of flame still sparked and crackled beneath her chain mail body suit. Her whole body was covered with the small wisps of flame, even her shoulder length silky red hair.

"Is it working, wizard?" she spat.

The wizard continued and said nothing to the woman.

"Ra-Corsh?" she repeated.

"Curse you, woman!" Ra-Corsh said. He pulled his hands from under his robe and pointed at her chest. "If you cannot tell that all is working as planned, may I suggest you look around? My gronts are causing massive destruction upon this weak and simple village."

"But the swordsman...do we have him yet? Or are your precious gronts even smart enough to be looking for him again without being told to do so?"

"Unfortunately, they are not looking yet. Gronts are a very..."

"But you told them! They are disobeying you!"

Ra-Corsh looked toward the ground and shook his head, and then looked up at her, his chin still near his chest. He slowly raised his chin as he spoke.

"These are not your normal gronts. They are Kronn Gronts. Yes, they are stupid, but they are the most ferocious creatures you will find. They are not only bred to fight and to kill other living beings, but they are resistant to any Kronn, as the Kronn is in their being from birth. Killing is what they do, and it is what they enjoy the most. It is not too often they find other races besides their own to kill and I seriously doubt that they are even thinking about capturing our prize until they get their fill of killing first."

"We don't have much time. I suggest you expedite the process. I don't want this getting out of control!"

"Fyaa! Be patient. You just need to wait. And don't forget the girl. We have to have their sacrifice or this will be for naught." Ra-Corsh shook his head again and turned to Fyaa directly. "Look at me! I am a human in command of a wild band of gronts. I know these gronts. If I didn't, I wouldn't be alive right now. So just trust me, and wait, and let me and my gronts do our work. They will find the girl and then I will let you search for him when the time comes."

Fyaa turned away from the wizard and her wings exploded from her back, sparking and crackling as the flames shot out in fury, and she flew away towards the village.

As she flew through the festival site, she shot fireballs onto all of the booths, although they had already been mostly destroyed, and then she flew deeper into the village and torched the wooden structured buildings and even the small homes as she circled around. She smiled as she watched them burn and the people scrambling out of them and running in fear for their lives.

*****

On the opposite side of the village, far from where the attacks were happening, Alaezdar heard the screaming as he ran from woods. Without going into the heart of the village, he ran first to his small cottage on Tharn's farm, but he feared he might not reach it in time. He ran furiously as he heard the screaming and smelled the smoke from the fires. Finally he entered into his room, dove under his bed, and reached blindly for his sword. He felt only the empty hard floor.

Was it gone, he worried. He had just pulled it out a few days ago. How could it be gone? He looked under the bed again and still could not see anything but darkness. He reached in again, further back, and felt it.

He grabbed the scabbard and the sword. Just touching it brought back memories to him again, both good and bad, but there were many he wished to forget. He had thought he was done with his past and he had been more than ready to forget it all and begin anew.

Bloodseeker was the name of his sword. It called upon the magic of the land to seek out blood, but once it had tasted blood again, Alaezdar knew it would want more. Many a time the magic has helped him in battle. He knew not how it worked, or where it came from, but it did just as promised every time.

Now he felt it calling once again.

He heard the screams outside and knew it was time to act, but still he paused briefly and looked at the inscription on the scabbard. Even in the dark, he could almost see the inscription and the words he knew by heart. *To Honor, To Death: Rock Blade.*

"To battle again," Rock Blade said aloud and he withdrew the blade.

As he pulled the sword out and dropped the scabbard, two sharp and jagged smaller blades extended outward from just under the cross-guard with a clink. He felt the rush of the sword. He smiled as he felt his surge of raging anger. He stood up and ran out of his cottage and back to the village, his own rage further awakened by the power in the sword.

***

While Morlonn was still at the wall, he had grabbed his sword, bow, and two full quivers of arrows before he set off into town. As he now reached the outskirts of the village, he heard screams coming from the town fountain, but he had a hunch that the monsters that had attacked would no longer be at the fountain, but would be making their way to the outskirts of the village.

Morlonn went to his own house first and jumped his fence just as the gronts came down his street. Finding a good defensive position behind the chimney stack on the roof of his cottage, he fired arrows at the unsuspecting gronts as they ran by searching for innocent victims to slaughter. He was surprised how well he could see during the night. The torches from the festival, along with the light from the burning buildings, lit up the night all around the village .

The gronts were running around throughout the village and showing no reason to the direction of their travel. Morlonn could tell that they were ecstatic and lost to their blood lust, and their excitement sickened him. To his frustration, he found that many of his arrows bounced off their rock-like, pasty white smooth skin, but he remained determined and continued to let loose arrow after arrow.

Eventually a select few did find their mark and his black, diamond tip arrows pierced the gronts' vulnerable soft spots on their necks and below their rib cages. The arrows rarely killed them with the first piercing, but Morlonn did find some satisfaction as the gronts squealed like pigs in pain and ran away, not knowing where the arrows had come from.

After he emptied both quivers, he jumped off his cottage, ran inside and grabbed a few more fistfuls of arrows to refill his quivers. He ran back outside and followed a few straggling gronts back into the dirt streets of the township. He had only gone down his street past a few houses when he saw Rivlok fighting a gront. Their swords flashed quickly as each tried to defeat their opponent. Morlonn notched another black diamond tip arrow and took aim for the gront's neck. Releasing, he saw the arrow whiz passed Rivlok and hit its mark, slicing deeply into the gront's throat. This wound was fatal and the gront gurgled and grunted as he grabbed at the arrow and fell to the ground. He wiggled back and forth on the dirt furiously before losing consciousness forever.

So many cottages, outbuildings, and barns were still burning so violently that a steady light glimmered through the smoke and haze throughout the village. Rivlok ran past a burning cottage, turned, and saw his friend Morlonn, forced a brief smile of thanks, and charged for another gront a few houses down the road in the same direction Morlonn was running.

Morlonn shook his head, dumbfounded. It looked as if Rivlok was actually having the time of his life, for Morlonn could not see any fear in his face.

Rivlok then picked up the pace and ran past Morlonn, who followed him as it seemed that he either knew where he was going or was experiencing the same blood lust as the gronts. Either way, he knew his friend would need help.

He followed him until he came upon Alaezdar, battling three gronts at once, but it looked as if Alaezdar was losing no ground in the battle. Rivlok ran to help Alaezdar and plunged his sword in the back of the closest gront, withdrew his sword and then prepared for another swing. The gront arched and threw both his hands skyward and screamed, but to Rivlok's surprise, the gront did not fall to the ground. Instead it growled with a renewed and more intense anger, turned around, and blocked Rivlok's half-hearted and meager second attack. The gront locked himself in with this new opponent who had wounded him.

Rivlok pounded the gront with a fury of attacks and the gront fell backwards. The wounded gront was beginning to show signs of his pain and he was bleeding severely. The gront's legs were now wet and slippery from the blood oozing from his back. Encouraged by the sight, Rivlok continued to pound on the gront and defended himself against every return blow.

Eventually Rivlok's attacks and the wound in his back proved too much to bear and the gront slipped on his own blood and fell onto his back, just waiting for Rivlok's sword to pierce his heart. Rivlok put every ounce of weight into his sword and felt it slice into the gront's flesh and crush a rib bone. The gront squealed for only a moment before dying.

Meanwhile Alaezdar was swinging his sword quickly and deftly at the other two gronts and successfully slicing them with his every swing. No action or movement was wasted. With a focused vision and the clarity from the light of the fires, he saw the gronts through the nighttime darkness, smoke, and haze, and although the gronts he fought blocked many of the blows, Alaezdar sliced and tore into gront flesh with every opportunity.

He cut into their flesh quickly and precisely, almost as if he enjoyed tormenting the gronts, a happy torturer to his victims. Bloodseeker sent ecstatic chills through Alaezdar's veins, and happiness and satisfaction vibrated though every fiber of his being. Sword and hand now worked in unison, inseparable, towards a reciprocal goal, to kill gronts and to satisfy a need.

The sword and swordsman worked together to slice through the gronts, and with every instance that Bloodseeker drew blood, Alaezdar felt his rage increase. It did not matter whether the victims lived or died, only that they bled. Though the cuts had little effect on the gront's hard outer skin, they were effective in producing blood for Bloodseeker and for Alaezdar and in slowing the gronts and weakening their morale.

Soon the gronts realized that the battle would eventually lead to their death, and even the insidious, blood-lust gronts were wise enough to know that this man was not a normal villager.

Morlonn rounded the corner shortly after Rivlok and saw Alaezdar and Rivlok in battle. He notched and aimed for the gront that was locked in close battle with Alaezdar. Releasing the arrow, he watched it hit the gront in his rib cage. The gront flinched and recoiled, and that extra movement gave Alaezdar an opportunity to plunge his sword deep into the gront's chest. He had to use both hands upon the sword and thrust forward with all of his might to penetrate through all his tough skin. As Alaezdar grunted and pushed the sword through the tough hide, the gront's eyes went wide, realizing his demise, and then closed. He fell like a rock to the ground.

Bloodseeker was now fully awake, and happy, but still not yet satisfied.

The remaining gront, realizing that he had just lost the advantage of his fellow gronts' numbers, charged after Alaezdar with his sword over his head in a last ditch effort. He brought the blade down with all his might with the intention of splitting his opponent's head. Alaezdar saw the gront with only enough time to put his foot onto the dead gront in front of him and withdraw his sword from his chest as he fell.

The attacking gront's blade was coming quickly and Alaezdar dropped to his knees and rolled to his right side. The gront's blade came down wildly, but still caught his left shoulder as he rolled. The gront had to adjust his weight in order to hit Alaezdar, and he lost his balance. He stumbled for a few steps as he tried to regain his balance. Still on the ground, Alaezdar swung his sword and hit the gront on his knee and the gront tripped over the sword as it cut his leg. He fell with a thud. Alaezdar had just enough time to stand up as the gront also stood and began limping towards his combatant.

Both gront and Alaezdar circled each other trying to anticipate each other's next move. From the corner of his eyes, Alaezdar noticed Morlonn and Rivlok in an ugly battle with a few more gronts that had just arrived. Rivlok was on the ground unconscious while Morlonn stood over his body holding only a hunting knife. The two gronts stood facing Morlonn and they took turns feigning several attacking moves, playing with Morlonn as a cat does with a mouse before pouncing.

Alaezdar continued to circle the gront he was fighting until his back was to Rivlok. Keeping this gront away from his partners, Alaezdar turned quickly and left the gront standing alone while he ran towards the unsuspecting gront fighting Morlonn. Alaezdar caught the side of his face with his sword and dropped him.

Alaezdar and Morlonn now faced two remaining gronts, but held fast to protect their wounded friend. The other gront that Alaezdar had been fighting now charged, making it three gronts facing them. Morlonn, not knowing what else to do, threw his dagger at the gront, but it only hit his chest and bounced away harmlessly.

In the distance, screams still filled the air and were joined by the sound of a strange instrument, much like a bugle or a horn, but sounding more like a rolling dragon snort. The wounded gront in front of Alaezdar and Morlonn immediately left the fray and ran towards the sound while the other two gronts continued to taunt their prey as the sound filled up the air.

Taking advantage of the new distraction, one of the gronts charged at them.

Morlonn saw that the charging gront would reach Alaezdar first and pushed Alaezdar off balance and out of the path of the gront. Morlonn dove for the gront's legs and tackled him to the ground just as the gront began to swing his sword with a fierce downward blow. The gront could not stop running in time and he tripped over Morlonn and fell to the ground with a grunt. Alaezdar recovered himself, realized what Morlonn had just done and plunged his own bloodthirsty sword into the back of the gront before he could recover.

"Get up!" Alaezdar yelled. "They've found us!"

Morlonn rolled over on his back and then sat up and looked down the alley. A dozen more gronts were coming at them followed by a flaming woman and a robed man. They ran as if they were on a mission and Morlonn thought they all might just run right through them.

"Run!" Alaezdar yelled and he grabbed Morlonn's arm and turned him away so they both could run in the other direction.

"What about Rivlok?" Morlonn asked, panicking, not sure if he should stand his ground to protect his friend or run.

"We have no choice! If we are lucky, they will think he is dead," Alaezdar yelled and pulled at Morlonn's arm to get him running.

They had rounded one corner when they heard Aaelie yell for Alaezdar and down the next alley, they saw Ambassador Krostos, Tharn and Aaelie. Aaelie struggled as Azrull was holding her with a dagger to her throat. All of Azrull's Trielian soldiers surrounded them and two other solders held Tharn with both hands behind his back.

"What are you doing? Gronts are coming and they will be here any second!" Alaezdar yelled as he ran in front of them, but he was stopped at sword point by one of the Trielian soldiers.

"Aaelie, are you alright?" Morlonn asked.

Aaelie did not respond. She looked more angry than afraid even though her face was wet from her tears.

"Tharn, what is going on?" Alaezdar asked.

Tharn jerked his hands free of the soldier and pushed him away with such force that the soldier lost his balance and fell onto his back.

"They want you, Alaezdar. You need to go with them. If you go with them, they will let Aaelie go."

"Go where?"

"Back to Triel. They feel you are dangerous to this realm."

"Then why don't they kill me?

"They will if they have to," Tharn said and locked eyes with Alaezdar.

"Finally we can finish this and get out of this dreadful place!" Fyaa said as she and the gronts rounded the corner and charged into the alley.

She and the wizard Ra-Corsh walked towards them and the gronts followed, still wanting to fight, grunting and moaning because they had been fettered, almost as if held back by a spell, while they walked behind Fyaa and the wizard.

"Why don't you secure him and turn him over to me now?" Krostos pleaded after seeing this new development and wanting a quick resolution.

Krostos stepped forward to meet the flaming woman. Her skin had small wisps of flames stretching out of her chain mail as if they were attempting to grab small victims and bring them to her. Her mail still glowed slightly after covering her flaming body for so long during the battle. The hair on her head no longer looked like hair, but small flames scratched across her skull as if the flames were living vipers.

Krostos began to sweat as he approached and he stammered slightly as he spoke.

"This is not the time, nor was it the agreement. You said we could have him first."

" *You* do not know who he is, and you have no business with him. Nor do you want to do anything other than what I want! Do you understand…little man?" Fyaa asked caustically.

Alaezdar's hands trembled with rage and he wanted to fight this woman and kill Krostos at the same time, but he knew that would not end well for the others, especially Aaelie. He went to sheathe his sword, but the two outer claws at the bottom of the cross-guard of the sword were still extended and prevented the sword from seating. He left it partially sheathed, but kept his hand on the sword.

"What do you want with me?" he asked.

Fyaa laughed and looked at Ra-Corsh.

"Does he not know who he is?"

"I told you that he does not know. I told you that after I saw him a few days ago in the village. I had him seeing visions, but he transformed the visions much more deeply than I had expected. He really thought he was under an attack by his guild. This one holds great power, yet he has no idea he has. Be careful with him, Fyaa."

"Oh, this is even better than I had hoped," she said and laughed with childish excitement.

Fyaa walked towards Alaezdar, but Alaezdar walked backwards matching each of her forward advances.

"I will not tell you who you are to me, my love. Not yet, but you will come to understand in time. Come with me, and all will be done here at this tiny little trove that these worthless people inhabit."

Tharn walked up to Alaezdar and whispered to him, "I'm sorry. They knew you were coming long ago. When Torz came here the first time, he was looking for you then, and he promised us peace if I turned them over to you."

Ra-Corsh heard Tharn and added, "Tharn has been a great help in finding you. He has been listening to the Watchers Guild's every prediction about you and communicating your arrival."

"But you destroyed our village," Tharn responded angrily.

Ra-Corsh laughed. "You can thank this crazy witch woman for that. I had nothing to do with the plan of destroying your worthless village."

"Do you still want this girl?" Azrull asked Krostos, who was still clearly nervous and impatient.

Krostos turned and took a few steps back to Azrull to look to Aaelie. He walked over to her and lifted her chin.

"Oh, yes. I am keeping this one."

Tharn snapped around.

"That is not part of the deal!"

Alaezdar withdrew his sword and charged for Azrull. Rage filled his heart as he lifted his sword above his head. Azrull smiled, pushed Aaelie away, dropped his dagger, and withdrew his sword. He blocked Alaezdar's swing as it arced a few inches from his skull. Alaezdar stepped back and attacked repeatedly, but Azrull blocked every attack.

"No!" Fyaa yelled as Aaelie took advantage of the fight and escaped down the alley. None of the Trielian soldiers tried to stop her because they were closing in to help Azrull in his fight. Two Trielian soldiers jumped in front of Azrull and took over his attack on Alaezdar.

"Is there nothing you can do, wizard?" Fyaa screamed at Ra-Corsh.

He dropped to his knees and began an incantation that immediately began to affect the gronts and some of the Trielian soldiers. They began to tremble in fear and they dropped to their knees. Even Azrull felt a slight tingle of anxiety from the spell and started to back away from Alaezdar.

Alaezdar felt it too, but instead of fear, he felt his head tingle for a moment and a fog clouded his eyes, but then his rage took over and all he saw was Azrull through a dark tunnel of smoke.

"Get him!" Fyaa yelled, but no one responded. Ra-Corsh was working the spell and the gronts and soldiers were terrified. "You stupid human!" she cursed and she took to the air after Aaelie.

At that moment, Ra-Corsh stood up and clapped his hands over his head. As he did so, a wave distorted the air and then spread throughout the space and down the alley. Azrull fell to his hands and knees, but he quickly began to recover, shaking the cobwebs out of his head.

Alaezdar stood unaffected, stared at Ra-Corsh in front of him, and then turned to Fyaa behind him. Aaelie lay on the ground a few feet away from Fyaa. He saw Tharn, Morlonn, and Krostos all on the ground by Azrull, all unconscious, but Tharn looked like he might be starting to recover.

Tharn shook his head once and started to crawl over to an unconscious soldier near him. He withdrew the soldier's dagger from his belt and then climbed on top of Krostos's chest and placed the dagger to his throat.

Rage filled Alaezdar's entire being and he could feel it pulse through his hand and into Bloodseeker. He knew the best thing he could do was to charge after Aaelie and save her from Fyaa, but his anger led him instead to Ra-Corsh.

He ran towards him, raising his sword over his head, and when Ra-Corsh saw Alaezdar charging, he knew his first spell had had no affect on him. He raised his hands and worked another spell and an orange aura shimmered above Alaezdar's head and then slithered through the air down onto Alaezdar's hands. It wrapped tightly about his wrists and stopped Alaezdar's hands from swinging the sword just as he had began to drop it down and crush Ra-Corsh's skull.

"I need help, woman! I cannot hold him here forever!" Ra-Corsh shouted, still concentrating.

Fyaa jumped up, flew to Alaezdar, grabbed him from the back and wrapped her arms around his chest. He felt the back of his hair start to burn from her flaming skin and her fierce grip squeezed his ribs and caused him to lose his breath.

His skin began to burn and his eyesight began to dim and sparkle from the pain and the loss of oxygen.

"You are killing him!" Ra-Corsh yelled!

"I thought your power was supposed to prevent him from dying!" she said.

As they spoke to each other, Alaezdar felt the spell weaken and her grip loosen. He realized that he still had his sword in his hand and he changed his grip on it to an overhand hold and tried to poke the flaming woman behind him. It proved to be too awkward a movement and instead the sword slipped out of his hand and fell to the dirt with a thud.

Fyaa turned slightly to avoid the sword as it fell, and her movement gave Alaezdar a little room to elbow her repeatedly in her ribs until she let go of him. He turned around then and tackled her, knocking her onto her back, and he began to punch her in the face with his fists time after time.

Finally he grabbed her flaming head and smashed it to the ground five or six times before Azrull came up behind them and kicked Alaezdar off her.

Alaezdar rolled over on the ground, found his sword, and then located Ra-Corsh again. He was the one Alaezdar had initially wanted to kill, and he charged at him again.

Ra-Corsh realized that he had no more spells or power over Alaezdar and that he was now a weak and helpless man. He turned and ran down the back alley and off towards the village center.

Fyaa watched from the ground as Alaezdar ran away from her. She knew she could easily attack him again, but she also realized that any more aggression towards Alaezdar might kill him, so she let him escape.

She wanted him dead, and she did not want him realizing who he was or, even more importantly, who she was to him, not yet anyways.

"This is going to be too much fun!" Fyaa said and laughed as she stood up and began to alter her strategy. "Wait. The girl? Where is the girl?" Fyaa muttered to herself.

●●●

"Krostos! Wake up!" Alaezdar heard Tharn say as he ran past the two of them.

For a second Alaezdar came out of his blood rage to look at Tharn straddling his old friend. Tharn slapped Krostos in the face until he came to consciousness. His eyes were foggy, but as soon as he realized that it was Tharn on top of him, he started to get up. Tharn put his hand to his chest and pushed him back to the ground.

Tharn raised his dagger and slowly plunged it into Krostos' throat and began to slice from right to left and then up to the bottom of his chin. Blood squirted out of his throat and gave Tharn a warm shower all over his arms and chest. Krostos made a gurgling sound as he tried to speak before he bled out within the next few seconds. He dipped again into unconsciousness, and then into death.

"This changes everything!" Azrull said to Tharn. He'd arrived too late to help the ambassador. "You could've had it so good. Now you can just suffer the consequences of your decision and live in this burned out village without our support." He pointed at Tharn, stepped up within a few inches from his face and smiled. "You have actually done me a favor. Mount up, soldiers!"

He ran from the bloody scene and left Alaezdar standing next to Tharn.

Soldiers rose from their stupor and ran after Azrull. Those on horseback collected those on foot and they were all out of the village within a few minutes. Ra-Corsh too had escaped.

Alaezdar looked at Bloodseeker, and the two smaller, extracted blades sucked up tight into the base of the sword with a single click. He sheathed his sword, but he felt frustrated, angry, and unsatisfied.

Aaelie came out from hiding behind a building after having watched the whole scene and she began to run down the alley. Fyaa smiled.

"There is more than one way to catch a swordsman," she said and she flew to Aaelie and swooped her up. Aaelie screamed as her skin became singed from the woman's grasp, and Fyaa took her out of the village and flew high into the sky on her way into the forest, where she found a massive oak tree and placed Aaelie on a strong branch.

"Just hang there for a few minutes," Fyaa said. "You can try to escape, but I will be back before you can get down. Or you can fall and kill yourself. Up to you. Either way, I will return for you."

Fyaa then took to the air and flew back to the village. Aaelie watched her fly away and then looked down and saw that she was indeed way too high to escape.

Chapter 11

Alaezdar and Morlonn looked around in shock at the devastation of their village and then saw the blood on Tharn as he held his dagger. They looked back again toward the village and saw the dead body of Krostos.

Alaezdar stood there, just waiting for something more to happen.

It did. Fyaa returned.

"Time to go! Time is of the essence!" her voice came from the sky.

The flaming witch flew over Alaezdar and Morlonn, just out of their reach. She hovered over them; her flaming wings flapping and dropping sparks to the ground, as she observed the two combatants. Then, without a word, she flew off. Alaezdar wasn't sure -- because the fires were not putting off as much light as they had been earlier -- but he could've sworn that she winked at him.

Many gronts were now running towards them, and many ran right past them as if they weren't there, except one gront, still thirsty with blood lust. Alaezdar withdrew Bloodseeker again and prepared for the one gront's charge. The Gront attacked Alaezdar, but he blocked the attack and countered back with a low stab, which the gront blocked as well. The two battled for several minutes until the war horn belched again, whereupon the gront stopped his melee, screamed a deep and loud pig-like squealed grunt, and ran away.

Alaezdar dropped to one knee and watched the gront run. Morlonn was now finally becoming fully aware of his surroundings and he remembered the injured Rivlok. He tugged at Alaezdar's arm and the two of them ran back past a few alleys to where they had last seen him. They found him as they left him and still unconscious.

"Is he even still alive?" Alaezdar asked over his shoulder while looking down at Rivlok's body lying in the hard dirt.

Morlonn wiped the blood from Rivlok's head with his sleeve and then ran over to his knife, which was still in the dirt about five feet away. He used it to slice off Rivlok's whole left sleeve, and he wadded the cloth and applied pressure with it to the left side of his wound. The wound had actually stopped bleeding and had begun to coagulate.

"He will be fine," Morlonn said. "It looks like he took a blow from the flat side of the sword. Once I dress this wound, he will be okay. He will just have a gigantic headache for a few days."

Morlonn cut more cloth from his shirt, applied it to the wadded cloth on the wound, tied it around Rivlok's head, and secured it all in a tight knot so that it would continue to apply pressure. When he finished, he sat down and shook his head.

So many thoughts were racing through his mind about what had just happened. How could their peaceful village have just suffered such a violent attack? He sat in the dark, listened to the crackle of the burning buildings, and smelled the smoke as they burned in the night. They had known they were always in danger due to their proximity to the Goblin Tribes Forest, but they never had anything of value that the tribes that resided in that evil tangle would want. Confused, he returned his thoughts to his friend Rivlok.

"Why would they bother to attack him with the flat side of the sword and not kill him outright?"

"Gronts will do that," Alaezdar answered sharply. "When they know that they have outmatched their opponent, the kill then becomes a game to them and they like to see how many moves it will take to actually kill their opponent. The more moves it takes…the better."

Rivlok stirred and Morlonn put his hand behind his head and helped him to sit up gently and slowly.

"Hello, my friend," Morlonn said.

Rivlok said nothing, but sighed deeply and reached for his head. He felt the drying wetness of the blood.

"No…" he said, and then leaned back into Morlonn's lap. "I lost."

Alaezdar smiled, stood up, and walked past Morlonn and Rivlok. Rivlok's head wound was not serious. Even Alaezdar's wound was not as bad as he had first suspected even though his left shoulder still had blood trickling down his arm and back. Alaezdar put his sword down tip first in the dirt and leaned the hilt against his hip. He took his right hand and ran it over the wound and with his index finger pulled away some of the skin flap. He felt inside the wound. It was only a shallow cut that one of the villagers, most likely Tharn, could easily stitch, but it would not need that for he could already feel his sword healing his wound from within.

He had not realized the full potential of his sword, but he did know that often -- usually if the sword was satisfied with blood -- the power of the sword healed his minor wounds. Alaezdar sheathed his sword and applied pressure to his shoulder. While he did this, he looked at the village burning and the remaining townsfolk finally shaking loose their fear as they ran about putting out the fires in hopes of saving the remains of their homes and village.

"This is even worse than it seems…" Alaezdar thought aloud.

Houses, shops, barns, outbuildings, and booths burned throughout the village. Smoke choked the air and filled Alaezdar's nose with ash as he breathed. Feeling a sense of dread, he walked away to try to find some sense of peace, or at least a hope that his newly found home and friends weren't now completely devastated.

He had only to walk around the first corner when his most dreadful feelings were confirmed. Lying in the street was a young boy with a wooden sword in his hand.

"Rowlf!" Alaezdar yelled as he ran towards him.

His shirt was soaked with blood from a single stab wound to his stomach. He was lying in a pool of his own blood and was near death. Alaezdar knelt down beside him and placed his hand behind his neck. As he did so, Rowlf's eyes opened. He squinted, trying to see in the darkness and smoke. Somehow, even in his condition, he knew his rescuer.

"Alaezdar?' he whispered.

"Look at you, Rowlf. There is blood all over you."

"Yeah, he got me good, he did," he whispered.

"No, you are going to be fine. It is gront blood all over you, not yours."

Rowlf smiled and choked and coughed up a little blood that trickled down his chin.

"I did what you told me. I fought well, but he was just so big."

Alaezdar brushed Rowlf's hair back with his hand.

"You did well, my young friend. You will be a great swordsman yet."

Rowlf said nothing. His eyes glazed over, but he was still looking to Alaezdar for approval as he slipped away.

Alaezdar laid his head down and stood up, still looking at the boy. Shaking his head, he clenched his fists.

"Tharn, I told you no good would come of this," he whispered to himself. "This will not happen again. I promise."

Alaezdar then leaned down to Rowlf, closed the boy's eyelids, and stoked his hair again.

"This is the second time, and I promise you, Rowlf, I will not let another child die because of me. I have to leave you now, Rowlf. Others will be by soon to take care of you and your other friends who died today. I am sorry. This is my fault."

"Alaezdar?" A dazed voice startled him from behind.

Alaezdar turned around and saw Rivlok with Morlonn behind him. Rivlok's head had started to bleed again from his not staying down and he held a bloody piece of cloth to it to stop the blood. He wobbled slightly as he walked and was still a bit dazed.

"This is all your fault, Alaezdar," Rivlok slurred. "That boy, the village, Aaelie, all of this is your fault!" Rivlok shouted and pointed his finger into Alaezdar's face.

Clenching his fists, Alaezdar took a step toward Rivlok. He was ready to pound his head right on his wound, but Morlonn stepped in between him.

"You are right, Rivlok! This is *all* my fault. The wizard, the witch, the gronts, they are all here for me," Alaezdar said, trying to restrain both his temper and his frustration. "Why they are here, I do not know, but I do know this…"

Alaezdar pushed Morlonn aside, grabbed Rivlok's shirt, swung him over his right hip, and threw him to the ground. As soon as he hit the dirt, Alaezdar was on top of his chest.

"But I will be dead before you will ever get in my face to tell me what *is* or what is *not* my fault!" Alaezdar yelled in Rivlok's ear.

He grabbed Rivlok's shirt by the collar and began to shake him so that his head bobbled back and forth, hitting the ground again and again. Morlonn jumped in, grabbed Alaezdar by his waist and pulled him off Rivlok.

Alaezdar recovered his senses quickly and stood back up. He looked at Rivlok as he dazed in and out of consciousness, and then Alaezdar turned around and walked away. There were bigger problems to take care of now, he thought to himself.

The gronts were now gone. Fyaa and Ra-Corsh were gone as well. They had seemed to make a very organized and hasty exit. He wondered what Fyaa had to do with Ra-Corsh and what Ra-Corsh had to do with the gronts. None of this made sense. All were unlikely partners for attacking an unlikely target.

He had never seen Fyaa, or Ra-Corsh, but he did know of them. They were both enemies to the land. Any person of worth, especially swordsmen of hire such as himself, had heard of them, but no one had ever had heard about them working together. They were different beings with different motives. Alaezdar could not figure out their connection.

Ra-Corsh, last Alaezdar had heard, had been the active henchmen for a group called The Staff of Torz, a group dedicating themselves to finding the Ten Books of Magic, called the Compendium: Known throughout the realm as an eternal quest, not just by the Staff of Torz, but a quest by all the wizards of Wrae-Kronn.

Although now only a handful of wizards existed, they searched incessantly for that ancient artifact, the Compendium, which held many of the missing keys to the mysteries of this world. Many in this world prayed that the Staff of Torz would not find the ten books.

The Staff of Torz had destroyed villages in the name of their quest, had disrupted lawful expeditions and merchant caravans with their magic, and had raided their camps for supplies. Ra-Corsh was Torz's right hand man. Torz had been a professor at the Wrae-Kronn Islands Fortress of Prophetic Studies until he had been banished from the islands.

Ra-Corsh was himself a good part of the reason that Torz had been banished. He had been Torz's best and most prized student. Ra-Corsh finished top of his class, and as was traditional for all of the top students in their class, he earned the right to look into the Floating Book to read and attempt to interpret the prophecy from it.

Ra-Corsh, as had all the other top students before him, read the profound revelation to the future of the land. Then, shocked and overwhelmed, he tried to take the Floating Book from its stand, but found that the book was fixed to its position and would not move. Panic began to set in. He managed to do the next best thing he could think of and ripped out the pages that contained that prophecy along with some pages that contained very powerful spells. One of those was the Spell of Demon Summoning.

Later, while supervising Ra-Corsh's reading ceremony with a handful of other great Master Mages, Torz realized the immediate trouble that Ra-Corsh had just placed himself in, and he snatched up his student and disappeared with him in a flash. He left the island knowing they would never be allowed or able to return. Once they were safely away from the island and out of the Master Mages' magic sight, Torz reprimanded his young and very unwise student.

The damage had been done, but now Torz decided to use this event to his advantage. They both knew that the prophecy was of the fourth Quarterstar and its relation to the human king and Kronn, and they planned to exploit it. The sacred information had never been revealed beyond the Mage Masters and a select few graduates of the school.

Now Ra-Corsh knew it and Torz now had it. In his possession he could keep it hidden from all other mages and student mages forever.

Torz and Ra-Corsh took the pages and traveled the land as outcasts. They were searched by mercenaries throughout the land, but they evaded capture and death around every corner. Along the way they picked up a few followers and together became a powerful guild.

To make the prophecy work in their favor, they had planned to return the fourth and true god of the land, Dar Drannon, but only to destroy him. After years of traveling the land, they decided to split up and embark on this most important mission. Torz would go to the northern kingdoms and elicit their power, might and force to prepare for the return of Dar Drannon. Ra-Corsh meanwhile would enter the Goblin Tribes Forest, search out the origin of Gralanxth and summon him to their cause by using the Demon Summoning Spell to help them enter the Halls of Dar Drannon and steal the Ten Books of Magic.

Alaezdar, of course, had only heard tales of Torz and Ra-Corsh and had known a little of the history of their banishment from Wrae-Kronn Islands, but he never knew their mission or what the extended prophecy stated in the Floating Book.

Fyaa, on the other hand, he knew a little more about. Although he had never seen her, or seen Torz and Ra-Corsh either, he did know of her exploits through the tales of the land, but even what he knew was not much more than anyone else in the land knew. She had come to Wrae-Kronn by chance through the Aaestfallia Keep, a keep originally built by the elves to protect and house the Triestones. It was only by chance that she had come through the keep during a period almost four hundred years earlier when the Triestones were weak from the Markenhirth extension, and the barrier between worlds had opened.

It was then that Fyaa and three Birds of Fire, as the land had come to call them, came through the keep. It was an eerie coincidence because the Triestones' function was to protect the Aaestfallia Keep from opening without an elven mage to work it open. It was during this temporary weakening that she and her birds fell through the keep and into Wrae-Kronn.

Even stranger was the fact that the keep had opened for only a few seconds and then promptly closed. Some say she had been banished from her own land and sent there, but that was pure speculation by the people of Wrae-Kronn. Fyaa's vicious winged beasts came through the Aaestfallia Keep minutes before she did and they, not knowing where they were or what had happened to Fyaa, either took off looking for her, or as some said, escaping from their master.

Fyaa flew off chasing her charges, but she could not find their trail and she has been looking for them ever since. The Birds of Fire themselves have become a great mystery to the people of Wrae-Kronn because they wreaked havoc for only a short span of time and have since disappeared. Some believe that they are lost in the old abandoned dragon lairs, while others believe that they flew off into the Wrae-Kronn Sea only to grow tired and drown in the great waters. There are also some who believe that they are lost within the Halls of Dar Drannon and that they have made a perfect home within the grimshadows and their like, guarding the Ten Books of Magic. Yet still a select few say that they have met up with the Grimshaeds of Mervyyx.

Alaezdar could not figure out this new relationship between the gronts, Ra-Corsh and Fyaa. While still deep in thought, Alaezdar heard a scream from a few houses down the street. He took off running toward the scream and found Aaelie's mom running up and down the rows of streets and burning cottages and yelling for her daughter. Alaezdar caught up to her and stopped her by spinning her around and putting his hands on her shoulders.

"Where is Aaelie?" he shouted.

"She is gone. I can't find her! She can't be dead, Alaezdar!" she screamed and then covered her face and whispered hoarsely behind her hands, "She can't be"

"We will find her," Alaezdar simply said in what he knew was a weak attempt to reassure her mother that she was fine.

Alaezdar unsheathed his sword and left Aaelie's mom to go search for her daughter, but when he had gone around the corner and out of sight of her, he began to run in a panic throughout the village looking for Aaelie.

***

The people of Valewood worked for hours past dawn putting out the fires before they began salvaging personal items and saving livestock and crops. Though many homes had burnt completely to the ground, the village as a whole was not obliterated. Many of the markets and shops had burned to the ground and were still smoldering, and chicken, horses, goats, and cows were roaming through the village. The water towers and parts of the wooded ducts leading from the towers to the canals had also been destroyed and there was now a muddy mess wherever a tower had once stood. The stage, and every other structure where the once happy residents had celebrated, were now smoldering piles of unrecognizable destruction.

Alaezdar, Morlonn and Rivlok searched the village and its outer perimeter for Aaelie, but they could not come up with any sign or clue to her whereabouts. It wasn't until after they had exhausted all of their options that they came across a farmer who claimed to have seen Aaelie being dragged away by three gronts, led by the fire woman.

Hearing this information, the three men decided to part ways and round up all of the villagers to discuss what to do next by organizing a meeting back at the center square for early evening. Rivlok first went to Aaelie's mother to console her, and Morlonn went to his parents' home to help with their partially burned home. Once Alaezdar had told as many villagers as he could, he went back home to Tharn's farm and found it untouched.

The rest of the morning the villagers worked tirelessly to put out the remaining fires and to tend to the wounded and bury their dead. Overall, there were thirty wounded, three of them so seriously that they feared they would not make it to see the next day, one missing, and twelve dead.

By midday most of the town was asleep. Many just collapsed in their homes from exhaustion from not having slept for over a day and those who still had a home offered it to those who did not. As a community they would re-build the homes of the unfortunate, but the building would not start that day. Many rose just before sunset and began about some regular business, and although they stumbled around town in a dazed stupor, they had never felt more emboldened before as a community.

As the sun set to the west, a faintly brownish hue from the lingering smoke hanging above them painted the sky orange, creating a beautiful sunset. The inhabitants of the half-burned community of Valewood were assembling at the center of town right at the stage where they all had been when the attack occurred.

Tharn climbed up onto the slightly damaged fountain in the square and began to address the crowd.

"Friends of Valewood, last night was a horribly tragic event. We have lost many loved ones and even one guest from the kingdom of Triel. Many are beginning the grieving process for family, friends and property. However, we must work to together to rebuild what was destroyed and get back on track. We will rebuild, and we will survive!"

"What about Aaelie?" Marlie, Aaelie's mother, shouted from within the crowd. Tharn looked down at the grieving woman but he did not know what to say. He wished he could just forget poor Aaelie, and secretly he even wished that they had killed her instead of abducting her. He did not know why they had taken her, but he could only imagine the horror she must be going through. Knowing the type of monsters that had taken her caused his imagination to run wild with the horrible possibilities of her fate.

"Where is she? What can we do?" Marlie asked and broke down in sobs.

"I don't know," Tharn said, finally, almost in a whisper.

Rivlok ran to Tharn and climbed up the first two steps to stand next to him.

"I do!" he said. "We track those creatures down and get her back! Morlonn is an avid hunter and an excellent tracker. If anyone can find them, he can. And last night I saw Alaezdar fight like…"

No!" Alaezdar shouted, cutting Rivlok off. "You do not know what you are saying."

"Yes, I do, Alaezdar! I saw you fight last night with such swordsmanship as I have never seen. You are not who you say you are. Your skills are not those common for a traveling farm hand or a nomad, as you claim."

"You do not know the power of these creatures. Look at what they did to you. You were no match for them. If I hadn't gotten lucky with a few gronts, you and Morlonn would both be dead right now. It is just that simple."

"Stop pretending, Alaezdar. Before I got hit, I saw you fight with skill, not luck."

"What can we do?" Morlonn shouted. "We can't just let them take her while we stay here and allow them to do whatever they want with her!"

"No, we can't!" Kunther burst out, his words followed by an outcry by many others voicing similar opinions.

"You cannot simply go past the Sippling River and into the Goblin Tribes Forest. You will not survive a day alone," Alaezdar interjected, even though he knew he was opening himself up to fall into a trap that probably would not have a good ending.

"Then tell us, Alaezdar, how you know this," Rivlok challenged and the crowd began to grumble in agreement with Rivlok. Rivlok raised his hands to silence the crowd and looked directly at Alaezdar. "Lead us, Alaezdar. I plead you. If you don't, I will go alone, and whoever wants to go may, but I will go no matter what, even if I have to go by myself. I feel you know more than I do about what is out in those woods past the Sippling River. Many of us have never crossed the river, and none of us have *ever* ventured into the Goblin Tribes Forest just beyond the river. So, you may be correct in saying that we will die, but if you do not go with us, our blood, *and* Aaelie's blood, will be on your hands."

"I will go!" Kunther shouted and he ran to Rivlok. "Whether Alaezdar goes or not!"

Morlonn went to stand next to Rivlok and Kunther. He gave Alaezdar a pleading glance as he turned to face the crowd on the fountain step.

"You and I have not been the greatest of friends," Rivlok continued, Morlonn standing beside him, and he looked directly at Alaezdar, "but I know you love Aaelie, as well, and you must feel as I do, whether you say it or not, but I know you do."

Alaezdar stood silent for a few moments and then walked over to Rivlok, still on the fountain, and stood in front of him, looking up.

"You don't understand how grave this endeavor can and will be," Alaezdar said flatly.

"I don't care. What other choice do I have?"

Alaezdar lowered his head, took a deep breath and turned to the crowd. "Does anyone else want to go on this suicide mission?"

No one answered from the crowd, but an old, familiar voice from behind him spoke.

"I will," said Tharn.

Alaezdar winced and shook his head slowly.

"Anyone else?" he asked as he turned around and saw the hard determination in Tharn's eyes.

"Then we will go. How many is that…five?" Alaezdar acquiesced. "That will have to be sufficient. We don't need to bring any more people than we have to. Go home now, get your swords and weapons, and sharpen them. Bring whatever you think you need, but pack lightly. Then get some rest we will leave before first light."

"No, we leave now!" Rivlok interjected.

"No, we will not!" Alaezdar retorted and felt his face get flush with anger. "That would be foolhardy. I cannot say enough about the seriousness of this quest we are about to embark on. We may not survive past the next day. Besides, you must take in account their traveling party consists of ten to fifteen gronts, one wizard, one witch, and their prisoner, who will be slowing them down. They are on foot and we will be on horseback. We will catch them in two days, if not more quickly, if we are well rested and make less frequent stops than they will make. If we leave without rest, we will be hurting our chances of catching them by not being sharp enough to find them by staying on their trail.

"So collect your food, armor, supplies. Tharn, can you get the horses ready?"

"Yes, I can. I will choose my best and strongest horses."

"Good." Alaezdar looked to the crowd. "Let's all get some rest. We will do everything we can to bring Aaelie home to you."

The crowd began to mumble and disperse. Alaezdar looked at Kunther and was about to say something when Rivlok grabbed Alaezdar by the arm and swung him around to face him. Rivlok was only inches from Alaezdar and he looked into his eyes with a fierce intensity that told Alaezdar he no longer would be patient with him.

"Wait! I want you to tell me who you are. Right now!" Rivlok hissed so that no one except Alaezdar could hear him.

Testing Rivlok's patience, Alaezdar turned his back to Rivlok before telling him. "You don't want to know."

"Alaezdar, I mean it! Tell me!" he snapped.

Alaezdar stopped, but did not turn around.

"I need to know," Rivlok said calmly, using every ounce of his restraint to do so.

Alaezdar turned and saw that Rivlok, Tharn, Morlonn and Kunther were all looking at him and also waiting for his response.

He stared at the three men and at Kunther, who was not quite a man, but yet a strong young teenager. He pondered his response. How much should he tell? He questioned keeping nothing a secret or keeping everything a secret. At this point he truly feared they were all doomed to die within the next few days, so it wouldn't matter how much he told them, he reasoned. Surely his secret would go to their graves with them.

In the darkening evening, he began to tell his story.

"I am known as Rock Blade from Rager's House of Renegades. I was a hired warrior, swordsman, and assassin. In short, if the price was right to our leader, then I was their servant, no matter what the cause. I was a killer, murderer and hero, all wrapped into one, yet perceived separately and differently, depending on whose side of the mission we were on. That's what I was, but no longer."

Alaezdar waited for that information to take hold. He had just blurted it all out, and they stood in shock, not only because they had actually received the information they wanted, but because they realized their village had such a famed mercenary in their midst. Even they had heard of Rager's House of Renegades, and Alaezdar's description of the guild was exactly how they understood it to be, as well. Many heard the tales of this guild and some had glorified them as they passed them on, yet all feared them.

They had indeed done many good things throughout the land, but as Alaezdar said, it all depended on the side of the mission one was on and who was telling the tale. Some said they were nothing but a group of murderers and thieves, while others told tales of great heroic deeds disposing of the evilest of men.

"I left Rager's House of Renegades because I had killed a member of my own in a brief moment of conscience. I attacked, killed and disrupted a raid against one of our mortal enemies, Reikker-Kol."

"Why did you kill him?" Kunther asked.

Alaezdar took pause at the directness of the question, but smiled at the youth's carefree attitude, even in the delivery of the question. He should have been fearful of that information. Even speaking to a member of Rager's House of Renegades could be a dangerous and risky moment. Just mentioning a member's forename, such as the Rock in Rock Blade, could be grounds for a quick and silent death. Although usually a painless one due to the quickness and severity of the attack, because once the name was uttered or even heard by anyone outside of the guild, they were to be dead before it could be repeated or heard by others.

"Red Blade was our mission leader. Our orders were to carry out an assassination of two children of our enemy, Reikker-Kol. Well, the raid had not gone as planned. Eight of us entered his palace disguised in the armor of his own army. Our founder, Carsti Balron, known throughout the land as The Rager, had sent a letter to Reikker-Kol weeks in advance, while he was away. He was not due to return for at least a month. The Rager told him in the letter that his castle would be taken over by our guild by the time he returned and we would hold his children hostage until such time as he returned and surrendered himself to us.

"He never came to rescue his children. In fact, he sent an outside force to seek us out and kill us. We found ourselves trapped in his castle. The man was so ruthless that he didn't care about the safety of his own children. Red Blade was about to kill the boy when I realized that I could no longer be a part of this wicked plan. I struck first and killed Red Blade and escaped the castle."

"How long ago was this?" Morlonn asked.

"Actually, not long before I came here to Valewood. I wandered for quite a while, and I initially planned on leaving Valewood and wandering some more. But I liked what I saw here, and I settled here. Even as such, I planned to just stay here for the winter and move on because I knew that the Ragers were looking for me. I ended up staying longer because everyone made me feel at home and feel part of your village. I was eventually going to leave before trouble came to us, but it looks like it came anyhow, just in a different form than I'd expected."

Alaezdar exhaled deeply, still in thought, and then looked at Kunther.

"Kunther, I want you to go to Daevanwood and search out Carsti Balron and ask him for help. Tell him to come find us on the other side of the Vixtaevus gap, and tell him that I will freely surrender when he comes as long as everyone else in our party is left unharmed."

"You can't do that!" Kunther objected. "You said that they want to kill you!"

"Yes, they do, and they most likely will. It is okay. I am ready. I am tired of running. If nothing else, you guys have shown me what a normal life should be like. I have never had that. My life has been chaos ever since I was a boy, back when my mother was killed by the wizard Torz, and my father, also a wizard, left me as an orphan."

"I won't do it. You belong with us now, you are part of us, and we will help you," Kunther said.

"You will die trying. I keep telling you all, the life I have lived is so very different from the one you live. These people are ruthless and have no feelings or care for you and your life."

"Won't they kill me on the spot, as you say, since I know your true identity?" Kunther asked.

"That's right," Rivlok interrupted. "What you are telling us is flawed. If they are so ruthless, what is stopping them from killing Kunther right then and there as he stands?"

"No. Again, Rivlok, I am telling you, you do not know these people like I do. Yes, I did tell you that they will kill anyone just for breathing our identity, but Kunther has information that is more important to them than his life.... my whereabouts. That will be his key to everything they want right now. In fact, it is most likely the very most important thing on their agenda right now, and that will be Kunther's greatest asset in keeping him alive."

"I still won't do it. I want to go with you," Kunther pleaded, like a child wanting a treat from his mother.

"You must, or you will stay here. Besides, it is more important to our lives that you go. Like it or not, they are the only people who can help us. Other mercenary guilds will want more money than we can offer, especially now that Valewood will need all its available resources to rebuild."

"How will I pay?" Kunther asked reluctantly after giving in to the argument. His face showed the sad realization that he wasn't going to be chasing after Aaelie with the men he looked up to.

"My name and location will be all you will need. That will be the only payment that will satisfy them anyhow, and it will be more than enough to save your life, as well as hold something over them. But be careful, that could also be very dangerous information for you. Hold our whereabouts tightly to your chest, for once they are done with you, they will kill you. As soon as you have led them to the Goblin Tribes Forest, you must escape."

"Why?" he asked.

"Again, for your safety. You know my name, and they do not want you to know it."

Kunther felt dejected, but knew what Alaezdar was asking was important or he would not have asked him. Still, he could not help but plead one last time to go with them.

"Since I can't go with you, I want to ride with them until I find you."

"No, you don't. We most likely will not survive this quest. If we have any chance of surviving, it is because the Ragers will bring their experience and numbers, but when they have me, they will kill you because of me. You must not ride with them much past the Sippling River."

"Then I will leave right now," he said. He'd finally realized the importance of his mission.

"No, not yet. Pack up, find the fastest horse in the village, rest up for a few hours, then go. You will leave before us because you will need the head start."

"I will," Kunther said and turned around and ran back home to get ready for the most important and life changing event in his life.

Chapter 12

Kunther awoke after two hours of fitful and restless sleep. He wanted more, but he could not rest with the anticipation of his mission upon his shoulders. He tossed and turned, and if he fell asleep, he would only awaken ten minutes later. He did this many times until he eventually gave up trying.

Before lying down he had done as Alaezdar had suggested and found Tharn's fastest and strongest horse and packed her up. She was obediently standing right where he left her when he awoke. He went outside and mounted her and saw the early Doreal evening had an empty darkness about it. The night air was very dark and chilly and the village still reeked of smoke from the smoldering fires, so much so that it created an eerie haze as he sat on the horse pondering the trek in front of him. He was about to nudge his horse forward when he saw a figure walk out of the smoky haze at the end of the road.

"You are leaving too soon," Alaezdar said as he approached the young man.

"I can't help it. I can't sleep," he said

"Just as well. Neither can I. You might as well leave now, but you need to go and go quickly. Do you have a sword?' he asked.

Kunther smiled and withdrew his sword from the scabbard strapped onto the barrel of the horse's left side.

"I have Straight Edge," he said with a proud smile and handed it hilt first to Alaezdar.

Alaezdar took the sword and felt its weight and balance while swinging it from left to right, then down and up. Taking it with both hands, he throttled the hilt. He could tell even in the dark by the feel of it that it was not a work of beauty and was actually quite crude, but the weight was right and he knew that Rankin had made the sword and it was a worthy blade. The sword would be effective in battle in the right hands. Unfortunately, he feared that Kunther lacked much experience and he might be sending him to his death along with the others.

"Remember and do exactly as I have told you," Alaezdar said and handed the blade back to Kunther hilt first. "Talk only to Commander Carsti Balron and no one else. They will try to get information out of you, but be vigilant and confident. You must speak only to Carsti Balron."

Kunther agreed as he centered his horse from straying sideways.

"Thank you, Alaezdar."

"For what?"

"Having faith in me. I know this isn't what I initially wanted to do, but I do realize that this is vital to getting Aaelie back alive."

"You're right. We are counting on you."

Kunther nodded to Alaezdar and then kicked his horse and raced off down the road out of Valewood towards Daevanwood. Alaezdar turned around and started running back to Tharn's farm, where the others would soon be heading. His thoughts were on Kunther and his meeting with Commander Carsti Balron and he wondered again if he might be sending Kunther to his early death.

Or, was he prolonging his life by not allowing him to go into the Goblin Tribes forest. He knew Carsti Balron, out of all his faults, to be a fair man and a good leader. Although he was a ruthless and shrewd man, he would listen to reason when it was presented to him properly. He just hoped Kunther would be wise enough to give him good reason at the onset to let him live to tell the tale of where Rock Blade would be.

He ran quickly along, thinking these thoughts, until he saw Tharn's farm just as a tint of sunlight began to creep up over the horizon.

When he got back to the farm, he found, not surprisingly, that Tharn was already awake and packing up all of the horses for their trek. Without a word Alaezdar helped Tharn finish packing their supplies, and just as they had finished, Rivlok came with his horse pack over his shoulder, dressed in a still dusty suit of leather armor.

"Where did you find that old thing?" Alaezdar asked.

"I bought it, why?" Rivlok responded in a terse voice.

"No reason, really, other than I haven't seen armor like that in years. It looks like armor from the Korlond Empire."

Rivlok smiled and then quickly took the smile away. "Well, it may be. I don't really know, but it is better than nothing."

"I agree. You are right, but I have something a little more current and efficient. After we last spoke, I went to Rankin and Kord, the leather-smith, and asked them to come up with some swords, shields, breastplates and arm guards for all of us. Before we leave, we need to go over and pick them up. I am sure he is still working on them. We didn't give him much time to make them perfectly efficient, but with a little luck they might stop arrows."

"Why don't you go pick them up now?" Tharn suggested. "I will get some food and torch supplies and then meet you there."

Alaezdar agreed, and he and Rivlok mounted their horses, ponied two more horses and then headed to the smithy shop. On the way they stopped at Morlonn's house and found him standing outside of his partially burned home. They gave him a horse and proceeded on to find Rankin and Kord, who were finishing their final preparations, but they had most everything ready.

"I have all of the breastplates, shin and shoulder guards, daggers and swords all done," Rankin said as he wiped the sweat off his gray eyebrows with his blistered hands. "Some of these I already had in the back room just collecting dust. Kord is just finishing up with the last scabbard."

Alaezdar picked up a breastplate and inspected it. He looked at the front side and turned it quickly to look at the backside.

"Quick work," Alaezdar stated bluntly, neither complimenting nor criticizing the work.

"I did what I could with such short notice," Rankin defended.

Alaezdar continued to examine the breastplate and did not look up.

"Understood, but these breastplates are too heavy and will limit movement. I just hope we don't get into any hand to hand combat." Alaezdar paused and looked to Rankin. "The gronts may be short and stocky, but they are very maneuverable when locked in hand to hand combat."

"It is all I have," Rankin once again defended himself.

"I have more scabbards and leather leggings," Kord said as he entered from the back room. Alaezdar turned to Kord and put down the breastplate.

"Do you have any scrap pieces of leather to use as breastplates?"

"I can make some."

"Do it. Just make them one sheet thick and use two leather straps as ties. Simple, but light weight, and effective for what we will be against." Alaezdar turned to Rankin and put his hand on his shoulder. "We will need the breastplates, and we will be taking them. Thank you. You did great with all these, especially on such short notice."

Alaezdar, Tharn, Rivlok and Morlonn did not have to wait long for Kord to finish the breastplates, put them on and make a few minor adjustments. They packed the rest of the armor, shields, and daggers onto the spare horse and were soon on their way.

Within minutes they were crossing the Sippling River not far from the spot where Alaezdar and Aaelie had last spoken. The sun had just crested over the Goblin Ridge Mountains, finally bringing in the early Doreal warmth with the morning's sunrise. They rode for six hours before their first stop. Morlonn found evidence of broken branches from what looked to be someone being dragged in the dirt, but soon he lost that trail just as if it had magically disappeared in front of him.

They decided to break up into groups of two's and continue in a diagonal sweeping pattern and crossing back every half mile to try to get the trail back, but after a few hours they gave up. Alaezdar called everyone together, dismounted his horse and asked the others to do the same. Rivlok jumped off his horse and charged towards Alaezdar. He was clearly frustrated with their slow progress.

"Why are we stopping now? I don't understand. Ever since we decided to go with you, you have done everything possible to slow us down!" Rivlok shouted.

"Back off, Rivlok!" Alaezdar said and jumped in front of Rivlok's face, shutting him up.

"Morlonn," Alaezdar said, "Any new signs yet?" He turned away from Rivlok and left him alone brewing in his anger with his fists clenched tightly.

Morlonn walked up to Alaezdar and looked ahead of them.

"Nothing yet."

"I want you to lead from here on. Go up a few hundred yards in front of us, if you need. Rivlok, I want you to ride with Morlonn. Tharn and I will follow from the rear. Ride towards the Goblin Ridge Mountains, stop if you find their trail and wait for instructions once Tharn and I catch up to you. If you don't find their trail, continue on to the Vixtaevus Gap. I am sure we will find their trail there, as there is no way around for hundreds of miles but through the pass. Once you get there, stop and wait for us. Under no circumstances do you cross into the gap without us."

"The Death Pass?" Tharn asked.

"It is the quickest and only route into the Goblin Tribes Forest. I don't know why they have Aaelie, but I am sure that they are in a hurry to take here there."

"Surely, we aren't going to walk right through the Death Pass and not expect to get attacked?" Morlonn asked, showing a little fear in his voice for the first time.

Alaezdar mounted his horse.

"No, I am not expecting that. In fact, I am expecting to catch them before the Death Pass, but if we don't make it in time, we will have to cross the pass and I fully expect to be attacked, but we will be prepared," he said and pointed to the packhorse. "We will be wearing our iron breastplates, and we will -- cautiously and very quickly, I might add -- be moving through the pass. Whatever will be waiting for us there, goblin, ogre, gront or chrok, will have to have a keen eye to see us."

"They will most likely be waiting for us if these gronts know that we're following them."

"I am sure they would inform their own kind of such things," Tharn added and he too mounted his horse.

"Not necessarily,

Alaezdar said. "The Goblin tribes don't always communicate with each other because they are often fighting each other, so Fyaa and hers may have to fight their way past as well."

"Then let's go!" an impatient Rivlok shouted as he mounted his horse and rode to the front, expecting the others to follow.

"That boy is going to get us into a lot of trouble," Tharn said as he grabbed the reigns of his horse and packhorse and waited.

"He means well," Alaezdar commented, but he also felt uncomfortable about Rivlok's anxiousness and aggressive attitude.

Morlonn had just left the group to catch up to Rivlok when they all heard a loud squeal and then Rivlok's yell for help.

"It can't be them already!" Alaezdar said.

He withdrew Bloodseeker and charged his horse into the woods where a gront was attacking Rivlok. He felt Bloodseeker's power rush through his veins as he charged and he immediately saw Rivlok on the ground, his horse running away, and a gront on his knees, but about to stand. Rivlok was conscious, but was lying in the fetal position with his hands covering his head.

"Get up!" Alaezdar yelled as he swung Bloodseeker at the gront. Morlonn arrived a few seconds after him and was nocking his arrow as he rode towards the gront. Alaezdar's sword and Morlonn's arrow hit the gront at the same time. The arrow hit the gront's chest, but only bounced off. Alaezdar's sword hit the gront at the shoulder, but only knocked him down.

Rivlok heard Alaezdar yell and he realized he needed to move, fast. He scrambled to his feet, grabbed his sword and charged the gront, still on the ground. His blow hit the gront in his ribs, but his blow, like Morlonn's arrow, only bounced off his rough hide. Alaezdar jumped off his horse and met the gront in hand-to-hand combat just as he was about to return the strike from Rivlok.

The gront and Alaezdar now fought intensely. The gront growled and grunted with every blow and the massive overbite of his fangs dripped drool down his chin with every swing. Finally, with one deft stab he made Alaezdar jump back, but before he could charge his opponent, Rivlok's sword finally found its mark. His blade entered into the gront's back just below the shoulder blade and his arm flew up as he dropped to his knees.

Alaezdar brought his sword down on top of the gront's head, but his blade only bounced back at him. The blow only brought the gront back into the rage of battle, and he straightened his grip of his sword, put one foot on the ground, and had begun to stand up when an arrow hit his left cheek. The gront grunted and groaned again, but this time dropped his sword and clutched at the arrow.

Rivlok and Alaezdar both took advantage of the opportunity and began cutting into the gront's hide until they finally penetrated it enough times to kill him. They beat him senseless and continued slicing him and his blood made the ground muddy beneath the gront's carcass.

Alaezdar and Rivlok stood above the bloody creature and stared into his now lifeless, coal black eyes. His animal hide armor was now wet from his own blood and sweat and it looked like the body of a giant rat. His mouth was open, exposing his giant teeth and the sharp fangs showed a superior fierceness even in death. Even the space where a nose should have been gave the gront's face the impression of a fierce demon.

Even more intimidating to Rivlok had been the fact that when the gront was fighting them, he stood almost six feet tall, making him appear to be a walking animal with pale grey skin a the fighting ability better than most common human warriors.

"What happened?" Alaezdar asked Rivlok without looking up.

"He jumped me from the top of a tree," Rivlok answered, shaking his head.

"What…a tree?" Alaezdar looked sharply at Rivlok.

"Yes, a tree, just as I said. He jumped out of the tree and knocked me off my horse. I got the wind knocked out of me. The next thing I remember was you yelling."

"Gronts aren't known for climbing trees. In fact, they have never been known for having the patience to wait for their enemy and ambush them. They have gone into battles in large groups, of course, but this is the first time that I have heard one going it alone."

"What does it mean?" Morlonn asked. He rode up a little closer to where they were talking and his horse stomped his feet as if to make a point to Morlonn that he did not want to get any closer to the dead gront.

"I don't know. I don't know of any spell that Ra-Corsh could have over this gront that would last once Ra-Corsh left the area. The farther the wizard travels from the area, the weaker the spell, but that doesn't explain how tough this one was to kill. I hit his head with my sword and it bounced off like I had hit an anvil…this is all too strange."

"What about Fyaa?" Tharn asked after finally coming to the group for the first time since the fight began.

"I'm not sure. Fyaa is very mysterious. She is not part of this world, so I suppose anything is possible," he admitted.

"Alaezdar," Morlonn broke in. "I think I can find this gront's trail and that can lead us to where he came from.

"Good. Scout ahead and we will wait here. We will rest up and eat before we continue on, but be careful. They could be setting up another ambush. This gront could have been a plant so they would know where we are, or he could be sent just to slow us down. Either way, it seems like they know we are following. Oh, and see if you can find Rivlok's horse while you are at it."

Morlonn smiled, jumped on his horse and sped off to the east. While he was away, Alaezdar, Rivlok and Tharn searched the body of the gront. Alaezdar took the animal-hide off its back, but found it useless because it was merely the rough hide of a boar. Their own leather and iron armor would serve as greater protection to them then the gront's so-called armor.

When Alaezdar pulled the pelt off the gront, though, he found the brand of the Fire-Gront on his chest. The mark had been branded with a hot iron directly on his chest and it had left a scar that was hairless, so the brand was clear and evident. It was the shape of a human hand with a fireball through the center. Alaezdar knew this was a definitive mark of the tribe of gronts led by the wizard Ra-Corsh.

The tribe got their name when Ra-Corsh had stumbled across a small tribe of wandering gronts. They were a small group banished from a much larger tribe. This small tribe had seen him wandering the forest alone, and they decided if they could kill such a wizard, they could bring his body back home and win their places back into their tribe.

In a burst of confidence the gronts took the opportunity to attack the wizard, but the fight did not last long as Ra-Corsh's magic was too powerful. The final blow was when Ra-Corsh sent a flame spear towards them, catching some of the forest trees on fire. He then cast a freeze spell onto the gronts, so that they could not move, while the fire burned around them.

They pleaded for mercy and Ra-Corsh promised to extinguish the fire and let them live if they would serve him. With visions of revenge upon other tribes, and eager to have such power on their side, the gronts eagerly agreed to the deal. Ra-Corsh extinguished the fire and hammered out the guidelines for his new servants. The first test of their loyalty was to take a brand on their chest to signify their new organization, the hand of Ra-Corsh and the spell that had begun the creation of the Fire-Gronts.

Alaezdar brought the brand to the attention of Rivlok and Tharn.

"For some reason," he said, "Ra-Corsh holds great power over these gronts. I don't quite know what that power is, but they seem loyal enough to die for him, even by doing things that are very uncommon for gronts, like this, setting up ambushes in trees."

"Maybe they know you, Alaezdar," Rivlok stated with a cocky half smile. "And they don't like you."

Alaezdar shook his head. He was not in the mood for Rivlok's half joking insults.

"Look here," Alaezdar said and reached for the gront's pouch on his belt. He opened it up and dumped its contents on the ground. Out came a rat's head, a half-eaten fish, and a piece of meat wrapped in a large leaf, with maggots crawling all over it.

"Lunch!" Tharn laughed.

Rivlok grimaced and Alaezdar just smiled.

Chapter 13

Throughout the night and long into the next morning they ran.

Aaelie could smell the sweet pinesap as the sun rose silently. The morning dew dripped off the clustered pine trees, and the trees steamed as the morning sun evaporated the beads of moisture from the previous night. The gronts pushed hard through the thick foliage as if it did not exist. Three gronts led the way with their short swords and cut down anything that might block their path or slow down the main group.

A few hundred feet behind was the main group that had Aaelie. Behind them another group followed that made certain that if the one ahead of them slowed down, they were going to make her feel the wrath of gronts with idle time. Gronts were easily bored, so if they felt that they needed something to keep occupied, they knew they might find some entertainment through Aaelie. Therefore, to protect Aaelie, and some of the gronts from getting into trouble with Ra-Corsh, the group to the rear pressed on harder than the others ever would.

As soon as they had captured Aaelie, they tied her hands and waist together with reinforced twine. In the beginning they dragged her for the most part against her will. She fought, kicked and tried to escape while screaming at the top of her lungs, but no avail. No one heard her. The villagers were still fighting the fires, protecting their homes, or hiding and still in shock about what had just happened to their peaceful village. They would be working all night long and into the day licking their own wounds.

It wouldn't be for many hours before any one of the villagers would realize that she had been taken.

Eventually Aaelie gave in and remained silent, but she did nothing to help the cause of her abductors. She let them drag her on her back while she dug her heals into the dirt, if not to slow them down, then at least to leave somewhat of a trail for someone from the village to follow.

When the gronts got tired of dragging her, they stood her up, beat her and threatened to do worse to her if she would not walk. Two gronts held her from each side with her hands outstretched, and tied them to their waists. She ran along beside them, unashamed, even though her dress was torn to tatters from the waist down and her braided hair had long since come undone.

Two more gronts then tied a twine around her waist and kept it taut so that she could not move in any direction except to follow. If she strayed to one side or the other, they cinched the twine tight about her waist. More often than not that took the air out of her lungs and brought her to the ground. Sometimes the gronts would pull the twine tight out of boredom and for the sheer delight of watching her in pain and listening to her scream. The gronts would laugh amongst each other at the thrill of playing with their new prized toy.

As they ran, Aaelie watched the gronts with disgust. Their awkward bodies and oversized thighs caused their torsos to wobble as they ran, and if she hadn't been in so much pain, she would have laughed at how utterly pathetic they looked. Even worse, their odd shaped figures caused their bellies and chests to shake and bounce in unison.

How could these creatures even fight effectively, she thought to herself. Amidst all the pain and torture she was going through, she felt even more embarrassed that she had been captured by something so crude and clumsy as these gronts.

The gronts, meanwhile, continued to taunt her every chance they got. She even began to dread the time that they took to rest, for the gronts, not being preoccupied with keeping their wobbly bodies moving forward, found many other fun things to do with their prisoner. The first time they stopped, they decided that she was hungry and tried to force a live frog down her throat. The frog wasn't past her lips when Aaelie found the opportunity to kick one gront between the legs. She managed to laugh as the gront fell down. The frog, as well, fell unharmed and hopped away to safety.

The second time they stopped, most of the gronts circled around her, ripped what was left of her evening dress to shreds, leaving it barely clinging to her body, and only her undergarments still kept her from being completely exposed. They pulled her hair and punched her face with their pale, milky white fists and waited to see how fast her face would swell and bruise. When it did, they pointed and laughed, proud of their accomplished work.

Aaelie eventually noticed that their leaders did not approve of this action. As she lay in the dirt, bleeding and swelling, the gronts continued to kick her in the ribs and back. She tucked in the fetal position and rolled with every kick, but exposed a new area each time for the gronts to exploit. Coming close to losing consciousness, she heard the demon woman come close and the gronts scrambled and ran away when she approached. None of the gronts wanted anything to do with this witch they knew as Fyaa.

Fyaa's body tensed up and the small hairs on it ignited. Her tight-knit chain armor turned bright red and was close to melting off. He body seemed to expand from the heat and it looked as if she was floating a few inches above the ground. Aaelie heard her scream a name -- the name of the wizard she guessed, because a man in dark robes then appeared and cowered before her.

"I want no more torturing of our prize!" she yelled through gritted teeth. Her facial features were no longer visible through the flames. "We need her alive! Ra-Corsh, if you cannot handle your gronts, then all of this will be for nothing. You will not get what you need and I definitely will not get what I need. If we fail in this, you will not live to see another day...no, you will, but you will beg me to let you die before I am through with you! Do you understand?"

Ra-Corsh went to one knee before she was finished speaking.

"I will take care of it," he said and he stood and ran to corral up his gronts while Fyaa stood above the curled Aaelie. In her haze, Aaelie knew that she was in trouble. She had heard tales of Fyaa and her Birds of Fire, and this Ra-Corsh gave her a horrible feeling of dread and heartbreak.

Their last stop was not a planned stop. They had been traveling for a full day when Ra-Corsh and Fyaa began arguing. Fyaa once again engulfed herself in flames, and her now flaming wings sprouted out of her back and she flew away and did not return for nearly an hour. During that time the gronts once again tried to have their way with Aaelie, but Ra-Corsh stopped them every time they tried anything.

In their last attempt, the gronts had surrounded Aaelie, but Ra-Corsh angrily spoke to them in their native language and by the sound of it to Aaelie, and by the way the gronts were reacting, he wasn't offering pleasantries to them. When he finished speaking, the gronts grunted in fear, but danced about in what looked to be a mix of fear and excited delight. They pushed each other around, knocking some to the ground, and others even kicked the ones that were down and seemed to be laughing as they did so. Eventually three gronts picked up one of the fallen gronts and threw him at the feet of Ra-Corsh.

The chosen gront fell prostrate before the wizard, grabbed the bottom of his dark robe and kissed his feet as he did so. Ra-Corsh raised his hands above his head and pointed to the sky with both hands. Calling upon his Kronn, he felt it surge from the ground into the soul of his being and course through his veins.

The gront stood erect and did not move. Ra-Corsh touched his hands together and sparks began to charge between his fingers, eventually forming a small sphere of sparks. He grabbed the gront's head, said a few words and then sent the gront running back towards the village.

Ra-Corsh walked over to Aaelie as he removed the hood of his cloak. Aaelie turned her back to him, but the gront that was holding the rope to her waist snapped it and she bent over in pain. Realizing what the gront meant by whipping the rope like that, she turned to face Ra-Corsh.

"My name, as you may have heard, is Ra-Corsh," he said as he scratched his black tightly shaven beard with his knuckles downward repeatedly. His hair was thin and had a slightly receding hairline. His mustache formed the shape of a T beginning above his upper lip and continuing down from the center underneath his lower lip to his chin. He looked at Aaelie with mock compassion in his dark brown eyes. "I assure you, no more harm will befall you from my crude grontish friends. I sent the one who beat you on a very crucial mission. He will either succeed or die."

He paused and looked at Aaelie for a response, but got nothing from her.

"I suspect that we are being followed. During our raid I noticed among your villagers is a swordsman. Who is he? Where is he from? He surely is not a typical farmer, native to your village."

Aaelie turned her head away to show her defiance.

"Look at me!" he shouted.

Aaelie did not turn her head, but instead clinched her eyes as tightly as she could. She expected him to strike her for her defiance. Instead, Ra-Corsh began to mumble and twist his right hand until Aaelie began to feel an urge to turn her head.

Unable to resist, she turned and looked at Ra-Corsh.

"Ahh, isn't that better my love?" Ra-Corsh gushed. "Now tell me, who is following us?"

Aaelie tried to turn her head away, but could not and the rage inside her made her eyes water. Ra-Corsh mistook her tears as fear and placed his hand on her cheek.

"It will be fine, little sweet one. You have no reason to fear me."

Aaelie turned back around to spit in his face.

"I don't know who it is!"

"How can you not know?" he said, wiping his face with the palm of his hand and taking the spit and rubbing it back on her lips. He smiled and he flattened out his palm and ran it past her neck and around to the back of her hair. He pulled hard and forced her to look upwards.

"I am sorry that this may hurt. You are so very beautiful and your friends must care about you very much."

Aaelie bit her bottom lip to keep herself from releasing any sound that might give him some satisfaction in thinking she was showing weakness.

"Please, tell me, and maybe I will have some idea if my servant gront that I just sent back will live or die. You must understand that this is his punishment for harming you. He can redeem himself by killing your friends, or even wounding and slowing them down. Otherwise he will be punished by sacrificing himself when they kill him." Ra-Corsh let go of Aaelie's hair and smiled at her. "You see, either way, I will gain valuable information. If my friend dies and does not return, I may not know exactly who is following us, but I will know that the swordsman is with them."

"I...truly...do...not know," Aaelie managed and glared at Ra-Corsh.

"Oh, but I think you do," he responded mockingly. "I also do not think you know the severity of the situation you are in. You see, Fyaa is very angry with me and if she harms me, then nothing will stop the gronts from tearing you to pieces. Trust me, they would love nothing better than to do that. It would not be a quick death for you."

"I do not know!" she snapped. "Probably the newcomer to village, but I do not know him!"

"Now we are getting somewhere. Where did he come from?"

"I don't know. He never said."

"You are not being very helpful. You need to help me, and I think in time you will."

Aaelie lowered her head and began to sob.

"I will not. My father wouldn't help your kind the last time a wizard like you came to our village, and I won't help either."

Ra-Corsh almost could not hear her, but he bent down again and lifted her chin. "So you think you know of my type? Curious. Who do you think we are?"

"A sorcerer came to our village and harassed my father and others, and then another group of swordsmen who were looking for them followed a few days later and killed my father. Now you and this witch come to our village and destroy it."

Ra-Corsh smiled.

"Yes, terrible things happen wherever we go, but we have a just cause. That man who came to your village is my mentor, Torz, and he will change this realm for the better, you will see. Do you know why he came to your tiny little village?"

"He was looking for somebody he thought was hiding in our village."

"I see." Ra-Corsh rubbed the whiskers on his chin. "Yes, we have been looking for this man, in fact, I believe the man I am looking for is following us. I have decided to take matters in my own hands. Instead of killing to find him, I have decided to steal something he cares about and make him come to me."

"Why me, why?" Aaelie screamed at him.

She covered her face and began to cry heavily, her chest heaving out of control.

"Well. We need to move on. Maybe we can finish this conversation later and you can tell me if this swordsman really is who I think he is, after you've tired out from running."

Ra-Corsh turned around and commanded the gronts to move on. Aaelie once again followed at a slow jog, but the gronts did not ease up with their occasional taunts or with hitting her as she ran.

Chapter 14

Alaezdar and company continued trekking east, slowly following the trail Morlonn had left them, when Morlonn himself returned. They still had a few hours of daylight left so they were encouraged when he returned with news that he found their tracks. He reassured Alaezdar that the ones they pursued were still on foot and were only a day ahead of them, if not less.

Alaezdar and the others mounted up. Since Rivlok's horse had abandoned them, he rode with Tharn. They took advantage of the rest of the daylight and ran hard, but they stopped shortly before the sun went down.

"This is where we will camp for the night," Alaezdar said when they came to a clearing next to a small brook.

"But there is still light! We can ride. In fact, with Morlonn leading we can ride into the night!" Rivlok protested.

Alaezdar stepped off his horse, tied it to a tree, unsheathed his sword from its saddle scabbard, and took a defensive stance.

"Come to me, Rivlok. Attack me."

Rivlok snapped his head back in confusion.

"Now! Do it now!" Alaezdar demanded again.

Rivlok stepped down from his horse and turned around to unsheathe his sword. Alaezdar charged Rivlok while he had his back turned and pushed him to the ground. Rivlok's sword flew out of his hand.

Alaezdar did not attack Rivlok to harm him, but merely to prove a point, and even though the attack was not done to harm, he still felt the excitement of Bloodseeker coursing through his veins. It took all of his inner discipline to remind himself not to hurt Rivlok.

Alaezdar straddled Rivlok and put a knee to his chest.

"From here on out you must be prepared for anything. A gront almost killed you this morning, yet you still question my motives. It is time for some quick training, and we can only do this when there is light. We rode as long and as quickly as we could without ruining our horses, and now I need some time and light to teach you all a few things that may save your lives in the next day or two."

Alaezdar stood up, releasing Rivlok, gave him a hand up and pointed his sword at Tharn.

"Take up your sword, old veteran."

Alaezdar taught them the same basic maneuvers as he had the children in the tournament. He taught them the importance of balance of the body and staying on the ready by bending their knees and keeping the soles of their feet touching the ground as much as possible. Then he showed them how the weight of the sword must be mastered in order for it to be used as an advantage. Otherwise, it would quickly become a hindrance to their effectiveness.

He taught them to keep the sword close to the body and watch their opponent to try to calculate his moves to defend and to then look for open spots to attack. He told them never ever to lose control or attack in a blind outrage. He even taught them how to use the surrounding environment, such as the rocks, bushes and trees, for defensive positions, and to try to keep the sun in their opponent's eyes if possible. Finally, he taught them the simple moves of thrusting, swinging and parrying.

They all caught on quickly, but still lacked the many skills that only came with experience. However, with a few more hours of training Alaezdar knew they could learn enough skills to fight the crude fighting style of the gronts. Teaching them the fundamentals of swordsmanship was fairly easy, but the hard part would be teaching them not only how to defend themselves from an experienced swordsman, but to defend themselves from the demon woman and the magic of a very powerful wizard. He knew he was leading these men on a very dangerous and deadly mission, but exactly how dangerous, not even he really knew.

They practiced until dusk rolled in and cast long shadows on them as they battled each other. He pointed out errors, but he also directed them how to fix their flaws. They kept going until the shadows from the trees were no longer, and then the pure night darkness prevented them from continuing. They withdrew their sleeping rolls, made a small fire and ate some fruit that they had brought with them from the village. They sat wordlessly by the fire and watched the embers glow and flicker before them.

"How far is it to the Death Pass? Morlonn finally asked Alaezdar.

"We should be there the day after tomorrow."

"Will gronts be there?" Rivlok asked.

"Some, but there will be others there that are much, much worse.

"It doesn't matter what they are," Tharn said and began shaking his head and pointing a finger at Alaezdar. "They're all monsters and they mean to kill. Rivlok and Morlonn haven't witnessed death like you and I have, Alaezdar, and I hope they won't have to either."

Alaezdar nodded silently before he answered.

"I am afraid that they will witness not only the death of these foul creatures, but I fear we may witness the death of one another. We may see ogres, orcs, maybe goblins, but I don't know specifically what we are up against. You have all heard tales of the Death Pass and how it got its name. Most of what you heard are pure tales, but some of what you heard is true. Tharn is right. I have seen death. I wish I had not, but I have, and the Death Pass is only one of the places where I have seen it."

Alaezdar paused to look at the stars faintly shining through the hazy smoke from their fire.

"Well, are you going to tell us about any of it?" Rivlok asked, nonplussed.

"Yes," Alaezdar said blankly and looked up at the sky for a few more minutes before addressing them. "The Vixtaevus Gap, or the Death Pass, as it is so aptly named, is one of the most beautiful places in Wrae-Kronn, but it is also the gate to the Markenhirth forest, now more commonly known as the Goblin Tribes Forest. This is where many tribes of the forest have set up non-stop watches for intruders. They wait, only to maliciously ambush them and intimidate them from entering their homeland. The pass is a mile wide, but the cliffs on each side tower the gap and that is where the beasts hide. The term 'goblin,' in this sense, is an amalgamation of all the tribes working in unison at the pass. This is the only place in the whole realm where they will work together without infighting.

They shoot arrows, throw spears and drop rocks down at the trespassers, usually slaughtering them all or, at the very least, forcing them to turn and run to save their lives. It is not known how they can organize themselves for who watches the pass and when -- especially since beyond the pass they are constantly battling each other -- but the Gap has always been known to have at least one group on watch at all times, all hours of the day."

Alaezdar looked again to the sky and then back to Rivlok. "I was with Rager's House of Renegades the last time I was here. Six of us went searching for the grimshaeds and had to pass the Death Pass to get there."

"Grimshaeds are real?" Morlonn interrupted.

"Oh, yes, they are definitely real."

"Are they truly as hideous as they are in the tales we hear?"

Alaezdar shook his head, a little annoyed to be pulled off topic.

"Yes, they are…and most likely even worse than you can imagine. Most of the time, you will not see their true form because they conceal it so well within their cloaks, but if you get close enough, they will shed their cloak to intimidate you, as a wolf will raise its hackles before a fight. Their skin is wrinkled and deformed and looks as if they have been burned, melted and then dried. Their wrinkled head is bald, with the exception of a few strands of hair extending out. Blood and pus oozes frequently from random parts of their body, their teeth are ferocious and sharp, their noses are long and curly. The eyes of a grimshaed are deep sockets in their foreheads with black marble-like eyeballs. They carry all types of weapons for they have arms and hands like humans, but they also have long claw-like fingernails, like their beast fathers. They are the spawns of goblins that have captured human females and then bred these twisted creatures. They live in the dead village of Mervyyx, a once proud, functioning dwarf village that is now in shambles and ran by goblins and grimshaeds."

Alaezdar glanced at his three companions sitting around the campfire, but he eyed Rivlok especially to gauge his response to what he had just told them.

"Anyways, when I was with the Renegades then, we had word that they were all traveling to the Goblin Tribes Forest and that the goblins had left their posts in fear. When we got there, we had found that not to be the case. It may have been at the beginning, but what we found were three dead grimshaeds and about five hundred ogres, orcs, gronts and goblins who had just massed together at the pass to chase away the grimshaeds, which they did. Amazingly, they only ended up killing three. The rest of them must have returned to home at Mervyyx. Of course, we did not know this at the time and wandered deep into the pass to examine the three dead grimshaeds. When we saw the mass of others gathered there, at the same time they saw us, they were still excited from their small, but for them big victory because even goblins are terrified of grimshaeds. We knew then that because of this massing we were in bigger danger than we could've imagined, even in our worst nightmares. In their lingering excitement, they attacked us for all that they had. We ran, but we had already gone too deep into the pass before we realized what was happening."

"Didn't you see the massed goblins?" Tharn asked.

"No," Alaezdar stated quietly. "We wanted to see a dead Grimshaed up close for we too had only thought them to be a legend. But to see one…well, we were blind to everything else. In the end, four of my partners died that day. Only I and my close friend Shadow Blade escaped with our lives."

"But that was five hundred goblins. Surely we won't see that many?" Rivlok asked.

"No, not likely, but the one we see will be just as dangerous and we have to find a way to travel a full mile deep into the pass before we are through.

"What? A whole mile?" Morlonn, now in shock, asked. "How can we do that?"

"I'm not sure, to tell you the truth, but that day when we got attacked, I thought I saw a cave about half-way into the pass. If we need to, we can hide there and regroup to go further. But now we need to rest," Alaezdar announced. "We will sleep until just before daylight."

"Why so much sleep? We need to keep moving. We aren't on a camping trip," Rivlok protested.

"Yes, you are partly right. We do need to keep moving, but we won't be here very long. We aren't on a camping trip, as you stated, but we must keep up our energy. That just might be our biggest challenge before we catch up to Aaelie, for before we are done, you are going to feel like you need to sleep for a week just to walk straight. We will only stay here for five hours, and we will only have four hours of sleep tonight because we will post night watch. Rivlok, you stand first watch. I will take second. Morlonn, take third and Tharn, take last. So I suggest we eat some of the nuts and berries that we packed and get to sleep."

As Alaezdar readied himself to sleep, he realized it had been a long time since he had slept underneath the stars. He had done it many times when he was with Rager's House of Renegades and it had always brought him peace, even when they were in the midst of some of their most stressful and dangerous missions. He had begun to feel some the excitement of returning to a mission like those that had been all too common in his life. Although he often felt the sense of being at ease from the camaraderie of being with fellow swordsman, he found that the stars calmed him in the night before a big battle or mission. He had always had a sense that helped him feel immortal and protected, but for some reason, it brought him no peace this evening. All he sensed was doom.

How had it come to this?

He had left an experienced guild to escape the violence and mayhem of dangerous missions and killing, and now he was leading three untrained men into a rescue mission against a powerful wizard and a group of battle-trained gronts. He had Rivlok, the hothead, Morlonn, the hunter, and Tharn, a wizened, aged veteran. He felt he could count on Tharn for wisdom and for some physical abilities, but his age would not allow for great stamina on a trek with limited sleep, especially after they'd reached the heat of battle. It made him sick with worry that he was leading a man of great stature in his village and of great past of experience to his death.

He continued thinking and visualized them reaching the Death Pass. Centuries ago, the tribes of the Val Elves inhabited and prospered in this area. Soon, though, the Val Elves found themselves battling the Goblin and Gront tribes more often and that forced the Val Elves to be an aggressive race of elves, just to protect themselves. The Val Elves no longer inhabited the area for they had migrated north and made an alliance with the peaceful Sor Elves who lived near the Northern Sea. Though they merged with the Sor Elves, they remained the more aggressive race of elves, but even so found a common thread between them to coexist.

There had been many tales of the elven artifacts and structures, hidden and exposed, that had been left behind by the Val Elves. One was the Elven Catacombs, tombs of great elven kings and princes and great warriors buried in honor in tombs deep within the dark underground tunnels. It had been rumored that the catacombs lay somewhere deep in the Vixtaevus Mountains east of the gap, but no non-elf had ever found them. Many treasure seekers had tried, but all had failed to find the coveted burial grounds. Now all that remained in the area were rumors and death, death to any outsider to this area who dared to explore it. The goblin tribes were quick to find any explorer, treasure seeker, or wanderer who came into these lost mountains and dense forests.

The elves had later migrated into the deep west after the humans from the south had attacked the Sor and Val elves of the north and chased them out of their northern home. These humans were not the barbaric human tribes that lived with the goblins. They were much more intelligent and organized and even though they were individual tribes, they were able to organize under one very strong and dangerous man. This man, a distant relative to the First Human King, Dar-Drannon, and his daughter Traelyn, was able to organize all of the tribes together with the help of some dragons, and they attacked the elves and chased them out of their land, sending them on their migration westward.

They eventually found their new and current home in the forested mountains of the Mollidennum Woods and Lake Quarterstar. They had been there now for nearly a thousand years. No human had bothered them there, in this new territory of theirs, because the humans had all been fighting each other and were not able to form a force united under the same banner. Only for a short time, eighty years, did they rule under one banner under the name of the Korlond Empire. Even that had been a long time for humans to unite, and they still could not prevent the inevitable for a warring race doing what it did best, war. They again split into two kingdoms, and then split repeatedly again, and have not since reunified despite the conquering spirit in every one of their kingdoms.

The elves, meanwhile, were severely dejected to have been defeated by an inferior, human race. They had long believed that they were the superior race because since they had first merged, some of their elven mages were masters of both Wrae and Kronn magic and they therefore possessed superior magical abilities that no human should have been able to overcome. When they lost their battle at the Kingdom at Aalararae, they felt that they had taken a blow from their gods Val-Eahea and Raezoures, and they felt like they had now been forsaken.

In their new world, far away from their homeland, they believed that any elf who died without the use of Wrae was placed in a forever-sleep in this land and was not allowed to travel on to their afterlife. Even though this was a dire predicament to be in, the elves -- having a lifespan of thousands of years -- felt that they had time to figure out how to get their immortality back before they were each to die.

If they died in battle, however, their souls would then remain in limbo, lost in between two worlds, and they would become Wraeths. The only elves who had found peace in the afterlife were those who had died before the great migration west and were entombed in the catacombs. Those who died after their first migration to the north were still allowed entrance to the afterlife, but those who migrated west to Lake Quarterstar would lose all entrance to the elven afterlife.

The elves searched deep within themselves, religiously, magically, and as a unified race, and reasoned that all the events that proceeded were but a planned process from their gods Val-Eahea and Raezoures. Even though it cost them many lives and many heartaches to leave their two previous homes, they felt – or at least they hoped -- it was all for the better good.

Alaezdar remembered being told that the elves' migrations had meant leaving their first and natural source of magic in the form of the Sippling tree, which was planted by Val-Eahea and Raezoures. Those elven gods had planted the tree to preserve the land through magic and to control the seasons while regulating the harsh cold of the frozen core of the earth, known as the Markenhirth. They also lost an even more important artifact, The Triestones, when they had moved from the northern coast to Lake Quarterstar.

Once they had to leave the Aaestfallia Keep and remove the Triestones from it, they lost the connection through space and time of this realm to other realms. The Triestones were the magical source that powered the Keep, and it was this power that kept an open door for their gods to visit them without losing their immortality. Those who entered the keep could travel to other worlds or within this world, but in a different time. The Triestones that powered the Keep became a magical channel surging from the Sippling tree to the four powerful stones placed inside the Keep. The elves had been able to construct a powerful device to carry and house all four of the stones, which could not be separated if the the magic was to remain contained.

Currently the Keep where the stones were once kept was now only a symbol of the once great elven magic. It was little more than an ancient ruin, Alaezdar knew. When the stones were removed, the elves figured out that their removal not only negated the power of the keep, but their absence also severed the link to the Sippling Tree, forever. The Aaestfallia Keep was now only a stone structure, empty of all magic except on rare occasions when a magical surge would burp through the Keep and the doors of time and other worlds would pass or touch Wrae-Kronn. Only those rare events proved that the Aaestfallia Keep and the Sippling tree were still somehow connected.

Alaezdar had heard that it was through this burp of power that Fyaa and her Birds of Fire, a flaming witch and three beasts from another land and time, had entered Wrae-Kronn. She only wished to go home, and everyone in Wrae-Kronn only wanted her to leave, but no one knew how to help her achieve that end, for no one knew how to open the Aaestfallia Keep so that she could return. The elves would offer no help either.

No human kingdom had been powerful enough to kill her, not even all the massive armies of the northern human kingdoms. It was not that she was so strong and powerful, but that she was so quick with her destruction. None could find a way to snatch her out of the air or find a hero strong enough to defeat her with sword or other man made weapon. She had been known to devastate entire villages and fire was her favorite weapon.

On occasion, though, her opponents would outnumber her and surround her and thereby nullify her fire power. In those rare instances, she used her ability to shape change into anything she wished at will -- most commonly a small bird or even an insect -- to avoid capture or death and thereby escape in flight to safety.

As powerful as Fyaa could be, for the most part she had not seemed intentionally harmful. She did not aggressively attack. Her purpose within this realm was unknown, but what many had told Alaezdar was that she could not move forward with whatever malicious plan she might have because she needed first to find her demon-like birds.

Those powerful, massive, winged bipedal creatures, which had come to this world moments before she had entered it, had flown away in confusion. Few people have ever seen the birds. The birds had been destructive at first, lighting on fire everything they saw and everything they touched, and they had destroyed many crops and villages. It was as if they were children who had discovered fire and were playing with it only because it was new and entertaining. This had gone on only for a short time before they for some reason stopped. Afterward they had disappeared from Wrae-Kronn completely.

Fyaa had searched the land for her birds and she swore that she could not, would not, leave this realm without them. Everything she did was somehow linked to the birds. Fools would tempt her by voicing a simple rumor of their whereabouts, or an ignorant fool might summon her, for selfish purposes, to entice her to attack their own enemy by promising her the whereabouts of her birds. Whatever the reasons, they would end up with many deaths and Fyaa would leave without her birds.

Alaezdar stared up into the night sky and remembered his first meeting with Fyaa.

He had not actually seen her, but he did see the charred remains of a battlefield where some numb-brained elite had coerced her into partaking in a battle as ransom for information about the birds. Man, horses and the like lay smoldering on the ground after the small skirmish. The Trielian spearman and archers, with Fyaa's help, had defeated a small group of bothersome raiders of their kingdom who had been a problem to the Trielian king for many years. They lay upon the battlefield, totally annihilated, but her help did come at a great cost to the king after Fyaa had learned of his deception.

Alaezdar had still been part of Rager's House of Renegades, who had been summoned for a price to help in the cause of ridding the Trielian kingdom of the raiders, but they had arrived too late and they had missed Fyaa's fury against the raiders. The battle had just ended and they quickly surveyed the area and saw that not only were they too late, but their services were not needed. Without receiving payment, they went back to their base at Daevanwood.

Later, after the battle, Fyaa had found out that the information about her birds had been fraudulent and she attacked the castle at Triel and had torched the commander who had made the promise to her as well as a dozen of his soldiers before she shape-changed into a small insect and escaped as the remaining soldiers began to re-group and take the initiative.

Lying there under the stars, Alaezdar could not imagine why Fyaa was active now. Was it another case of promised information about the three birds which had sent her on another quest? He shuddered to think of who would be so brave or stupid to tease Fyaa with information, only to now to have her intervene into this small defenseless village and kidnap an innocent woman and drag her into the goblin tribe's forest.

He closed his eyes and drifted off into a restless half sleep, trying in vain to block out images of the many different scenarios of the death he could see for himself and his friends.

He wasn't even quite asleep when Rivlok's hour was done and Rivlok gently kicked him in the ribs to wake him for his turn at the watch.

Alaezdar sat up, brushed his hair out of his eyes and nodded at Rivlok. "Get some sleep. It won't be much, so hurry."

Rivlok said nothing and walked away. Alaezdar thought he heard him huff and grumble after his back was turned and he walked back to his blanket and roll.

Alaezdar stood up, grabbed Bloodseeker, strapped it to his back, and walked the perimeter of the camp to check on the others to assure that they were fast asleep. Morlonn snored lightly, but Tharn snored loudly and Alaezdar gave him a gentle kick in the ribs to quiet the telltale noise. Tharn stopped, grumbled something incoherent, and rolled over.

The night's chill had set in. Alaezdar looked up momentarily and breathed in the oak scrub and the Manzanita's musky smell mixed with fresh pine. He was tired, but he knew he had to go forward. He would stay up for his hour and then get some rest because otherwise even he would be too tired to press on.

As he continued around the perimeter of the encampment, he watched and listened intently. He walked deliberately and cautiously so as not to stir up any animals or kick any noisy wood debris from the soft forest floor.

The stars this evening were so bright that he did not have to strain his eyes to see out in the distance. Extending his perimeter in a circular fashion, he scanned for any signs of trouble and listened for any movement. Even as silent as he tried to be, twice he startled a young jackrabbit that jumped up and hauled off in front of him. He wished he had his bow and arrow. A young rabbit stew would be delicious if only they had the time to cook it.

He shook his head. It was too early to be thinking about food already. They were going to be out at least a week with no more than nuts and berries, and a big rabbit dinner was not in the equation.

He walked the perimeter three more times without event, but as he began his fourth round, he heard something. He unsheathed Bloodseeker, crouched down and listened, but heard nothing more. With the exception of turning his head slowly in both directions, he did not move for many minutes,. He stayed in the crouched position and then lay flat on his stomach and listened to the sounds at ground level to see if he could hear any footfalls or the crumpling of leaves.

Again he sensed nothing. Satisfied, he stood up and sheathed his sword.

Alaezdar then saw him. He was standing directly in front of him, so close he could almost sense the man's breath upon his own face. The man seized the moment of surprise and grabbed Alaezdar's head with both his hands, one on each side just above his ears, and Alaezdar stepped back to escape the man's grip. He tried to reach for Bloodseeker behind his back, but he could not break free of the man's grasp.

The man whispered, "No!"

He stood right in front of Alaezdar but let go of his head. Alaezdar stepped back and withdrew his sword.

"I am not here to attack you," the man said. "If I were, you would be dead by now. I have been watching you since you woke up and I stood almost directly in front of you while you were on your stomach. You were easy prey, if I wanted you dead. Put your sword away."

Alaezdar paused. It was not often that he was caught so easily and feebly, but he did put his sword away even though he was not comfortable with the situation.

"Who are you?" he asked the man.

"Yes, a fair question so early in the meeting," the man said in a hushed tone so as not to disturb the others' sleep.

He was dressed in crumpled dark cloak with this hood back. In the dark,

Alaezdar had a hard time making out the features on his face, but from what he could tell, his face looked as wrinkled as his cloak. He had short dark hair and he seemed fit, given his build.

"I am Gartan, the Kronn Seeker, and you are Alaezdar."

"How do you know me?" Alaezdar was now even more puzzled by this strange intruder.

"Gartan the Dark said you were heading this direction. So I began looking for you…and here you are."

"But. Gartan the Dark is back in Valewood. How is that possible?"

Gartan smiled.

"I thought you knew us better than that. We can communicate through the land. I myself am especially good at reading the land. I have been doing this for quite a while. That is why I am here. I live here, in the goblin tribe's forest, and have all of my life. It is my job to seek out Kronn and everything that is Kronn, discover the origin of its birth, and predict its death. I have long since learned that this realm's origination began not too far from here. The Kronn, the land, and some of the people here are intertwined, and since it is Kronn and everything about Kronn that I seek, I am very good at listening to the land and the Kronn.

"So you are here to find me? Why?" Alaezdar asked. He was starting to relax his aggressive stance.

"I have a message for you that will save your life."

"And what is that?" he asked unconditionally. He trusted all of the Watchers Guild's messages because during his experiences with Rager's House of Renegades, he found that their knowledge had been almost always uncannily true.

"Listen to Bloodseeker, but it is not with Bloodseeker from which you will find answers."

Alaezdar shook his head in confusion.

"That's it? What is that supposed to mean? That's a bit contradictory isn't it?"

"Yes, but no. As far as anything and everything matters, that is what I must tell you. If I was to die right this minute, I would not have succeeded in my personal mission, but I will have accomplished what Kronn has asked me to do. Anything that I tell you from here on out is merely noncommittal. My only other instructions were to find you tonight in the dark so that I could see your eyes as I tell you this. I have been told that you are either the savior of the realm, or the destroyer of it, or both."

"Why do you speak in riddles?" Alaezdar asked. He was now frustrated. He remembered speaking with Tharn earlier about elven prophecy and how it had aggravated him just thinking about it again then.

"I do not know. All I know is what I have been told through Kronn. Although I do know a bit about you that you may not know about yourself."

"Like what?"

"Well, I know that you think your sword is a magical sword."

"Well, I don't know if I would call it magical, but it has been with me for a long time. It was given to me by my mentor, Lark Blade, but he did not tell me that I would feel differently when I use it. When I do, though, I am changed within."

"So, your Kronn courses through it?"

"I suppose, though I am not that familiar with Kronn, or what it means to me, or how it works. My father spent some time explaining it to me, but I didn't listen. I don't care for wizards and their special enhancements, and I certainly didn't care to be a wizard, as he wanted me to be."

Gartan paused after Alaezdar's response as if he were assembling pieces of his own mysterious puzzle.

"I have been searching for Kronn," he said, "its existence, its meaning and its genesis. It has been said that its origination is somewhere near here, near the catacombs, and I have not strayed far from this area for many years. Because of this I know quite a bit about the subject."

Alaezdar's head swam. His eyes began to see moving shadows on Gartan's face and it distracted him to focus on Gartan's face in the dark.

"What are your plans now, now that you have presented your message to me?" he asked in hope of ending the conversation.

"Well, with your permission, I would like to travel with your group."

Alaezdar sighed. Of course, he thought to himself.

"What means of protection or weapons do you have for yourself?"

"Just a knife and my cloak."

"Oh, that should do fine," Alaezdar mocked. "You really shouldn't travel with us. We don't have much food ourselves, much less enough to add another person."

"You won't have to worry about me. I can defend myself and I know this area very well and can come up with some food that you won't have to hunt for yourself. It will be nourishing enough to last your whole trip."

Good enough Alaezdar thought to himself. Tired and impatient, he gave in. He figured that Gartan just might turn out to be useful in that respect alone.

"Then get some sleep. We will be up in two hours."

"Actually, I have already slept. If you would allow it, you can sleep for two hours and I will watch over you."

Alaezdar thought about rejecting the offer, but he was tired, and it would be good to let the others sleep through, as well. They were going to need it. He was a bit hesitant about trusting Gartan, but he had known other Watcher's Guild members and he had never known any of them to be malicious in any way. Besides, he could really use that extra hour of sleep.

"Done," Alaezdar said. "Wake us in two hours."

Alaezdar went back to his bed roll and looked up at the stars. He closed his eyes and cleared his mind. This time he fell asleep without a further thought.

Chapter 15

Gartan woke them up late. It was still before sunrise, the air was still and chilly and the color of the sky was no longer dark, but was beginning to show a faint hue of orange and blue. He bent over to wake of Alaezdar, and Alaezdar jumped with a start. He knew immediately he had slept too long.

"What is wrong with you?" he yelled and he grabbed Gartan by his cloak and pushed him to the ground. As he shouted, the others woke up and began stir.

"You need your rest," Gartan said as he sat up. "You are not going to catch them before the Death Pass."

"Of course, we aren't, now that we've slept so late."

"You weren't going to make it either way. You have been taking too long in your chase."

Alaezdar growled and cursed under his breath. This group is destined to die, he thought to himself.

"Get up everyone. We have to hurry! Grab your packs, load your horses, and we will eat later on the way," he said as he kicked the ground while grabbing his belongings.

Everyone jumped up and scurried to roll up their belongings. They loaded and saddled up the horses and were on the trail within minutes. They removed some non-essential items from the packhorse to make room for Gartan and they could now move a little bit faster by not having to pony the horse any longer. Rivlok still rode on Tharn's horse, but complained viciously as he climbed up behind Tharn. Morlonn led the way because he had the fastest horse and he scouted the trail ahead as he rode. Everyone rode all day at a quick pace.

Alaezdar noticed the cloak that Gartan wore seemed to shimmer against the backdrop of the trees. Sometimes it even seemed to him that Gartan would disappear. Knowing better, he tried to ignore what he was seeing, and he allowed his mind to wander on simple things. No matter how he tried, though, his thoughts became clouded with memories he wished he could forget.

He kept thinking about his father, but why his thoughts kept drifting to him, he did not know. It was annoying him. He needed to concentrate on the next few days ahead, but some foreboding details kept creeping into his mind, and these thoughts did not include anyone that was with him. It was as if what was about to happen did not matter in the grand scheme of things. All he could hear was his father's voice reprimanding him for wanting to be a soldier.

"You are wasting yourself," his father had told him often. The ironic part, Alaezdar knew, was that he had never really instructed him to be any different either. He just gave his son constant harassment and criticism of everything he did.

Alaezdar tried to think of things his father might have said that would give him a clue to his current situation. Why was he in it? Why did his thoughts continue to come back to his father? He didn't know. He could not remember much of anything about those days, but there had been constant turmoil when his father was around. Most of the time he was gone, but every time he did return, there was never a happy reunion.

It was after his mom had been killed, that he realized why he kept returning to his father. It was something Fyaa had said at the sacking of Valewood, something about him not knowing who he was. She must have known he was the son of Val-Vector-Sor. The wizard Torz had killed his mom to exact a punishment upon Alaezdar's father, but there may have been – or still be, Alaezdar thought -- a connection between Ra-Corsh and Fyaa through Torz.

"Ah, ha!" Alaezdar yelled aloud. At the exact moment of his revelation he noticed that Gartan's cloak was indeed changing appearances and camouflaging itself into the scenery behind him.

"Gartan, stop!" he commanded.

Gartan pulled the reigns of his horse and waited for Alaezdar to catch up, but before he could say anything to Gartan, Morlonn came out of the woods from scouting ahead.

"Did you find anything?" Alaezdar asked as he approached.

"No, their trail has gone completely cold. I have gone ahead, circled to our left and right flanks for about three miles in each direction. I even climbed a few trees, but still no sign."

"Maybe I should go back to the last known tracks and start again."

"No, that will take too much time."

"Then what do we do now?" Morlonn asked. "They must be covering their tracks magically. That is the only thing I can figure, because they just disappear."

"Then we just need to ride to the Death Pass as quickly as we can. We can make a meal, rest the horses for an hour...but only an hour," Alaezdar emphasized and looked at Gartan. "Then we can ride through the forest during the night as quickly as we can and just head straight for the pass."

Alaezdar cursed himself silently for taking so long to follow their trail. They should've just headed for the pass as fast as they could and cut them off.

He seemed to be making the wrong decision at every corner, but he also knew that if they went straight for the pass, he risked being wrong. They could end up waiting in vain at the dangerous pass and would have missed them entirely. They would have no way of knowing where they were. That was a gamble he chose not to take, but looking back now, it seemed more evident that that would have been the better choice.

Where else would they have gone if not directly past the Death Pass and into the Goblin Tribes Forest?

In the end, Alaezdar concluded they were all going to die heading into this mission chasing Fyaa. Maybe he was trying to save their lives by stalling. He shook his head and tried to shake the folly out of his thoughts.

Alaezdar dismounted, tied up his horse to the closest tree and pulled out the last bag of oats from his pack. He opened it and tied it to the tree so his horse could eat, and then he went straight to Gartan for some answers.

Gartan was dismounting from the packhorse when he walked up to him.

His hood was over his head and Alaezdar reached for the top of it and pulled it back. "Tell me. What is all over your face?"

Gartan flinched and stepped away with his back against the hindquarters of the horse. The horse sidestepped as if it had been pushed to move away.

"My face?" he asked.

He looked into Alaezdar's eyes and realized instantly why he was not supposed to see them when he had given him the message. He felt afraid of Alaezdar, and he did not know what was going to happen to him.

Gartan's face seemed to have ink tattoo markings of leaves covering every inch of it except for a small dragon over his left eye and facing his right eye. Its wings tucked in and its tail hung around the outer side of his eye and turned back in at the cheekbone continuing under the eye. The dragon tattoo Alaezdar recognized as the exact tattoo that Gartan the Dark and all of the other Watchers guild members had, but usually the dragon was the only marking any of them ever had.

Gartan's cloak also looked to be made from leaves, but it wasn't. During the day Alaezdar had noticed that it changed as they traveled, almost as if the leaves were moving and changing their color and hue to match the background. There was also a crumpled effect to it, as if to erase any straight edges a natural cloak would have.

"It is my cloak. Like your sword, it channels my Kronn. That is what changes my face and causes the cloak to change around from the environment. When I need it to be, I can be almost invisible. I am not really, but it blends in so well that I can barely be seen, although I can be smelled and that is unfortunate as far as hunting goes. But if I am upwind, it is quite effective. Would you like a rabbit for dinner? I am quite good with a bow and arrow, if I can borrow Morlonn's?"

"I don't need your help finding food!" Morlonn interrupted. "In fact, I am going right now for food before it gets too dark."

"So, if you take off your cloak, your face will change as well?" Rivlok asked while throwing Tharn's saddle on the ground.

"Yes, the only mark on my face is the dragon. By the way, may I ask if the dragon is sleeping?"

Alaezdar looked at Gartan quizzically, but answered.

"I suppose so...it is just lying on your eye."

"Thanks," he said.

Morlonn had just grabbed his gear and had one foot ready to leave, but he stopped abruptly and asked, "Instead of taking my bow, why don't you let me borrow the cloak while I hunt?"

"Just like Alaezdar's sword, it isn't magical in the sense, that is, of its own being. It cannot work without an addition to it, such as Kronn. So, it most likely won't work for you, just as the properties that make Alaezdar's sword seem magical won't work for you either."

"Right. I see," Morlonn lied and impatiently continued leaving so he could bring the group something decent to eat for a change. He checked his bow, mounted his horse, spurred quickly around, and rode off deeper into the forest.

"What do you mean by that?" Alaezdar asked as he watched Morlonn leave.

"It is your Kronn, not the sword, that makes your sword do what it does. Where did you get the sword?"

"My mentor gave it to me as I was inducted into Rager's House of Renegades. He told me it was a magical sword, but he himself could not find it useful in its magic. I think that was his way of saying that he either doubted it was authentic, or he couldn't use it."

"Did it work for you right away?" Gartan asked.

"Yes and no. I felt it immediately -- the coursing through my veins -- but it took a few months, maybe a year, before I started realizing its potential for how it worked. I still feel that I have even more magic as yet to be revealed."

"I think you are right about its capabilities. I would guess that it does indeed have some great power that is yet to be unlocked, as is the same with you. The sword is just the device to express your Kronn. You yourself are a device of Kronn. So, depending on the power of one's Kronn, one can determine your strength or even an object's power, such as the sword. Look, hand the sword to me. Let me look at it before I give it to Rivlok."

Alaezdar withdrew Bloodseeker and gave it to Gartan.

Gartan took it and immediately felt something he was not expecting. The sword felt hot in his hand, and instantly he began to feel anger, but within seconds, the sword and his anger cooled. This was not consistent to what he had learned about Kronn, yet it was another piece to his puzzle discovered.

Kronn was an individual thing and he had never felt someone else's Kronn like that before. Perplexed, he handed the sword over to Rivlok. Rivlok took it, but was hesitant to be part of this lesson.

"Do you feel anything, Rivlok?" Gartan asked.

"No, of course not. I don't believe in this stuff."

"Of course you don't, because you don't have any Kronn to make it work," he said sarcastically.

"But, I might believe in your cloak. Let me wear that," Rivlok said and returning Alaezdar's sword to him.

Gartan took off his cloak and handed it to Rivlok. Rivlok took it, but when he saw Gartan's leaf markings disappear, his face went flush with astonishment. What was once a cloak that looked like leaves now looked like a common brown wool cloak. He put it around his shoulders and lifted the hood over his face. Nothing happened. Rivlok rolled up the sleeves to look at his arms, hoping to see the markings, but he saw nothing.

"See, Alaezdar," Gartan said. "His face is plain, and even if he wanted to, he cannot make the cloak make him invisible. He does not have the tools, or Kronn, to make it work."

Rivlok took off the cloak and threw it back to Gartan.

"Someone needs to make a fire to cook up Morlonn's catch!" Rivlok said and stomped off impatiently. "Come on, Tharn. Let's get something going and hope Morlonn isn't too long with a couple of rabbits."

"Kronn is of the land," Gartan began. "The Sor elves were the first to use it effectively. Some humans know how to use it, but it is said that is only because they have elven blood somewhere in their lineage. The Watcher's Guild learned it from the dragons because they passed it to us when they left the land."

"I have heard some of that, but I did not know about the dragons," Alaezdar stated.

"Oh, you knew it all along, and even if you would've thought about it long enough just now, you would've came to that conclusion. Think about it. The dragons were created at the same time Kronn was created, but for some reason they never really belonged to the realm. They sought to leave the realm from the very beginning and many, many years ago, our founder Dragos Gartan released them through the Aaestfallia keep and they left this realm forever. They returned to a land more suitable to them and when they did so, they relinquished their power of Kronn to Dragos Gartan. He in turn passed the power to all of his guild members and future guild members. But that doesn't matter so much now. What matters is that you understand what you are."

"I know what I am. I am a failed swordsman looking to redeem a quiet life," he answered quietly.

Gartan laughed, but then stopped quickly for fear of offending him.

"That you will never have."

"What do you mean?" Alaezdar asked. He felt a little annoyed, but mostly embarrassed for speaking about the personal pain of his failures.

"You are much, much more to this realm than a swordsman or a quiet farmer hopeful."

"How is that possible? If I want to hide myself from everyone and everything, no one can stop me."

"No. That is where you do not understand how Kronn works. Look, here is a simple test. I have just learned that there is pain in your heart that causes rage. Think about it. What is the name of the mercenary guild you joined? And I know the answer, so don't try to fool me."

"Rager's House of Renegades"

Yes, Rager's. The name Rager's is no coincidence, and your sword is called Bloodseeker. Who gave it that name?"

"I did."

"Of course you did…why?"

"Because once I start battle, it seeks blood and will not stop until it gets it. It makes my body vibrate and hurt until it finds its first kill or marks its first wound."

"And then how do you feel?"

"I want more. I get angry and I feel my blood change. It turns…I don't know how to describe it…except…inside out, but more importantly, I feel anger."

"You are raging mad," he added.

"Yes…I never thought of it that way, but yes, that is it. So, that is Kronn?"

"Yes and no at the same time. It is your Kronn and it is communicating to you through the land. You are one of the few humans who can do this. Your rage is something of an enigma, though. I cannot feel where that part stems from. Your sword, though, is a bit different. I did feel the Kronn in it earlier when I held it, but there was something else involved. There is no doubt that it is a magical sword. The question is whether it is not only Kronn magic or both Kronn and Wrae magic, or maybe the sword is even a bit magical in a hidden way."

Gartan let Alaezdar think on that for a few seconds before he asked, "Do you have elven blood?"

"I don't know. My father has Kronn. My mother did not, as far as I know, and I really don't know much more about my family line."

"I really do wonder, and am very curious, although your heritage doesn't matter as much as that you realize you are important to this realm in a way greater than you know."

"Do you know?" he asked.

"No, I don't. I only know that when those who have Kronn use it, it is specifically identified with their personality and inner being. Some can heal for good, some can only use it for ill or pain, and some can control others to manipulate them to do good or bad. It all depends on the individual. You, on the other hand, are none of those, yet possibly all of those things. Right now, you are too angry to see the truth. Only you will know your true Kronn when you find it. And in that respect, that is what I am doing here in this forest. To find my Kronn, and maybe help you find yours. I have been on this mission all of my life, and I think this mission may be close to its end."

Alaezdar raked his fingers through his hair and nodded in understanding, but his head was swimming trying to put together all of his thoughts. As he looked up, he noticed an unusual gathering of small birds in the trees and they all seemed to be looking at him. Their soft chirping had a calming effect to his thoughts.

"I think I have had enough to think about for one day. All I want to do right now is get Aaelie back to her family."

"Fair enough. I am sorry to lay all of this at your feet, but I truly believe that is why I have spent my life out here searching and learning about Kronn…so that I can meet you today."

"Thank you…I guess," Alaezdar said

He walked away and went to check on Rivlok and Tharn to see how they were coming along. He hoped that Morlonn came back soon with something good to eat because he was very hungry for something with substance. He was getting tired of the nuts and the roots that Gartan had found along the way today.

Gartan ran up to Alaezdar and put his hand to his shoulder.

"Don't move. We are in big trouble."

"You are just now figuring that out?" he asked.

"Shhh…look in the trees."

"Yeah, tons of birds. So?"

"It's not what you think. They're Dok Churners."

Alaezdar's blood chilled. He knew exactly what those were. Even though he had never actually seen them before, he had heard about them and what trouble they could cause. Most people who had seen them had never lived long enough to tell their tale. They were most dangerous when young hatchlings and still in the care of their mothers. They were small birds then who had no means of feeding themselves, and they fed upon the fresh blood of recently killed prey killed by their mothers. At their young age they were too small to kill on their own.

The mothers hunted and killed their prey by decapitating their heads by wrapping their long, barbed tails around the preys' necks. The mother bird was featherless, unlike their young, who lost their feathers around the same time that their tails grew. The mothers flew high overhead and looked like small sleek dragons with wide, shiny, soft black wings. They'd silently glide overhead and wait for the right moment to strike.

Once a mother spotted her prey, she would land directly on its forehead and wrap her large wings completely around its head, covering the eyes, and then wrap her tail around its neck. The tail is so long and strong that it wraps around its victims neck sometimes twice, The sharp barbs on the tail are evenly spaced, and the tail squeezes tightly while the barbs penetrate the neck of the prey. The mother then quickly severs the head from its host.

Once the head is removed, the feeding frenzy could begin. Before an ounce of blood is spilled onto the ground, the small birds land on the prey's shoulders and begin sticking their long beaks into the neck. Their long tongues enter into the cavity and sucking out the blood. Within second the body is drained of all its blood.

Alaezdar withdrew Bloodseeker and called for Tharn and Rivlok. Within seconds, they were there, but they stood silently, wondering why the urgency.

"Get underneath this horse and stay there!" Alaezdar whispered through clenched teeth.

Gartan, Tharn and Rivlok did as he said.

Alaezdar went into the woods to see if he could spot the mother. He knew if the Dok Churner found him first, he was not going to live, even if he had stayed with the group. There was no defense foe these birds once they landed on you. They latched on so tightly, all one could do to kill one was to slice it with a sword, but to do so could also kill the person the sword was attached to. The best one could hope for would be death by the sword or, even better, a severe concussion from the sword blow. In most cases it spelled death.

As he ran through the trees, he looked to the sky, but did not see anything flying in the air. He did notice that in all of the trees surrounding him there were small birds, no larger than finches. They seemed to be watching him and chirping louder and louder as he ran. They began to make so much noise he feared that the mother had to be close.

Then he saw her. She was in a spinning dive coming right towards him. He raised Bloodseeker and immediately began swinging blindly. The Dok Churner dodged his swings and began to swirl above his head. Alaezdar felt his sword tremble in his hands as if it were itself frustrated as he tried unsuccessfully to knock the bird out of the air time after time.

In a panic, he ran back to where the group hid underneath the horse.

"Run!" he yelled as he ran towards the horse. "Run deep into the woods and hide, but stay together!"

Everyone scattered in all directions from underneath the horse, but they came together again shortly and disappeared deep into the woods. The Dok Churner became confused for a second and it stopped flying after Alaezdar. Instead, she flapped her wings, staying in one spot surveying the situation. Alaezdar took advantage of the situation and sheathed Bloodseeker easily, which surprised him. He sensed Bloodseeker wanted no part of this battle. He then jumped onto the horse and went in the opposite direction from the others.

The Dok Churner did as Alaezdar had hoped and followed him. He ran the horse through the thick trees, and the branches of the full pines scratched both him and the horse as they raced by. As the bird flew right behind him, he could hear her big wings flapping in the air. The horse jumped and nickered when the bird whipped her tail and hit Alaezdar behind the head with a thump.

The bird continued to whip her tail numerous times as they ran, and each time he could feel that more of the tail was making contact. The back of his head began to bleed. He knew he wasn't going to get away. The bird was gaining on him and he feared one more tail whip would be around his neck, although he was surprised that she hadn't caught him yet and already had his neck wrapped and his head covered by her wings.

Out of desperation, Alaezdar jumped off the horse and withdrew Bloodseeker once again. The horse ran a few yards, but then circled around and waited for him to remount. He smiled and thought it was fortunate how well this horse was trained. Rivlok's horse had clearly bolted and never returned when Rivlok had been knocked off by the gront. He'd have to ask Tharn about that later, if he lived.

The bird circled around Alaezdar's head just out of reach of the sword. He could feel the bird laughing at him and her younglings watching the battle, they seemed to be cheering on their mother as they flew around her and in between trees in their chaotic anticipation of a feeding.

Then something unexpected happened. The mother clearly had Alaezdar in her sights as her prey, but her younglings spotted the horse just a few yards away and were circling the animal as if to tell their mother that they wanted the horse. The mother, seeing the cue of her young, whipped her tail and smacked Alaezdar across his left cheek. One of her barbs hit him below his eye and left a deep gash.

She flew to the horse at breakneck speed like an arrow flying through trees.

She landed on the horse's head and wrapped her wings around its eyes as she curled her tail around its neck and squeezed tightly. The horse nickered once and reared up on its hind legs and its head began to bleed. When its forelegs came to the ground, the horse lost consciousness and its front legs folded over.

The Dok Churner screamed a loud, high-pitched screech as she tightened up on her grip and began to saw her tail back and forth. The horse's head gave way and fell to the ground. Blood first sprayed out of the horse's neck in a minor explosion before pouring out of the body in a steady flow.

The young birds landed on the horse's body and began the feeding. They had long tongues that stretched out of their beaks five times the length of their bodies. Alaezdar watched in fear as their tongues went down the throat of the horse and they began drinking the blood as if their tongues were large straws.

The mother sat on the horse's hindquarter watching Alaezdar as if to say to him *this was your lucky day*. Alaezdar nodded to the Dok Churner, sheathed Bloodseeker, and was surprised again that the sword let him put it away. He looked at the mother Dok Churner once more when he felt her gaze still upon him. There seemed to be a mutual respect with the bird, as if it were displaying an intelligence not found in a typical bird.

Shaking his head, he turned and ran back to the group. Down another horse, he cursed at himself, as he ran.

Chapter 16

Kunther rode hard, and the harder he rode, the better he felt. The steed he rode was the best in the village. The horse was in her prime and had been chosen specifically for the long trip to Daevanwood. Kunther knew he had to ride as fast as he could, but he also knew that he could not ride the horse hard all day. If his horse collapsed from exhaustion, he would be nowhere except stranded in between two points, and his mission would be a failure. He had gone too far to let his horse die from exhaustion now or at any point of the trip.

He had left Valewood six days earlier, when the village was still in a state of emergency. He rode off with a fresh body, a motivated soul, a fresh horse, and five days of food. He even brought "Straight Edge," the crude, homemade sword that Rankin had made for him. It wasn't as fancy or as magical as Alaezdar's Bloodseeker, but it was his.

The first day he rode the hardest in his blind ambition to succeed in his mission. He rode maybe a little too hard, for the more often he stroked his horse, the slower she went. He decided to give up and let her rest for a few hours. He could use a nap, and it was getting close to sunset.

He was tired and sore by the time he stopped, and he cursed himself for being so out of shape. He worked hard every day as a blacksmith apprentice, but he realized it took a little more stamina to ride a horse all day, at least a different kind of stamina than he was used to. His inner thighs and butt hurt badly, and it was only the first day.

When he finished tying up the horse, he made a small fire to cook on and he began to think. Feeling all of his pain, he began to dread the rest of the trip and although the road to Daevanwood was a relatively easy trip -- aside from the pain -- he dreaded the unknown of what will happen when he reached Daevanwood. What if Rager's House of Renegades would not receive him? He knew he had dangerous news to tell and their just knowing it could be justification enough to kill the messenger. Alaezdar told him that he might be risking his life just to go on this mission. Kunther didn't care though. He would do his part to make sure that Aaelie was rescued and safely returned home.

The roads to Daevanwood were actually the easy part. He knew they were marked clearly, and even though the condition of the roads was usually quite worn from the trading caravans constantly travelling on them, the surface would be no problem for a single rider on horseback.

Within the first few hours of the second day, Kunther had gotten behind two trading caravans and was forced to swallow their dust until he passed the many wagons of the train which were bumping along the dusty road. Both times he had to wait until he could find a place where the forest was clear enough to take his horse off the road so he could pass. The caravans generally did not let commoners pass with ease. Only soldiers and raiders had that much authority over the road greedy caravans.

By sunset of the sixth day, Kunther had reached the small vale community of Hollenwood. The town seemed smaller than Valewood to Kunther, but the attitude was the same. Hollenwood was the last vale village before entering the borders of the big southern kingdoms. After Hollenwood, he would ride thirty miles until he reached the Torellan Forest and after the small forest, he would be in the land of soldiers, warriors, mages and mercenaries.

Even though Hollenwood was so close to the kingdoms, the inhabitants somehow remained an untouched vale community. They would see the people of the kingdoms passing through their small community in caravans, for the main road passed right through the center of town, and generally these travelers did not stop. When they did, the village shop and inn keepers made the most of their efforts to earn any coin they could from the travelers by offering food, shelter, goods and services, even if they rarely stayed more than for one night's rest. The kingdom folk had little desire for Hollenwood other than its pleasant view of the peaceful surroundings, its cold ale and a good night's rest.

Kunther rode his tired and weak horse down the main street of Hollenwood. He was out of food and in need of immediate nourishment, and he needed to stock up for one more day. The sun had just disappeared behind the Raezoures Mountains and the dusky evening brought a comfortable feeling to Kunther as he rode past the shops of the village.

The main street only had a dozen shops that carried the necessities of the village. He first passed the blacksmith, who was retiring his leather apron and closing his shop. Kunther smiled at the man. He knew how good that feeling was to finish the day's work and retire to a hot meal, something he sorely wanted right now. He knew he must first find an inn, and then a stable to keep his horse for the night, and maybe even make a trade for a fresh horse so that he could get up the next morning and charge towards Daevanwood completely fresh. He was now so close he could taste it.

It didn't take him long to find an inn, right across the street from an elaborate building that looked like an establishment where prostitutes might do their business. He saw a big pink sign that had a picture of a white foamy waterfall spraying down off a mountain cliff and into a calm and serene pool below. The sign on the front read simply "The Bathhouse of the Serene Falls."

Kunther passed the bathhouse and tied his horse to the post at the inn across from it which the proprietor had titled "Old Man's Inn." He walked inside. The inn was quiet, aside for a few customers enjoying their evening ales, and a fire was burning in the hearth. He could smell a roast cooking in the kitchen. Kunther looked toward the bar and saw that no one was behind it, but he walked ahead anyway and sat on a barstool.

"Excuse me, boy, or warrior, should I say? Are you a soldier?" someone asked from one of the tables behind him. Kunther turned around and saw a middle-aged man with a slight beard and a mustache, as dark in color as his long black hair. He sat amongst the other men of the same age drinking their ales. The man who spoke had no ale, but was smoking. Kunther figured him to be the innkeeper.

"I am neither," Kunther returned.

This caused a few quiet chuckles amongst the men.

"Then place your weapon in the rack, if you would," the man said in a voice that was not polite, yet was more firm than offensive. He pointed to a small rack next to the door which had hooks where one could hang their sword. Only a small dagger and scabbard hung there and Kunther headed towards the rack. He untied the scabbard from his belt and put Straight Edge upon the rack.

"Where are you headed, boy?" the man asked as he got up from his table and walked behind the bar. "Ale?" he asked and pulled out a glass from below the bar.

"Sure."

Kunther eyed the man, not sure if he should divulge his mission, but he realized he should tell some of the story to be polite and not to offend anyone there. He did indeed want a good night's rest tonight and a fresh horse to finish his trip. Conversation he knew would help to get honest answers.

"Daevanwood," he replied unemotionally.

"Daevanwood? Why in Markenhirth would you want to go to such an evil city as Daevanwood?"

"I seek mercenary help," he answered, barely louder than a mumble. "Of course!" the man exclaimed, laughing and slapping his hand on the bar. "Why else would any young man such as yourself go to Daevanwood, except to hire a mercenary? But do you mean, you seek to hire or to be a mercenary. Which to be honest, a warrior is what I thought you were intending to be in the first place. I mean the way you walked in here with your sword and all. Walking like no man alive could defeat you."

Kunther gave the man a polite laugh along with a look that let him know that he really wasn't pleased with the comments.

The innkeeper poured his ale and handed it to Kunther.

"Copper," he said smiling.

Kunther reached in his pouch and gave the man his coin.

He took the coin and watched Kunther drink his ale. Kunther's shoulder length red hair made his round red face look even redder than if his hair were darker. He was not overweight, but he was not in great shape either.

"If I may ask," the man said, breaking the silence. "What sort of mercenary help do you seek?"

Kunther paused mid swallow, looked over his glass at the other men to see if they were listening to the conversation. They were not. They were beginning to argue about who could cut a log in half faster, and they were about to go outside to prove it in a match. Kunther tried to second-guess the innkeeper as to whether or not he was just curious or if he had other plans in mind. The innkeeper reached under the bar, withdrew another rolled cigarette and lit it as he waited for Kunther to answer.

"I am seeking out the help of Rager's House of Renegades," he said

The innkeeper quickly exhaled his first puff of the cigarette and nearly choked.

"Boy, are you mad? You must be in great trouble or have high standards of your swordsmanship. You seek high company, probably the highest in all of the Known Lands! Besides that, I don't think you can afford them."

Kunther withdrew and began to regret his eagerness to divulge.

Seeing Kunther's discomfort, the innkeeper smiled.

"It's okay, boy. I didn't mean to frighten you. It is just that those boys are serious, not to mention very expensive. I am curious why would one boy need help with a group of miscreants such as those Rager boys? They aren't the type you mess around with lightly, unless you really know what you are doing, and no offense, boy, but you really don't look like you know what you are doing."

Kunther smiled politely. "Thank you, sir, but my business is my own."

The innkeeper chuckled slightly. "If that is the way you want it, boy, but I can offer you some advice if you seek it. I have seen many people pass through here seeking out swords for hire among the various groups among the two Daevan kingdoms, and if you don't know what you are doing, you could find yourself in a pit with no one ever knowing what happened to you."

Kunther took a sip of his ale and stared at the hearth.

"I may be in deeper than I can handle," he admitted after a while.

"What do you need them for that you can't handle yourself? You look to be a boy from one of the vales."

"The gronts attacked our village and kidnapped one of our own," he answered. He was beginning to feel the effects of his ale.

The innkeeper frowned.

"Now why did you want to go and make up a story like that? Gronts, goblins, orcs coming out of the forest. Why, next you will be telling me the flying demon Fyaa came out of the woods taking prisoners to sell them to the slave trade. Boy, if you don't want to talk to me, then just say so, but don't go making up stories about creatures that never cross the Sippling river attacking your village. Dangerous as they are, they would never attack a village of humans. They fear our numbers, boy, or else they would be ruling all of the Known Lands by now."

"Yes, sir," was all that Kunther could muster after his tirade.

"Well, regardless, you don't want my help. No problem for me. You are just another traveler with a big tale, and believe me, I have heard them all. You better hurry and get your rest. I don't want to stand in your way. Tomorrow is a big day for you. Those people aren't exactly the nicest people around."

"Thanks, I guess." Kunther felt relieved, but not altogether comfortable with his situation. "If you don't mind, I do have need of your help for one more thing. Do you know where I could board my horse for the evening?"

"Well, something I can do to help the brave boy. I do, actually. I can keep it here for the night for you, or you can go to the stables about a mile down the main road, outside the village. But the stable master there is a cranky old man and is probably already asleep. He rises very early you know."

"Then I suppose I will leave it with you. How much?"

"Five copper for the horse, and five copper for you for the night's stay." Kunther gave him two silver pieces.

"That's for your help and to cover a little extra if you don't mind walking my horse around back and brushing her down for me."

The innkeeper picked up the two silver coins and smiled.

"Don't mind at all, boy."

Kunther didn't trust the innkeeper's smile, but he was very tired, so when the innkeeper gave him his key and number, he left for the room and his first night's rest in a bed since he'd left Valewood.

Upstairs, the room was simple. There was a bed with one sheet, one dirty blanket with small holes, and one pillow stained yellow with age and use, but for Kunther it looked ready for royalty. A bath, he figured, he would have to get across the street. He thought about walking over to take a bath, but decided that it wasn't all that necessary. It would be nice, but he was on a mission to save his friends' lives, and to indulge in such luxury while his friends were in such trouble would eat at his conscience.

Daevanwood was still a little more than a full day's ride, but with a fresh horse he could make it just after dark. That might be a little dangerous, he thought, but he had to take that chance. His friends went into the Goblin Tribes Forest facing immense danger so he felt that he should take a few extra chances if that could speed up the help for his friends.

Kunther undressed, pulled back the covers to his bed and crawled in. He put his head on the pillow and began to drift off into a deep and much needed sleep. Kunther only awoke once that night, just after he had fallen asleep. He awoke with the realization that he had left Straight Edge downstairs, but he was too tired to wake up and get it. He slept and did not awake again until the sun shone through the window upon his face, when he woke with a start.

He looked out the window. The townsfolk were already beginning their morning errands. "Damn, I overslept!" he shouted to himself in a panic.

He ran to the other side of the bed looking for his clothes. He found them on the floor ruffled and soiled and he sat back down on the bed, put his head in his hands, and stared at his dirty clothes. He did feel refreshed and energized -- regardless of how late he was getting started -- but he couldn't believe that he had slept so long. He must have been more tired than he had thought.

He reached for his pants to put them on when he remembered that he had left Straight Edge downstairs. Quickly he pulled his trousers over his legs and sat back down on the bed to put on his boots. He had finished putting on the second boot when he realized his pants seemed lighter when he had put them on.

Fearing the worse, he checked his belt for his money pouch and found nothing.

"Oh, no," he said and jumped off the bed to search the room for his money pouch. It wasn't but a few gold pieces, a half dozen silver and a handful of copper, but it was enough to help with the trade of a fresh horse, and maybe one more meal once he reached his destination.

After searching the room, and finding nothing but lint balls, he finished dressing and charged downstairs to find the innkeeper.

An old and weathered bald man with a gray beard was behind the counter washing mugs. Kunther ran past him and to the sword rack where he had left Straight Edge. As Kunther had feared, he reached the rack and found it empty. Now furious, he raced back to the bar.

"Where is my sword? I have been robbed! Where is the innkeeper?"

"Whoa! Slow down there, young man," the old man exclaimed. "I'm the innkeeper and what is this talk of a sword and of being robbed?"

Kunther, still red eyed with fury, spoke in haste.

"My sword is gone! My money pouch is gone as well! I was told to place my sword in that rack against the wall. Then, when I woke up this morning, I find that my money pouch is gone and a different innkeeper is running the bar."

"I'm sorry, but I don't know what you are talking about. I am the innkeeper and have been since this building was built."

"Then you should help me," Kunther demanded. "Why is that?" the innkeeper asked. He was starting to get a little angry with the young man giving him orders. "You come in here last night, take a key, and leave a copper for the room. Why should you get service, when a room costs five copper pieces, not one! You should have..."

"I did pay five copper for the room!" Kunther objected, cutting the man off. "And then I paid five copper for the horse boarding, and I even gave the man who I thought was the innkeeper two silver for his trouble. If you are the innkeeper, then who was the man that sold me the room last night?"

The innkeeper smiled.

"It could've been anybody. Every night at dusk, I go across the street, have a nice dinner, and bath. I know everyone in Hollenwood, and I am a respected old man, so I just leave my inn open for the customers and they respect my inn. While I am away, they watch it for me. Customers often simply leave their money for what they use or drink."

"Then who sold me the room and board?" Kunther repeated impatiently.

"You damn kid! I said it could've been anybody. What did he look like?" he asked no longer too friendly.

"Middle aged man, with a light beard, dark hair, and tall."

"That fits a lot of men in Hollenwood, boy. You've got to do a lot better than that. Any scars maybe?"

"No," Kunther said without spirit and frustrated.

"Well, there are a lot of travelers coming through here. Maybe you just got taken."

"Is that all you can say? 'Maybe I got taken,' and drop it there!" Kunther exclaimed.

He placed both hands on top of his head, now completely uncertain how he was going to make his way to Daevanwood.

"What else can I do? Until you can tell me who it is, or what he looks like, I can't help you." The innkeeper paused, looked to Kunther with a half smile and continued. "I tell you what. You can have the room you had last night free. Here is a copper back."

The innkeeper reached in his pocket, set a single copper piece on the counter and looked at Kunther as it rolled on the counter and then spun to a stop.

"But I gave ten copper, and two silver!"

"Not to me, you didn't. And did you say something about a horse and stable?"

"Yes, my horse. Where is she? The innkeeper, or whoever he was, was supposed to board him up in your stable out back."

The old man began to laugh and walked over to his stool and sat down, pulled out a pipe, packed it with tobacco and lit it. He looked over at Kunther, smiling while he puffed and exhaled.

"I am sorry, young man, but I don't have a stable out back. The closest stable is up the road a little," he said, pointing to his right.

Kunther became furious. He could not believe his ears. Embarrassed and even more frustrated, he ran outside and through an alley to the back of the inn to verify what the old man had said. When he reached the back, he only saw garbage carts, trash, dirty rotting food and hundreds of flies. He stood staring in disbelief and felt totally lost and alone.

"What now?" he asked himself. He had no money, save a copper piece that couldn't buy him a dry sock. He had no sword and no more food. His friends could be dying right now and he was in a small village suckered and beat.

The innkeeper had told him of the stable up the road. At least that much seemed to be true, as that was the only point consistent from last night and this morning. But what could he do now? Last night he'd been told that the old man was not a happy man. Or was that another lie to discourage him from going there?

Kunther watched the flies swarm the garbage and thought of an idea. It seemed to him to be his only option. A dangerous option, and not one he would be proud of, or even one he would ever imagine himself doing, but in the end, it had to be done. He must find the stable and steal a horse. It would have to be as simple as that.

He had never stolen anything before, but now out of desperation, he would be forced to do so. If only he could do it without being caught and trapped in a jail cell and left with absolutely no chance of helping his friends. He decided he would have to try. Otherwise, he would never get to Daevanwood at all.

Revived with a little hope and a lot of adrenaline-motivated ambition, Kunther walked back to the main street and headed south towards the outer edge of the village. The walk down the main road during the late morning hour became interesting to him despite his other mixed emotions.

The people were about and shopping the streets or tending to their daily chores. Men were on horses and carriages scuttling about up and down the road. Everyone seemed to have something important to do. That would be a good thing, he thought to himself. The last thing he wanted was to stand out in any way or look suspicious. Especially since he was about to do something deceitful. He knew he was already looking a bit suspicious from his obvious inexperience and his guilty conscience.

When he reached the edge of the village, the number of people began to decrease and the only traffic he saw was a carriage or two leaving and entering the village. Oak trees bordered each side of the road out of the village which eventually led into the rest of the forested woods that bordered it. He stayed on the main road and walked on.

He walked long enough to work up a sweat from the still warm Doreal season and the heat made him think of the Fifth of Doreal Harvest Celebration in Valewood just the week before. Life was so simple then. Before the horrible events of the last week, the hardest thing he had to worry about was getting to guard duty on time for Morlonn. Life was simple and exciting.

He missed that way of life and he knew it would never be the same.

Kunther looked up from his gloomy thoughts just in time see a rider on horseback who was in such a hurry he brushed past him and almost knocked him down. The rider never looked back. Kunther figured he was probably laughing spitefully to himself and he'd better pay more attention to his surroundings. He walked on and rounded the next corner the stables came in to view.

They were in a large clearing within the woods. A huge long barn, as long as three regular size barns put together end to end, stood out amongst a dozen other out-buildings that were scattered around the large stable. Behind the stable were two round pens and in one of them were a dozen horses. Five men were working with the animals, training them perhaps, Kunther thought. Off to the left side of the barn was a grass trail that led to a beautiful large cottage surrounded by huge willow trees. Flowers of various colors grew in the scattered shade.

He walked straight to the stables where he figured the horses would be kept. He hoped that everyone would be so busy that maybe he could walk in and simply ride back out. He knew the chances of that were unlikely, but it didn't hurt to hope.

Approaching the stables, he noticed that the large doors were open and nobody was around, so he calmly walked inside, looking as non-conspicuous as he could so as not to attract any attention. The center aisle of the stable was clean, with finely groomed sand, and on each side of the aisle the horses were boarded in individual stalls. Half the stalls had horses occupying them and a few of the other stalls showed evidence that horses had recently occupied them. Whether they were in the corrals or out riding, he could not tell for sure.

He made a quick inspection of the first few horses he saw and went over stood in front of the stable that held what looked like the youngest and fastest horse. A red mare with a white diamond between her eyes looked at him cautiously as he lifted the latch and walked in the stall.

"Easy, girl," Kunther reassured the horse. He looked around and found a bit hanging on the wall in the corner. He started to grab the bit and reins when he heard someone walk into the building.

Looking through a crack in the wood, he saw two men, one an older man, the other about the same age as himself. The older man, short and gray haired with a hard face and leathery skin, went to an empty stable, opened the door and grabbed a bit and reins. He gave it to the younger man and motioned him to go back outside with it.

"Is this all I need?" he asked, puzzled.

"What else do you want, you fool? Just go!" the old man responded impatiently.

The younger man left. The older man stood looking around the stalls for a minute as if he knew Kunther was there, but shortly he turned and left.

Kunther, relieved, went back to the horse.

"Thank you for being quiet," Kunther whispered to the horse as he petted her nose. The horse flinched at his touch and Kunther moved slowly closer to the horse with the bit and reins.

"Okay, girl. Easy now."

Kunther put the bit in the horse's mouth and dropped the reins to the ground. The horse made no fuss.

"Now, to get out of here," Kunther said and he exhaled to help relieve his tension.

He turned around, checked through the crack, and saw no one, so he quietly lifted the latch of the door. He went out to the doorway of the barn and looked in both directions. To the right he saw the corrals where everyone was working. To the left side he saw the oak woods and the road where he came from.

"All clear," Kunther said in quiet, but anxious anticipation and he went back to the stall, opened the gate wide and stood beside the horse, petting her.

"Okay, girl are you ready?" Kunther whispered, his hand on her neck. He grabbed the far side of her neck and pulled himself on top of the horse's back.

"Let's go!" he commanded, excited once he had settled himself comfortably on top.

The horse began to walk out of the stalls. Kunther turned her towards the outside of the stable to the road leading to the oak woods. The horse had only taken three steps outside when the old man came walking back toward the stable.

"Hey! What are you doing?" he yelled.

Kunther froze, not knowing now what to say or do.

"Come, Jessupi," the old man commanded in a firm but soft voice.

Kunther felt his adrenalin begin to flow and with a burst of energy, he kicked the horse and yelled, "Let's go!"

The horse did nothing. Then she started walking calmly towards the old man.

"Good girl, Jessupi. What are you doing with my horse?"

Kunther began to sweat. Once again he did not like his situation.

"I am looking for a job," was the only answer Kunther could think of. "So you want a job, do you? How do you explain that you are on my horse right now without my permission?"

Kunther said nothing and his mind raced for an answer.

"I was hoping to ride out to you and impress you with my riding skills. I learned them on my father's farm," was the best he could come up with.

Kunther saw the old man's face relax a little and he felt impressed with himself that he was doing this well under the intense pressure of the situation.

"First off, you look like you are stealing my horse. You might get your ass beat instead of a job, pulling a stunt like that on my ranch. Besides, you won't impress me by riding the tamest horse I own. Get down from there. If you want a job, I'll give you one. I can always use a good, strong young hand, even one as dumb as you. What is your name anyways?"

"Kunther," Kunther said as he dismounted the horse and handed the reins to the man.

"Don't give them to me. That's your job now. Take her back and brush her down."

"Brush her down? But I didn't ride her."

"First rule of being in my employ, do as I say and don't give me any lip!" the man said and looked into Kunther's eyes. Beyond some fear and intimidation, Kunther saw a hardness in the man's eyes that showed years of hard work and hard times, but he did give off an air of compassion.

"When you are finished, meet me at the corrals. Don't go anywhere. I'll be watching you. Also, just so you know, that horse won't leave the ranch without me. Just in case you really are a thief. Don't even try, I will hang you up by your toes, and don't doubt me. I have done it before."

Kunther walked the horse back to the stable, wondering if the horse could really be as trained as the man claimed. She did come right to the man when he called, even when Kunther had kicked the horse to ride past the man.

Kunther decided not to take any chances, not now at least. Tonight he would try something else when the dark of night would act as a better cover.

He did have to hurry, though. He had to get to Daevanwood soon and he had not anticipated this delay. Time, he knew, was not a luxury he had. He took the bit and reins off and hung them back on the wall, grabbed the brush and gave the horse a quick brush down. When he was finished, he left the stable, locked the latch behind him, and walked out to the corral.

He saw the same men that were there when he had first arrived at the ranch. Two men led horses by ropes, trotting them gracefully in circles within the small corral. In the large corral, the three other men were riding their horses in between barrels. Another man was on the ground, yelling commands, and in the third corral, the old man lunged a black pony.

Kunther walked to the man and greeted him with a nod of acknowledgment.

"I want you to show me your riding skills with this horse," the man said, pointing to the horse in front of him. "He is not yet fully trained, but I think he may yet be the best horse I have," he paused to watch Kunther's reaction, but he only saw a blank face waiting for further instruction. "Well, with good training, he can be the best. Now, how well you ride will determine if I will put you in charge of this horse or not. Understood?"

"Yes," Kunther said and wondered if he could ride this horse well enough to impress the man. He had been around horses all his life, but he had never learned any fancy riding skills like what he had seen Tharn do, or even what some of the soldiers did when he had seen them riding.

He began to doubt what simple skills he did have. All he knew how to do was to trail ride.

Kunther realized that he was over-thinking his whole situation. It did not matter if he got the job or not. In the end, all he wanted was a horse, and this pony might just do the trick. He just had to get it out of the corral and run from there. "Now just climb on the fence and jump on the horse. I'll hold the reins and then give them to you when you get on him and are settled," the old man instructed.

Kunther climbed on the fence while the old man cinched a rope around the horse's neck. He held the reins from the other side of the fence. Once Kunther was in place, the old man tossed the reins over the horse's head so that Kunther could grab them. The horse jerked backwards a little as Kunther slipped his legs over the horse and grabbed the reins. The horse began to

191

jump and buck.

The rope tightened in the old man's hand, but after a few tugs the cinch came loose and the horse took advantage of the open corral and started jumping and bucking wildly.

Kunther pulled back on the reins, but it did not make any difference and it did not take long for him to lose his balance. He dropped the reins, grabbed the horse's neck with both arms and hung on as the horse continued to kick and buck with all of its strength. He rode for a few more seconds, just holding on, but he was able to glance past the horse's head just long enough to see the men crowding around the corral. They were all laughing at the spectacle.

In that moment of lost concentration, Kunther's nose met the back of the horse's head as it came up during one of his kicks. Kunther felt pain searing past his eyes up into the top of his head. He began to pass out and he felt blood drip to his upper lip.

Barely keeping his consciousness, he fell head first to the ground stretching out his arms in front of him to break his fall. His left hand hit the ground first, but the momentum of his wild fall twisted his wrist and he fell onto his right shoulder, knocking his head to the dirt.

Kunther lay in pain as he stared at the dirt. Beyond he saw the corral fence in the distance and the horse running towards it and out the gate. His wrist began to hurt with a sharp burning pain and he could feel it beginning to swell. His head ached and he could feel the dirt sticking to the blood on his face.

Just in the distance, barely within his sight, he could hear the old man and the others laughing. "Get out of my face, horse thief!" the old man said as he walked towards Kunther.

"My wrist. I think it is broke," Kunther said as he tried to breathe and speak at the same time. He could feel his chest was also tender and he found the whole experience far too painful to ever try again.

"Small punishment for trying to steal my horse. Get this boy out of here!" the old man said to two of his workers.

They immediately ran to Kunther, grabbed his arms roughly by the armpits, and dragged him out to the front of the house at the edge of the road. They dropped him onto the dirt without warning.

Kunther did not move for many minutes as he lay there in pain. His first movement was to feel his nose. It hurt, but he found that it had stopped bleeding. He noticed that the sand that had packed into his nose from the fall must have blocked the flow and helped the bleeding to stop. His wrist ached and it felt three times its original size. His ribs sent searing pain to his side with every breath.

He was afraid to move for fear of feeling more pain or discovering new bruises. Feeling the pain throb throughout his body, he told himself that he would stay there a few minutes longer. The pain was intense and Kunther felt that he could sleep.

He did not fight it, and he drifted off into a half sleep with visions of the attack of the goblin tribe in Valewood. He saw the burning hutches, homes, and the evil creatures running through the streets, screaming like wild animals, as he hid behind a booth that was selling pottery. The owner of the booth was dead and lay on the ground with an arrow in his throat. His eyes were wide open and his hands, frozen already from rigor mortis, wrapped around the base of the arrow. Kunther lay on the ground next to the dead man and watched from underneath the booth.

He also remembered seeing a man in a dark robe who did not fight, but only walked slowly behind the monsters. Kunther had only seen him that short moment during the battle, and all he did was follow his gronts and walk slowly behind them, moving his hands in precarious motions and mumbling strange words aloud. Kunther remembered the fear he felt seeing the man and seeing another figure who came out from of the wilderness.

The witch, he remembered, was a tall, beautiful woman who had skin of fire, barely noticeable, but on fire just the same. Kunther stared at the woman and forgot his fears briefly as he watched the nearly naked woman as she approached the man in the dark robes.

When she reached him, she had a short conversation with him, a conversation that Kunther had not remembered until just now. She had told him that if they couldn't find the swordsman, they needed the girl, not any girl, but a specific girl. Kunther didn't understand what that meant. Why Aaelie, he thought.

Before they finished their conversation, one of the villagers charged them. Kunther watched in fear as the fire upon the woman's skin began to ignite brightly. Her back quickly caught on fire, and out of the flames, a set of wings formed upon her back. Her face twisted and wrinkled, becoming disfigured, and large fang-like teeth grew out of her mouth.

The attacking man stopped in mid stride and screamed as she grabbed his throat with her talon-like hands and bit into the side of his head before she dropped his lifeless body to the ground. Kunther turned his head. He did not look out into the street again until the whole affair was over.

The remembrance of that day now made Kunther weep in his painful delirium.

Kunther woke abruptly when a rider on horseback almost ran him over, but then continued past him up the road to the ranch. The man brought his horse to a stop in front of the house and loosely tied it to a post. "Merkal!" he yelled. "I need your help!"

The man dismounted and ran in between the house and the stables and out towards the corrals. Kunther lifted his throbbing head and noticed that the man's horse was fully saddled and had two bags hanging across its shiny flank.

Kunther forced himself to stand up and walk towards the horse, but every muscle in his body pounded as he moved. His wrist throbbed harder, now that he was standing, and the pain made his stomach upset. He thought for a moment that he might vomit. It took him several minutes to limp to the horse, and he felt every step. It seemed to him at one point he was not going to make it without passing out.

"Easy now," Kunther said when he finally reached the horse.

He took the reins off the post. He took a deep breath and winced in pain, but he forced himself to grab the saddle horn, place his foot in the stirrup, and weakly lift his body up and over the saddle. He slumped over the horse's neck, but then he slowly pulled himself erect.

"Let's go!" he commanded and he turned the horse around and headed out of town and away from the ranch. This time the horse ran, and Kunther might have even enjoyed the ride if it were not for the pain that seemed to increase every time the horse jarred his ribs with its long strides.

Within minutes, he was leaving Hollenwood, relieved to be riding away from the stinking village for the last time. Now he just had to reach Daevanwood.

It should be a relatively easy ride, he thought. First, he had to travel through thirty miles of the Torrelenwood forest and then for another thirty miles past that to Daevanwood. It was mid afternoon and he would have to ride all night just to make it before sunrise. It was good that the sun stayed in the sky until mid evening during the early days of Doreal or his travelling would be slowed considerably by a sun that set as early as it did in the Ethinar.

Kunther was pleased that he had a fresh horse to ride through the night. Though he did not know how far its previous owner had ridden him, he guessed it wasn't too far because the horse wasn't all that sweaty when he had mounted it.

Kunther's ride was once again, back in his own hands. All he had to worry about was staying on the trail and not falling off his horse. If he could accomplish those two things, he knew he could make it to Daevanwood. After that, the rest of his fate -- and his friends' -- would be up to Commander Carsti Balron.

Chapter 17

For four days Fyaa, Ra-Corsh and the Fire Gronts dragged Aaelie through the deep woods of the lowland shrub forest of Valewood that eventually led into the tall, tightly knitted pine trees and often rocky terrain of the Goblin Tribes Forest. Now they stood at the point of the forest where the link between two forests met, the Death Pass.

That dangerous gap was where the low rolling mountain forest of the Valelands ended and met the steep rugged mountainous forest of the Goblin Tribes Forest. Two towering, rocky cliffs faced each other like brothers facing each other in combat, and the pass between them divided the two cliffs with a narrow path that invited a simple entrance to the wickedly thick forest that so many dangerous creatures called their home.

Ra-Corsh signaled his gronts to stop and take cover. Scrambling noisily through the trees, the gronts drew their crude blades and crouched to await further instructions. The two gronts guarding Aaelie pushed her to the ground face down, knocking all of the air out of her lungs, and the gront behind her took a handful of her hair and pushed her face further into the rocky dirt. The other gront turned around and straddled her back with his sword to the back of her neck.

Fyaa immediately sensed danger and her wings un-tucked from her back and caught fire. She took to the air, flew in between the massive cliffs, and scouted the gap thirty feet above ground. She left a trail of sparks dropping from her wings.

Ra-Corsh watched her fly into the massive gap as late afternoon shadows stretched themselves over each other. Large, crag-like boulders with towering pine trees made up the high formation of the cliffs and on the lower steps of the cliffs grew bush-like vegetation. The large forest could be seen through the end of the chasm like a dark, ominous wall forbidding any intruders or daring them with their lives to enter.

A small trail snaked its way through the center of the valley where tall pine trees had once stood. The stumps of these massive trees were left behind when the tribes had first burned the trees and cut them down, and some of the trees still lay where they were cut. The Goblin Tribes had burned, cut and removed the trees to gain the tactical advantage in an ambush by taking away all possible hiding spots in the pass.

Most travelers who came through the pass did not survive unless they came through at a time when the tribe on watch was napping or during a shift change when the guards were distracted. But either napping or distracted, they rarely missed an opportunity for an exciting kill. Even members of the same tribe would send some of their own through the pass for discipline or to be fired upon just for the sake of practice. The Goblins loved to do that for it was good fun and excitement on any normally dull day.

Fyaa's first pass through the canyon was uneventful, but on her return trip, the ambushers were eager to be redeemed from their earlier laziness and they filled the air with arrows and spears. Fyaa flew too fast for them and returned to the entrance unscathed when all the arrows either sailed behind or dropped well below her flight path. When Ra-Corsh saw her returning, he began concentration on his magical Wrae and zoned his attention onto Fyaa.

Fyaa flew over Ra-Corsh's head, just above the tree line, and small, dart-like projectiles left his fingertips at a high rate of speed toward the rocks on both sides of the cliffs. They hit their targets and exploded in the areas where the Goblins were readying for the next pass from Fyaa. Ra-Corsh's projectiles sent rocks, dust and debris flying high into the air and down into the canyon. A few goblins tumbled down the cliff and were crushed by debris falling on top of them.

Afterward a large cloud of dust obscured the opening of the gap.

Next Ra-Corsh reached deep within his Kronn, concentrated on the dust and made it as dark and thick as mud, like a hovering rain cloud. Lightning even coursed through the dust cloud and Ra-Corsh smiled a little. That little trick turned out to be better than he expected.

The lead gront saw the cover that Ra-Corsh had created and took advantage by signaling all the gronts to rush into the gap. Out of the woods they charged, but only briefly showed themselves in the open clearing in front of the dust cloud. The goblins behind the rocks and bushes began firing their arrows and spears at the open spot and toward the beginning of the dark dust cover.

Three gronts slipped into the dust, but a fourth and fifth gront took numerous arrows to their chests which penetrated their thick hide. Wounded and in pain, they continued on their feet still while running for cover.

The two gronts that were guarding Aaelie were the last to charge into the dust bank, and when they did, Ra-Corsh covered Aaelie with an invisible shield to protect her from the projected missiles. He watched Aaelie's body shimmer briefly as she entered into the cloud. A green aura then wrapped her body before she disappeared from sight completely.

"Are you coming wizard or are you afraid?" a calm voice whispered from behind Ra-Corsh. He was easily brought out of his momentary concentration because his three spells in just a matter of minutes had nearly drained him of his mental and physical senses.

"Go, you witch…" he managed. "I can only do a little more."

Fyaa smiled at Ra-Corsh. Her body began to shimmer and then began to mold into a new shape.

"Then I won't wait," she said. Small wisps of flames shot out from her wings and left small trails of smoke behind her. Then, while she was flying, her wings shrank and her whole body sprouted feathers before she turned into a small sparrow flittering away through the canyon.

Ra-Corsh exhaled and began a new incantation that involved a series of mechanical maneuvers with his weak and aching fingers. After a few minutes of aggravated and uncomfortable contortions, Ra-Corsh's body lifted off the ground and he too flew up into the sky above the valley. None of the goblins saw him and he flew quickly above their heads above the cover of the woods in front of the entrance of the pass.

Ra-Corsh's concentration on the dust cover protecting the gronts began to change even darker, and the lightning shooting within the cloud sent out bolts that targeted any living object. They hit both gronts and goblins indiscriminately, but they only lasted a few seconds. When they ended, nothing remained of the cloud.

It had not killed any of the targets, but it did daze a few of them and left a handful of gronts on their knees, attempting to stand and to clear themselves of the newly exposed danger. The goblins saw this and began tossing their spears and launching their arrows at the gronts.

Ra-Corsh thought to himself that he had reacted too soon. He knew that casting numerous spells would lessen the intensity of his previous spells. He also would not be able to control his Kronn as effectively as if he were rested. He was tired, and he let that damn witch intimidate him into hurrying. Now he would lose some gronts and possibly even Aaelie with his carelessness. Fyaa would blame him for losing Aaelie -- even if it was from her intimidation -- but, of course, she would not see it that way.

Below him, two gronts dropped to the ground under a new barrage of spears and arrows. Many more still were wounded, but running. The spell around Aaelie still held strong, which was lucky, Ra-Corsh thought, since the goblins were now aiming directly at the vale-girl. And it was just luck, he knew, because the spell that protected Aaelie was a simple spell and did not require much concentration to cast it or to keep it.

The gronts were now completely in the open and another gront went down. Ra-Corsh sighed. Just a few hundred feet more and they would be into the forest on the other side.

He could hear the gronts grunting and groaning in their fear to scramble away from the projectiles and get across the clearing. Such pathetic creatures sometimes, he thought. They were hardy, combative and aggressive creatures in hand to hand combat, and great in large numbers, especially when they were on the side with the advantage, but when they were at a disadvantage, or just slightly weak in numbers, they quickly became quite cowardly.

As Ra-Corsh approached the forest, still undetected by the goblins, he looked down and witnessed a handful of his gronts either lying in their own blood pools or squirming in pain as they relinquished the last breaths of what he thought were their pathetic little lives. He briefly considered returning to help a few that might survive their wounds, but just as quickly, he thought against it. It would not serve any purpose to get himself wounded or killed, and the surviving gronts knew this and would honor his decision. They knew they would only be alive because of him. They counted on his magical abilities, and they knew they could not survive this mission without him.

They also did not want to have to face Fyaa without his protection from her. If he died, they would clearly dissipate and attempt to escape, and that would cause Fyaa to go on a rampage and hunt down and kill all of them.

Yes, Ra-Corsh thought to himself, it was time to cut his losses and leave the dead and wounded behind.

Once on the other side of the Death Pass, he regrouped the surviving gronts and lined them up so that he could get a good count of them. The pine trees on this side of the pass were taller and thicker than the low scrub pines on the other side and they had an old growth smell to them. The ground underneath felt soft under his feet from hundreds of years of needle droppings. The pine dew smell permeated the air. Ferns grew sporadically, scattered across the whole floor, as the canopy above offered little more than slightly variegated sunlight.

Ten gronts was all he had left from his initial two dozen.

He had already lost a handful of them in the battle at the village -- even though he had not expected to lose a single gront there -- and now he would need as many as he could to make a stand against the goblins, and possibly against the swordsman, if he lived long enough to make it through the pass with his amateur villagers.

Ra-Corsh rubbed his bearded chin with his knuckles. He decided that he was not going to worry any further about those chasing them. They were now in his territory. Even if they were foolish enough to follow and make it through the pass, there would be numerous other tribes eager to engage them and slaughter them all without much bloodshed on their side, no matter how experienced their swordsman. He knew he needed Alaezdar to survive and follow them to the end, but at this point he really did not care. He was getting tired of this whole endeavor.

Besides, they still had a five-day trek to meet their rendezvous with the goblin tribe, the Bloody Fang Tribe. Ra-Corsh laughed to himself just thinking about their tribal name. All the tribes had picked up names for their clans which had been fashioned after some of the human and elven warriors they had defeated. They had learned to read and appreciate the fancy artwork on the banners of kingdoms picked up off the ground after they had slaughtered their enemies, many of them to the last man. Some tribes had local homes while others wandered as nomads, but no tribe had organized or mapped out borders to mark where each tribe lived. All that had really mattered -- or was respected -- was the size of the tribe and its quest for total dominance of the surrounding area.

The Bloody Fang Tribe was not the fiercest tribe in the forest, but it was likely the most cunning. Its leader, Commander Pencog, had given himself the title of commander, not as a real rank, but rather as a title chosen from hearing it from those that he had been victorious over. It had become common for goblin leaders to assume such titles once they had learned a common language, and Pencog had followed along in this practice.

Before encountering the humans, tribes had annihilated each other through incessant battles amongst themselves until they discovered this new prey to attack in the form of humans. All of the tribes within the forest battled against each other with no permanent allies. Even though one tribe might ally with another tribe one day, at the dawn of the next day both tribes might end up fighting each other again.

The humans had crossed into the forest seeking knowledge and adventure at first, in the form of glory and fame. Mostly they searched for lost artifacts in the forest itself or within the fabled ruins of the Halls of Dar-Drannon to the Northeast.

Soon other kingdoms came in looking to gain land and the advantage of establishing a foothold in the forest behind the massive defensive vantage point of the Vixtaevus Gap.

As bad luck would have it, all of the tribes Pencog had belonged to had become extinct or were broken up through fighting. It was only through Pencog's deceitful intellect that he managed to survive as long as he did. He would find ways to survive, even if it meant surrendering and becoming prisoner to an opposing tribe one day until he found a way to deceive his captors and escape the next day using various methods of deceit or cunning manipulation.

His most common life-preserving tactic, which he used more than once, was to leave the battlefield during the height of its chaos. Instead of fighting in a blood rage as his fellow combatants did, he would turn and leave the battlefield. He felt no dishonor in saving his own life. Turning away from a battle once the blood lust had entered the chaotic fray was a learned trait, and one that many goblins could not do,

One other tactic Pencog had used to stay alive was false loyalty. Fighting, hunting and killing were all that most goblins knew how to do. If they possessed any loyalty at all, it would only be to kill the enemy's leader and protect their own leader until their death seemed imminent. In that case, their mindset would often change to self-preservation at all cost. Pencog changed loyalties as often as he changed his battle stained shirts.

Pencog was an excellent fighter, and by surviving so many battles, he had learned that he could read the battle while he fought. He had an eye for knowing when his tribe was about to be destroyed. Realizing this, he saved his life many times. When the end was looming, he would resort back to his old tactic of discreetly wandering from the battlefield before the tide would turn and before escape would be deemed impossible.

During one battle in particular Pencog became most proud of using such tactics in life preservation by using his intellectual advantage over other goblins. A rival tribe of goblins had clashed with Pencog's tribe during a raid and they had battled all day and well into the night. The deaths became more prevalent and Pencog witnessed that many of his fiercest leaders had failed, but their subordinates had failed to notice, blinded as they were by the darkness and by their blood lust. Pencog took advantage of the situation, slipped away, and left the rest of his tribe to be slaughtered.

He escaped the battle by discreetly running into the deep woods and then skirted around the battle site and slipped in amongst the ranks of the opposition He began fighting his own men and helped to finish off the last members of his tribe. The opposing tribe realized the battle was over and victory cheers filled the putrid and blood scented air. In the darkness they pillaged the dead bodies and afterward began their trek back to their own tribe's encampment.

As they walked along, Pencog walked as the last goblin in line, and one by one, he silently stabbed each one in the back until he reached the final few. He then slipped away into the woods unnoticed. He had wanted to stay just so he could watch the leaders finally turn around and notice the trail of dead bodies he had left which stretched for miles.

He found this tactic so successful that he used it a number of times, enjoying the cunningness of his wit with every kill. He even enjoyed fighting shoulder to shoulder with his enemy. An unsuspecting goblin, not realizing that Pencog was not one of his own, would thrill Pencog to no end. The fact that the goblins did not recognize him did not matter, for they were often in such bloodlust that they assumed if he wasn't trying to kill them, then he was on their side. The ruse worked too beautifully for Pencog.

Years later, after switching tribes over a dozen times, he found himself with a very powerful and semi intelligent tribe. The 89th Bloody Fang Tribe was notorious amongst the other tribes for being ruthless -- though not the most ruthless -- and they were undoubtedly the largest and most successful tribe in the Goblin Tribes Forest. Most of the semi intelligent tribes had formed a military structure such as the 89th Bloody Fang Tribe had, but few were as successful given to their overwhelming size.

Once the goblins became semi-organized by learning the battle tactics of the humans, the human kingdoms found value in that for their own training purposes and they would send warriors into the goblin homeland to practice battle tactics on the often hapless and unorganized goblins. This became such a common experience that over time the smarter tribes learned from their mistakes and started not only beating the human warriors, but also destroying them down to a man.

The devastated humans left behind their banners and standards. The goblins liked the names and the colors of the banners and began to duplicate the names and adopt them as their own. Sometimes they created names for themselves which matched their own feelings for their tribe, hence the 89th Bloody Fang Tribe.

The goblins also took notice of the humans' fighting disciplines, such as how they fought in groups or squads, and they even discovered the advantageous technique of scouting and flanking before and during a battle. The goblin tribes also noticed the ranking structure and the different uniforms and armor that the human leaders wore, versus the common soldier's garb. They picked up these new techniques and ideas and used them within their tribes to create further echelons and new rules for leaders and subordinates.

Pencog had also accepted and adapted to this new style of hierarchy in the tribes and he worked it to his advantage by moving his way up from a common warrior to a group leader and finally to Supreme Warrior, who was next in line and confidant to the tribal leader.

He held this position until the tribal leader died in his sleep from a poison drink that Pencog had served him before they retired that night. The tribe assumed that he had merely died in his sleep. The warring goblin tribes believed it was a disgrace, though, as it was a shame to die so peacefully when a warrior was still young enough to fight and lead others. Only women and the old died in their sleep, they thought.

When they learned of their leader's passing, the goblins began fighting amongst themselves in an attempt to establish a new pecking order. Pencog quickly put an end to the fighting when he jumped two fighting goblins, instantly killed one and sliced the other so that he bled so profusely, but lived long enough to feel an excruciating pain. All the dying goblin could do was lie in his own pool of blood and scream. His loud, terrifying screams caused the others to stop fighting and take notice.

They saw Pencog standing over the screaming goblin, painfully hanging on to the last moments of his life. Looking up at Pencog, he tried in his final moments to spit out a final insult as he realized his life was almost over, but he could only spit blood that splattered on his chin. As he bled out, his screaming subsided and was soon replaced with moaning as he slowly slipped away.

All of the goblins watched in amazement and wondered how Pencog had so quickly disabled the two goblins, and then how fast he had killed one and how painful he had made the other. Most goblins killed quickly and succinctly so that they could move on to the next kill.

At that moment, the goblins knew they had found their new leader.

Ra-Corsh looked at his gronts. He knew things would work out in his favor either way. He would still find Pencog, who would deliver his prize of Aaelie, and as an added bonus kill the swordsman if he can make it through the pass and catch up with them in time,

The remaining gronts stood awaiting orders even though some of them were barely strong enough to stand.

"Those wounded come forward and I will heal you," Ra-Corsh

commanded.

Three gronts came forward with open wounds that, although not deep, were still openly bleeding. Ra-Corsh wrapped their wounds with bandages and curing ointments he had taken from the elven healers at the Fortress of Prophetic Studies on the Rae-om Islands. Then he laid his hands upon them and upon two others who were claiming to be weak and nauseous from exhaustion.

It now took all of his strength to call his Kronn and effectively heal the beasts that so repulsed him. Their skin leaked a sweat that almost made him vomit and the looks in their eyes of a fear of him disgusted him. His work was labored, and slowed from the distraction of his disgust, and his healing took longer than expected. When he was finished, he knew he was spent.

"I am weak," he said quietly. "Set camp here for the night."

Ra-Corsh had just found himself a place to sleep when he noticed Fyaa approaching. He could tell by the way she walked that she was angry. She stopped short of walking right through him and put her face next to his. She looked downward slightly, as she was an inch or two taller, and he could smell her breath. It reeked of ash mixed with death.

"Why did the goblins attack us?" she asked.

"What do you mean?" Ra-Corsh returned, his eyes nearly closed from exhaustion. He was on the brink of unconsciousness. He turned his back on her to found a tree to lean against.

"Don't turn your back on me, wizard!"

"Fyaa… enough…" Ra-Corsh said apathetically, and he plopped down against the tree behind him.

"Goblins! Those were goblins in the rocks! I thought you had an alliance with these tribes. That is one of the reasons I was using you. We have been betrayed!" she said in a vicious whine.

It took everything for Ra-Corsh to force open his eyes, look at her and respond to her stupidity and naiveté.

"No, Fyaa. They don't care about me or us. In fact, they fear you…and because of that fear, they would not hide from you or cower, as you may think, because they hold the numbers. They would just as quickly have you erased from this world. They don't even care about their own brothers, so they definitely will hold no allegiance to me or to you."

Ra-Corsh closed his eyes again, lowered his head and bent forward before standing up. He felt like a weak old man as he stooped halfway and had to put his hands on his knees to stand erect. Looking at Fyaa in disgust, he walked passed her in a weak stupor.

"Check on the girl for me, will you?" he asked without turning or waiting for acknowledgment.

The flames on Fyaa's skin lit up.

"What! I should kill you where you stand, you puny little wizard man!"

Ra-Corsh stopped and lowered his chin to his chest in mock submission. He was frustrated, but he would not turn to face her.

"Please do. I am spell stricken and would welcome a quick death," he said quietly.

When Fyaa did not respond, Ra-Corsh continued to slouch his way over to another place to rest.

Chapter 18

"They've definitely been here," Morlonn said to Alaezdar.

He crouched behind a bush at the foot of the Death Pass after they had noticed the scuffled trail of gronts in the moist ground before them. Behind them a few yards Tharn, Rivlok and Gartan waited.

Alaezdar turned and asked them to come forward, but they stopped short, too nervous to approach any closer than they had to. This was the first time that they had seen the Death Pass and now they understood the magnitude of the rumors and tales they'd heard about how destructive and dangerous the pass could be.

"It looks like it was quite a battle," Alaezdar said and pointed out the scarred and burnt rocks on both sides of the cliffs, along with the dead gronts in front of them.

Morlonn nodded in agreement and he squinted to see what he could in the dying late afternoon light.

"I don't see signs of any one, or thing, still alive in the pass."

They scanned the pass, looking for more signs of active goblins and for the illusive cave, but they saw signs of neither. Alaezdar hoped the cave was still there. He did remember seeing something the last time he had been in the Gap that resembled a cave, but he was unsure of what he had seen. Was it a cave, he wondered now, or just a small crevice in an indenture in the rocks. Still, it was his best hope to try to find it so they could use it as a regrouping point.

"I can't tell, but you can never be too sure. They hide well," Alaezdar said.

"Then should we wait until night fall?" Morlonn asked.

"No, their vision is better at night than ours. We might have to wait it out until first light tomorrow, maybe that way we might catch them sleeping."

"Rivlok isn't going to like that," Morlonn added.

"No, I am sure he is not, but he can charge hard in there alone if he wants."

Morlonn shook his head. He knew that Rivlok might try to force the issue.

"Let's tell the others the grim news," Alaezdar said. He stood up from his crouched position and led Morlonn back to the other three.

They all looked to Alaezdar, anxious for his decision.

"We will go in early in the morning and hope we might catch them sleeping," he said.

"No, we need to go now!" Rivlok protested, just as predicted. "I am tired of you putting off this mission. It is almost as if you are doing everything to prevent us from catching her. Let's get her now. You keep telling us we are going to die in the process. Well, I say let's start chasing her now and start dying. If I am to die in this, I want to die in the process of saving her. Let's get to her now!" Rivlok ended off almost shouting as his voice had escalated louder with every word.

"I think he is right, Alaezdar," Tharn added. "I think it is time we put it all out there and charge hard for her."

"They're right, Alaezdar," Morlonn added quietly.

"What do you think, Gartan?" Alaezdar asked. He looked at Gartan as the green and black leaves crawled on his cloak.

"It is not for me to answer. Now that I have found you, I am here to observe and report."

Alaezdar kneeled to the ground, pinched up some dirt between his fingers, and thought for a moment.

"Then let's do it," he said throwing the dirt down. "Grab your horses. Morlonn. We need you on foot with your bow to provide cover. The goblins will be focusing on us at first and won't be attacking you if you stay behind us a bit. I will take your horse. Rivlok, take Tharn's horse. Gartan, you ride with Tharn on the pack horse, but first unpack everything you need off the horse and leave the rest. We won't need it anymore. It is time we save Aaelie or die trying!"

They mounted the horses and waited a few minutes for the sun to stretch across the east side of the pass. The setting western sun would be bright on the eastern side, and Alaezdar counted on the glare to help them through the pass. He instructed everyone to ride on the western side of the center.

Nobody spoke as they waited. It was only a few minutes, but it seemed to take forever, and the others were right, that the longer they waited, the farther away Aaelie would be. She had already been through this pass, and there would be little stopping them to reach wherever they were going. Also, now that Alaezdar and the other four had made it through the pass, they themselves had no idea where they were going.

Alaezdar was not even sure that Rager's House of Renegades would even find them. He had hoped everyone would meet right there at the pass, battle it out and end it before even going through the pass. But the time was now, as Rivlok and Tharn had said. It was now all or nothing.

"Now!" Alaezdar said as he nudged his horse forward into a trot and then slowly gained speed as the others followed. He charged his steed into the clearing. The horse's strong legs strained as he nudged him to run as fast as he could. Rivlok, Tharn and Gartan were close behind.

They were beginning to think that they had picked a time when the watch was vacant. They began to pass the dead gronts that were scattered within the pass, yet nothing had happened.

Alaezdar searched ahead for the cave as he charged on. He did not get far when he felt a tug at his tunic and heard a whish sound just behind his head. Looking up, he saw dozens of arrows shooting from the right side of the canyon.

"Ride to the right side of the canyon!" he yelled to the others. "Morlonn, start taking them out!" he shouted as he jerked his horse to the right.

His horse grunted as it charged towards the rocky cliff canyon. The others followed as the arrows now flew directly over their heads and were missing them by a few feet because the angle for the goblins was too great. They continued to press on through the canyon as fast as they could until they reached a spot in the valley that was only a few hundred feet wide.

Morlonn fired his arrows while running behind Alaezdar and keeping as many goblins as he could from getting any shots off, but every time he would get one to take cover behind the sharp rocks, two or three more would pop up somewhere else.

"Look out!" Tharn's voice rasped as he pointed to the cliffs on the left side.

Looking in that direction they all saw creatures with long green arms, stretched faces with long pointed ears, and outstretched noses raising their spears and ready to throw.

"Trolls!" Alaezdar warned. "Stay on this side and keep riding!"

The trolls all raised their colorful, battle-proud spears in unison and paused while their commander shouted orders. Watching the intruders with intense scrutiny, their commander, though he lacked intelligence, just waited, a self-trained skill from his years of experience commanding the watch at the Death Pass. He gave a short, nearly unintelligible rasp of his voice and they launched their spears into the valley.

The barrage of spears came down from the rocks like a massive hailstorm. Alaezdar slid off his horse opposite the side that the spears were falling, but exposing him now to the side where the arrows were coming from. Within seconds of doing so, a spear hit his horse in the chest and the horse's front legs buckled and he fell face first into the hard dirt. Alaezdar fell to the ground and rolled as arrows lunged around his body, some barely missing him while others pounded into the flesh of his horse. Regaining his composure, he knew he had to keep moving. He stood up and ran.

Tharn saw Alaezdar go down and he charged towards him, but when his horse bolted forward, Gartan slipped off the back behind him. Tharn turned around and saw Gartan rolling in the hard dirt. He stopped his horse and struggled briefly, trying to figure out who he should go after, but he noticed that because of the cloak Gartan wore, none of goblins or trolls saw him. Tharn immediately turned back towards Alaezdar. The pause was only a few seconds, but it was enough for the trolls and goblins to hone in on him. He was now the most visible and the slowest target.

Tharn looked up just in time to see arrows and spears fill the air in all directions around him. The only thing he could think of doing was stopping the horse and pulling it down on top of him. He grabbed the reins, turned the horse's head, and brought her weight down on top of him. The weight was suffocating and he heard many of the spears and arrows hit their mark.

Gartan arrived as Tharn began to scratch and claw his away out from under the dead and bleeding horse. He grabbed Tharn's hand and pulled, but the weight was too heavy.

"Leave me!" Tharn yelled to him.

Gartan took Tharn's hand in both of his, knelt beside him, and began to hum from deep within his chest. Tharn felt his hand turn an icy hot that began to run from his hands down to his feet. Within a few seconds, he felt numb, but he noticed that the weight of the horse had become heavier.

"Wait, what are you doing?" Tharn yelled.

Before he realized what was happening, he looked at the dead horse and saw that it had turned into a block of ice and had begun to crack and fall apart around his body. Freeing himself, Tharn released Gartan's hand and scrambled on to all fours for a few feet before rising to his feet and running. He only looked behind him to see that Rivlok was still on his horse, passing him, as he charged towards Alaezdar.

"Alaezdar, grab my hand!" Rivlok shouted as he approached Alaezdar.

Alaezdar saw Rivlok coming at great speed. He continued to run and only turned around when he knew that Rivlok was close enough to reach out to take his hand. Rivlok grabbed his hand and pulled with a swing to try to bring him to the back of his horse, but the speed and the weight of Alaezdar was too great. He let Alaezdar's hand slip loose just before he was about to fall off of the horse himself. Alaezdar's feet came off the ground from the speed of the horse and he fell onto the ground, hard on his chest.

Rivlok stopped and began to turn around when the goblins began to hone in on their now slow moving target. Arrows besieged Rivlok. Ten arrows pierced his horse and one sunk itself into his forearm. Rivlok shouted in pain and felt a new sense of fear -- a fear that adrenaline could not hide -- fill his being as the horse stumbled onto his forelegs. Rivlok rolled off and took cover behind his horse. Somehow, the animal wasn't dead, but had only begun to panic trying to get away.

Alaezdar lay on the ground tasting dust and hearing the arrows pelt the ground all around him. He watched as Rivlok struggled with his terrified horse. Alaezdar feared all would be lost in this pass and panic began to set in. His vision blurred and seemed to turn white around the edges, as if he were entering a bright tunnel. Rolling onto his back and then again onto his stomach so as to remain a moving target, he tried to find some sort of shelter to hide in.

After dodging a few more arrows, he looked over to the side of the cliff for protection and he saw the cave.

"Tharn!" he yelled as he stood. "There, right there! Charge to the cave!"

Alaezdar noticed that Rivlok had also seen the cave and was already running towards it, leading his horse by the reins. The animal was still in a frightened panic. Morlonn also saw Rivlok running and assumed he had found the cave, so he ran towards him and pulled up beside him, all the while firing arrows randomly to provide cover as they both headed for the cave.

All five men now ran for the cave while the arrows and spears continued to rain upon them. When Rivlok and Tharn were only a few feet from the cave, they stopped abruptly at the entrance. It was barely three feet tall and three feet wide.

"This is the cave?" Rivlok cursed.

Arrows pelted the rocks around them. Morlonn fell to his stomach and crawled into the cave. Alaezdar and Tharn came running to the entrance and Tharn followed Morlonn in. Rivlok quickly unstrapped his bags from his horse and threw them towards the cave just as the goblins took a bead on him, a standing target now, and they pelted the horse with arrows. He took his bags and shaking his head in disgust and frustration, he crawled into the cave.

Alaezdar kicked the last bag back into the cave just as Rivlok's feet disappeared and then he guided the horse between himself and the cave entrance. He took his knife out of his belt and sliced the horse's throat. The horse's eyes widened, and the animal jumped and grunted for a few seconds before losing its lifeblood and fell to its knees. While slipping himself into the hole, Alaezdar guided the horse down so that it provided a large block covering the cave entrance.

Once inside, they all crawled only a few feet until they found that they were in a wide circular area where they could stand, even though they had to bend over. Frantically they searched their bags in the darkness for their torches. Tharn found a torch with its wrapping first, and within a few minutes he found the oil. After he found the flint, he doused the torch with the oil and lit it.

As the light began to chase away the darkness, but not the shadows, the men found that they were surrounded by the walls of a cave which had been chipped away. Rough edges marked where axes or spears were used to chisel the cave by hand.

Rivlok walked over to Alaezdar and stood directly in front of him.

"Some cave we have here, Alaezdar!" he said and he leaned his head towards Alaezdar. "It doesn't even look like it goes anywhere."

"I told you I wasn't sure if it was even here!" Alaezdar snapped back. He grabbed Rivlok's tunic by the chest and pulled him to the ground face down. He rolled over on top of him and put his knee on his back and hissed into his ear. "Get into my face again, Rivlok, you had better be prepared to kill me!"

"Alaezdar! Rivlok!" Morlonn yelled. "Knock it off. We have to get together on this or we are just going to die. It won't take long for the goblins to figure out where we are."

"That's right," Tharn added. "We only have a few minutes to figure out a way deeper into this cavern before they find us, so you two need to put your dislike for each other aside for now!"

"How do suppose we do that, with Alaezdar's knee in my back?" Rivlok asked.

"Wait…" Morlonn interrupted.

Alaezdar stood up, turned Rivlok loose, and drew his sword.

"I heard it too," he said.

The five of them stood silently while they listened. The sound of footsteps worked towards them from behind one rock wall. Whoever or whatever it was, they really were not trying to be all that quiet. It sounded as if they were dragging their feet instead of stealthily walking through the cavernous tunnels.

"Well, there you go, Rivlok," Alaezdar whispered. "It looks to me this tunnel does go deeper than we can see."

They waited in silence, not moving for many minutes as the sound of the dragging feet became louder. A piece of the cavern wall suddenly moved inward and two sets of red, beady eyes reflected in the torchlight coming from behind the now open wall.

"Hello…?" came a voice from the shadows.

"We want no harm," came another, slightly similar voice.

"Come out of the shadows and show yourself!" Alaezdar commanded.

Out of the darkness came two short, stocky figures. They had noses that looked like sticks that extended from behind their large round eyes. Their eyes went inward and were unnaturally close to their stick-like long nose. A small horn protruded from the top of the head of each, not centered, but slightly askew to the right. It was so small and off centered that it looked more like a large bump than a horn. They had hair all over their bodies and had on very little but tattered clothing.

They looked like dead animals that had just clawed their way out of a deep grave.

"Chroks!" Alaezdar gasped, disgusted at the site of them.

Chapter 19

The watch along the outer perimeter for the Fortress of Blade at Daevanwood, home to Rager's House of Renegades, was never a warrior's favorite mission. In fact, though the most skilled men took the position, it was given to them as punishment or was drawn unluckily in a lottery if no punishments were to be served at the time. The guards who watched the outer perimeter were vulnerable to sneak attacks from raiders on route to the castle. The watch was their primary purpose in the fortress's protection.

Men on the watch had to be prepared at any moment for such attacks, and any lag in their duties could mean instant death from an attacking scout silently attempting to clear the castle guards before the main raiding party launched their attack. Because of this those on watch had to keep a clear head, open ears and keen eyes. They had to know the territory and use every bush, tree and rock to their advantage. It became a hated duty because Daevanwood itself was such a hated province and township and held in great contempt by the other kingdoms throughout the Known Lands.

Commander Carsti Balron, one of the main leaders of the City of Renegades was known throughout the land, and his success in surviving without the protection of a kingdom made many land hungry, tax-collecting kings envious and red with anger, especially since his fortress was highly protected by bands of the exiled or unwanted characters of the land.

The occupants of Daevanwood swarmed the streets as the unwanted thieves, wizards, rogues, warriors, merciless mercenaries and assassins who had been banned from other kingdoms, never to return. These low life types of inhabitants ruled the streets and had vowed to protect the city and not destroy their own so that they would always have a home to go to after their subversive work was done within those same kingdoms that would not have them.

Even with all the training these men received before standing the watch, the actual event was never easy. The animals in the woods stirred at awkward moments, and even a light breeze between the forests could sound like an army of men.

Of course, there were other dangers as well.

One could never be at ease from the larger animals or beasts of prey that lurked within the dark thick woods that surrounded the fortress. One could not predict when a band of stray goblins or gronts would come trouncing through the forests in search of treasures or for sacrifices for their religious ceremonies. These beasts, though uncommon to the area, often traveled across any land in the name of their annual cultic celebrations.

These thoughts crossed the minds of many perimeter watch men duly informed of any and all such dangers beforehand, including Deriyn, who now hid in the shadows of the moonlight shining high in the sky above the dark fortress.

He looked toward its dark and ominous silhouette as it towered above the trees and wished he'd been posted as a guard anywhere within the walls instead of being out in the woods with the creatures and dangers of the land. He began to think of his home and his family, who lived just outside the city limits of Daevanwood, when he heard a noise that made his heart jump and his pulse quicken. It was a noise like the sound of a bush being moved by a hard wind, but no wind blew tonight. He had hoped that it was a deer, or a fox, or something harmless, at least.

Silently he withdrew his sword and hid behind the closest bush. If possible, he would first try not to be discovered, but if he was, he would fight to the death.

The noise was getting louder and closer, he could tell from the volume, whoever or whatever it was obviously did not care about being discovered.

The moonlight soon provided Deriyn with the silhouette of a man, a soldier.

"Deriyn. I know you are near," the man whispered as he passed by, not seeing Deriyn.

Deriyn stepped out from the tree he was hiding behind and stood in back of the clumsy lurking soldier. He sheathed his sword.

"What are you after, your death?" Deriyn asked caustically.

"I'm bored," Gharz stated flatly. "Besides, no one will be bothering us tonight. It is too quiet and I need to talk."

"It's too dangerous to be out talking. This is how we are going to get ourselves killed if we don't get back to our post."

"Post? You know that we have no specific post. The whole forest is our post tonight."

"Still, we should not be this close together. It ruins the structure of... Wait, did you hear that?" Deriyn stopped talking when he heard another sound off in the distance.

"Sounds like a horse," Deriyn said as he withdrew his sword again from its scabbard. This time quickly and not as quietly as he had done the first time. "It's coming from the road and by the sound of it, he is riding fast. Quick, get ready to light the signal. I'll go to the road to see if I can get a look at him as he passes. If he gets to the castle before our signal, Commander Balron will surely have our heads."

Deriyn ran swiftly, but noisily to the road, thrashing his scabbard and pack against the trees and bushes as he ran. While Deriyn ran off in the distance, Gharz prepared the bow. Its arrows all had phosphorous tips and each arrow had a different color to alert the guards of the castle to different things.

Gharz withdrew an arrow with a green tip to signify a single rider and then waited for Deriyn's signal to be sure. Deriyn made it to the road just seconds before the rider rode past him with great speed and without caution. After seeing the rider, Deriyn ran back to Gharz to inform him.

"Just one!" he said, out of breath.

Gharz lit the tip of the arrow with his pocket flint, strung the arrow as it caught on fire and let it fly. A bright green light streaked across the sky towards the castle.

Atop the wall of the fortress, two guards saw the arrow peak in the sky and then fall to the ground in front of the castle. It burned out as quickly as it had touched the ground.

"Go! Now!" one of the men guarding the wall said to his subordinate and sent him running to the watch commander. The man ran across the battlement and over to the commander's tower that overlooked the forested valley.

"Single rider sir, unannounced," Pilter gasped, out of breath, to the watch commander.

"How long ago was the signal sent?" Sergeant Mourt asked impatiently.

"Only moments ago," he said. He turned to face First Warrior Konrod.

"An unannounced rider is coming towards the castle," Sergeant Mourt told him. "I am on my way down to the gate to greet him. I wanted to inform you so that the watch relief may know of the upcoming situation."

"Very well, carry on, and keep me updated."

Sergeant Mourt gave a brisk salute and left for the gate before First Warrior Konrod could return his salute.

Reaching the gate, Sergeant Mourt was surprised to find that the rider had already reached it and was arguing with the guard. The guard saw Sergeant Mourt approach, relieved to see that help had arrived.

"Sergeant Mourt, could you please explain to this beggar that I cannot let him through."

Sergeant Mourt looked at the rider, obviously tired from what seemed to have been a long strenuous ride. His clothes were soiled and worn, and the dirt upon them was sun dried. It was obvious to Mourt that the rider had not even attempted to wash off the dirt for what could've been weeks. His red hair was a long, oily and tangled mess. His horse's hair was wet with sweat and the animal looked near death with exhaustion.

"What is your business?" Sergeant Mourt demanded firmly.

"I wish to see Commander Carsti Balron," Kunther said. He looked to the ground, too exhausted to hold his head erect.

"Unannounced?" he asked incredulously.

"I have come a long way to see him, sir, I cannot turn back now."

"I can tell that you have come a long way, son. I can smell you from here. But if I let every stranger into this protected fortress wanting to see High Commander Balron, how long do you think he would be alive?"

"I realize your position, sir, but I have a message for him, and I need the

218

services of Rager's House of Renegades."

Sergeant Mourt smiled. "Well, this is getting better and better by the minute. But you still cannot see our commander, nor hire the services of Rager's House of Renegades, unless you can give me a very good reason to justify your passing, and I don't think you can come up with one that good, if I am to be honest."

Kunther looked into the eyes of Sergeant Mourt and saw that the man seemed adamant in his position, but he tried again.

"But my village, family, and friends are in grave danger and I have large amounts of gold and even dragon pieces to pay for services, not to mention the message I must give him that I know he will find most worthy of his time."

"If this message will interest him, then you can give me the message and I will relay your words to him."

Kunther straightened up in his saddle and raised his voice to address him further.

"I cannot give my message to anyone else but High Commander Carsti Balron!"

Sergeant Mourt took two steps towards the horse and looked blazingly into Kunther's' eyes.

"If your message is that important, then you can tell me now!"

"I cannot, but you can tell him that if he does not talk to me, not only will my people die, but he will miss out on something much greater than any amount of wealth, including some very valuable gems. I have all of this, but more importantly, the information is what he will treasure the most dearly."

Sergeant Mourt looked at Kunther despondently.

"Wait here," he announced to Kunther. "Do not let him leave your sight," he said to the guard.

He made his way reluctantly to tell First Warrior Konrod that he had failed in stopping the stranger and that First Warrior Konrod must go to the High Commander's chambers and wake him.

"You wake me for a lone rider?" the High Commander bellowed as he reached for his robe to keep himself warm from the cold and damp air.

He rubbed his eyes, looked at First Warrior Konrod and saw that although the man was a great warrior, there was a sense of concern for his job in his eyes. Carsti Balron took a deep breath and began again.

"Relax, First Warrior Konrod. You said this lone rider has a large sum of wealth with him?"

"Yes, High Commander," he said showing a little relief from Balron's quick change of attitude. "He claims to have some information that you will greatly receive. The man is just outside the door. Sergeant Mourt is outside watching him."

"Send him to the council chambers. I will meet you and the stranger there after I get dressed and prepare for his offer."

***

The walk to the council chambers was a long, but well awaited one for Kunther.

Sergeant Mourt and the First Warrior stood on each side of him as they escorted him through the many turns and stairs of the fortress. The musty smell locked within the walls added to the uneasiness within his stomach which left him feeling nauseous. The damp smell eventually went away as he walked further into the fortress because fires were lit in many of the hearths along the hallways.

Along the way he walked passed many memorials to valor and honor which decorated the walls. Swords, daggers, shields, pikes, and maces all hung in elaborate fashion as if they'd been stolen from the battlefield still crusted with mud. They were well organized and aligned next to tapestries of all colors which covered the large windows and which bore the insignia of different guilds, no doubt important guilds that Kunther thought, had made their home in Daevanwood. Artifacts collected from ancient elven ruins sat on shelves along the walls and paintings of dragons and brave warriors hung perfectly beside them.

They led Kunther up a long spiral of stairs that went straight up three levels of the castle and at the top a catwalk hallway stretched along the back side of the wall. The opposite side of the hall was open and had no rail to protect any one from falling to the ground some fifty feet below.

When they reached another hallway, they stopped and waited until an attendant came out of a door at the top of a stairway and motioned them to come up. They climbed the stairway up the two flights that eventually brought them to an open door and an elaborately decorated room filled with small trinkets, cups and ancient coins from faraway places, all collected during one of the many journeys that had been made to such places. At the end of the room was a large door that was wide open.

Kunther could see into the room and its comfortable environment. Long couches and soft chairs filled the large chamber. The High Commander stood with his back turned from the door and looked out of the only window.

A servant boy who had just finished lighting the fire saw First Warrior Konrod coming and picked up his flint and paper and left the room. Konrod knocked firmly on the opened chamber door and waited a few moments for the High Commander's permission to enter. Kunther waited in front of the door, anxious to finally have this talk and get this ordeal behind him. With any luck, he thought, he could convince this man to help his friends.

"Enter," the commander said with his back still turned to the three men.

Sergeant Mourt allowed First Warrior Konrod and Kunther to enter first. The First Warrior led Kunther inside the room, commanded him to stop, and took two more steps forward before announcing, "First Warrior Konrod reporting, sir, with the unannounced rider."

"At ease, First Warrior. You may leave now," the High Commander said and turned to face Kunther.

Sergeant Mourt stood by the open door and let First Warrior Konrod pass and then followed him, closed the door and left Kunther alone with High Commander Balron.

Carsti Balron turned his back again on Kunther and looked down upon the city of Daevanwood nestled within the forest. Most of the inhabitants were inside for the evening, but a few remained in the streets partaking in the wild life that the city so lawfully permitted, the very same wild life that had given the city of Daevanwood the reputation as the City of Renegades.

"Every time I look down upon this city, it reminds me of the goals and ambitions of my youth. I remember when I first came here. Like you, I was in trouble. It was a pivotal period of my life when I arrived and turned my dreams and ambitions into reality. In some ways, I was lucky. I did many things on my own, but it was not without good help. Within a few years here, I had turned from exiled warrior to a leader, a king of sorts -- if you will -- of this proud, but devious city. I try not to forget my beginnings, especially when it comes to helping those in need..."

Carsti Balron finally turned and faced Kunther.

"...especially when they arrive with promises of wealth and information."

Kunther saw a tall and proud man wearing a dirt brown robe with a purple sash around his waist. He watched as the commander eyed him intently, showing no sign of emotion. His red hair and beard was unkempt and that made him even more intimidating for it told Kunther that he must have been retired for the evening and now had been rudely awakened.

"Now that my lecture is over, I want to get to the heart of the matter that you have deemed to my good men -- men that I trust, I should tell you -- unworthy to handle themselves. Why do you seek me out?" he finally asked.

He did not seem to move a muscle in his face other than his jaws to speak.

Without hesitation Kunther began talking quickly. "I need your assistance. I have friends in the Valelands who are in grave danger and only your Rager's House of Renegades can save them."

Carsti Balron stepped behind his oversized lounging chair and rested his arms upon its backrest.

"My men are busy, so my fee is very steep right now. Do you even know my normal fee to lend my men out on dangerous missions?"

"I have an idea sir, but..."

"No, I don't think you understand," he interrupted. "The fee I ask is even more than can be obtained from a commoner from the Valelands. If you fully understood, you would never have traveled so far."

Kunther paused, but then spoke.

"I must speak regretfully and truthfully, sir. I have no money to pay you, but I come with a message, and for a favor in return for such message."

Carsti Balron's eyes opened with a mixture of anger and curious interest. He scratched his beard. Holding his short temper in check, he asked, "What favor could you possibly offer us?"

Kunther took a deep breath and spoke before he could change his mind or begin to fear for his life.

"For your services I will tell you the whereabouts of Rock Blade."

For a brief moment, Kunther swore that the air stood still and time froze.

Carsti Balron stood erect. The large chair he was leaning upon slid forward. His eyes widened and his face began to turn deep red, matching the color of his hair.

"How do you know that name?" he commanded.

"From Alaezdar himself. He sent me here, for your services. A witch, a wizard, and a tribe of gronts attacked our village, and they took one of our villagers into the Markenhirth forest. Alaezdar, or Rock Blade as you know him, assembled a few men to go into the forest to save our kidnapped villager. He sent me here, to Daevanwood, to seek you out, and only you. In return for your services, he promises to give himself to you if you save our friends in time."

Carsti listened to Kunther patiently, but anger still welled up inside him with every minute that passed.

"This is outrageous! I owe that traitor nothing! And he wants my help? I will have his head! Do you realize that anyone who knows that name carries with him a death sentence?"

Kunther stepped back and looked fearfully at Carsti and wondered what he was about to do. He thought that he might strike him and then call his guards to take him away, but instead his rage seemed to subside after he took a deep breath and looked into Kunther's eyes.

"What is your name young man?" he asked.

"Kunther," he responded respectfully and timidly.

"Kunther, I want you to allow my guards to take you to our temporary guest quarters and wait for my reply. This is a serious matter that I need to discuss with my aides, but before you go, I want you to quickly tell me what you know of Rock Blade and Rager's House of Renegades."

"I don't know too much more, sir. Alaezdar lived with us for about a year and during that time he was very secretive about his past. After the attack on our home, he only told us that he was once a member and that his secret name was Rock Blade. He said that he left the guild, but was now a wanted man, and that you wanted him back to be held accountable for a murder. He also told me to be very careful to tell no one but you that I knew about his identity because it was a sacred secret, and that I could be killed just for knowing the name. He even told me that telling you what I knew did not guarantee my safety, and that you might kill me instead of helping us. But I told him I did not care because I wanted to do my part to help."

Kunther stopped to take a deep breath before he continued. "I have been truthful to you, sir, and I hope no harm will come to me. To tell you the truth, on Alaezdar's behalf, no one in the village knew of his identity until after the attack, and I am the only one he told his secret to."

"Do not fear, Kunther," the commander said calmly, the tone of his deep voice now one of concentration. "No harm will befall you by Rager's House of Renegades. You are our guest and will be treated as such. Rock Blade will be beheaded for his murder and his treasonous act of allowing his guild name to pass to your breath. Under the circumstances, the crime will be his and no one else's. Now, go with the guard and rest. We will bring you food, as well, as I am sure you are hungry. I will talk to you later -- possibly tomorrow morning -- so get a good night's rest. You look as if you have earned at least that much."

"Yes, sir. Thank you, sir."

Carsti Balron watched Kunther open the door and face the guards.

He informed the guards of Kunther's status and where he was to stay the night, but as they walked away, he grabbed the second guard and asked him to have Talon Blade report to him at once. Carsti Balron watched them walk away, entered his chambers and closed the door behind him.

He stood alone, deep in thought and full of rage. He had been motionless for many moments when a knock came upon his door.

"Enter."

A man entered the room and gave a motivated and crisp salute. He was wearing loose fitting pants and a light silk shirt and he had his long brown hair pulled back into a ponytail,.

"Sir, Talon Blade reporting!" he snapped.

"Relax, Talon. I have an emergency mission for you. A rider with a message has given us word as to the whereabouts of Rock Blade."

"Where is he, sir? You must tell me so that I can avenge the death of my friend Red Blade!" he said eagerly.

"He is in the Markenhirth forest, searching out a goblin tribe that attacked his village and kidnapped one of their villagers."

"The Markenhirth Forest, sir? Alone? How deep into the forest?"

"No, not alone. He took a few villagers with him. The man seems to have no compassion for the villagers he leads into the forest. I am certain the goblin tribes will surely kill them all. It shows his arrogance and stupidity because Rock Blade has been into the Markenhirth Forest and knows how dangerous that can be."

Carsti Balron stopped to think of the last time he had to send any of his guild into the Markenhirth Forest. The Fierce Killers battalion of the Battleworth Kingdom had hired the Ragers to rid themselves of the attacking ogres. They had constructed a dozen makeshift boats that had crossed the Darv-Nar bay and attacked a small village near the city of Battleworth during the night, while the city slept. The Kingdom's city militia retaliated and destroyed half of the raiding ogres before they could return to their boats. Then their navy attacked with their ship, the Zarkon, and sank the other boats before they could return to their land.

The Fierce Killers battalion was dispatched to enter the Markenhirth Forest and attack the ogre tribe closest to the sea to give them the message that any attacks in such a manner would not go un-avenged.

The scouting mission with ten members of Rager's House of Renegades had succeeded in finding the ogre tribe and exposing them for the battalion, but the ogres took the lives of eight of Carsti Balron's well-trained men. The two surviving men returned with reports of acts of gruesome violence, much worse than what they had already seen in the thickest of battles.

Balron knew that men in combat were capable of committing some of the most heinous acts of terror in the name of their kingdom, and for their own survival, but these monsters had found ways to torture men while they were still in battle. They tortured them and left them to die in their wounds in the most painful of ways. They even did so without regard to their own lives, and it had seemed to Balron that in their bloodlust it was the ultimate goal to cause terror over anyone's survival.

"I do not know how deep into the forest he is, or what his final destination is," Carsti Balron began, breaking himself from his own thoughts, "but that information you must find for yourself. In one of our guest rooms, you will find the messenger. He is merely a boy. His name is Kunther. You can get all the information you need from him. When you have completed that, you may assemble all the men that you deem necessary for the mission. Do not be afraid to over-staff this mission. I do not want to lose any more lives for the sake of that treasonous Rock Blade."

"When should we leave?" Talon Blade asked.

"As soon as possible, but ultimately that is your choice. Also, if you want to take Kunther with you, you may, but he is tired from his long trip and may just slow you down. I want you to get Rock Blade as soon as possible so that his head may roll to justice."

Carsti Balron smiled for the first time since Kunther had first arrived.

"In fact," he added, "I want to see his blood, and I don't care if his blood is fresh or not, I just want to see it drip upon my hands! Understood?"

"Gratefully, sir."

"Then leave!"

Talon Blade saluted and left the room, eager to obtain the information that would lead to his long awaited revenge.

Chapter 20

The pair of chroks inched their way cautiously towards the men and shielded their eyes from the light of the torches as they approached.

"Back off!" Rivlok shouted. He drew his sword and took a step towards the chroks.

The two creatures recoiled and slipped back into the shadows.

"Wait," Alaezdar said and he punched Rivlok square in the back. "We need your help."

"What?" Rivlok snapped, turning around.

Alaezdar raised both hands, looked at Rivlok, and whispered. "Shut up and get behind me."

The two chroks once again crept out of the darkness, but stayed just out of the torchlight.

"Can you help us find a way to escape from the goblins outside?" Alaezdar asked while he cautiously stepped towards them.

Silence and their shuffling back and forth, in and out of shadows, was their only response.

"We have to hurry. They will be here soon," Alaezdar said.

An answer finally came.

"They won't be coming in here."

"How can you say that? They are just outside. I can hear them assembling."

More shuffling and then a short silent laugh.

"No, they won't. They are afraid."

"Afraid?" Alaezdar asked. "What are they afraid of?"

"The wraeths, of course," the two said in unison, giggling.

This time the silence came from Alaezdar and Rivlok.

"The wraeths that live in these caves terrify them," one shadowy chrok said.

More laughing and then the other one spoke with a slightly deeper and scratchy voice.

"Yes, they are very, very afraid of them, and us…yes, us also."

"Then can you take us to the quickest way to the north side of the pass?" Alaezdar asked.

"The quickest way into the pass is behind you," one answered while the other laughed.

"Of course, you are right," Alaezdar said, "but we will be killed. Is there another way around?"

"Yes, there is, but do you want to avoid the wraeths?"

"If possible, but I am not afraid of them. Take me to the quickest way out of here, whether we encounter wraeths or not."

"Alaezdar?" Tharn whispered. "The elven wraeths are not to be taken lightly."

"I know, but I can handle this," he snapped.

More laughing until the scratchy voiced chrok spoke up.

"Then you need to follow us. We will take you through the catacombs where the elven dead sleep and live."

"Yes…follow now...Oh, yes," the other chrok said. "To the catacombs we will go."

They both slipped into the darkness.

"Wait!" Alaezdar said. "We need to gather our belongings. Rivlok, Tharn, Morlonn! Grab all that we can carry. We will need all of our weapons more than anything else, so grab only what food we need for the next day or two."

"But we are more than two days from home," Rivlok said.

"I am not sure we will be returning. We just need to live long enough to reach Aaelie. Gartan, start grabbing what you need."

Gartan did not respond, but stood still as if in a trance. Alaezdar walked up to him, put his hands on his shoulders and shook him slightly.

"Gartan! Let's go!"

"I can't," he said, as if waking from a deep sleep.

"What do you mean, you can't? We don't have much time."

"Alaezdar, what I mean is that *we* can't. There is a reason why I have not been in these catacombs. I have been seeking Kronn my whole life, and I have known that the answers I seek are here, but I have never had the courage to seek them out from here."

"Then stay. I don't care. I think I am going to need you soon, but I can't make you go," he said and he turned his back on Gartan and pulled Bloodseeker from its scabbard.

He heard the familiar click of the small blades under the cross-guard snap into place with screaming urgency. His right arm surged with adrenaline as Kronn flowed into the sword. When the chroks heard the sound, they giggled with excitement like two young girls seeing an attractive young man. Before Alaezdar could take another step, they were standing within the torchlight and looking up into his face, smiling from ear to ear.

"Youu have magiiiic…" they hissed.

"Alaezdar!" Gartan shouted as if a terrible thing had just happened. "Stay away from them. Chroks absorb magic. That is how they live here unharmed amongst the wraeth's."

Alaezdar turned to Gartan, saw the fear on his face, and immediately noticed that his connection with Bloodseeker did indeed seem a little duller than before. He held up his sword to inspect it and noticing that the cross-guard blades had also retracted. That only happened when the danger subsided. He knew he was still in danger and that the magic must've been weakened in the presence of the chroks.

"Back away from me!" Alaezdar said and he shooed the two chroks away from him. The chroks backed away with hurt looks on their faces.

"We have to go now!" Alaezdar yelled. "Everyone, Gartan, stay or go. I do not care!"

"I will go with you," Gartan said and picked up from the ground the items of his which they had dragged in from the horse.

Alaezdar, Rivlok, Morlonn, Tharn and Gartan looked at the chroks who still stood staring at Alaezdar like he was a piece of meat to eat.

"Move!" Alaezdar shouted to the chroks.

As if being awakened from a trance, they turned and walked quickly into the darkness and down a dark tunnel that sloped downward slightly. As they walked away, he felt a little of the tingle from Bloodseeker return.

They all walked for an hour into the dark tunnel, passing many different openings that led deeper into the darkness. They seemed to switch back toward the east and then to the west, then the north, then south. None of the directions they took made sense.

Alaezdar followed the chroks directly, but purposely fell behind some to test again if his sword's power would return but then weaken, the closer he was to them. It ebbed and flowed constantly as he did so, making him nervous about the changing of the sword's power.

Morlonn followed behind Alaezdar. Tharn held the torch behind Morlonn, and Rivlok was followed by Gartan, who stayed as far away from the chroks as possible. As they walked, Alaezdar began to feel fatigued and he realized that he had not slept much since they left Valewood.

His eyes closed numerous times as he walked and listened to the footfalls of the chroks so that he would not lose them. His head spun as he walked, but he remained alert enough to keep putting one foot in front of the other. He went on for a few more switchbacks until the chroks stopped, stood still for a few moments, and then spoke to each other in a different and unintelligible language. Soon they started walking again and one of the chroks spoke up.

"My name is Igs," he said.

"Ohhh, yesss, my name is Smack," the other said before laughing. "Nice to meet you."

No one spoke again for another hour, until the chroks stopped again, stood in silence for a few minutes, and then turned to Alaezdar.

"Stay back," Alaezdar told them before they could walk towards him.

"Wraeths," was all the chrok said before he turned around and walked away.

"Follow," the other said.

As they walked, they could hear what sounded like a river not far away with white water rushing by. The chroks continued while Alaezdar and the others followed, and as they did, they saw they were coming out of the cave and into an open expanse. The air was no longer stale and a hazy purple light now shimmered in the tunnel.

They continued walking until they came completely out of the tunnel, but the path dead-ended at a straight cliff drop overlooking a great open valley.

At first, they thought they were outside again. A small brook meandered directly below them, and up above they saw stars shimmering in a cobalt blue sky. Alaezdar looked closely and realized that it was only an illusion.

He didn't know how he knew it was an illusion because to his eye, it was as real as he could see. For all he could tell, it did feel as if he were outside because the river rushing by created a slight breeze that invigorated him and made the air smell fresh.

"Alaezdar, this is the where the elves bury their kings and heroes," Gartan said.

"This is not where we need to be," Rivlok said as he walked up behind Alaezdar.

"I would never have guessed of this in my wildest dreams," Tharn added.

"We need to be careful," Gartan said, scratching the stubble on his chin. "I don't think we will be very welcome here."

"Where did the chroks go?" Alaezdar asked when he noticed that their scrubby little friends weren't around anymore.

"There!" Morlonn said.

He reached for an arrow behind him, nocked it, and took aim at one of the chroks as they ran across a small bridge across the river down below in the valley.

Alaezdar put his hand on Morlonn's bow and lowered it.

"No. I have a feeling they are going to find us again."

"What about the wraeths?" Rivlok asked and pointed his sword down at the valley. "They said that the wraeths were here."

"Unfortunately, I have a feeling we will find them whether we want to or not," Alaezdar said.

He sheathed Bloodseeker and pushed his way past Rivlok and Morlonn to the left side of the cliff's edge. He looked down and found a small rope ladder dangling all the way to the valley floor. It was tailor made for the chroks, with two ropes entwined together to forming a ladder with rungs only six inches long and six inches apart.

"Well, this could be fun," Alaezdar said.

He unbuckled his scabbard-belt, refastened it around his back, turned around and began his descent down the rope to the valley floor.

One by one, everyone followed him down the rope and assembled at the bottom of the cliff. From there they walked across the stone bridge that went over the brook where they had last seen the chroks. After crossing, they were surprised to find that the surface they walked on felt like they were standing on soft ground, not hard rock.

Smaller streams, void of any large boulders, meandered through the soft grassy dirt in the center of the valley. There were a few small stones scattered which they could use to step on to cross and although the streams were small, many were big enough that they had to put at least one foot in the water to cross. Others were bigger, but none of them were more than two feet deep.

They walked unobstructed until they found themselves in the center of the valley, and they stopped there to figure out where to go next.

"Where are we supposed to go now?" Rivlok asked. He looked at Gartan and not Alaezdar for answers.

"I told you. I have never been here," Gartan snapped, clearly nervous of these surroundings.

Tharn pointed to an archway on the far side of the valley which was nearly covered by a cluster of small pine trees that almost looked like bushes.

"I think we should start over there," he said.

Morlonn nocked an arrow and let it loose, landing it in the clump of trees. Smiling, he winked at Alaezdar.

"Just checking for our chrok friends."

"Let's hurry then," Rivlok said and he ran off towards the trees and archway.

He had only gone a few feet and jumped over another stream when he began screaming and twisting before being lifted off his feet. He hung suspended only a few feet above the ground, and as he did, his form began fading in and out for a few seconds before he fell to the soft ground, unconscious.

Alaezdar and Morlonn ran to him, but Gartan grabbed Alaezdar's wrist and yelled for them to stop.

"It is a trap!" he said. "The wraeths are here. We can't see them yet, but we will when they want us to."

"Is he ok?" Alaezdar asked, snapping around to Gartan.

"For now he is. If the wraeths wanted him dead, he would be. I think they are just testing us to see what we want. The wraeths aren't necessarily evil or malicious. They are just protective, with a slight bit of justified anger."

"We have to do something," Morlonn pleaded.

"And quick," Tharn said and removed his sword from its scabbard.

"No, Tharn. Put that back. They will give us a signal soon enough," Gartan said.

As soon as Gartan had finished speaking, a form materialized in front of them in the shape of an elven warrior dressed in leaf battle armor. He stood there staring at Alaezdar.

"The one with Kronn must come with us. Everyone else can leave," he said as he lifted his bow and shot an arrow into the wall to his right. "Find that arrow and you will find an exit to the catacombs. Follow it and leave now."

"What does that mean?" Morlonn asked.

As soon as he spoke, Alaezdar dropped to the ground like a boneless creature, and then he and the wraeth disappeared.

Immediately after they had disappeared, Rivlok began to stir and he stood up. "Don't move, Rivlok!" Morlonn shouted.

"We need to get out of here!" Rivlok shouted back in terror, realizing where he was and remembering what happened. "Did you see that?"

"We didn't see what attacked you, but we saw you. Are you okay?" Tharn asked.

"No, I am not. We need to go," he said, shaking his head again like it was going to vibrate off of his shoulders.

Morlonn walked over to the small stream and stepped into it.

"Take my hand," he said and reached for Rivlok.

Rivlok, now feeling a little silly, accepted the help, took Morlonn's hand and stepped across the small stream.

"Now we should go," Morlonn said and nodded to Tharn and Gartan. "Run to the edge of the valley by that rock face where the small pine trees were. We should find my arrow there."

Everyone broke out running to where Morlonn was pointing even before he finished his sentence. Tharn, with sword ready in hand, and Gartan, armed only with a knife, ran to the marked area, but Rivlok's sword was still in its scabbard as he sprinted in front of everyone else. Morlonn raised his bow, nocked an arrow and ran behind everyone, keeping his bow ready to fire at anything. It did not take long for something to appear, but it wasn't another wraeth, as they had expected.

Five hunched figures came running towards them from out of nowhere. Morlonn could not tell what they were at first. They looked to be little more than shadows with short swords and shields. submersed in the hazy purple light and charging.

"Ravages!" Gartan yelled. He charged the first one, but not until he had nudged passed Rivlok to give him time to pull his sword free of his scabbard.

The ravages charged at them, grunting and yelling as they came. They were goblinoid, dog-like creatures with bodies covered in stubbly hair tightly woven within their skin in black and tan broken stripes. They looked more like disfigured creatures and they stood uncannily on their hind legs. They flashed their teeth with fierce intensity as they ran. Their incisors had been sharpened for effect and extended out from their mouths, waiting to taste blood.

Morlonn let his arrow loose and hit the leading ravage just seconds before Gartan encountered it. His arrow pierced its flesh in the upper chest just below its neck, wounding it. Gartan tackled it and landed on top of its body as it screamed, realizing too late that it had an arrow in its chest. Gartan plunged his knife into its chest just below the arrow just as another ravage took its sword and hit Gartan on the shoulder, knocking him off the other ravage. Gartan grabbed his right arm and screamed in pain as he fell off the ravage.

Tharn reached the ravage that had attacked Gartan and blocked its second blow just as it was about to plunge its sword deep into Gartan's head. Morlonn sent another arrow and pierced its left shoulder. Tharn, taking advantage of the wounded beast, swung wide and sliced its throat. Blood spurted on Tharn's face as the ravage fell and died.

The three remaining ravages, seeing the blood on Tharn's face, began howling and making a sharp piercing sound that reverberated throughout the chasm. As they did so, they threw their shields to the ground, hunched down on all fours like dogs, and began grunting and yelling so deeply and loudly that the sounded more like vicious animals issuing a guttural barking as they attacked.

One of them jumped on Rivlok and knocked him down, bumping his sword out of his hand as he went to the ground. The ravage jumped on his chest and opened his maw to bite his throat out and take Rivlok's lifeblood from him.

With both hands now free, Rivlok grabbed the head of the ravage as it snapped its jaws like a rabid dog right in front of his face. Drool came out of its mouth and pooled up in Rivlok's eye socket.

Tharn and Morlonn both changed directions and went to Rivlok's defense. Morlonn shot another arrow, but missed this time. Tharn ran towards the ravage, kicked it in the ribs, knocking it off of Rivlok, and then jumped over Rivlok's body and plunged his sword into the side of the ravage as it rolled off Rivlok. The ravage moaned slightly and died.

"Get up!" Tharn yelled.

Tharn turned around and saw the two remaining ravages tearing into Gartan's clothes and flesh. Gartan screamed as blood and ripped cloth splattered on the ravages. Morlonn sunk an arrow into the side of one of them as Tharn ran towards the other and sliced its spine nearly in two with one hack. It folded over and died on top of Gartan. Meanwhile, Morlonn had sunk two more arrows into the other, but it seemed not to notice and it took another bite from the side of Gartan's neck.

Tharn took another swing at the remaining ravage, hit it in its side and then pulled back and plunged his sword into its chest as it pulled away from Tharn's first swing. The ravage barked at Tharn as if in defiance, but then it fell next to Gartan and died.

Morlonn placed his bow over his head and ran to Gartan seconds after Tharn had sheathed his sword and kneeled next to Gartan. He placed his hand behind Gartan's neck and held up his head while applying pressure to the gash in his neck. Blood squirted in between his fingers as Gartan choked, opened his eyes and looked up. He realized that he would soon be breathing his last breath. What was left of his shirt was soaked with his blood and the ravage's foul saliva.

He looked at Tharn and choked again, coughing up blood.

"Alaezdar…you can't leave him in here. This is not a place for Kronn anymore."

"We will find him," Morlonn answered.

"My dragon…is it still on my eye?"

"Yes, it is," Tharn answered, but as he did so, the tattoo on his left eye began to shimmer. The dragon uncurled, shook itself like a wet dog and then slithered into Gartan's eye and disappeared. When it had left his face, Gartan choked once more and stopped breathing.

Morlonn bent over and brushed his cheek in a gesture to say goodbye.

"Your dragon is gone and so is your life, but you will be remembered," he said.

He stood up and noticed that Gartan's cloak had turned solid brown and lost its entire leaf-like pattern.

"I am sorry, Gartan, but I am going to take this."

Gently, Morlonn removed the bloody cloak and put the hood on his head so that the cloak hung down his back.

"We need to go!" Rivlok shouted. He picked up his sword after Morlonn had taken the cloak off Gartan's body.

"Yes, we do!" Morlonn agreed and ran towards the rock wall.

"Keep your sword in your hand this time!" Tharn reprimanded Rivlok like a commanding warrior might his subordinate soldier.

As the others ran to the rock wall, Morlonn bent over Gartan again and placed his hand on his head. He apologized for having to leave him there, but he felt at peace with that decision. This was a burial place after all. It seemed to be mostly filled with elven souls and spirits.

Morlonn thought of what seemed to have been Gartan's warning to Alaezdar that he would be a crucial part of the world's salvation or demise. Alaezdar had made a habit of denying his part in this grand plan of the realm, but regardless of that, Morlonn knew, it seemed that Alaezdar possessed some form of this magic, whether he believed it to be true or not.

Standing up, Morlonn became determined to find Alaezdar and not leave the catacombs. He saw Tharn and Rivlok running to the wall, but he could not see where they might be going after that. He needed to catch them and rally them to find Alaezdar.

By the time he reached them, they were standing at the rock face and looking again for a secret entrance.

"There is no way out from here!" Rivlok shouted at Morlonn. He was clearly frustrated with the situation. "We need to find Aaelie and help her.

Tharn, what do we do?"

Before Tharn could answer, a cloud began to swirl out of reach just above their heads. Morlonn pulled an arrow and shot through the cloud with no result, but as the arrow disappeared, four wraeths in the form of elves materialized out of the cloud and stood before them. They were armed with shields and short swords and immediately attacked.

Two elves were on Morlonn before he could drop his bow and draw his sword, but Tharn, realizing that Morlonn needed more time, took his sword and attacked one of them.

Morlonn jumped back, dodging a blow from one of the elves which nearly missed his head. He took the few seconds gained by Tharn's attack to withdraw his sword and return with a swing to the elf's head. He was slightly off balance and his swing came up missing his target.

Rivlok, Tharn and Morlonn soon found themselves in an all out melee of attacks, blocks and counter attacks. The fourth elf continued to attack Morlonn, but Morlonn was able to block the blows from either elf, but they prevented him from taking any more offensive action.

All seven sparred for a few moments and then, without notice, the elves turned back into their wraeth mist and floated away, dissipating in the distance.

Confused, the three just stood and looked at each. They had no idea why the elven wraeths left. Morlonn then noticed the two chroks approaching.

"Why would the wraeths be afraid of the chroks?" Morlonn mumbled to himself.

"Why did you leave us?" Rivlok asked as the chroks approached. He held his sword chest high, pointing it at them. "You shouldn't have come back. I would like to kill you both right now!"

"You were supposed to follow us. We came back to get you to where you wanted to be," the smaller of the two answered.

"No matter. We have to get out of here!" Rivlok protested.

"We can do that," the larger chrok answered, his eyes wide with anticipation.

"Not just yet," Morlonn chimed in.

"What do you mean?" Rivlok asked. "We most certainly do have to get out of here."

"He is right, Morlonn," Tharn added. "We have to get out here,"

"We can't leave without Alaezdar," Morlonn said.

"I don't think we have much of a choice," Tharn began and shook his head, regretting having to make that decision. "We need to get Aaelie. If we take time to find Alaezdar, it may be too late. We have to choose one of them. If we wait, Aaelie is surely dead. We can always come back for Alaezdar."

"You should go then," Morlonn said. "I will stay and look for Alaezdar."

"That would not be a good idea," Protested Rivlok.

"You don't understand. We need him and I think he needs us. There are two chroks. You take one and he will show you out. I will take the other and look for Alaezdar. Igs and Smack, can you do this for us?"

"Yes, we can," Igs answered and Smack nodded enthusiastically.

"I will take you deep into the catacombs," Igs said, smiling through his furry teeth.

"Then it is settled. You need to hurry and find Aaelie. I will catch up to you as soon as I have Alaezdar."

"How will you be able to find us? We will be too far ahead. Not to mention that none of us really know where we are going," Rivlok said.

"Don't worry about him, son," Tharn said and put his hand and Rivlok's shoulder to guide him away. "Morlonn is a tracker. He can find his way to a rabbit hole in a rain storm."

Before they could say any further goodbyes, Smack walked down the cliff face a few paces and slipped in between a crack in the wall which could only be seen if someone hugged tightly along the cliff wall.

Morlonn watched them disappear and wondered if he would see them again, or if he really would be able to find them.

"Okay, Igs. Where are we going?" he asked once his friends were gone.

"They will be keeping him from seeing the Guardian. The wraeths do not want him to see the Guardian, so I think they will be trying to entomb him. So, we will be going deep into the catacombs. There we should find him."

"Well, then, lead the way, my furry friend."

David L. McDaniel

Chapter 21

Kunther awoke from a fitful sleep. He was thankful to have a cot, but it was stiff, uncomfortable, and noisy. It creaked every time he moved, always waking him up. The cell smelled of urine and mold. The walls looked like they were moving from the wet dew dripping from within. It was dark save for a small candle provided by the guard outside. They told him he was a guest, but they placed him in the dungeon and locked the door.

Granted, he wasn't treated like a prisoner in the sense that he had been well fed the night before and the cot was brought in with a pillow and he had more blankets than he needed, so in all those respects, he was comfortable.

Not able to sleep another minute he rolled over and placed his feet on the cold stone. Mumbling to himself, he found his boots and put them back on. He could smell his own stink and his clothes were damp, even though he had never removed them before falling asleep.

"Guard, what time is it?" Kunther yelled as he rubbed the top of his head.

"About an hour before sunrise," the scruffy guard outside the door answered.

"Can I have breakfast?"

No response came from the guard.

"Coffee then?" Kunther asked, knowing no response would come.

"I have to piss."

The latch on the door squeaked before being pushed open.

"Thank you," Kunther said as he walked out. The guard followed. "Are they going to leave me here very much longer?"

"I hope not. You are a pain in the ass. I am not accustomed to being a hand servant to my prisoners," he responded.

Not the answer Kunther wanted, but it was the one he expected. Time was running out, and he needed to get back on his horse and head back, hopefully in time to help Alaezdar rescue Aaelie. Walking back to his cell, he began to feel even more anxious about the fact that he might already be too late. He had been gone for about a week now, and they would have to hurry back at a blistering pace to make it back in less than that time.

How did Alaezdar expect us to make it back in time, he wondered. Alaezdar would have to stall his effort, but he knew Rivlok would be pushing them to hurry at every moment, and Rivlok would probably be right in doing so. It seemed to Kunther there would be no good outcome in this whole effort. If he succeeded in bringing the Renegades back to Alaezdar, they would surely kill him.

As the guard was about to close the door on him, he heard footsteps coming down the stairwell.

"Where is the traitorous rat's friend?" a voice rang out as he entered the hall.

"He is here. He just finished pissing," the guard responded a little timidly, which surprised Kunther given this guard had seemed to be such a brusque soldier.

"He is wanted upstairs," was all he said and he turned around and marched back up the stairwell.

"I guess you need to escort me one last time," Kunther said to the guard, smiling to himself.

"Shut up, rat," he said as he grabbed Kunther by the elbow and guided him around the corner and then pushed him in the center of his back repeatedly as he walked up the stairs.

When they reached the top of the stairway, he was met by a group of warriors dressed in red and black leather battle armor. Though they did not wear helmets, they did carry shields upon their backs.

"Here is your rat," the guard said as he bowed his head in humble respect. He turned around and went back down to his damp and dark duty station.

One of the warriors grabbed Kunther by the arm and led him through the castle without saying a single word until they passed the mess where servants were preparing the morning meal.

"Grab'm a roll!" one of the warriors yelled to one of the busy kitchen staff, but he did not stop walking. They continued at a brisk pace, not stopping to wait for his morning roll. They came outside and entered an open bailey as the sun's morning light began to crest over into the fortress.

Seven horses were standing there, loaded and ready to go. They had some protection on their chest and legs, but nothing covering their barrels except small bags. It looked like they were prepped more for speed than combat. Only walls surrounded the area except for a large double door wooden gate that was being swung open as they walked in.

"Mister?" a small timid voice came from behind.

Kunther turned around and a young boy held out a piece of bread for Kunther to take. Kunther looked at one of the warriors as if to ask permission to take the roll.

"Take it, you fool!" he said to Kunther as if disgusted that he hadn't taken it already. "Get out of here, you mutt!" the soldier yelled to the boy scurrying him along.

The boy wasted no time in turning about and heading back to the kitchen.

"Get this boy suited up!" came a loud voice behind them. A large strong man with red hair and a tightly shaven red mustache. Kunther could tell that this warrior was their leader and was strong and in better shape than all of the others who were subordinate to him.

Quicker than what Kunther thought possible, he was given a leather vest and a shield. His sword and scabbard, which had been taken from him before he was locked up, were returned to him.

He buckled the sword to his waist, strapped his shield over his head and walked over to where the warriors were congregating by the horses.

The warrior with the red hair extended his hand to Kunther. Kunther took it and shook it. The man had a grip so firm that it almost hurt his hand. As Kunther looked into his eyes, he noticed that he had a scar above the left side of his face that started above his lip and went down to his chin. His lip was slightly deformed from the scar tissue.

"My name is Blade. You will address me and only me. If these other nucks talk to you, you may answer, but do not strike up conversation with any of them. Do you understand?"

Kunther shook his head, but promptly received the back of Blade's hand.

"You will not respond to me by rattling your brains! Let's try this again. Do you understand?"

"Yes, I do," he answered and felt his lip beginning to swell.

"Get on that horse and wait," Blade said, pointing to the smallest horse It looked more like a pony than a horse to Kunther. He did as instructed, ran to the horse, and waited respectfully while Blade whispered a few instructions to his men before mounting up and heading out the gate.

Twelve warriors in all mounted up and waited for Blade to take command. Proud and strong, they respectfully sat atop their horses, perfectly still, awaiting Blade's next command. All of the warriors had different armor and shields for they all came from different areas and different backgrounds. Each shield had different decorations, from dragons on a blue field to dark mares spitting fire on a white field to a blue pixie flying on a green field.

They did have one thing in common. They all had the symbol of red eyes on a black background in the upper left corner.

Only five were archers, and Kunther noticed that their shields were strapped upon their horses instead of their backs, but on their backs were long wooden bows that were more elaborate than anything he had ever seen. They looked to be elven bows, although Kunther had never seen either an elf or an elven bow, but if he could imagine what one would look like, these would be exactly that.

As soon as they crossed the gate, Blade gave the command to pick up their pace and the horses charged forward, running at a blistering pace down the road. They continued with that pace for many miles before slowing slightly to a quick gallop. The riders all continued without comment until the sun went down and they allowed the horses to rest. They ate a few rations, drank from their skins, and continued again down the road, but this time they allowed the horses to walk.

They continued in the dark with only the starlight to guide their path. The Doreal air began to chill the evenings. Kunther enjoyed the slow pace, even though the faster pace during the day made him feel better about his plight about getting back to Alaezdar. Now, though, he was beginning to tire from holding on to his horse as it ran on its little legs trying to keep up with the group.

They rode in the dark for many hours until Blade dropped back and stared at Kunther in the dark.

"How did you come to meet Alaezdar?" he asked.

Kunther began to feel intimidated by his gaze.

"He just arrived in the village one day."

"Oh, he did, did he?"

"Did he ever tell you who he was?"

"No, not until after the raid on the village."

"Did he tell you who he really was after that?"

Kunther paused as he remembered what Alaezdar had told him about knowing this information could cost him his life. He also remembered to use this information as leverage for keeping his head intact, even though he really did not know any more about Alaezdar's whereabouts than what he had already told Carsti Balron.

"Do not worry, young man. I do not intend to kill you. Though you are recognized as an enemy to the guild, it is more of our intention to watch you for the time being rather than kill you. So, I ask again. What did he tell you about himself?"

"He told us that he was a swordsman for hire with Rager's House of Renegades and that he was on the run for a bad thing he did," he said quickly, hoping to avoid the big man's wrath.

Blade laughed so loud that the others in front of him turned around in their saddles.

"Eyes front!" he snapped.

He did not say another word for about an hour. Kunther could feel his rage as he watched him squirm in his saddle.

"I will tell you what he did," he said, breaking the long awkward silence. "He killed my best friend, and I believe he is not done killing. He will kill all of your friends before he is done, because that is what he was trained to do…he is a killer. That is what he will always do." Blade paused, and turned on his horse to face Kunther. "He is not to be trusted, he has his own grand plan, and you small people do not matter anything to him. Know this, young Kunther, he is not your friend."

"Oh," was all that Kunther could bravely muster.

"Yes. I suppose that is all I could expect from you. You don't know anything about my friend. Yes, it is also true that if Alaezdar had talked about my friend, it would not have been positive as they did not like each other. I didn't like him much either, for that matter. Alaezdar came into our guild as young rat such as you, but for some reason he moved up within the ranks more quickly than any newbie accepted into our guild. He attracted the attention of our guild seer, and ever since, he became untouchable from all of us. I think that is what was the hardest to swallow, the fact that it didn't matter that he was good with the sword or that he had earned his way by surviving missions where others had died, but that he was elevated to the elite just by the word of our seer, according to his own plans. Though, I will admit, he was very good with the sword. Then they gave him that sword that was supposed to be magical…" Blade laughed cynically and was silent for a few more minutes before resuming. "Yes, he murdered my friend, and, trust me, I will get my vengeance."

"How did he kill your friend?" Kunther blurted out without thinking, but he was very curious.

Blade stiffened, took a deep breath, and rode silently, listening to the creaking of his leather saddle for a few minutes before answering. Kunther felt it was almost as if he were talking to himself.

"We were on a mission to finally put an end to our main adversary, Reikker-Kol. We invaded his castle late one night when he was away. His elite guard and most trusted warriors were striking a bargain with the Kingdom of Triel to help them with protecting their merchants who were having problems in a mine in the Goblin Tribes Forest, not far from where we are headed now. By doing this he left the castle to be protected by lowly, inexperienced, shall we say, scum. It was just too easy how we were able to sneak into his castle, enter his children's chambers and hold them hostage. Carsti Balron sent another runner to give a message announcing our demands to Reikker-Kol before we had even left for the raid. This of course had to be timed perfectly so that we would raid his fortress and secure his children as hostages at near the same time that he would return. The demand was that Reikker-Kol surrender himself to us and that we would leave his castle, unharmed, and take him to Daevanwood to be executed."

"I am assuming that it did not go as planned?" he asked.

Blade turned his head to look at Kunther in the dark. Kunther could feel his gaze and he thought for a moment the big man was going to reach over and yank him off his horse.

"No, it did not," he answered. "Reikker-Kol got the message just as planned, and as timed, but instead of returning to the castle, he sent a handful of his warriors to find us and kill us. We heard them coming up the stairs for us and in a panic, Red Blade killed one of his children."

Blade paused, stopped his horse, and looked at Kunther.

"You realize what just happened then, my young friend, don't you?"

"I think so," Kunther responded. He feared that he did indeed know the answer.

"I told you the true name of one of our members."

"But you just told me that he was killed."

"Doesn't matter. Before this is over, I will have to kill you so that you do not pass along this information." Blade laughed and kicked his horse to start again. "Don't worry, my young friend. I am not going to kill you, not just yet."

"But, you said you wouldn't kill me…" Kunther whispered. He shook his head in frustration.

They rode in silence for nearly an hour before Blade began again.

"I didn't finish telling you the ending of the story," he blurted out with excitement. "After Red Blade killed the little boy, Rock Blade summarily and without notice, took his sword and disemboweled my friend. He bled out within minutes and died in my arms without saying a word. After that, the battle raged. Reikker-Kol's second-class guards barged through the door. We were outnumbered three to one, but these warriors -- if you want to call them that -- fought like children and we easily killed them all within a few minutes. It was almost as if Reikker-Kol wanted us to survive. Why he would do that, I do not know, because in the end he lost one of his children, his heir. It would've been a good day regardless, had Rock Blade not killed Red Blade. I saw a day where we invaded his beloved keep and killed his heir, but who would've figured that one of our own would kill another."

"How did he get away?" Kunther asked.

"Humph, you would think it not possible, eh? Well, he did escape during the fighting. Their numbers were indeed great, but they were weak, and unfortunately for us, and fortunately for Rock Blade, they kept us preoccupied enough for him to escape while we slaughtered every man who came through that door. I sent another one of our members to search for him while we escaped to safety, but he came back empty handed…he had escaped our grasps. Never again will he get away from me. Next time I will not let that happen, I will kill him just as soon as I see his evil brown eyes."

Blade remained silent a little longer before he rode back up to his guild members. They spoke silently for a few moments and were then quiet for many hours after that. Kunther remained behind, just enough to stay out of their way, but not far enough to make them feel like he was trying to get away.

He wondered if Blade would really kill him after helping him find Alaezdar. Why would Alaezdar send him on this mission to have his enemy hunt him down and kill him? He understood that Alaezdar expected Blade to come in with reinforcements to help with the fiery witch and the gronts, but would Alaezdar really expect to give his life in order to save Aaelie? Kunther assumed that he would, but also he hoped for a better outcome. He could not see how, though, unless Kunther could manage to kill Blade before he could kill Alaezdar.

Kunther continued to follow, occasionally nodding off and wondering when these crazy warriors were going to stop. How could they continue without sleep? He realized that his pony was trained to follow the pack no matter where they went, so he took a chance and laid his head on the back of the pony's neck and, surprisingly, found he could sleep.

He was awakened with a start and he found himself on the ground, surrounded by the group laughing at him. Someone had pushed him off the pony.

"Grab your roll and sleep, you slouch!" Blade yelled at him. "The sun will be up in an hour and we will be on our way again."

"You can do this on an hour of sleep?" Kunther asked, rubbing his eyes.

"We can go three days without sleep, you fool. It seems you can't go a few hours without hugging your mount to rest."

Kunther stood up, grabbed his roll off of the back of the pony and laid it down by the nearest tree. He was asleep faster than he thought possible, but was awakened again with a start.

"Shut your mouth, boy," someone whispered, his hand over Kunther's mouth.

Kunther nodded that he understood and he sat up. The sun had not yet risen, but early morning light trickled through the trees and sparkled through a light dewy haze. All of the others were up, swords drawn and shields up, facing the road, each hiding behind a tree.

Kunther couldn't see anything, but he could hear something coming down the road. Disobeying his command, he went to his pony and found his sword. He wished he had Straight Edge instead. It already seemed so long ago that Rankin had made his sword, but it had been stolen back in Hollenwood, and he would never see it again.

Blade spoke to another member, named Blade, Kunther surmised, as he was the only man he was allowed to talk to. They were all named Blade as far as he was concerned. It was a confusing mandate when surrounded by more than one person, but who was he to argue? The two crouched behind the tree in conversation and pointed down the road, and Kunther could hear the sound of horse hooves and a rackety old wagon in tow, creaking in agony.

One of the other men came from behind him and crouched next to him, put his hand on his shoulder and smiled.

"We are going to have a good old fashioned raid with a small group of Trielian warriors. Stay back, boy. These warriors aren't slouches. You are going to see some experienced fighting on both sides. I guarantee you a good show this morning."

"What is your name?" Kunther asked without thinking of the consequences. He was just curious at first, but then he thought, "What does it matter? Blade said I was to die soon anyhow."

The man smiled, but said nothing.

He then stood and ran from tree to tree, keeping concealed. Kunther stayed hidden behind one tree and waited. He wanted to fight, and he heard Blade's voice echoing in his head telling him that he was going to kill him sooner or later, so what did it matter if he fought or hid? Really, he thought, why did they need him along on this mission anyways? He didn't know where Alaezdar really was, other than somewhere in the Goblin Tribes Forest, and yet somehow Blade seemed to know exactly where to go. Ever since they had left, they had been charging like a pack of wolves to sheep. So why did any of it matter?

Kunther heard the wagon approach even closer. Six men on horseback in Trielian dark blue and black, light battle armor rode spread out, three on each side of the road, followed by a tired, worn out looking uncovered wagon carrying what looked to be dark rocks.

Dark rocks, Kunther had seen before, but only once. He had seen a wagon similar to this one behind Rankin's smithy. He had never thought much of it then, but he did remember asking Rankin what type of rocks they were, and he now remembered how angry Rankin had gotten, and how he had summarily dismissed him and threatened him with the hot end of his poker.

Two men sat on the wagon controlling a team of two horses while six more warriors trailed behind, scattered in no particular order. As soon as the wagon reached Blade, he gave a hand signal and two other men loosed their arrows and took out the drivers. All of the Ragers were then onto the road before the two drivers hit the ground. The horses stopped when the reins fell to the path.

Arrows continued to fly, knocking two of the warriors off their horses. Even though they were on horseback, the Ragers had used their advantage of surprise to attack their opponent from the ground and force them off their horses, either by slicing their saddle tack loose or by killing the horse outright.

The archers continued to let loose more arrows. They had capitalized on the initiative and had done their damage, but now the Trielian warriors who were still on horseback had begun to regroup and engage their attackers by charging into the brush and assaulting the ambushers.

Five warriors charged directly towards the archers while the remaining five, now on foot, continued to defend themselves. The two archers, now realizing they were in trouble as the men on horseback came directly at them, began shooting off as many arrows as possible, not taking too much time to aim, but still hoping all or some would hit their mark.

One of the Trielian horseback warriors charged on top of one of the archers and tried to hit him with his sword, but the archer dove flat down to ground, safely, and the sword caught nothing but air. The other archer was not so lucky. He continued to fire while on his knees, still aiming for the warrior charging him, and one of his arrows hit its mark, but only glanced off of the helmet.

The warrior stayed focused, even though the glancing shaft had caused him to take his eyes slightly off his target. After reacquiring his target, he raised his sword and swung downward. He split the archer's skull. Blood splattered on the horse as the archer's body slumped against the tree next to the animal and slid to the ground.

The other archer, who had been lying on his stomach, stood up as the horseman passed him and ran deeper into the woods. By the time the warrior had turned his horse around, the archer was gone and out of sight.

Kunther watched him run right by him and jump on his horse, patiently waiting for his master. Kunther noticed that all of the horses were so well trained that they waited untied, standing just outside of the fray.

"You had better get on your pony and either start fighting or start running!" the archer yelled before he reined his horse back towards the battle. One by one, the men found their horses and charged back into the fight.

They attacked the Trielian warriors with a vengeance Kunther had never seen before. As they fought, each one knew where their members were and either had their back or would knock out their own opponent. No one had to worry about anything other than killing their own man.

The Trielian warriors returned the fight bravely and did not disengage their battle until they were either dead or wounded so badly that they could no longer fight. They did not kill their opponents once the fighting stopped, though, and Kunther wondered why they did not totally annihilate their opponents. Why did they allow the unasked mercy?

Kunther noticed that two men were lying in the road, unmoving in the dirt, while Blade was fighting two Trielian warriors. Though men from the Rager's guild had the upper hand in the battle, all were preoccupied in their individual battles to help their leader, who was now at a disadvantage.

Kunther, finally finding his courage, looked at his sword and thought about Straight Edge again, and how that sword in his hands was a mere toy, and this sword, as crude as it was, was not a toy to look at, or a weapon he could pretend someday he'd use in battle. Today was the day. He ran to his pony, grabbed his wooden shield from the pony's back, and ran into the road.

Both of the Trielian warriors were in front of Blade, but he held a defensive stance, receiving and blocking every blow that came at him.

Spinning and dodging, he countered every attack with a grace that Kunther found amazing.

As Kunther ran towards him, one of the warriors got the best of Blade by using his shield to knock him on his back. The other warrior then went in for the kill by swinging toward Blade's head as he fell to the ground, but Kunther reached him first before he could bring his swing down.

Kunther lunged his sword into the small of the man's back, where his armor exposed his flesh since his arms were above his head. The warrior screamed as his knees buckled and his body went limp and he fell to the ground paralyzed. The other warrior saw Kunther and redirected his attack to him. Blade was still on the ground.

Blade took advantage of Kunther's attack and swooped his leg underneath the warrior and knocked him to the ground. He fell on his side with a grunt, but still held onto his sword and had rolled over to stand back up when Kunther kicked him in the ribs as he moved up on to his hands and knees. Again he rolled over in pain, this time dropping his sword to grab his chest, but he did not need his sword anymore. Blade, now standing up, drilled his sword into the warrior's neck and killed him instantly.

Blade pulled his sword out of the man's neck. Blood now covered both the sword and Blade's feet. He looked around and found that the battle seemed to be over. He saw the rest of his fellow Ragers returning on horseback.

"They're all gone now," one of them said as they faced Blade. "The ones on horseback escaped."

"How many?"

"Only two or three of them."

"I don't think they will be returning after the beating we just handed them. Take anything of value you can find from the dead and hide it somewhere where we can find it on our return trip."

Blade walked over to the wagon and grabbed a chunk of gray rock with his gloved hand. He made sure that none of his skin touched it and he held with care. He lifted it up so that Kunther could get a good look at it.

"Do you know what this is, my young friend?"

Kunther had seen it before, but only in Rankin's shop when he had been an apprentice and Rankin had taken great care in keeping it hidden and out of sight.

"I have, but I don't know what it is," he admitted.

Blade smiled.

"This is ore mined from the mountains in the Goblin Tribes Forest. It is called Goblin-Touched Steel. The Trielian King takes this from your village to make swords. Why is this ugly rock so precious, you might ask. Well, I will tell you. The rock is toxic. If you just merely scratch yourself with this rock, your blood will carry the poison to your heart and make you sick and weak. Sometimes it can even kill you. This is a powerful ore, you see, and all a warrior has to do is wound his opponent and the battle will be quickly over. Tharn is the master of this ore and of its production."

Blade took his sword and swiped it over his thigh to wipe the blood off. Kunther just stared at Blade, curious as to how he knew this.

"Oh, you thought Tharn was just a simple farmer running a tiny, benign little community, did you?" he said laughing, as if reading Kunther's mind, "Oh, he is much more than that. He has been mining this little ore for his Trielian friends and sending it to them three or four times a year, at least…maybe even more, I would imagine. The whole farming scene was just a ruse to cover his mining operation. Did he tell you that he was a soldier in the Trielian army?"

"Yes," Kunther answered, not sure if was actually supposed to answer, "but he had retired."

This made Blade laugh so hard that he started to cough. When he finally stopped, he looked over towards Kunther and smiled.

"Yes, I suppose he did retire in some sort. He retired out of the regimen, but he retired as a high-ranking commander and was rewarded for his diligent service to settle down to some easy duty in the Valelands. But make no mistake, boy, he was fully commissioned by the king of Triel to do the king's business by sending him poisonous weapons."

"This is hard to believe," Kunther admitted.

"Of course it is. Tharn is a very deceitful, very political old man who has been trained years to do what he is doing. Don't feel too badly, Kunther. Alaezdar is just as deceitful as Tharn is, and I look forward to killing both of them before we head back home."

Now feeling awkward, Kunther kicked the dead warrior at his feet and looked at Blade.

"What now?" he asked.

"Good question, my young man. Kneel."

Kunther felt all the eyes of Rager's men upon him. This is it, he thought. Blade was going to kill him right there and then after he had told him so much.

Kunther dropped his sword and kneeled.

"Pick up your sword!" Blade commanded.

Kunther lowered his head, looking to the ground, but then shook his head.

"If you are going to kill me, then just do it."

All of the men laughed at Kunther.

"Just pick up your sword, boy," Blade said, laughing.

Kunther kept his eyes to the ground and reached for his sword. His fingers crawled over to it like a spider until he reached the hilt and picked it up.

"Place one knee on the ground and put your other foot flat. Then place your sword flatly upon your knee."

Kunther did as instructed, but kept his eyes to the ground.

"Now look at me."

Kunther looked up, gazing at Blade, as the large man, standing above him, loomed ever larger with his sword drawn inches from Kunther's face.

"Would you die for those you fight with?"

Kunther nodded.

"Answer me, boy!"

"Ye-yess...I would," he stammered.

"If instructed, would you kill Alaezdar to save my life or another member's life? Think carefully before answering."

Kunther was silent. He knew he would not do that, Alaezdar had been kind to him, but he feared that if he said no, Blade would certainly kill him.

"Yes, I will gladly do so to protect the Rager's House of Renegades."

"Will you hold the honor of the guild above all others?"

"Yes."

Kunther straightened up as he realized what was happening.

"Will you die before breaking the honor of the guild?"

"Yes, I will."

Blade took the flat of his sword and smacked Kunther on the side of the head, knocking him off balance and causing him to drop back down on both his knees.

All of the men laughed as Blade offered him his hand.

"Stand now with us and never break from us, unless in death. I have knocked your old self out of your body and now you stand renewed as a member of Rager's House of Renegades!"

Kunther took his hand and stood, picked up his sword, sheathed it and put his hand on his head. That is going to hurt awhile, he thought to himself.

"We will fill you in with the rest of your vows once we get back. We have a much longer ceremony that involves many more swearing of oaths and a long night of drinking. But that will have to wait until later. Right now, we need to get back to business. But first, we will introduce ourselves."

Blade grabbed Kunther's shoulders and spun him to face the group.

"Gentlemen, I introduce to you Thorn Blade, his name given to him by me. Talon Blade, as he came to us as a thorn in our side, delivering news of Rock Blade, but now he will fight as one of us. In front of you are all of the members that were with Rock Blade the day he killed Red Blade. Half Blade, our only half elf in our guild, Stolen Blade, Battle Blade, Shadow Blade, Mark Blade, and our fallen archer, Twin Blade."

Kunther nodded but felt overwhelmed. He began wondering what he had just agreed to. He had often pretended he was a great warrior, using wooden swords with his friends, but he had never really thought he would actually become one. Well, at least he was now part of a guild with the opportunity to become one.

"Now take that wagon, hide it deep into that ravine back there and cover it the best you can," Talon said, barking the orders for the others to follow. "You," he started, pointing to Kunther. "Take one of the horses from the wagon and transfer your belongings from the pony to it. No Rager is going to ride a pony."

Chapter 22

"I despise waiting," Fyaa spat out as she twirled her red hair and created tiny sparks in between her long supple fingers.

Fyaa and Ra-Corsh stood at the edge of a grove of tall pine trees so clustered together that what little sunshine filtered through them only spotted the soft ground and the small fern vegetation with small, flickered dots of light. They waited on the edge of a rocky cliff that overlooked a small rumbling brook twisting its way through the small valley.

The gronts had stayed behind in the safety of trees. They not only feared the fiery witch, but they also feared the prospect of their upcoming meeting.

"What could they possibly want from us before we meet?" she asked.

"They are there on the other side of the brook waiting for us to do something," Ra-Corsh answered. He pulled his cloak over his head to cover his forehead and pointed to the other side of the grove where a few goblinoid creatures crawled on their stomachs, inching their way in and out of the bushes.

He paused and shook his head slightly underneath his cloak. He was frustrated with her impatience and ignorance. How could she have been in this realm as long as she had and know so little? He knew she had most likely touched every inch of this realm at least twice in the time that she had been searching for her beloved birds of fire.

"How do you not understand these creatures yet? They need proof that we mean business."

"I thought you already established that before you left."

"I did, but these are stupid creatures, filled with hate and mistrust. You have to gain and regain their allegiance and their trust with every meeting."

"Very well," Fyaa sighed.

Fire sprang out of her back into the shape of her wings and they began buzzing and crackling as they formed behind her in the shape of hummingbird wings. She raised her hands and lifted off the ground, slowly at first, but then dove head first down the cliff and flew directly above the brook. She stopped short of the grove and hovered three feet off the ground.

She crossed her legs at her ankles and put her hands on her hips as if taunting the goblins to stand up and attack her while she made an easy target for them.

"You spineless weaklings, what are you waiting for?" she shouted and she raised herself a little higher and pointed towards the trees. One goblin archer stood up from the bush he was behind, nocked an arrow and shot it towards her. Fyaa raised her left hand and created a firewall that sparked and hissed. Dark smoke twirled above her as she waited until the arrow pierced the wall. It instantly caught fire, turned to ash and drifted to the ground.

Moaning in frustration, Fyaa turned and flew back to the top of the cliff and pointed at one of Ra-Corsh's gronts. The gront timidly stepped forward, but then found himself floating in the air towards Fyaa. He started squealing in fear as he was propelled towards her against his will.

"Shut up!" Fyaa told him.

She made a fist and then opened it and slapped her hand on her thigh. The gront's whole body became consumed with fire. He screamed in pain and terror for only a few seconds before his body became limp while it continued to fly across the sky as if it were being dragged.

"Stop, you damned witch!" Ra-Corsh yelled.

Ignoring Ra-Corsh, Fyaa grabbed the gront's body and threw it across the brook and into the grove of trees, catching them on fire as well. All of the goblins then stood up and turned loose a full barrage of arrows and spears towards her.

Laughing hysterically, Fyaa flew into the fray, dodging all the projectiles.

"That's more like it!" she yelled, relieved, and sent a large fireball into the trees.

The Warrior's Bane

Within seconds the brook was filled with hundreds of goblins, some frozen in fear, some swinging and stabbing their swords and spears into the air, not even close to hitting anything. Others shot arrows at her to no avail. Every single one caught fire and disintegrated before reaching her.

Fyaa flew as fast as a hummingbird in between the goblins, antagonizing them with her flames as she passed by.

Behind her two gronts were hacking at the base of a large pine tree with their axes. She heard a large snap and a crack as it splintered at its base and fell off the cliff and into the brook. Suddenly there was a bridge from the cliff down to the brook. Excited for the taste of battle, the gronts began running down across the span of the fallen tree and into the fray of battle.

Fyaa turned to look for Ra-Corsh on the cliff, but did not see him. Gronts and goblins were now in full melee in the brook, and she watched with childish glee as the gronts, to her surprise, fought well and killed most of the goblins they faced with certain ease.

However, the gronts were still outnumbered twenty to one. She was about to even the odds a bit when she noticed two things simultaneously. The grove where the goblins had once staked their ground had escalated into a full-blown forest fire, but Ra-Corsh and a goblin in full combat armor were somehow standing amongst all the flames. The goblin wore a half helmet, a metal breastplate, and metal leg guards and he hid behind his shield with his short sword ready.

Ra-Corsh stood a safe distance away from the goblin, but he had his hands above his head. It seemed to Fyaa that he was chanting again, something he did often that absolutely annoyed her. The second thing she noticed infuriated her so badly that she vowed that she would later take her revenge on him. She realized too late that the spell he was summoning was directed towards her. Her personal fire went out and ice consumed her and froze her like a block of ice before she fell with a splash into the brook.

"I think you have had enough for now, Fyaa!" Ra-Corsh yelled to her as she lay frozen in the brook. Staring at him in rage, she began to work out her revenge.

The goblin yelled something in a language no one except the other goblins could understand, and the fighting stopped. Goblins and gront separated, but all stayed clear of Fyaa and the consuming forest fire.

Ra-Corsh turned and faced the forest fire and raised his hands again. The smoke from the fire sucked towards him like a vacuum and consumed him, but within seconds the fire began to dull as all the oxygen around the trees dissipated. Ice then began to fall from the sky and knocked all the embers from the pine needles to the ground, soundly putting out the fire.

The ice block surrounding Fyaa began to thaw and melt away as the water from the brook washed over it. Breaking free, she stood up and tried to call out her wings, but she found she had not yet received her full power so she ran as fast as she could towards Ra-Corsh. Just before she reached him, the goblin warrior had his sword on her chest. She stopped herself just short of running herself through with the top of his sword.

"What is wrong with you two?" she yelled in rage.

Ra-Corsh turned around, satisfied that the fire was extinguished.

"You stupid witch, this is Pencog. We are here to finish what we started with him!"

"I will kill you before I am through!" she vowed and pointed at the wizard.

"Then you won't find your stupid birds," Ra-Corsh said, shaking his head to mock the obvious. "When we are done with Pencog, he will tell you where your birds are and then you can go. Believe me, I want nothing more than for you to leave my sight. Go bring the girl down here so we can start negotiating."

Fyaa took a deep breath and exhaled. She found her power was beginning to return. She called the flames and they began to shoot out from the fine hairs of her body and then the hair on her head took solid flame. The chain mail on her naked body glowed bright orange again. She turned away and walked into the brook, the water hissing with each step she took.

As she walked, she cursed herself for once again becoming a pawn of the people of the land who should not have been here in the first place. This was her land, her creation, and hers to devastate. She needed partners in order to finish what she had started.

Why did she always become the fool with these witless inhabitants?

If only she could return back to the Time Keep and go back in time and start over. This whole task had been one fiasco after another. She needed to take care of this once and for all and wreak havoc and revenge on all the inhabitants of the land this nasty realm had become.

She began to walk across the fallen pine tree, but halfway up the tree she could feel that that the power of her wings had now fully returned. Fire once again exploded out of her back and her small wings sparkled and hissed and began a loud hum as she lifted herself up to the top of the cliff.

Aaelie was bound to one of the pine trees. Two gronts stood next to her and went to one knee in submission as Fyaa approached.

"Cowards!" she said.

She flew up to them and landed directly in front of the two gronts. Aaelie's eyes went wide in fear, as well, even though during her capture she had had little contact with Fyaa.

"Go to your master!" she said and she pointed down at the brook. The gronts immediately rose and scrambled to get away from her.

"Why must we do this?" Fyaa muttered to herself as she bent over to get a look at the terrified Aaelie.

Aaelie spat in her face, but began to sob. Fyaa recoiled slightly, repulsed by the girl's reaction.

"I show a little compassion, and this is how you show your gratitude?" Fyaa asked as she grabbed Aaelie's bindings. The ropes around Aaelie's wrists caught fire when Fyaa put both her hands on them, and the girl screamed as the fire burned her flesh.

"Oh, does that hurt?" Fyaa asked in mocked compassion.

She grabbed the ropes on Aaelie's ankles and burnt those off as well.

"You're hurting me!" Aaelie screamed.

Fyaa grabbed Aaelie's hair and lifted her to her feet.

"Shut up, you stupid, pitiful weakling!"

Aaelie's hair began to burn in between Fyaa's fingers and it sizzled as it shriveled up and burned away, curling up into small black knots that looked like black worms as they floated away in the breeze. Fyaa continued to grab new hair to burn as the sizzled hair floated to the ground.

Aaelie screamed and kicked and tried to free herself from Fyaa's burning hands. Where Fyaa had touched her neck, just below her left ear, and the back of her head and her face above her chin now all burned badly. She could feel her skin starting to peel away.

She didn't panic, though, until she could smell her own skin and hair burning away with every touch. With all of her kicking, Fyaa only held on

tighter, and the burns went deeper. Finally, when the skin on the back of her neck peeled off into Fyaa's hands, Aaelie jerked her head and escaped.

"Perfect! Run, Aaelie, run!" Fyaa yelled after her.

Fyaa lifted herself off the ground, flew to Aaelie, grabbed her by the wrist, picked her up and flew off with her now five feet above the ground.

"You're burning me!" Aaelie cried.

Fyaa ignored her screams of pain, flew her back to the brook and held her twenty feet above a surprised Ra-Corsh and Pencog.

"You want her?" Fyaa yelled above Aaelie's screams. "Then get her!" she said and she dropped her into the brook.

Aaelie screamed even louder. She fell into the brook with a splash and a thud. The small boulders sticking out of the shallow water knocked her unconscious.

"What have you done?" Ra-Corsh yelled as he ran to Aaelie. "We need her unharmed and unspoiled!"

"Then heal her, wizard."

"It is not that simple, witch!" Ra-Corsh yelled at her. He was nearly whining. "I can heal her, but I will need to rest afterwards and I may not be able to return before the ceremony."

"Not my problem now, is it wizard?" Fyaa shouted.

Her wings exploded out of her back and she jumped up like a hawk and flapped her flaming wings. She took to the air and disappeared above the cliff.

***

Ra-Corsh watched as Pencog issued orders to a handful of goblins and they scrambled over to the girl and dragged her out of the brook. Aaelie's arms and head bounced off boulders before she was pulled along the soft dirt past Ra-Corsh and into the woods. Ra-Corsh thought he heard her moan and she twisted her head as she passed by, and that gave him some hope that he would be able to heal her wounds quickly.

He needed to work fast, and she needed to heal almost instantly. He knew the importance of her health before the sacrifice of the tribal ceremony. Their god Gralanxth demanded an unspoiled human female sacrifice in order for them to summon his help. If they sacrificed this child properly, they believed Gralanxth would rise again from the Markenhirth and wreak havoc upon

259

the opposing ogre tribe. Pencog had made it clear to Ra-Corsh how important it was that they complete their quest with the girl intact.

Ra-Corsh also remembered how Torz had months earlier set up this meeting between Pencog and him. Torz had assured Pencog that he would send his young, but talented wizard to help them infiltrate the human village and to steal the young girl.

"You have two missions to accomplish here," Torz had said as they stood on the rocky shores of Rae-Om Island.

Every young acolyte and their warrior charges had looked for the one who had ripped out numerous pages of the Floating Book after his visionary graduation. Holding the pages in his hand, Torz had thanked Ra-Corsh for his deed. He had earned the right to look into the Floating Book, he'd said, by being number one in his class, and he'd told him that the Floating Book held all of the prophecies of the known lands. Many of them contradicted each other, though, as they were written from both polar extremes of the beliefs of Wrae and those of Kronn. Each had different predictions of the future, but uncannily, both had the same ending. How each side triumphed, though, depended on which side of the belief they were on.

"You will need to head to the Goblin Tribes Forest and find Pencog," Torz had told Ra-Corsh. "He will not be hard to find once you enter into the forest. In fact, chances are he will find you. I told him I would send you to him to assist him in raiding a human village and stealing a girl for their sacrifice. Although not just any girl will do, you need to find the girl who is related to Bor Annessie. She is a very distant relation to him through the female line of Traelyn, daughter of the first human king. It should not be hard to figure out who she is. Bor was killed a few years ago, shortly after we were at their village looking for that young mercenary who is hiding in that village. He is the same one I was looking for a few years ago. I just miscalculated when he would be there. Abduct the girl and the mercenary will follow. It should not be hard to do if you plan properly. Make sure the girl is sacrificed and then, first thing during the chaos of the battle, do not hesitate to incapacitate the mercenary, capture him and bring him to me."

Torz had paused and looked to Ra-Corsh sternly.

"Both of these individuals are important to obtaining our goal of releasing the Blue Wraeth. Do you understand?"

Ra-Corsh had nodded.

"I want this to happen as much as you do. I understand that we must kill the girl and use the mercenary to manipulate the prophecy to our will."

"Good," Torz said. "You have read the prophecies and now know how important this is to us. Together we will work to complete the destruction of the age of the Markenhirth, and to bring in a new era for us."

Ra-Corsh had known he had no choice but to complete the mandate.

Now, raising his hood, he followed Pencog to their makeshift campsite to begin healing Aaelie. When he approached the camp, the goblins ran towards him and encircled him while chanting in the tribal language, of which Ra-Corsh knew very little. His own gronts were nowhere in sight. Cowards, he thought to himself. Just like them to turn and run when he needed them the most.

"Get away from me!" Ra-Corsh shouted and pushed his way through the crowd of chanting goblins. He grabbed one of them by his leather breastplate and swung his body around him. throwing him to the ground. To his surprise, the rest actually cleared away and gave him room.

"Move out of my way," he said anyway. "I need to heal the girl!"

He felt a new surge in his own confidence.

Ra-Corsh found her lying on a makeshift bed of sticks, ivy and ferns which Pencog had been using as his sleeping pad. He approached her and noticed that her hair had been shortened and singed so badly that all the tiny hairs had turned black and now curled tightly upon her head. The hair that remained untouched by fire was knotted up in the sticky blood from the wound on the side of her head. Some blood still ran down her chin.

The burns he might be able to heal, he thought, but he would not be able to keep them from scarring. He could see they were so deep in some spots that her skin would be permanently damaged. With magic, he could only hide it for a short time and give her the appearance that she was unharmed.

He knelt next to her and smoothed out her hair. He straightened out the clumps and the knots as a loving father or mother might do.

"Can you hear me, Aaelie?" he whispered as he bent close to her ear.

When she did not respond, he soothed her forehead with his palm and began to call upon his Wrae to begin her healing. His Kronn was stronger, but Kronn could be unpredictable so he called upon the magic created by the gods Val-Eahea and Raezoures.

Nothing happened for the first few seconds, but his healing powers rarely began immediately. He knew his healing spells took extra concentration, and the powers could therefore take a few extra moments to tap into.

Once he felt the surge of power coursing through his veins and being, he began first to chant the healing spells to close up the wound in her head to stop the bleeding. Within seconds the blood stopped oozing from her head wound and began to clot. Ra-Corsh took his hand and smeared the remaining blood that lay on her face into her skin. He rubbed in small circles until all traces of blood disappeared from her face.

"Now the hard part, young one," he said softly as he smoothed her hair once again. He continued to channel the power from his body into hers, and his face began to twitch and convulse as he laid both his hands on the top of her head. He soon felt the response of the gods reaching into his inner being and pulling his strength to heal the other wounds that were so deep within her body.

He did this for nearly an hour before she began to stir and open her eyes. Ra-Corsh removed his hands, fell back from his kneeling position, sat and pulled his knees to his chest.

"I am done," he said.

He fell onto his back and lay in the fetal position for many minutes.

"What happened?" Aaelie asked.

She began to sit up, but soon felt dizzy and laid back down.

"Stay down, child. Fyaa betrayed us both. Pencog! Where are you?" Ra-Corsh yelled. At least he felt like he was yelling, but his call came out barely louder than a whisper.

When no one responded, he rolled over onto his knees, kneeled on all fours for a few seconds before raising one leg to the ground, put both hands on his knee and forced himself to stand up.

"Where are my Fire Gronts?" he asked.

He walked away, slumping with his head down, until he found a clump of granite boulders and wormed himself in between two that had a perfect crevice where he could lie on his back and feel somewhat protected.

Aaelie watched him leave. She realized that no one was watching her and that he had left her unprotected and, better yet, unsupervised. Taking advantage of his sloppiness, she began to crawl on all fours. She began to feel her eyes prickle and spots danced in her vision. Pushing through the fuzziness, she stood up, looked around and ran into a clump of bushes where she stayed with her head down until her vision began to clear. Then she backed herself into the bushes so that she could bolt and run if necessary when she felt it would be safe to do so.

Fear began to creep up into her chest as she realized that the longer she waited, the sooner they would realize their error and start to look for her. They would scour the woods and find her quickly and she knew she needed to react now, but her fear still seemed to paralyze her. She took a deep breath, steeled herself for what she had to do, stood up and ran out from the bushes.

She did not know which way to go, or how far to go, but she knew she would have to figure that out as she went. First, she just needed to get out of there. She ran from the area where she had last seen Ra-Corsh, but that took her into a clearing where a group of goblins were sitting and chewing on the bones of their last meal. In shock, she panicked and took off the other way. She turned left just before she reached the area where Ra-Corsh was last seen. In her haste she knew she had made too much noise. She heard the goblins drop their bones, snort out their incomprehensible yells and begin to chase her.

The forest began to thicken where she ran, but she continued to push through, moving the branches out of her way as they scratched her face and arms. She scrambled through the thick woods as fast as she could, but within a few minutes she began to feel light headed again. She heard the goblins closing in on her, so she reached deep into herself for the energy to press on through her dizziness.

Her mind racing as to what she should do, which way she should go, but no answers came to her other than to run and to keep running.

The goblins began to yell and chatter and she could tell they were now right behind her. She heard them crashing through the woods with reckless abandon because their skins were hardened to this environment. Hers was not.

She felt a small ray of hope when she reached another clearing in the woods and she was about to sprint through it to make up time when she fell to the ground. She wasn't sure why at first, but as her face hit the dirt, she quickly realized that she had been tackled, but not by one of Pencog's goblins, but rather by one of Ra-Corsh's gronts. The gront had her by the legs and grunted loudly.

Other gronts charged into the clearing about the same time that twenty goblins did, but the gronts had already surrounded Aaelie, their backs turned to her and ready to fight off the goblins. Some of the goblins stood with their short swords and shields in hand, but others did not because they had been too caught by surprise.

Aaelie took advantage of the standoff, shrugged out of the gront's hold on her and started to pass them all. She had only taken two steps when one of the gronts grabbed her shoulder and spun her around and down, slamming her head onto the ground.

The goblins started to close in, but the gronts held their ground and prepared for the imminent attack, but just as the goblins were about to pounce, a horn blast pierced the air. The goblins immediately took to one knee and waited.

Within seconds, Pencog forced his way past the goblins and stood before the gronts.

"Move aside," he said in their common language so that he knew everyone would understand. He had heard Ra-Corsh speak it to his gronts on numerous occasions.

They hesitated at first, but when Pencog bared his teeth and hissed at them, they backed away. Aaelie sat with her knees up to her face and cried as Pencog approached her.

"Stand up," Pencog hissed.

Aaelie shook her head in between her knees. Pencog bent down, grabbed her arm and gently pulled her up.

"Come with me, and I will protect you."

Aaelie did not fight him, but allowed him to walk her back to where she had been. Her head began to clear as she walked and she began to rethink her situation. She had to find a way out of her predicament, but still no clear answers came to her mind.

She had begun to give up hope that Alaezdar and Rivlok would come bravely to her rescue. She tried to imagine their arrival, but every time she thought of them heroically appearing at a given moment, she realized that just the odds of the numbers against them would be insurmountable.

As hard as she tried, she could not keep thoughts of doom out of her head. She tried instead to think about the good times with Rivlok, the happier times with him as her best friend, and sometimes more. She thought about her infatuation with Alaezdar, and she would circle back around to the hope that, the expert swordsman, would come to her valiant rescue. As always, though, her thoughts would return to her current situation.

Hope again began to fade away as Pencog led her to a small wooden chariot that had a metal cage on top of it. He unlocked the door and guided her up the steps as if she was his special lady. He held her hand as she entered the chariot, but then closed the door and locked it shut.

Her fear was now complete with the failure and the doom that lay heavy upon her heart.

Chapter 23

Alaezdar floated in the sky, high above the realm. He felt the salty sea breeze sting his eyes as he drifted above the ocean that sprayed the rocky shores of the Rae-Om Islands. He had never been there, but he realized where he was when he saw the gray, mortared and rock-lined Fortress of Prophetic Studies that towered from amongst the fog.

He continued to glide through the salty breeze towards the mainland, drifting inches above the crashing waves, until he rose higher and higher above the realm where he could see every inch of the known lands. To the west was Lake Quarterstar and farther than that was the never-ending forest. To the east and northeast were the lands that disappeared into the uninhabited frozen wastelands.

In one blink of his eye, everything froze for Alaezdar. Land and ocean blended into one. His eyes hurt from the blinding glare of the never-ending ice. Though he felt no cold, his blood chilled. Unsure why his blood would freeze in his veins like that, he realized that he was witnessing something deeper.

He was witnessing the birth of the realm.

He looked below him then and saw a battle waging. Four figures scrambled in the snow and ice, three against one, all using incredible magic against each other, magic such as he had never witnessed before, He knew it existed, but only from the tales that had been told to him by the Watcher's Guild.

Below him, one lone figure, a human, defended himself against a dwarf and two elves. The human seemed to be taking a beating until he changed his shape from a humanoid figure into something entirely different, something obscene. Whether he did it to himself or because of the attack from the three other combatants, Alaezdar could not tell.

From above, he witnessed a large black swirling circle that spun out of control until a massive black demon formed from within it. The monstrous figure then sprouted up from the twisted black mass with wings on his back and large horns on his head. Alaezdar recognized the creature, not as a dragon, as he had first thought, but as the massive, human-like demon that would become known as the Markenhirth.

Above him, a shooting star screamed through the sky and sparks crackled in a tail behind it as it fell in front of him. From the battle below, a fireball now raced up to meet the star, but it crashed into it and split it into four pieces before it returned to pierce the Markenhirth's chest and explode through his body.

The Markenhirth crashed to the ground and disappeared as the four shards found their respective places in the land. One was North, one West, one South and the last, near where the battle had just occurred, crashed into a small mountain range and left a black, gaping and hissing hole in the snow below.

Alaezdar saw that the mountain range was very near the Vixtaevus gap, just where he and his party had entered while chasing after Aaelie.

His body began to descend, slowly at first, and then quickly until he crashed like the star itself at the same exact spot. His body was ripped to pieces and then reformed deep in the catacombs.

He awoke inside them in a place he did not recognize. He floated horizontally on his back, inches off of the ground, looking up at a sky that was not sky, but a rocky cavern. He could not see the ceiling, but instead saw the illusion of sky.

Four icy walls surrounded him and the room swirled from a warm, foggy mist mixing off the cold icy walls. From them stepped a figure cloaked and dark.

Alaezdar now saw the small streams meandering into the icy walls and disappearing below the cracks at the base. Four long, headless snake-like figures appeared from out of the cracks and wiggled out into the soft grassy dirt under him. He could see from the corner of his eyes that as the snakes reached the center of the room, they began to grow.

His arms and his feet dangled down now and almost touched the grass. He felt as if he were lying on a board no larger than his spine. As he watched the snakes growing, he picked up his arms and crossed them over his chest. The serpents continued growing longer and thicker until they transformed into human skeleton-beings before they transformed into solid creatures.

One at a time, they completed their transformation and as they did, these newly solid creatures stood around him and waited for the others to transform.

"Why is he here?" the first that had transformed asked after the others had all arrived. He wore a crown of gold and silver woven into a tightly tangled vine, the ancient crown of elven kings.

"I have brought him here to end the prophecy," said the warrior that had brought Alaezdar from the center of the catacombs. "You and Meztrae need to decide this one's fate."

"I have asked our great hero, Eranon, to bring him here to us," said the cloaked figure.

"I should've known it would've been you, Meztrae," the elven king admitted. "But how did you enter here? You were not entombed here."

Meztrae laughed.

"You were a fool when you were alive," he said after he'd finished laughing, "and you are still a fool now as a wraeth. Unlike you, I can leave these crypt caverns or catacombs that you call your *sacred* place. I have been granted the power to roam the realm as a spirit, free from Wrae, but using the power of Kronn which was granted to me by the Blue Wraeth."

"Blue Wraeth or not, you do not know who this man is," the wraeth king said.

"This one can release us from our bond here," another elven wraeth said. He was wrapped in a long ceremonial cloak with elven scripts covering the hood and body.

"You too, Kroejin?" The king shook his head in sadness as he remembered the earlier betrayal by both of his advisors. "Neither of you do understand the prophecies as I do."

"You are a fool, King Keiyann Krowe," Metztrae said pointing at him. "You are the reason we are trapped here because you released the human Dar Drannon from this realm instead of killing him. Now we are trapped in this realm until he returns, unless we change the prophecy! This man, this descendant of Dar Drannon, must be terminated per the prophecy. In doing that we will release our bond and be allowed to leave this entrapment and enter our rightful eternal home, our home, not of Val-Eahea, but of a place where the true elven people should be returning."

"And how does killing the man who will bring the return of Dar Drannon bring about this end for you?" the King asked. He was obviously not following Meztrae's reasoning and he was going to let him know that.

"There are many reasons for this man to die," Kroejin stepped in to say. "If he lives, it will bring destruction to this realm. He is a wanton murderer. His actions prove this fact as he has selfishly brought his friends into the catacombs for his own selfish purposes. They will die very soon, *and* he will continue to do things such as this until he has destroyed the entire realm. But, more importantly, if he dies, Dar-Drannon will not return. Therefore the Sword of Valkronn stays wherever it is, never to see this land again. If that is done, the Blue Wraeth will return to his natural form and rule the Known Lands from his rightful elven throne and return the elven people to their natural prominence."

"I do not see how that can be done." The King countered," You may kill this man and end the prophecy -- that I do not deny will happen -- however, I do not see how unleashing the Blue Wraeth upon this land will accomplish what you seek, other than gaining ultimate power for your faction."

"I don't expect you to understand," Meztrae said and stepping in between the Kroejin and the king. He stared at Kroejin as he spoke. "Knowing our end plan is not something that it is necessary for you to know. This one here," he said, pointing his finger inches from Kroejin's nose, "does not know when to stop talking. He has always sought your favor, when in all his time serving you, he was always betraying you."

"Meztrae, you were the one that broke my heart. Not so much with your betrayal, but with your ignorance of the prophecy. Why do you think Kroejin was entombed here? It is because when it came to recognizing the truth, he would always follow it, no matter how much you tried to entice him to change his path. He followed the truth at all costs. After your death, Kroejin turned away from the Agin-Sorae. He told me all about your plans to prevent the return of the first human king and secure all the shards and bring the power to the elven nation. I understand that need. However, all you would be doing would be bringing power to the Markenhirth, not bringing power to the elven nation."

"It does not matter how much you know. You can do little to stop us while you are entombed and entrapped in your crypt. Meanwhile, I am free to roam as I please with the power given to me by the Blue Wraeth."

The king walked over to Alaezdar and looked down at his face as he floated a few feet off over the soft ground.

"Meztrae, you will not succeed in your plan, as only a descendant of Dar Drannon can touch the shard without it being placed within the Quarterstar Talisman. Val-Eahea set that up as a restriction for us so we would be constantly reminded that the only through the prophecy will the elven weakness be reversed. Until then, the shards may never be transported from their original, sacred landing places. Prophecy states that they will not be removed until the line of Dar Drannon comes to remove them. Only he may remove them and then join all of them together. I know you want the shards, as well. You need this man to accomplish your task of returning the Blue Wraeth to his original form and to bring him to power. That is why I know you will not kill this man, as you allude to us right now that you would do."

"You are correct in that, my king. You have once again exposed my treacherous spirit." Meztrae smiled at his one time king and nodded his head before he bowed it and spread his arms out in mock supplication. "You are most powerful and wise, and I submit to your supreme knowledge and wisdom in this matter."

"It is time for you to leave this place, Meztrae. It is not this man's time here in the prophecy. He does not belong here and we need to return him to the outside."

"That is where you are wrong again, my king. I plan on keeping this one safe inside the catacombs, where you will not be able to reach him and where we can keep him until we need him. We will make him your new Guardian!"

"There is no place here that I cannot roam."

"Except that you cannot cross the river to reach the Guardian of Val-

Eahea's Quarterstar. No one but a descendant of Dar Drannon can cross. I know this, and you know this."

As Meztrae spoke his last word, King Keiyann Krowe's body shimmered as if it were being disintegrated into a million pieces, disappearing completely and then reappearing two feet above Alaezdar's body and then, finally, disappearing inside him.

Alaezdar stood and spoke in Keiyann Krowe's voice.

"With this body, I can travel wherever I choose, within the catacombs and without, and I will return him to the outside, keep him far away from you, and make sure he and his friends do not die. You will have to wait even longer to accomplish your goal!"

Keiyann stood up with Alaezdar's body and began to walk it towards the far side of the icy wall, but Meztrae disappeared, only to return standing in front of the icy wall to block the king's and Alaezdar's exit.

Keiyann stopped for only a second as he faced him before Meztrae's shape changed into a much smaller form of the Markenhirth. Keiyann saw the form only long enough to realize what it was before the whole room went dark. The blackness surrounded him and he was completely blind. He was forced to either fight his way out of the body or leave it in order to see.

He chose to fight. Raising Alaezdar's arms, he searched deep within Alaezdar's being and looked for the Wrae magic he could call upon. He found the magic he needed but it was surrounded by the Kronn, and he could not immediately call upon it for use. He attempted to pull it out, but he felt his form being tossed about the cavern landing and he was thrown up against one side of the wall and then slammed into the other. He heard Meztrae speaking, but he could not make out the words.

Keiyann continued to try to break past the Kronn to release the Wrae magic so that he could fight back, but he found the hard shell of Kronn stopping him at every moment. He knew he would either have to break past the Kronn to access the Wrae Magic and fight or give up and leave Alaezdar's body. Otherwise Meztrae would destroy it.

Darkness consumed Keiyann, and he begun to lose sight of everything as Alaezdar's body continued to be slammed from one side of the cavern to the other. He tried again to call upon the Wrae, but he could not release it. He could feel Alaezdar's body weakening with every blow against a wall.

He needed to do something and he decided to call upon Alaezdar himself. He re-awakened the swordsman's consciousness

Alaezdar stood up, not knowing where he was. The darkness now surrounded his being, too, and he felt cold. He realized he was in some frozen interior and he began to shiver. A shadow passed before his eyes, but before he could react, he felt himself being picked up and shoved against a wall on the far side of the room. His body slumped to the floor and he began to lose consciousness again as he curled up on the soft, cold floor.

"That is enough!" Kroejin shouted to stop as he expanded his body and exploded into a flash of red light lighting up the whole room. It was the last thing Alaezdar saw before he lost his vision and faded out into blackness.

"What is wrong with you?" Meztrae shouted and ran towards Kroejin, stopping short just as he rematerialized into his elven form.

"You two are fighting over the same end result," Kroejin said. "Whether you want him alive or dead, you have forgotten one crucial thing, and that is where I stand in this whole ridiculous prophecy game."

Kroejin raised his hand and pointed at Alaezdar. He raised him into the air, but his body slumped as he floated unconscious and his feet dragged across the cold floor as if he was being pulled towards Kroejin. Alaezdar's body slipped passed Meztrae.

"What does your opinion matter? You are a weak-minded fool who only follows your master, your king…your failure to the elven kingdom of a king!" Meztrae shouted.

"I want to rest in peace and I do not care if this man dies or lives!" Kroejin said as he raised his arms and slammed his fists together to create a bright light that pushed Meztrae against the wall and pulled Keiyann Krowe out of Alaezdar's body.

The two spirits remained slumped on the cavern floor and Kroejin dove on top of Alaezdar's body and disappeared. Meztrae looked at the now blank space and saw Kroejin had taken Alaezdar with him.

They reappeared on the other side of the river before the Guardian, who sat at a stone table reading a book with his elbows on the table and his fingertips wrapped around his forehead. As they arrived, he stood up and Kroejin pushed the dazed Alaezdar down to his knees.

"Stay on your knees like a dog, you human scum," he said.

Alaezdar, still in a haze, stared at the ground.

"What do you want, Kroejin?" the Guardian said. He stood and placed his hands behind his back.

"You are the only one trapped here who can tell us the truth. Since you are not a wraeth, and since you are the only one with access to these books, you can tell us if this man is the one the prophecy speaks of."

The Guardian studied Alaezdar from a distance and seemed to pierce his eyes.

"I cannot tell."

"You are lying! I know better than that!" Kroejin shouted.

"I am not lying. I only know what I know from the books that have been brought here from the scholars of history and the scholars of prophecy, and I know these books very well, as I have spent too many lifetimes reading them. Many of these books are written with much bias -- as if when they write something down, it will be believed, no matter what, and if it is believed, it will happen. Much of what I know and have discerned not only comes from these books, but comes from the Kronn that emanates from this ground."

"Then tell me what you know," Kroejin demanded.

"I know that the one the prophecy speaks of will fall from that star above," he said and pointed upwards to a shining star in the black sky.

Kroejin and Alaezdar also looked up. The appearance of light from the star, bright against the black sky, shone down upon them.

"That is not going to happen, and you know this. Are we made to wait here forever unless we make something happen?"

The Guardian smiled.

"You may be correct," he said, but he was no longer smiling. "Sometimes that is how prophecies are made to work. They would never come to pass if they were not mentioned, but other prophecies may happen, too, whether or not anyone knows about them."

"You and I both know that is not a star."

"You are correct, but it has been set up by Val-Eahea and by those who write the prophecies to make it consistent to the prophecy of resurrecting the four shards into one star."

"What will happen if I take him out of here and push him back through that star?"

"Then we will know if he is the one the prophecy speaks of. I for one would also like to know that."

Chapter 24

Fyaa had waited for darkness to cover the encampment, but then had to wait four more hours for the goblins to settle down for the night. She knew that she should not wait that long. She needed information from Pencog, but gaining it would be a delicate issue. Pencog's unpredictability made him a dangerous foe, and just as dangerous as an ally.

She laughed in disgust as she watched the gronts mingle with the goblins, a race so unintelligent, she thought, that she could not understand how they could even function in any organized manner of combat other than their frenzied killing. Pencog and Ra-Corsh did earn her respect, though, given their talent to control these beasts to do their bidding and to fight for them. She had witnessed them fight against her at the brook and she had seen how the goblins and gronts fought against each other. Now she watched them as they mingled together playing games in the dirt, wrestling, laughing, and speaking in languages that were all foreign to her.

They continued on with their games past sunset. Some then lit small fires amongst the pine trees so that they could continue on even longer, confident in their combined numbers that no outside forces would disturb them. After a few more hours of their unbidden, raucous games, they grew tiresome, and one by one worked their way to certain spots amongst the trees and rocks and fell asleep.

Making her move she found Ra-Corsh amongst those rocks, exhausted and passed out, just as she had hoped. She bent close to his face and studied his features in the dim firelight. The light cast eerie shadows on his face, but she was able to recognize all of his facial features perfectly. Her whole body shimmered in flame for a few seconds and then she rematerialized herself in an exact duplicate of Ra-Corsh.

She only had one more thing to do to complete her transformation. Capture his voice.

"Ra-Corsh, wake up!" she urged him and she shook his shoulder. In his exhausted slumber, he made no movement until she shook him a second and third time and finally hit his head against the rock that he had curled up against.

"Witch, I cannot deal with you now!" he said. He was trying to shout, but he barely was able to grumble.

Fyaa shook him again. He rolled over and turned his back to her.

"Go away and leave me now," he said a little louder.

"Go away and leave me now," she repeated, saying the words slowly until her last spoken word sounded exactly like his voice. Now she was finished.

She stood up, straightened the cloak she now wore which was part of the disguise she had created in her transformation, and rubbed her chin the way she had seen Ra-Corsh do so habitually. She smiled in spite of feeling a little nauseous from looking exactly like him.

This was her realm, her domain, her time to take back what truly belonged to her, and she needed to start by finding her birds so that she could finish what she had started. She needed to find Pencog, but finding him in this cluster of filthy creatures was not going to be easy. Goblins were scattered everywhere, sleeping in the dirt, in between rock crevices and leaning against the trees.

It seemed logical to Fyaa that the leader of this goblin fighting force would have some elevated sense of superiority and would sleep in a commander's tent or some other protected structure, superior to his charges. She wandered through the camp for nearly an hour until she came across a group of goblins standing in a circle deep within a tight cluster of pine trees and tall growing ferns, all just outside the glimmer of the dimming fires.

Two of the goblins broke rank and pointed their spears at her neck. Her initial response was to easily knock them flat on their backs, but she knew that would not be Ra-Corsh's reactions, so she stayed calm and asked them to be seen by Pencog.

The goblins, not understanding her common language, just stared at her while continuing to hold their spears against her neck while they slowly walked even closer toward her. She took a step backward.

"Pencog!" she shouted. "Wake up! I have something of importance to tell you."

In the shadows, she heard a growl that sounded more like a cat in heat than any sound a goblin would make. It was followed by a few guttural words in the goblin language and the guards raised their spears and stepped backwards to their original positions.

"I have no idea what you are bothering me for, Ra-Corsh. Why can't you just rest until tomorrow?"

Fyaa panicked slightly. She had no real reason to wake Pencog other than for her own personal deception.

"I cannot sleep until I figure out what we are going to do tomorrow. I have a few issues with my gronts which might present some problems," she lied.

"Humans are the mostly annoying of creatures, Ra-Corsh. I promise and warn you right now that when Gralanxth returns, I will have nothing to do with you and your stunted race except to exterminate you," Pencog said.

He picked wax out of his right ear with one hand and rubbed the bridge of his over-large elongated nose with the other.

"Please forgive me, great commander," Ra-Corsh said taking a knee even though doing so almost caused her to regurgitate the bile that had formed in her throat. "Please let me speak, I will speak quickly and concisely."

"No, do not hurry. I am awake now. We must drink and eat while we talk."

The last thing Fyaa wanted to do was to eat goblin gruel or drink blood from some form of a creature that had crawled out of the ground. She continued with her deception, distastefully, and played along.

Pencog made a few commands to his guards and they scrambled as if they were going to be punished terribly if they did not return soon enough with food. Pencog kicked a few logs and rolled them towards Ra-Corsh. Two more goblins rushed to the logs and set them upright so that Pencog and Ra-Corsh could sit while two others rushed to build a small fire.

"This is not necessary," Fyaa protested in Ra-Corsh's voice.

Pencog lifted his hand to silence him and waited for the two goblins to finish building the fire. When the fire started to catch and the flames crackled before them, Pencog asked for the drinks. One of his goblins brought forward two goblets, each filled with a thick brown substance. Pencog took them both and handed one to Ra-Corsh.

"Drink," he said, frowning.

Ra-Corsh took the goblet, looked at its contents, and held it against her lap.

"Drink," he repeated, "or you and I will not exchange another word."

Ra-Corsh lifted the goblet and took a small swallow. She felt the thick liquid ooze down her throat and gagged. She forced herself not to spit it out.

Pencog watched her gag, throwing his head back and laughed as she did so.

"You are so much fun!" he growled in between the deep breaths of his laughter. "Is it really that bad?"

"You have no idea," she said and wiped her mouth with the back of her hand. "I am sure you won't mind if I don't finish this drink."

She grinned at him as she put down the cup.

"Oh, so Ra-Corsh has no time for his goblin friend Pencog, no time to share a drink, but you have time to wake me," he said. He was no longer smiling.

"Please, forgive me. Sometimes I get anxious in my plans…our plans, and I forget my place."

Pencog stood up and kicked Ra-Corsh in the chest with the flat of his bare foot, knocking her off of the log stump and landing her flat on her back. He jumped on top of her chest and wrapped his legs around her neck as he grabbed her head. He rolled over on top of her and placed both his feet on her chest. As he pushed her from him, he sent her flying into the air with the great strength that came from his goblin legs.

Ra-Corsh landed flat on her back and looked up to the dark sky. She sat up and rubbed the back of her neck, incredulous of the stupidity of this creature.

"Are you done yet?" she said as calmly as she could manage.

Pencog stood up, put his face a few inches away from hers, and smiled.

Fyaa almost gagged after tasting his breath.

"You are such a bore," Pencog said and took his seat back on the stump. "What must we talk about, my boring friend? After we are done here, I will never deal with you again. In fact, I may even kill you before we are done because you are so dull, you do not deserve to live any longer, let alone experience the joys of fighting and killing."

Ra-Corsh straightened her robe and pointed at Pencog.

"Pencog, you may want to kill me before we are through, but you will not live to fight another battle…if you even try."

Pencog stood up, kicked his stump behind him, and went after her again by picking her up by the collar and pushing his face into hers.

"Now Ra-Corsh is starting to have fun!" he said.

He turned his back to her and walked away.

Ra-Corsh found her stump and set it back straight before sitting down. Pencog came back and circled her, breathing hard and grunting every time he exhaled. She watched him circle her, continuously, and it began to annoy her so much that she considered breaking her ruse and attacking Pencog with every ounce of terror she could muster.

Absolute ridiculousness, she thought to herself. How much more of this must she put up with? Ra-Corsh must be an absolute idiot to align himself with this low intelligence monster.

She waited and waited while Pencog paced around her.

Eventually he found himself bored and had calmed down his fighting urge enough to sit and listen.

"If you would've finished your drink, my ugly friend, you would've found that the properties in the drink would've made you more susceptive to us wrestling around, shall we say. You know this is what we do. You must've forgotten."

"Then I am fine with not drinking. I have grown tired of your extra protocols to communicate."

"You truly are a boring race," Pencog said, admitting defeat. Well, if you are going to be so boring, tell me what you have to say so I can get back to sleep."

"It is about Fyaa. I am not sure she is on the same page as we are."

Pencog laughed again and did not stop for another few minutes. When he did, he looked at Fyaa seriously, not smiling. "I don't think you are truly with us either, so what does that matter?"

"It is more serious than that. I believe she intents to betray us."

Pencog spoke after laughing through his sharp-toothed grin. "You are a strange man. Everyone wants to betray the goblin race. We deal with this even among our own people. And you are just now figuring this out?"

Fyaa was beginning to get frustrated with the whole conversation. She began to realize that she could not have any semblance of an intelligent conversation with this creature and she decided she would quicken the pace of it, if she could, and get to the point.

"All she wants is to find her birds," she said

Again, Pencog laughed and this time did not stop.

Finally, he stood up and when he did, Fyaa stood too and braced herself to be tackled again.

"Are you slow?" Pencog said in between his bursts of laughter. "Everyone knows that! That's why she foolishly accepts helping out people she doesn't want to help. But none of that matters because she is not going to find those birds."

"How do you know that? No one knows where they are hiding. No one has seen them for years," Fyaa said.

"I know because I am a goblin. Only goblins know where they are. This is too much fun. I love watching Fyaa squirm. Ra-Corsh, do you know where the Grimshaeds live?"

"Yes, I know Grimshaeds and I know where they live. They have overrun Mervyyx. I have been there and I have seen it."

"Ra-Corsh, The Boring, has been to Mervyyx? There may be hope for you yet," he said.

Fyaa watched him grinning in the dark shadows cast by the firelight.

"Her birds are in Mervyyx?" she asked.

"Yes, Ra-Corsh. You are a bit slow, but yes, that is what I am telling you. They are imprisoned by the Grimshaeds."

Fyaa was not sure what she should do next. All she wanted to do was kill Pencog and snuff out his arrogant goblin attitude. If Pencog were telling the truth, though, she realized, finding her birds in Mervyyx would be harder than anything she could ever have imagined.

The Grimshaeds were a creation from a hideous and terrifying event that had happened over two hundred years ago. Mervyyx was once a populous human and dwarf port city north of the Dwarven Har-Ron kingdom. The two races had lived in peace and had worked together mining the rich minerals out of the dangerous goblin infested Goblin Ridge Mountains. An outright goblin attack had always been anticipated, but when the last attack occurred, the humans and dwarves found that they were poorly equipped to manage the attack during the Markenhirth Grimshaed.

The goblins had attacked in massive numbers and destroyed all the mines, burned the village and killed most of its inhabitants. Very few escaped. The goblins also dragged away a few of the human and dwarf females and took them deep into the Goblin Tribes Forest where they tortured and raped them for pleasure. The goblins noticed, to their surprise, that their playthings' bellies began to swell.

All of the dwarf women died in childbirth and half of the human women died, as well, but what those women who survived produced were children that no mother could love. These creatures became to be known as Grimshaeds. Fyaa had been told that no one knew exactly how many existed, but it was believed to be somewhere over twenty, but less than fifty.

She had once stumbled upon these creatures during her travels. They had come upon her and encircled her. She thought at first they were men completely covered in cloaks, but once they had surrounded her, they shed their cloaks and revealed their identity. Their skins appeared to be the hide of a human, but burned so badly that it seemed to have melted and then dried in place. Their ruptured skin oozed out at various parts of their bodies and their heads were completely bald except for a few patches of hair growing out at random. Their teeth were ferocious and sharp and their noses were long and curled out of their faces, protruding from between their deeply socketed eyeballs, which looked like black marbles.

Fyaa had never seen any creature that terrifying before, and they had her doubting her confidence to defeat them. She took flight immediately and left the Grimshaeds standing and scratching their bald, grotesque heads.

They too wondered what they had stumbled upon.

Fyaa now started to walk away from Pencog, but he grabbed her wrist.

"What is wrong?" he asked her. "Are you so weak in the stomach that you can't even talk about them?"

"No, I am just tired. I am going to rest."

"But I haven't told you the best part."

Fyaa had no interest in hearing what else this scum was about to tell her, but she waited a few seconds to see what he had to say. Maybe it would help her figure out how to rescue her birds, but right now she had no desire but to leave and fly away to somehow retrieve her birds from captivity.

"Tell me quickly then," she said.

"I do not intend on telling that witch where her birds are. In fact, with your help, I plan on killing her and impaling her body on our standard so I can display her rotting corpse on the pole forever as our tribe's most prized trophy." Pencog laughed and began again. "Just imagine the fear we can thus spread, not only throughout the tribes, but the human kingdoms as well. We will have awakened Gralanxth, who will fight beside us, and we will have Fyaa, in deathly spirit, chasing away all the weak before every battle! Oh, how glorious that will be!"

"You are sick. That is a dangerous plan!"

"Yes, I am, and yes, it is," he agreed. He stood and put his hands on his hips to display his inflated pride to the imposter in front of him. "Now, go get your rest, my puny little human friend."

Without a word Fyaa turned and stormed away. She was eager to get away from this Pencog and even from Ra-Corsh. As soon as she was out of his sight, she changed back into her original shape.

Now, she thought, she would enact her revenge not only on Ra-Corsh, but on Pencog and his ilk as well. As much as she wanted to flee right now so she could rescue her birds, she thought better of it. She would stay until the battle to enact her revenge and destroy everyone -- even including this so called demon Gralanxth, who had never been part of her plan in the first place.

Chapter 25

Morlonn followed the chrok through the many twists and turns of the maze-like catacombs which had him turned around in his head with every turn. They had walked for what seemed like hours, but he was relieved that so far it had been uneventful and they had had no dangerous encounters.

Since Morlonn was only following the chrok, he allowed himself to think about other things, and he began to wonder if it really had been such a wise idea to separate as they had just done. It did not take long for him to conclude that, actually, he just did not care. He knew what he was doing had to be right. He needed to find Alaezdar. That was all that mattered.

He also decided that he didn't care that Tharn and Rivlok weren't up to helping Alaezdar. He strongly believed that they were putting themselves in great peril by abandoning the one person who they really needed in a fight. Sure, Tharn was a veteran, but he was past his prime, and Rivlok, though young and strong, did not have the experience they needed to overcome the great odds they would be facing when and if they met Aaelie's captors.

Morlonn contemplated the situation with hesitation and anxiety. He did not know what was going to happen once he found Alaezdar and he considered all of his worries as he followed the chrok without hesitation.

And, he realized, he truly did not know the motives of these chroks. Were they leading all of them into a trap? Were they servants to these wraeths rather than the hunters of them? Morlonn could only guess, and at this point had no choice but to follow. Besides, he had confidence in his own abilities to handle whatever came his way. Whether it be more ravages or more wraeths, he would fight and give them the fight of his life.

The chrok stopped and stood still for a few seconds. Morlonn saw that they had come to a triple fork in the maze where the path went in three different directions. Igs began to sniff as if he were a dog that had lost the scent, but Morlonn realized that it wasn't a scent he had lost, but rather a scent he had gained.

"What is it, Igs?" Morlonn asked.

"Wraaaaeth," he moaned and shivered with excitement.

"Focus…are these the wraeths that have Alaezdar?"

"Nooo."

Before Morlonn could say anything more to get Igs on track, he saw three elven warriors, each in battle armor, each one blocking one of the three corridors with their sword tip on the ground and both hands resting on top of the pommel. They stood silently looking straight ahead.

Igs looked to the left and as soon as he did so, one elf raised his sword and took a battle stance. Igs stopped, confused, stepped back and feigned straight ahead. The elf on the left returned to his sentry pose while the one he now faced took a battle stance. Igs jumped up and down twice and then backed off. He watched the elf return to his relaxed pose.

Igs then turned back to Morlonn smiling from ear to ear.

"This is a trap," he said

"What do you want to do?" Morlonn asked.

"You must be kidding. I am going to fall for the trap. I always do."

"What do you mean?" Morlonn asked, thoroughly confused.

"We cannot stay in the catacombs too long without them finding us before we find them. If we find them first, we can consume their magic for a short while, but if they find us first, then they'll use their magic to trick us. We *always* get tricked."

"Well, Igs, don't get tricked this time."

"Ahhhh….yeeess," he whined. "I can't help it. I want to chase them and find the real one."

"You mean one of them is real? You can't tell the difference? I thought you could sense their magic."

"Well, of course I can, but they are all magic. Only one of them is a wraeth and I cannot tell which one now."

"What will happen if I attack one?"

Igs smiled, jumped up and down and clapped his hands.

"Oh, would you, would you? That would be sooo much fun!"

Morlonn wanted nothing more than to take his sword out and smash the chrok's tiny little ugly skull, but he knew that would solve nothing. He did the next best thing. He withdrew his sword and charged with it over his head at the elf directly in front of them. The elf picked up his sword and effortlessly blocked Morlonn's overhead strike.

Morlonn was surprised that the collision of the two blades felt so real. He had not expected a solid figure to respond. He had assumed they were ghosts with no solid form. The elf recovered from the blow and without hesitation fought back with a thrust towards Morlonn's body.

Morlonn did not have a shield to block the thrust so he spun around to the left, just missing the elf's stabbing sword, and he was knocked off balance enough to see that another attack was coming his way from the elf on the left who had now been awakened by Morlonn inadvertently crossing into his view.

Morlonn lifted up his sword just in time to block the elf's blow.

He was now fighting two elves at once, and he began to worry. Out of the corner of his eye, he saw Igs smiling ecstatically, his head turning back and forth toward each elf as he tried to spot the real one.

"Keep fighting! This is good!" Igs shouted amongst the noise of the blades clanging in the corridor at every block, attack and counter attack. "How long can you do this...you are very good!" he exclaimed and jumped up and down clapping.

"Shut up, you furry runt!" Morlonn said, out of breath.

He blocked another blow from one elf, and the force of his movement pushed him back into the third corridor, activating the third elf. Morlonn realized he was now in deeper trouble than he could handle and he found himself backing up toward the center corridor. He held his sword up and, sliding his feet along the dirt, backed up and prepared to launch a counter assault if they attacked him again.

Instead, they walked towards him and inserted themselves between him and Igs.

He was about to take the initiative and attack instead of waiting to see what they would do when he noticed that once all three elves had entered the corridor, two of them had begun to shimmer. These lost their solid figures, turned into a bluish haze, and then combined all into one like a vacuum sucking into the third elf.

Igs screamed.

Morlonn could not tell if it was a scream of fear or delight. All he really knew was that it was loud.

Igs went to all fours and his hair stood on end as if each strand was a twisted wooden thorn, and he then leaped up onto the lone wraeth, still holding its solid form. The wraeth fell to his back and the horn on Igs' head glowed bright orange as Igs lifted his head to show a massive row of teeth that also glowed and crackled in orange flame. He buried his mouth into the throat of the wraeth and began sucking until the elf returned to a bluish misty form and became totally consumed by Igs.

Igs stood up, but fell back into a sitting position and smiled at Morlonn.

"Can we do that again?" he asked. "I can't wait to tell Smack about that. He will be sooo jealous!"

Igs fell fully onto his back and laughed hysterically.

"Yes, yes! That was sooo much fun!" he kept repeating until Morlonn kicked him in his ribs.

"Get up and focus, your freakish rat!" Morlonn told him.

Igs stopped laughing and rolled over, stood up, and without further word walked down into the left corridor.

Igs led Morlonn for another hour before they came to long flight of stairs that led up a steep incline. Igs stopped and started sniffing again. He had found the scent of another wraeth.

"They don't recognize me," Igs muttered in a low growl.

"What should we do?" Morlonn asked and he took a knee next to Igs.

"Your friend is up there, as well, but now he is in trouble. He is with one of *them.*"

"What do you mean by one of *them,* Igs?"

"Those that rule here. Those that are powerful in Wrae too powerful for me to steal. Those that are angry to be here, but yet can control their Wrae in ways that I cannot fathom."

"Can we chase them away? How many of them are there?"

"There is only one, but you can chase him away if you want," he said and turned to look at Morlonn. He was smiling again from ear to ear. "Yes, you can chase him away, just like you did the last one. This one is much more powerful, but ohhh, that would be so much fun to watch you do this. Where is Smack when I need him? He is going to be sooo mad to have missed this."

Morlonn ran his hand through his hair, grabbed a handful and pulled hard. Why must I put up with this ridiculous creature, he thought to himself and grabbed Igs by the scruff of the neck and picking him up off his feet.

"How powerful is this wraeth?"

"Oh…one of the *most* powerful he is…yes he is." Igs pointed up the stairs. "He needs you. Your friend is in trouble. He can only be saved by you."

"Can you help me?"

"Me? How can I help? I have never faced those that rule here."

"I don't know, Igs. You can't just watch and wait for me to do something before you attack. We have to think of something."

Igs shook his head as he started to walk backwards away from Morlonn.

"No, no. It is time that I leave."

"But don't you want to watch to tell Smack all about it?"

"No, not anymore," he said and took a few more steps backward.

Morlonn walked towards him.

"But Smack will be so jealous. Just you wait. You will have so much fun telling him all about this adventure, especially if you help me defeat this wraeth."

"Oh, no, I lied to you. You cannot defeat this one," he said. He was almost crying in fear now.

"Igs, we have to, and together we will. Now, imagine that. Smack will have nothing on you that can beat this. Together we can do this, trust me."

"I..I..I…can't," he said, his head shaking uncontrollably.

Morlonn grabbed him by the scruff of his chest again and pushed him down He pointed his sword at Igs' neck.

"You must. And you will!" he shouted.

Igs closed his eyes, froze, and stayed in that position as if Morlonn had already killed him.

"Are you ready?"

"I will go as I have no choice," Igs said in a tone different than any Morlonn had ever heard.

He no longer sounded like a young child wanting to play a new game. Instead he seemed like a tired and grumpy old man, except that his voice was abnormally clear. Morlonn stooped over and helped him to his feet.

Igs would no longer lead. He demanded that Morlonn head up the stairs first, and together they climbed up the flight of steps, Morlonn in front of the little chrok. With great caution, they mounted each step as if they were counting the paces to their doom. As far as Igs was concerned, they probably were.

When Morlonn was five steps away from the top, he heard talking. He could not make out what was being said, but he knew it wasn't Alaezdar's voice. He turned around and held his finger to his lips to make sure Igs knew he needed to be silent.

Igs looked up at Morlonn giving him a look as if to say --you really need to tell me to be quiet?--

Morlonn strained to listen more, but he still could not hear. He took off his sword belt from around his waist and held it in his hands as he went down on all fours and climbed two more steps. Igs did not follow.

At this point Morlonn did not care. He had no real plan for what Igs could do to help him anyways, nor did he know what he was going to do other than fight. He heard the wraeth speaking again. He seemed to be explaining something to Alaezdar, like a teacher lecturing a student, and then Morlonn heard a third voice that sounded as if it were in a tunnel.

He climbed one more step and peeked his head around the corner to get a quick look. He saw one elven figure in long gray robes, elaborate and ceremonial, with runes and figures sewn across them. The elf looked regal, but also charismatic.

Alaezdar knelt before him with his hands on the ground and looked down into a hole in the hallway. A light above them shone through the ceiling and seemed to be directed towards the hole in the hallway in front of them. The light, Morlonn realized, was daylight.

Morlonn hoped that they were now near to exiting out of the catacombs. All he had to do was find a way to steal Alaezdar from this creature and then – hopefully with Igs' help -- they could find a way out of this mess.

"Move out of my way!" Igs suddenly shouted. "If we are going to do this, let's do this!"

Shocked at Igs' newfound courage, Morlonn stood and let him pass. Morlonn unsheathed his sword, dropped the belt and followed Igs, now running towards the wraeth.

Kroejin stopped talking when he saw Igs and Morlonn charging at him.

"Chroks!" he shouted and he skirted around behind Alaezdar, planted his foot on his back and quickly pushed him down into the hole.

"No!" Morlonn shouted.

He ran past Igs and raised his sword over his head to bring it down with all his might on top of Kroejin's head, but he only sliced purple mist as he was dematerializing.

A second later he disappeared altogether from the hallway.

Chapter 26

Smack led Tharn and Rivlok to an exit from the catacombs where he was able to crawl through a small hole. He crawled outside and then came back in, straightened out his clothes and looked at the two. He was still limping and bleeding from the leg wound he had gotten from the goblin's bite.

"You can leave now," he said as if he were letting his houseguests know he was done entertaining for the evening.

When Rivlok and Tharn only exchanged glances, Smack grumbled and slipped back through the hole and entered for a second time, as if he were training a stupid dog.

"See. Simple. You can leave now," he said.

Rivlok bent down and looked through the hole. He could see the morning daylight shining through even though the crawl space wasn't more than four feet long. He could make out dew dripping from the foliage that hung over the top and concealed the hole from the outside view. He shrugged his shoulders, looked at Tharn and struggled to squeeze through the hole.

Once he was out, he stuck his head back in and motioned to Tharn that he could follow. Tharn wanted out, but there had to be an easier way, he thought. He was worried because they had just fought their way through a hive of venomous snakes and into a den of sleeping goblins. Smack had helped them scare away the snakes without incident, but even Smack didn't know about the goblins. He said later that they must have been staging for a big battle because the goblins never massed this far away from the pass.

"Sometimes they fight each other," he said as if it was no big deal or as if there were no danger that would befall them, but the fight before that point had been vicious enough.

They did not want to run into any more trouble now. They just wanted out. Tharn had to use every ounce of experience and courage to stand and fight and to not let Rivlok know that he was terrified.

When they had first come across the snakes, they thought they were going to have to turn around. They had been walking through tight corridors for hours when they came out into a large opening where the walls seemed to have been chiseled away by hand. The area opened up into three parallel corridors where the walls on all six sides had open crevices dug into them. In the holes were the skeletons of elven soldiers. Each wall also had a row of shelves full of skulls and skeletons reaching all the way to the end of the corridor. Each row went up to the ceiling as high as they could see and disappeared into the illusion of the sky.

"These are the Forgotten Heroes," Smack announced as they walked down the center row. "They have been here for hundreds of years. These ones do not turn into wraeths, but the elves say that someday they will."

They had marveled at the elves bones, lying in their crypts, and were thankful that they were not going to rise. Each of the remains had on the same or similar battle armor that they had been wearing when they died. The elves that had placed them there had not even bothered to replace their armor with anything ceremonious or decorative. It all just covered their skeletal remains as it rotted away in the dark.

Tharn and Rivlok stood admiring the crypts when they heard Smack hissing.

Snakes had began to both drop from the sky and come out of the walls and immediately after Smack had started his hissing, the ground had begun to turn from hard stone to mud.

Tharn looked down and noticed that his feet sank into the mud up to his ankles. A handful of small black snakes slithered out of the mud and curled up around his ankles and twisted around his calves as they worked their way up his legs.

Rivlok had cursed at the top of his lungs and yelled for his companion. Tharn had dropped his sword and was fumbling to reach for his dagger from the scabbard behind him which he kept on his waist belt.

"Don't move," Tharn cautioned Rivlok.

They heard Smack running towards them yelling at the top of his lungs, "Wraeeeethssss!"

As he dragged out the "sss" sound at the end of the word, Tharn and Rivlok froze in terror. What they now saw brought them more fear than the snakes that were working up their legs. Smack's mouth had turned into a gaping hole in his head as if his whole face were nothing more than an open pit with teeth that not only covered the outer edges of his mouth, but also rotated in a circle like the outer edge of a grinder. They could no longer distinguish any features on his head such as eyes or a nose.

He ran towards Tharn and Rivlok, his mouth continuing to make the hissing sound, and as he did so, a bright orange light swirled inside his mouth and the snakes closest to him were sucked up out of the mud and off the walls right into his mouth. They made noises not like common snakes, but more like loud whining dogs as they flew through the air and into the vacuum Smack created until they eventually disappeared into his mouth.

The faster he ran and the closer he got to Rivlok and Tharn, the more snakes he sucked up and the louder the screaming of the snakes became. Tharn felt the snakes on his legs tighten their grip, as if frozen in fear, and they stopped moving upward. Smack ran and ate snakes with an amazing appetite until he stood in front of Tharn and Rivlok and tilted his head upwards.

What now stood before Tharn and Rivlok was a freak of nature, a headless body with an orange and black swirling mass between its shoulder which sucked up snakes at an amazing rate. The snakes around Tharn and Rivlok soon lost their grip on the legs of the two and became caught in the vacuum before they disappeared into the orange cyclone. The mass of snakes were either swallowed up or had worked their way past Smack's vacuum and had slithered back into the walls for safety.

Without warning the orange swirling stopped and Smack's head returned to normal with a sharp pop. Proud and satisfied, he looked over at Tharn and Rivlok.

"It's time for you to go," he said, "but you need to move before the mud turns to stone or else you too will become a forgotten warrior."

With the snake-show concluded, Tharn and Rivlok realized that Smack was right. Their ankles had begun to harden in the mud. Rivlok stepped out of the mud first, but Tharn started to have a harder time pulling free and the thick mud began to tighten even more around his ankles.

Rivlok jumped back into the softer mud and grabbed Tharn from behind, his arms underneath Tharn's arm pits, and wrapped his hands around the back of his neck and pulled him out. As soon as he was free, the ground returned to its solid state.

Smack said nothing more. He turned around, ran to the end of the hallway, and turned right, leaving the open crypts behind them.

Tharn and Rivlok ran without abandon to follow Smack. They suspected that he knew exactly where he was going, but that was when they came upon the goblins snoozing in another large corridor that looked to be their staging area.

Neither Smack, Tharn, Rivlok, or the goblins had expected a battle, but that is what they all got. The goblins seemed to be the most surprised, sitting as they were against the walls, pounding, twisting, and tweaking the leather of their armor. Some had the armor in their laps. Some were teamed up and tightening the leather pieces up for fit.

Smack had seen them first, and when he did, he fell flat to his stomach and rolled to the left against the wall.

Tharn did not hesitate. He knew from instinct and experience that if he retreated, he and his cohorts would lose the element of surprise. He withdrew his sword and yelled as he attacked by slicing the neck of the first goblin he saw, nearly taking his head off. The goblin crumbled to the ground as his head bent backwards and rested on his shoulders. He fell face first and his blood splattered on the ground in red splashes.

Tharn's initiative gave Rivlok the opportunity to realize what was happening and gain some ground as well. He did not have the experience Tharn had and he froze for a second, but only a second. Once he realized what he should be doing, Rivlok attacked, and attacked vigorously, either from pure, violent aggressiveness, or purely out of fear, Tharn could not tell, but attack he did. He killed three goblins, splattering their blood against the cavernous walls, and they sat, paralyzed on the floor before any of them thought of standing up to defend themselves.

By the time the band of goblins had realized what was happening, there were only six left to fight back, and Tharn wasn't going to lose the initiative. He kept attacking and pushed two more goblins back against the wall, slashing and hacking them with his sword until they gave up the fight and slumped to the ground, either dead or dying.

Rivlok had three goblins upon him by the time Tharn finished his attack and could get close enough to help him.

"Smack, do something!" Tharn yelled.

Tharn ran over to help Rivlok and stabbed the first goblin he met in the back just before the creature could swing his short sword onto Rivlok's head. The goblin dropped his sword and crumbled over, reaching his hands behind his back as he fell. Smack stood up with his back to the wall, but did nothing more until one of the goblins that had been lying on the ground, wounded, grabbed his leg and started biting it and chewing into his calf.

Smack screamed. Tharn turned away and broke from helping Rivlok. He charged the goblin and sliced the creature in the back of the neck cutting his spinal column in half. The goblin stopped biting and slumped over. The hot, wet blood spraying from his neck mixed with the bite wound on Smack's leg.

Tharn turned back around to help Rivlok, but he saw that all the goblins were either dead or dying. Rivlok stood there smiling. The blood splattered from one goblin dripped from his left ear.

"I really can do this," Rivlok said and he sheathed his sword.

"Yes, and you'll get used to it," Tharn said.

He put his arm on Rivlok's shoulder and guided him back to Smack. They both bent over to inspect his wound.

"I hate, hate, hate goblins," Smack repeated a number of times before Rivlok finally hit him in the chest and told him to shut up. Smack whimpered and stood up.

"Can you walk?" Tharn asked.

"Yes, I can. Follow me. It is time for you to go," he said and he limped down the hallway.

They didn't have much farther to go before they reached the hole that led out of the catacombs. Tharn had been excited to see the dark little escape route, but then he realized he wasn't going to fit through that hole.

"How am I going to get out here?" Tharn asked.

"Not my problem. I have helped you all I can, and now it is time to me to find Igs."

"We are still so far away from Aaelie," Tharn said. "I am not sure how we are going to find her, but I will look for another way out while you check things outside." Rivlok nodded and scrambled through the hole. It was a tight fit even for him and Tharn had to push against his butt in order for him to squeeze all the way through.

Once outside, Rivlok turned around, stuck his head through the hole and told Tharn that he would only be a short while. Then he was gone.

Tharn wasn't going to wait around. The hole was the remains of an exit at the end of a hallway that had collapsed hundreds of years earlier and had left large boulders blocking the original exit. He backtracked a few hundred feet through one of the main corridors and went back to the goblin staging area to get a shield, just in case he ran into more goblins or ravages.

When he entered the area where their dead goblins lay scattered on the floor, he was surprised how much goblin blood had been spilled. He hadn't seen that much carnage since he had been a warrior in the service to the Trielian King. It made him proud of Rivlok. He had fought well, Tharn thought, but he also felt scared because of how much Rivlok had liked it. Unabated rage such as his, without experience, Tharn knew, tended to get young warriors killed before their prime.

Tharn stepped in between the dead and performed several mercy killings on those few still clinging to life, but nearing the end. He picked up two small shields and then came upon one that he recognized as Corben's, his mineshaft foreman at the goblin-touched steel ore mine. Shocked, he turned it over a number of times. He couldn't believe what he saw and a revelation came to him about the swords.

He picked up the nearest sword to him, wrenching it free from one of the dead goblin's hands, and inspected it. His fears were confirmed. The swords were goblin-touched steel. He knew those swords were made only in one place, but he inspected the hilt anyway and saw the Trielian Kingdom stamp upon it.

Tharn dropped the sword and heard it clanging on the stone floor of the hallway as he ran back to the hole to find Rivlok.

His mind raced. There were so many questions and possibilities about his finding. Foremost on his mind was the question of whether his own king had betrayed him by allowing these goblins to have finished swords. He supposed that the goblins could have stolen them after one of their kills, but he did not think that was the case because the Trielian army did not go further east than Valewood. That is what they had him for.

Second, these goblins could somehow be connected with the goblins who had stolen Aaelie. When he had first found Corben's shield, he had begun to suspect that this corridor was part of a tunnel that ran through the catacombs and led to the goblin tribe. This was a staging area for them. Even Smack had said it wasn't common for the goblins to congregate there.

Tharn was willing to bet this tribe had something to do with Aaelie's kidnapping and he was going to gamble on his gut feeling that this was the case.

He ran back to the hole Rivlok had gone through and he crawled through it as far as he could. He stuck his head out the end and looked around. Tall, majestic pine trees stretched to the sky above him, and a shimmering hazy light shone through millions of pine needles. He wanted to yell for Rivlok, but he was afraid to attract any attention either outside or behind him. He waited.

After about an hour, Rivlok returned.

"I got lost," he said, frustrated.

"Could've used Morlonn, eh?" Tharn asked.

"Get back in there."

"What? Are you kidding? Why?"

"I think we can find another way out," Rivlok said, "a way that might take us directly to Aaelie."

Chapter 27

Alaezdar had fallen to the bottom of the cavern and lost consciousness but he was awakened by someone cupping his head with a soft hand behind his neck. He had been in a haze for quite some time and did not realize where he was or where he had been for the past twenty-four hours. He heard rushing water nearby and the air smelled fresh since it was moving, but it also had the trace of ancient air to it, air that had never seen the light of day.

His vision blurred as he struggled to look around, but he could not see much more than a rocky cavern on four sides around him and the dark sky above where a bright moon shone. As his vision cleared, he noticed that the moon above was not the moon at all, but rather a hole in the top the cavern where outside light shone through.

The man who held his neck now smiled as if he had just been reunited with a long lost relative.

"Sit up, my friend," he said and he moved his hand from his neck to his back to help him sit up.

Alaezdar sat up, looked at the man, and noticed that he looked similar to his father, but without any facial hair. His jaw was gaunt and chiseled, and his hair was long and gray. The skin on his face was tight, yet seemed wrinkled, and his eyes were dark brown. Despite his obvious age, his presence was youthful.

"Who are you?" Alaezdar asked.

"I am the Guardian of the Quarterstar Shard and Keeper of the Elven

Kings and Warriors, Custodian of the Catacombs," he answered with a proud, yet tired smile.

"That is quite a title," Alaezdar commented, not really impressed.

"It wasn't always that elaborate, but I have added a few titles since I have been here," the old man added, smiling.

Alaezdar rubbed his head as a rush of memories began to wash back into his thoughts.

"Aaelie! I have to find Aaelie. Where are Morlonn, Tharn and the others?"

"In time you will find them."

"How much of this is real? Where am I?" Alaezdar asked as he began to remember his situation.

"All of this is real."

"I was just with…an elven king and an elven prophet, I think. Was that real?"

"You may have been, and yes, this is real. The past few weeks have been very busy around here. Many things that happen here are linked with the Time Keep and are in some ways happening concurrently with it. The elven king and his old advisors are feuding over you right now."

"Why me?"

"Because we -- or you, more importantly -- we are the sons of Dar-Drannon and Traelyn, the Great Mother. Traelyn is Dar Drannon's daughter, and we are from her line thereafter."

"I don't know what that means. I don't know who Traelyn is."

"Traelyn is the daughter of Dar Drannon and she had sons with the elven prince, but the elves shunned her and sent her away from their kingdom. That's what caused the war between the humans and the elves. She lived the life span of an elf and kept the war alive for too many years, but in the end, she and her children did the bidding of the land's prophecy that eventually led you to me. This means that you are both the destroyer and the savior of the realm and of the elven kingdom. Though, whether you are the destroyer or the savior depends on the translation of the prophecies."

"I don't care about the prophecies," Alaezdar said. He was shaking his head and wondering how he could ever escape the prophecy madness.

"Oh, you will." The Guardian laughed. "Whether you want to or not, you really have no choice. The realm will be in a total frenzy, either by helping you or trying to destroy you. Unfortunately for you, it looks like whether or not you are savior or destroyer, both lines of prophecy end in your death."

"That is exactly why I am not going to get involved in this prophecy game that the elves have created."

"Unfortunately, I am certain that you have no choice in the matter. Here, stand up. I want to show you something."

The Guardian stood up, took both of Alaezdar's hands, and lifted him to his feet. Alaezdar wobbled a bit as he regained his balance and his vision first blurred and then sparkled.

"You will be fine in a few minutes. I want to properly introduce myself."

"I thought you already did."

"I did, but that is not who I originally was. My original name was Daegon. I was tricked into coming here because those who thought to thwart the prophecy thought I was you."

"I am nobody," Alaezdar said and looked into what now seemed to be familiar eyes.

Daegon turned around and said, "Follow me. Here."

He stepped over to a table where a large tome lay closed. Behind the table were volumes of other books, all stacked neatly on rows of large shelves that had been carved into the wall. The books were free of dust and age and they looked to be as fresh as if they had just been written and bound that day.

"This book -- and all these other books -- tell a different story. All of them mention you one way or another, but none of them tell the same story, except for that fact that each story is based on this quote."

Daegon stood behind the table, opened the tome, pointed to a verse and read aloud.

"A time of peace and prosperity will be ushered in by the sons borne of the Human King's Daughter. The last of her lineage will awaken the power of the Quarterstar by uniting all of the shards and this will restore the balance of the land."

Alaezdar shook his head. He heard his father tell him of such a prophecy, but he never believed any of it, nor cared.

"All want this event to transpire," Daegon began again. "There are those who believe that the uniting of the Quarterstars will indeed unite the land in peace, but he who commands the Quarterstars as one will be in charge of the land and will rule everyone. He will have the power to rule as a dictator. There are those who believe that this savior will unite the races, though, and will allow all the races and kingdoms to live separately, but harmoniously. However, once again all these prophecies involve you."

"Then they are all wrong," Alaezdar said, clenching his jaw.

"That is what I thought, my son, until I read them. Believe me, I have read them all, over and over. Some more than others, because some are relatively recent. Throughout the years elves from different beliefs have brought books to me to read and decipher."

"And where do those books come from?" Alaezdar asked rhetorically, "I will tell you. They were written to make something happen politically or otherwise to strengthen someone's personal advantage."

"That is also what I thought at first. Believe me, I was not happy about being placed here over six hundred years ago, but I have had plenty of time to figure out the truth. And trust me, the truth has not been easy to determine. Those books were written by elves, a despicable race that I once hated, but I have long since learned to respect and, oddly enough, adore them. Elves are an inspired and spiritual race. However, I do not yet fully understand where the gods that they worship come from. I have learned that they are real, even though there are conflicting sources about them. It's as if the gods battle each other for power in this realm, and there is some spiritual conflict between the Wrae Elves and the Sor Elves which I don't quite understand fully yet."

"I do not believe in the gods, elven or other."

"You should boy, they are fighting over you, or us, or Dar Drannon, rather. Our Great Father must return in order to unite the elves, humans, dwarves and all the minor races, as well. Even the goblins are a bastardization of his being, and you are the piece that will bring it all together. Again, whether you live or die will determine the outcome of those fighting for their end. Yes, you are partially correct about these books being written by different points of views – by all of those wanting their own personal outcomes -- however, they all contain some truth to them. That is where I, having been here over six hundred years, will be your greatest benefit. All of the prophecies have Dar Drannon returning, one way or another, but some want to kill him when he returns, and others want to isolate him within the realm somehow. The other thing the prophecies have in common is that you are the catalyst for making his return possible. Many write that your death must be concurrent with that endeavor."

"This is all very fascinating, but it will take much more than you to make a believer out of me, especially if I am to die to make all of this come true."

"I understand. It took me over a hundred years for me to come to grasp the truth. Right about the time I should've been dying of old age, I realized I was going to be here for quite awhile -- especially when I started figuring out the time line in the texts that predicted such events. Once I stopped fighting it, and started learning, I began to listen to the events. I also began to figure out the two opposing sides of the prophecy and came to the revelation that the entire being of our realm is at odds with itself. Our realm, known as Wrae Kronn, is comprised of two opposing forces that work with, and against each other, in order to survive, while the same time each side is fighting for dominance. Wrae is magic and its beliefs are purely elven dominated. Kronn is separate in nature and is magic originated from the land."

Alaezdar remembered his father telling him the same thing, but instead of his telling Alaezdar that he was the catalyst, he had told him that he needed to keep a low profile always, and that he needed to learn both types of magic in order to survive. Alaezdar never listened to him and he was barely listening to Daegon now.

"I am sorry, Daegon. This has been my bane ever since my father began explaining these prophecies to me. I am not here to save or destroy the world. I am here to rescue a dear friend who is in trouble. How can you help me do only that?"

Daegon smiled so big that Alaezdar thought he was going to laugh at him.

"This event has been predicted, as well. Yes, Aaelie needs your help, and what you do next will change many things in the predictions of the prophecy. In fact, it will allow me to throw half of these books into the river here because they will no longer hold precedence to the future. In essence they'll become children's myths."

Daegon walked to the far end of the room, scanned the books, reached into a nook in the corner of the cavern and pulled out a talisman.

"This is the Quarterstar Talisman. It has one shard imbedded into it. It is the portion of the star that crashed into the land right at this exact spot during creation."

Daegon handed the talisman to Alaezdar.

"I have been waiting a long time to do this," he said to Alaezdar.

"What am I supposed to do with this?"

"Find and unite the remaining three shards."

"I am not going to do that. I have to help Aaelie."

Daegon laughed.

"Oh, yes, you are right. You must. And I believe you will"

"Where are Morlonn, Tharn and Rivlok?"

"Morlonn is nearby. A friend will be bringing him to us shortly. Tharn and Rivlok are already where they need to be."

Alaezdar heard a sound coming from above him and when he looked up, he saw Morlonn's head sticking through the lighted hole.

"Alaezdar, I found you!" he shouted down.

Meanwhile, Daegon continued, ignoring him.

"The Quarterstar Shard has powers that can only be harnessed once inside the talisman. I do not know all of what it can do, but I do know that it holds some of the power of the Aaestfallia Keep, or the Time Keep, as you call it. You can transport anywhere within the realm with it. However, not always in the exact time line you are currently in. Kronn controls that. That's where the power of the prophecies comes into play. If you still aren't a believer in the prophecies now, Aleazdar, you will be once you unharness the power of the Quarterstar. The magic in the Quarterstar is a powerful force that has been tasked to complete a mission. What that mission is, one can only guess, but the magic of the Quarterstars together want the prophecies to come true and they will thwart time and worldly events to make them happen as predicted. Be careful how you use this power once you learn it. It doesn't always bend to your will."

"This will help me find Aaelie?"

"If it is in the will of the prophecy to do so, yes. You will be transported at the exact time and place that the Quarterstar deems necessary. It may be minutes from now or it may be days from now. It may even be in the past. That I do not know. I have seen many forks in the prophecy concerning Aaelie. But you must be very cautious of Fyaa. She is the disrupter of the land. She is also a catalyst, but in different and dangerous ways. Do not help her. Do not trust her...ever!"

"How do I use this?" Alaezdar asked and held the talisman above his head so that he could look at the shard in the light.

"I don't know, but I have a feeling you will before you go. First I need you to do something for me."

"What do you need?"

"I am no longer needed here," he said and folded his hands in front of him.

"Aren't you the Guardian of elven kings and warriors?"

"Yes. But in reality I am merely the guardian of the Quarterstar. Everything else is secondary. Besides, these dead elves can take care of themselves. In some small way when you take the talisman, you will become their guardian, although you will not be confined to this imprisonment, as I have. I think I have done my duty, especially since I was tricked into being here."

"How can I help you then?"

Daegon turned and grabbed the stone chalice from a shelf by the books.

"I am so thirsty," he said and handed Alaezdar the chalice. "Take this cup and fill it with water from the river and bring it back to me."

Alaezdar took the cup and walked to the edge of the cavern where a set of crude steps was carved out of the platform leading to the river. He walked down the steps, dipped the cup into the river and filled it, and returned to Daegon. he handed him the cup.

"Thank you, my son. It has been a pleasure waiting for you and finally meeting you. Remember, you are the son of Traelyn, the son of Dar Drannon. Protect that knowledge and do what you think is best. Other than that, I can tell you no more." Daegon looked at the water in the cup, saw the purple swirl beginning to rise out of it, inhaled it through his nose and smiled broadly.

"I am so thirsty. I have not eaten or touched a drop of water since I have been here," he said.

He took a long drink from the cup, draining all of its contents, and turned the cup upside down as if to prove he had drunk every drop.

"It has been such a long time."

Within seconds his hair began to fall out of his head and his skin smoothed itself out like marble. He turned to dust and fell like a feather to the ground. Then, right before Alaezdar's eyes, Daegon was gone.

Alaezdar looked up at Morlonn, who still had his head sticking through the hole.

"What just happened?" Morlonn asked.

"That was my great, great grandfather, I guess you could say, and I think we are about ready to save Aaelie. Are you ready?"

"I have been ready for a long time, my friend."

Alaezdar put the talisman over his head. All he could think to do was to direct his thoughts toward Aaelie, and as he did so he saw her in his mind tied up to the outside of a caged wooden cart. The cart was on fire and she was screaming, and although she was not on fire herself yet, he could tell it would not be long before the flames reached her body. All around her goblins chanted and cheered as the sun began to rise through the trees.

Alaezdar opened his eyes and he and Morlonn were already there.

Chapter 28

Alaezdar looked at Morlonn in fear and amazement. They had been transported to what must have been the exact spot they had been searching for since they left Valewood. Aaelie had to be within their grasp, but how to rescue her still seemed to be an impossible task as she was surrounded by crazed and fanatical goblins dancing around her as the wooden wheels on the cart began to burn.

Smoke was beginning to rise up into the cart and conceal her. The last they saw clearly was her shaking the metal bars on the wagon. After the smoke consumed her, she began to choke and went to the far side of her enclosure where there was still a little fresh air.

"We have to save her!" Morlonn said, but he panicked after hearing Aaelie scream in terror, not knowing if she was burning yet. He knew if the flames did not consume her, the smoke would still asphyxiate her in a short time.

"Here take this," Morlonn said, as he scrambled to remove Gartan's cloak and hand it to Alaezdar. "Use this to get in there and save her."

Alaezdar grabbed the cloak and wrapped it around his body. As he did, his form began to disappear. When Alaezdar saw Morlonn smile, he knew that the effect he had wished for was attained. He reached for Bloodseeker and withdrew it from his scabbard. He could feel through the veins in his arm Bloodseeker pulsing in excitement.

"Stay here," he said.

He skirted along the wood line towards Aaelie's burning cart. To his amazement the goblins did not notice him, or at least he was obscured enough not to attract any attention from their celebration. Not far from the cart, he saw Ra-Corsh and another goblin figure that looked to be their leader watching the event.

This was going to be too easy. How could he have been so wrong? All he had to do was open this wagon, release Aaelie and get out of there before anyone would notice. The smoke might even provide enough cover for him to pull her out and no goblin would ever know the difference.

"Gralanxth the mighty and powerful!" the goblin next to Ra-Corsh shouted.

Alaezdar looked over and noticed a ball of black sludge forming between where they stood and Aaelie's burning cart. The sludge twisted, turned and flipped until it began to form into a large humanoid figure.

"Come to us, Gralanxth. You have been away far too long!" he continued to chant and the black sludge began to change from black to dark green.

This is not good, Alaezdar thought as he skirted behind the wagon, but all he had to do now was to get closer to the cart and open the bars. The closer he approached, the more the smoke thickened, but Aaelie was no longer screaming. He hoped that maybe she had passed out from the smoke and it still wasn't too late to rescue her.

"Aaelie!" he yelled as he neared the cart.

He took his cloak and covered his face as he approached. The flames were now burning the bottom of the wooden cart and he feared he might be too late. When he got close enough, he reached out and touched the metal bars, looking for her, and instantly he regretted doing so when he burned his hand sharply at the touch.

He struggled to look through the smoke, but he could not see her body, burning or otherwise. Where was she, and how could this be? He saw that the barred metal door at the back of the cart was open and he heard another scream that was not a female's.

"Gralanxth, come back!" Pencog shouted.

An immediate response came in a booming voice that permeated their surroundings as loud as any thunder that shook the trees. The loud voice filled the air.

"Your sacrifice is incomplete!"

The goblins stopped their celebrating, frozen in their tracks. Confused, they looked past the trees in fear before going from their hypnotic dancing trance to a combative frenzy. Some of the goblins charged the wagon while others ran deeper into the forest to retrieve their swords that lay in a pile near their encampment.

Morlonn saw the goblins scattering deeper into the woods and pinned his back behind a large pine tree. Something had gone wrong, but he knew that he had to take the new opportunity from this confusion and he nocked an arrow and came out from behind the tree. He took to his knee and started picking off goblins as they scrambled in even greater confusion now from his barrage of arrows.

Alaezdar was still behind the cart. He heard the goblins massing towards him and he rounded the corner of the wagon, sliced, and hacked through a dozen unarmed goblins as they ran to look for their escaped sacrifice.

"Aaelie!" Alaezdar yelled again.

He continued to hack away at the last of the unarmed goblins. He knew he had only a precious few minutes before the next wave of goblins came back with their weapons. The fire had now completely consumed the cart as the morning sun crested above the forested trees.

He watched for a second as Morlonn dropped goblins with great speed and accuracy, but he knew they were too outnumbered to come out of this unharmed. He had to find Aaelie and get out of there while he could, but he wasn't going to leave Morlonn alone.

He heard footsteps behind him. Turning around he saw Tharn and Rivlok. They could not see him because he wore the cloak, but they were clearly on a mission. What did they see, he wondered, as they ran behind him and disappeared into another grove of woods. Whatever it was, he would have to ignore it for the time being. He needed to get to Morlonn and help him out before he found himself at a point where he could no longer be helped.

He crossed over to the area where the creature Gralanxth had been materializing, but he had turned into a puddle of black slime on the soft, pine needle laden ground. He found a few more confused goblins that he stabbed at and cut them down as he ran. As one of the goblins next to Alaezdar ran towards him, ready to strike, Morlonn dropped with another of his precise arrow shots.

"This way!" Alaezdar yelled to Morlonn and he removed his hood so Morlonn could see him better.

Morlonn knocked another arrow and ran towards him while releasing the arrow and taking out another goblin.

Alaezdar suddenly felt the ground shake so violently that it knocked both him and Morlonn to their knees. The ground sent dirt and debris up into the air and immediately, materializing before them, appeared Ra-Corsh.

"What do we have here?" Ra-Corsh smiled as he rubbed his chin. "The mighty swordsman has finally caught up to us."

Alaezdar jumped to his feet and spun to face Ra-Corsh. He swung his sword downward to crush his skull, but his sword stopped inches from the unflinching wizard. At the same time, Morlonn shot an arrow from down on his knees, but the arrow never left the bow and the wood of his bow burst into flame. Morlonn stood up and dropped the bow and its blackened ash fell to the ground.

"Not possible!" Alaezdar shouted.

He tried a side swing at the wizard's ribs, but again found his sword stopping just inches short of his body. Realizing Ra-Corsh had powerful magic at his use, Alaezdar turned, ran to Morlonn and grabbed him by his arm. They both ran from the wizard.

They had only escaped a few feet when Pencog jumped out from the nearest tree, swung his sword at Morlonn and sliced his side as he ran past him. Morlonn fell to the ground and grabbed his side in pain. Alaezdar helped him up and they continued to run into the forest, but they quickly found themselves surrounded by a group of goblins. Morlonn withdrew his sword, charged for the nearest group of three goblins and began to fight them. Alaezdar followed him and attacked one of the goblins just as he was about to take an unblocked swing at Morlonn. Bloodseeker crushed his head and began to sing its happy tune by sending sharp tingles throughout Alaezdar's body. The swordsman slipped into a controlled rage, the type of rage he had found himself most comfortable with.

Alaezdar took out two more goblins as another group crowded around, eager to join the fray. Morlonn fought hard, but after the first few swings, his fighting turned into more of a defensive posture as the goblins began to take turns hacking at him. He knew he was defenseless in armor. He had no shield, and he only wore his hard leather tunic to block any attacks. His wound was now bleeding all down his hip, and he could feel his energy dissipate with every second.

Pencog caught up to them again and jumped in front of Alaezdar. He wanted to finish this battle himself. He had felt betrayed in his effort to bring Gralanxth back into this world and he now wanted to exact his revenge on the man who had somehow just disrupted his plans..

Pencog only had a short sword, but his small stature and quick reflexes prevented Alaezdar from hitting him on either of his first two swings. Pencog ducked, turned and twisted a number of times and kept narrowly avoiding even more swings from Alaezdar's rage-like attacks.

Then Pencog bit with his sword on Alaezdar's hip, causing him to stumble slightly. Pencog went in for a killing blow to the head, but Alaezdar recovered in time to block it. Bloodseeker screamed through his veins and he recovered quickly enough to send a furious counter attack that smashed through the top of Pencog's head and split half of it off down to the shoulder. The goblin beside him dropped to the ground and much of the blood from Pencog's head splattered onto the nearest tree.

The goblins that were fighting Morlonn stopped fighting and ran away after seeing their leader's head in such a brutal state.

"I think Tharn and Rivlok have found Aaelie," Alaezdar told Morlonn and he ran back to where he had last seen them, but he was once again stopped by Ra-Corsh.

Ra-Corsh raised his hands and Alaezdar thought he was preparing another spell, but instead he was motioning Alaezdar and Morlonn to stop.

"Alaezdar, wait," he pleaded.

Still in his battle rage, Alaezdar did not hear him and instead raised his sword and prepared it to come down upon his skull. Ra-Corsh realized that there would be no stopping him and dropped to the ground just in time to miss the blow before he dematerialized away from the danger.

With the wizard no longer in their path, Alaezdar and Morlonn ran into the clearing toward Aaelie's wagon. It no longer burned, but instead was a smoldering heap of blackened wood and metal. As soon as they reached the cart, they were surrounded by a score of goblins that were more than ready to use their numbers to rid themselves of these intruders, even if it meant they would lose half their own number.

***

"There she is, Tharn!" Rivlok shouted as he ran through the woods. Tharn ran to keep up, but increasingly he lost his ground to the young and now very excited Rivlok.

"Are you sure?" Tharn shouted back. He felt this had been entirely too easy.

"Aaelie!" Rivlok shouted as he saw her running away with her back to him.

She stopped when she heard him call out to her, but she did not turn around. Rivlok caught up to her, grabbed her shoulders and spun her around to face him.

"Aaelie, you are safe now," he whispered in her ear as he nuzzled his chin over her shoulders and held her tight. When she did not return his hug, he pushed her back to arms length, still holding onto her waist.

"Aaelie, you are safe now," he repeated again.

This time Aaelie smiled and pulled him tightly to her. Rivlok put his hand on the back of her head and cradled her next to him.

"It is time we take you home," he said, "but we have to hurry."

"I am not ready to go yet," Aaelie responded in a voice Rivlok did not recognize. "Rivlok, no!" Tharn shouted from behind him.

Rivlok pushed Aaelie away again and looked into her eyes.

"Aaelie, your voice…you sound different," he said.

She wrapped her arms around him again, grabbing him tightly and then burst into flames.

Rivlok screamed and tried to get away. He felt her arms latch on tightly around him and he felt his waist and hair began to catch fire where she held him. The more he struggled, the more tightly she held onto him, and the more he burned. His clothes began to catch fire, scorching his skin, and his face began to be consumed by the flames as he tried to pull away.

The ball of fire around him grew in intensity and he screamed as he felt the world around him darken and his pain increase.

"Let go of him!" Tharn yelled.

He charged at the two of them with his sword, but was pushed away by a bolt of fire which hit him squarely in the chest and knocked him to the ground. Tharn pulled himself up on one knee as he watched Rivlok screaming and squirming within the grasp of the burning Fyaa, who had made herself look like Aaelie.

As if Fyaa had heard him, she let go of the unconscious and dying Rivlok and exploded into a bigger ball of flame which erupted in such a great area that a dozen pine trees erupted into balls of fire.

Rivlok crumbled to the ground, a burning heap of flesh and bone.

Tharn's first instinct was to run to Rivlok to help him, but when the trees around him began to catch fire, he thought better of it. Rivlok was dead and could not be saved. Tharn ran, but he noticed that Fyaa, in the shape of Aaelie, had sucked in the ball of fire around her and had returned to the innocent looking girl Aaelie before she herself disappeared in a flash of bright orange and purple light.

Before Tharn had a chance to escape completely from the burning forest, he heard a loud crushing noise coming from a cluster of trees as if a large animal was running through the forest to escape the fire.

What came towards Tharn was not a large animal, but rather an army of ogres, forest ogres who were large muscular beasts with large mouths and fangs protruding from their faces. They wore no armor save vests of tough ox hide. They had black war paint on their faces, all in different designs that emphasized the terrifying features of their faces and bodies. Each carried a weapon, a wooden club, an axe, or a sword.

Tharn realized these were not ogres escaping a fire, but rather ogres charging into a battle. He ran a few feet farther, but heard the ogres gaining on him and he knew he was going to be trampled, if not cut down by them, in a short time. Being the warrior that he was, he did not want to die running.

He stopped in his tracks, spun around, withdrew his sword and swung at the first ogre that approached him. To his surprise, his sword found its mark quite easily and cut down the ogre facing him. Fifty more ogres ran past him, but only three stopped to avenge their fallen warrior.

Tharn took a defensive stance and waited for the ogres to attack. They did, all at the same time, with their short swords raised over their heads. Tharn blocked the first ogre's swing, spun around to dodge the second's swipe and came around to stab at the third ogre as he was caught off balance after missing his opponent. He pulled his sword out of his chest in time to block a second attack from one of the other ogres.

The two remaining ogres looked at Tharn and realized he was not a typical easy-to-kill human. They backed off a few feet to rethink their strategy.

Shortly, the ogres circled around him so that one ogre remained in front of him and another behind him. He watched them and smiled as he feigned a few attacks. Each ogre flinched under Tharn's thrusts.

Now feeling confident, Tharn spun around and attacked the ogre behind him first and engaged in a furious melee of attacks and counter attacks. With every swing and block he encountered, Tharn backed out of the melee and moved to his side. He knew that the ogre behind him was coming in for the kill, but each time he pulled away just as the ogre came in close enough to strike.

Suddenly both the ogres were now standing in front of him, but they danced their way back to their tactic of one to the front and one to the rear.

Tharn knew in his youth he could have knocked these ogres out within minutes. He still had the skills, and he might even argue that his youth was now replaced with patience in combat. He laughed to himself as he realized what he was doing now, using his patience to rest a bit. He was too old for this intense a battle, and he suspected that the ogres knew it as well.

After taking advantage of the stalemate that had led to a small respite for him from the fighting, Tharn took the initiative again and charged after the ogre in front of him. He brought down his sword from over his head, but the ogre blocked his blow. Tharn had used all of his strength in the downswing and the ogre had to take a step backwards too quickly and he fell to a sitting position.

Tharn kicked the ogre's sword out of his hand and brought his own sword down again with both hands into the ogre's chest. The ogre let out a loud gush of air, followed by a squeal of pain, and his throat filled with blood. He died making gurgling sounds in his throat.

Tharn quickly pulled his sword out of the ogre's chest and started to turn around to face the other attacking ogre when he felt a sharp pain in his back and then in his chest. He looked down and briefly saw the tip of a sword and then it was gone.

The ogre pulled his sword out of Tharn's back and then used his foot to kick him face first into the dirt. The ogre growled and grunted, celebrating his kill, before he ran off to join the others in the battle they had initially arrived for.

As Tharn lay in his own blood, almost face to face with the ogre that he had just killed, he thought about his life as a warrior. He was satisfied in the way his life was going to end. He would die from a mission trying to save Aaelie, and even though he had failed, he knew he would die as a warrior and not as an old rancher selling goblin touched swords to a corrupt kingdom.

His chest began to tighten and his vision began to fade. The last image he saw was that of a dozen men on horseback riding through the heavy smoke of the forest fire.

***

Alaezdar and Morlonn had fought off and killed over twenty goblins while maintaining their back-to-back defensive posture. Goblins attacked from all sides, and Morlonn struggled to keep focused on the shimmering, camouflaged shape from Gartan's cloak that he wore. Morlonn fought well, but needed Alaezdar's help a number of times to finish off a few of the goblins that persistently attacked at him. The goblins had kept coming, as if they had nothing else to do but kill the ones who had disrupted their ceremony to bring Gralanxth back into this realm.

Without warning, a massive surge of ogres came crushing in on them all and began to clash with the unsuspecting goblins. Alaezdar took advantage of the distraction and finished off the goblins that were still engaged in the fight with them. The two that were left were easy kills as they had clearly been distracted by the new development. Alaezdar stabbed the last one in the chest and slammed his shoulder into him before turning around and seeing that Morlonn had just finished off his last foe as well.

"We need to find Aaelie now!" Alaezdar shouted above the fray. "We might not get a better opportunity."

Morlonn nodded and they both ran off towards the smoke of the forest fire. The goblins and ogres clashed noisily and Alaezdar and Morlonn almost could have walked casually between their battles and not received a single cut because the others were so engrossed in their battle.

The two ran through the forest searching for Aaelie and calling her name, but their effort was futile. The sounds of the forest burning and the clanging of swords and shields were too loud for their voices to carry.

Soon they came across their two fallen friends. They found Tharn first, face down in the dirt. Without a word, they stopped, saw the two dead ogres lying next to him, and they each gave a solemn nod to the fallen warrior. A few minutes later, they found the burned corpse of Rivlok. Alaezdar knelt beside him and touched his skull. His hair had completely burned away with only a few curling strands left to cover his skinless and blackened skull.

"He was too young, too eager to fight," Alaezdar whispered. "I am sorry."

Before Alaezdar could return to his feet, the battle between the ogres and the goblins had taken another turn and moved in on them again. This time Ra-Corsh's gronts had entered the fray after they had come bursting through the burning forest and into the blackened area where Alaezdar and Morlonn stood.

Goblins, ogres, and the Fire Gront's all fought in a confused, massive melee. It looked to Alaezdar as if the ogres had slight control of the situation as their numbers were greater than any of the other combatants. The gronts were in the worst shape as they were taking on combatants from both the goblin and the ogre throngs.

Morlonn reacted first to the new incursion. He took his sword and stabbed one of the gronts in the back before he spun around and engaged one of the goblins that had a bow and quiver of arrows on his back.

Realizing what Morlonn wanted, Alaezdar sprang up and attacked the same goblin. The two of them had him down within seconds. To give Morlonn a few seconds to grab what he needed from the dead and bleeding goblin, Alaezdar fended off three more goblins after they had tried to change their tactics from ogre and gront to the humans.

Morlonn grabbed the bow and quiver from the goblin, took a knee and began firing away with rapid skill. He took out an unsuspecting ogre, a goblin and a gront in quick succession while Alaezdar chose his combatants more indiscriminately. Bloodseeker once again coursed through his veins and begged for more victims. Warm blood splattered on Alaezdar's face and put him into a nearly satisfied state of raging fury. He felt as if nothing could stop him as he mowed down each new combatant with ease.

Ra-Corsh then appeared from behind the trees and blasted Alaezdar with a searing, magical bolt that hit him in the side of his chest and knocked him to the ground, dazed, but not unconscious.

Morlonn saw what had happened and turned toward Ra-Corsh as his target. He fired a number of arrows directly at him, but each one stopped inches from his head and chest and meekly dropped to the ground at his feet. Morlonn scrambled for a new plan. He looked toward the woods and saw what looked like a girl running through the trees and the smoky haze.

"Aaelie!" he shouted and he ran towards her.

Ra-Corsh heard him call out, turned in the direction Morlonn was running and followed him into the heavy smoke.

Alaezdar was grabbing his hip. It hurt terribly, and already he felt Bloodseeker's healing powers begin to work, although not quickly enough. In pain, he stood up and followed in the direction of Morlonn and Ra-Corsh.

He arrived at a tight cluster of burning trees that surrounded a massive mound of granite rocks stretching in a semi-circle in front of them and towering fifty feet in height. Ra-Corsh was now cornered there, but he had Aaelie in front of him and his knife to her throat. Morlonn stood in front of them with an arrow nocked. He pulled back on his bow and waited for an opportunity to strike.

"You cannot possibly hold her and your spell forever!" Morlonn shouted as Alaezdar came up behind him.

"I can hold out longer than you can hold that bow like that," Ra-Corsh bluffed.

They stood stalemated for two minutes, no one saying a word, while the smoke began to thicken around them and make it harder for each to breath. Alaezdar fought his pain, the dying rage and Bloodseeker's annoyance at the pause, while he raced through his mind, trying to figure out a solution.

He had not come to any good answers when he saw three gronts come through the woods dragging a barely conscious girl who looked like Aaelie.

"What is going on?" Ra-Corsh shouted in the gront language.

Before they could respond, the gronts threw the girl to his feet. Dropping his knife on the Aaelie he thought he had, he spun her around to face him to figure out his new confusion.

Alaezdar and Morlonn could not see at first what Ra-Corsh was seeing, but they saw his face go from instant anger to fear as Aaelie's face turned from the scared girl he thought he had into the face of Fyaa.

Fyaa smiled at Ra-Corsh, winked once at him, and exploded into a ball of fire so hot and intense that Ra-Corsh didn't even scream. His body caught on fire and immediately disintegrated into ash.

Fyaa flew out of the ball of fire and returned to her original form as her fiery wings expanded on her back. She flew up over the granite rocks and flew away.

Alaezdar and Morlonn were blown back by the blast, but they were not burned any more than with few singed hairs on their head. The gronts panicked at seeing their leader dead and they ran. One of Ra-Corsh's gronts grabbed Aaelie by the foot and dragged her off into the flaming forest.

Morlonn was the first to stand up, but before he could chase her, he felt a sharp pain in his back as an arrow went through him. Morlonn arched his back and he fell forward, his arms reaching for the arrow sticking out of his shoulder blade. All at once gronts, ogres and goblins massed around him and Alaezdar as they tried to assess the new addition to the fray.

Talon Blade rode up through them to Alaezdar and pointed at Morlonn with his gloved hand.

"I hope he was as good as friend to you as Red Blade was to me!" Talon Blade said angrily.

He pulled out his sword and prepared to strike Alaezdar down, but a massive group of ogres charged in and grabbed at the legs of Talon Blade's horse while two ogres jumped up and tried to grab his arms and pull him off his horse.

Taking advantage of the attack, Alaezdar ran towards Talon Blade, but he soon found himself surrounded by ogres as well. He had conflicting thoughts. Should he help Morlonn or continue to press towards Talon Blade? He realized that with the attacking ogres, he could do neither. He waved his sword above his head to get the attention of the other Ragers who were now attacking and knocking down their opponents with ease.

To Alaezdar's surprise, Kunther was the first to come to his aid.

"Aaelie is being dragged away over there!" Alaezdar shouted as he pointed towards the burning forest.

"Are you sure?" Kunther asked. He looked toward the burning trees and saw that the smoke and flame were nearly impenetrable.

"Yes, I am sure. Grab Talon Blade and get her, because I cannot."

Kunther spun on his horse toward Talon Blade and helped him knock off the ogres that were attacking him. Alaezdar watched them fight for a few seconds, but soon found that he was surrounded again by ogres and goblins. Most of Ra-Corsh's gronts were now dead, bloodied or dying, or they had abandoned their futile battle.

Bloodseeker screamed in glee as Alaezdar turned and mowed down a few more ogres and goblins with ease as the rage inside him sent him on another fury of reckless abandon. He had just finished killing his fourth opponent when Talon Blade, Kunther and a handful of Ragers ran off into the smoke and the burning trees to find Aaelie.

Alaezdar fought and killed a handful more before the ogres and goblins realized that there really was not a need to be fighting anymore and, as if they had been commanded to stop fighting, they all turned and ran away from the battle and away from the burning forest, finally leaving Alaezdar alone. Now he could check on Morlonn.

Morlonn lay face down in the dirt as blood flowed from the arrow wound in his back onto the ground. Alaezdar pulled the arrow out of his back and rolled him over. He had already lost a lot of blood. His clothes were completely covered in his blood from an earlier wound and his eyes were glazing over, but he remained conscious.

Alaezdar laid Bloodseeker down on the ground since he knew he would not be able to put away the angry sword yet. He knelt down next to Morlonn, put his hand behind his neck and lifted up his head slightly. Morlonn looked at Alaezdar and tried to lift his arm to grab him, but he almost lost consciousness doing so.

"You have to save her," Morlonn muttered.

"I will, my friend," Alaezdar said.

"You told us it would end this way," he whispered.

Alaezdar shook his head. "If anyone could've done it, it would've been us. We shouldn't have separated."

"I had to go for you. We couldn't do this without you."

Alaezdar looked up at the sky and smelled the smoke from the burning forest. He shook his head, knowing that Morlonn was right, but he wished he had not taken everyone on this futile rescue mission. When he looked back down at Morlonn, his eyes had closed and he was gone.

In the distance, Alaezdar heard the last of the fighting. The voices of Rager's House of Renegades lifted through the air and he knew they had taken the advantage in the fray. The goblins and ogres had begun their retreat.

He heard Kunther's voice yell Aaelie's name, and he knew that finally her ordeal was over.

He picked up Bloodseeker and ran away from the voices back to the clearing where Rivlok and Tharn lay dead. When he got there, he found Fyaa, her wings flaming, floating above the bodies, waiting for him.

"You thought you could leave without us talking, Crimson?"

She tilted her head as she spoke.

"What are you talking about? I don't know you."

Fyaa lowered herself to the ground and stepped towards him. Alaezdar backed away as she advanced.

"We were lovers once, but you betrayed me. I know you don't remember, but you will, my love."

"You are just a crazy demon-witch."

"I know that is what they call me, but in reality I am more of a goddess. I created this pathetic world of yours, but you subverted it to what it is now when you destroyed my star."

Alaezdar shook his head, incredulous at the insanity of her words.

"I didn't do anything of the sort."

"You will understand in time. You have been in the elven catacombs. You have witnessed the wraeths spouting their demands to take this world away from us. They want Wrae to rule the world. But you and I are older than they. We can work together and take this realm for ourselves."

"Why would I want to do that?"

"Because you and I are not of this realm, but together we can take it back as we had intended. You and I created this world for ourselves to continue in, but the Kronn subverted our plan. They want to continue with their own plan to eradicate us and our goal. They want to use our magic to bring themselves to power."

"You are crazy! Let me be! I just want to get out of here before my enemies find me."

"Oh, don't be this way," she said, syrupy sweet and feigning disappointment. "You will find that you cannot escape your fate. You and I will finish what we started and then destroy this world. It is what we do. It is what we have always done, and what we will always do. It just happens to be that this world took on its own shape when the star crashed into its natural habitation. It wasn't supposed to happen, but it did."

"You have me mistaken for someone else."

"No, I have not, my love. You and I will finish what we started once you remember who you are. We will have our final battle again in this world and destroy it in the process. I know you don't remember, but when you do, you will know the truth."

Alaezdar heard the men returning from their battle and he knew he no longer had any time to linger there.

"I will take care of this," Fyaa said.

Her wings exploded and spit fire that sparkled off of her back. She rose another ten feet and encircled Alaezdar with flame so that he could see nothing but the fire. He looked at Bloodseeker and tried to return it to his scabbard, but it would not let him. Men and combat were too near. Never completely satisfied, it wanted still more blood.

He looked at his sword, turned it over twice and looked down at Rivlok's charred and unrecognizable body. He knelt down and placed a blackened skeletal hand around Bloodseeker's hilt and stood back up.

Fyaa turned and looked down at him. She knew what he was doing and she flew back to him and stopped inches from his face.

"Pick it up!" she shouted. Sparks and flame spit from her mouth and onto his face. He felt the hot embers bounce off his nose and forehead. They felt wet and hot at the same time.

"I will not," he said and turned his back to her.

She flew in front of him, pushed him down on his back and landed with her feet straddling his chest.

"Pick it back up, you fool!"

"Why is it so important to you?"

"You will die without it. I made sure that this sword landed in your keeping. It is yours. You cannot forsake it."

"I will no longer touch that sword. I have done enough killing. I will not kill for you and I will not be a part of others dying in my name. I am done!"

She kicked him in the side of the head and sat on his chest.

"You will!"

"Kill me now, and be done with it!"

"I cannot kill you until you know that you are Crimson. That is how the game works!"

"Then go away now," he said as calmly as he could. His head was ringing from her kick to his head and his left ear bled from her powerful kick.

She bent over close to his face with her chest touching his.

"You irritate me! You always have, and I cannot wait until *our* day. Our day of love and battle."

She stood up, kicked him in the head again with her left foot and flew away.

"I will fix this! Save yourself now," she called back.

Her wings exploded again in flame and she encircled him once more, sparks flying off of her wings, before she flew off towards the approaching members of Rager's House of Renegades.

Alaezdar sat up and rubbing both sides of his head. He crawled over to Rivlok.

"I am sorry Rivlok. I feared it would end this way," he said.

He stood up and ran away into the unburned section of the woods.

Chapter 29

The forest exploded into flames again. The trees in a ten-mile radius had burned brightly and then burned out, but the trees that were untouched by the first fire now ignited as Fyaa flew in erratic circles and set every tree, bush and stump on fire.

Smoke filled the area and Talon Blade shouted at his men to try to catch and kill the flying witch-demon woman. Arrows flew in all directions as they attempted to hit her, but she easily evaded every single projectile. She laughed as she taunted them with every attempt.

"Kill her and kill her now!" Talon Blade shouted at them again. He worried they weren't going to be able to accomplish that feat as long as she continued to fly around catching the forest on fire.

"We need to get out of here before we are surrounded by fire!" Shadow Blade shouted back to his leader.

"Not until we find Rock Blade!" he shouted back. He turned behind him and smiled at the broken, bruised, and battered Aaelie. "We need to find your friends, don't we?" he asked sardonically.

"He is dead!" a shout came from above.

"Why should we trust you?" Talon Blade shouted back to Fyaa, who now hovered ten feet above him.

"Because they are all dead! Dead and burned alive! Save yourselves while you still can!" she shouted and flew away, leaving them to contemplate her statement.

Aaelie put her forehead on Talon Blade's back and sobbed.

"Now, now, my child. We will see to this ourselves. Search the area! And quickly, before we all *are* burned to death!"

It did not take but a few minutes for them to find something. Shadow Blade called them all together. He had dismounted his horse and stood over Rivlok's charred body.

"Look, Talon Blade. Rock Blade is here."

"No!" Kunther shouted as he dismounted his horse and ran to the body. "How do you know for sure it is him?"

"Look. His sword," Shadow Blade said. He kneeled and ripped the sword away from its skeletal grip and lifted it up so that Talon Blade could inspect it.

"Are you sure it is his?"

"It is the sword he called Bloodseeker. I am certain."

Talon Blade dismounted and looked at the burned corpse and smiled.

"I wish I could've been the one to kill him, but at least I killed his friend. It is nice to see him burned to a crisp like this. How demoralizing for him, though."

He looked a little while longer and then turned to mount his horse.

"Let's get out of here now…before we end up like Rock Blade!"

"What about his sword?" Shadow Blade asked.

"Keep it for all I care!" he shouted, fully seated again in his saddle. He turned his horse and rode off.

Shadow Blade looked over and noticed that Kunther, now known to him as Thorn Blade, was clearly distraught. Shadow Blade motioned to him to look at something as the others rode away.

"Look," he said and pointed to the burnt scabbard on his hip. He then pulled it from the body. "This is not Alaezdar's."

"What do you mean?"

"I know it is burnt, but it is just a common scabbard. Alaezdar's had a very elaborate scabbard to go with his prized sword."

"Who is this then?" Kunther asked. He was just realizing the depth of the trouble his friends had run into when he noticed Tharn's body a few feet away.

"This is Rivlok," he stated, shocked at the realization of his friend's death.

"I think the same fate befell all your friends. We are lucky we got to Aaelie in time."

"I am glad we saved her."

"Now it is time to save you. Get on your horse and get out of here."

"What about you?"

"I am going to find Alaezdar," Shadow Blade said and picked up the sword. "And now you are going to get out of here and ride with Talon Blade, but first I need to make sure he doesn't kill you."

"What do you…"

Shadow Blade took the hilt of Bloodseeker and cracked Thorn Blade on the side of his jaw, nearly breaking it. Kunther fell to his knees, blood flowing from his lip. Shadow Blade hit him again in the face so hard that Kunther knew he was going to have a solid black eye for a month. He went down on his back, but Shadow Blade reached down and picked him up.

"Sorry, Thorn Blade, but you need to tell Talon Blade that I took this sword and am leaving this guild. You tell him that you tried to stop me, but I beat you unconscious and when you awoke, I was gone. Now, go!"

Kunther wobbled while Shadow Blade spoke to him. He helped Kunther up on his horse and hit the horse on the rear to send him back to safety. As he watched him go, he wondered if he was doing the right thing.

Rock Blade had been his friend for many years while they served with Rager's House of Renegades, but when Rock Blade killed Red Blade, he had to keep his solemn vow to hunt down and kill Rock Blade for his crime against the guild. Although it was a crime to kill another within the guild, Shadow Blade could not help feeling that Alaezdar was justified. He and Red Blade rarely got along either, and Red Blade was at best an untrustworthy rogue within the group.

Shadow Blade had not planned on his new decision to leave the guild. He had just come to it as he held Rock Blade's trusted sword. He now felt the need to find and help his friend.

Looking up, he saw there was now blue sky beyond the smoke. The forest fire had burned in the other direction. His only path would be to go deeper into the forest. He looked at Bloodseeker and then bent over and picked up the Rivlok's scabbard and sheathed the sword. It wasn't a good fit. The blade stuck out another six inches, but the two smaller clasps on the sword were clenched shut and Shadow Blade knew that meant the sword for now was either satisfied or knew its master had left.

He then found his horse, tied the sword and scabbard to the saddle, and mounted the animal. He kicked into his horse's flanks, spun around and charged as fast as he could away from the Rager's guild members and the fire and rode deeper into the forest to look for his friend.

Chapter 30

Corben crawled out of the hole from the mineshaft which was just a small aperture in the ground on top of a cluster of granite rocks. Along with many others, he believed that the hole was the very spot where one of the split Quarterstars had landed, pierced the mine and tainted the rock in it which they had called goblin-touched stone.

Corben and the other miners now surfaced out of the hole and hauled up the wooden boxes full of iron ore from the ground. His long, scraggly brown hair was covered in gray dust. He stood up, bent over, grabbed the rope that he had tied to a tree much earlier and dragged his box out from the hole.

The box came up slowly. His skinny, tired arms had been chiseling rock all day long and he was long overdue for some cold water from the stream that trickled nearby. He also badly wanted to kill and eat one of their chickens, cook it over their fire pit, and then rest for a few hours.

If they didn't have enough ore from today's haul, they would have to hit it again hard early in the morning.

"Let's go, you lazy slobs!" Corben yelled over his shoulder. The fading sunlight made him squint. "I'm hungry and we need to get Hormet cooking"

He finished pulling his box up, walked over to the hole, and looked down into it. He could see the lanterns swaying down in the hole and the rope ladder rocking as the men climbed up, one by one. He helped each man out of the hole, took their boxes and dumped them into a large carriage behind two oxen waiting impatiently in their yokes.

The sun still had not slipped behind the forested mountains when he and his crew finished loading the wagon with their day's work of iron ore. Corben looked at the load with satisfaction and wiped his beard as if he had just finished eating a hearty meal. He smiled at his men.

"I think we have enough to make that bastard Tharn happy," he said, grinning. "Now the only question is, do we want to head out tonight or wait until tomorrow?"

His crew grumbled and grabbed their tired backs and knees. He knew that they did not have energy to leave tonight, but they were too afraid to say anything different and make their foreman angry, but the expressions on their faces answered his question for him.

"My sentiments exactly," he said and rubbed his own back. "I want to eat our last chicken and sleep too long...way past sunrise tomorrow!"

All the men smiled, clapped each other on their backs and walked toward their horses that were tied up to makeshift wooden stalls that were no more than posts in the ground with food boxes and water buckets by their feet.

"Let's go find Hormet and get him cooking," Corben announced, but then froze as he saw something moving outside of their camp amongst the forested trees.

"Goblins!" he yelled.

He ran to grab his sword and shield from the pack he had tied to his horse. Before he reached the animal, arrows began flying through the trees and took out two of his men before they could move to protect themselves.

He was out of breath when he reached his horse. Three goblins jumped out from behind the trees and attacked him, but instead of fumbling for his sword, he turned and ran back the other way. He could see that his demise was only minutes away.

In minutes his whole crew lay dead and bleeding right where they had just stood. They never had a chance to run. The barrage of arrows had been too great.

Corben went to his knees and put his hands on the back of his head. He leaned over and planted his forehead in the dirt in hope that they would either spare him in his defenseless position or do away with him quickly.

It didn't take them but a few seconds to surround him and he could hear them talking in their squeaky guttural language. They sounded paranoid to him, but he could not figure out why they would be. He was nothing more than a shivering coward at this point, he thought. They had nothing to fear.

"Sit up!" one of them shouted in a common language.

Corben sat up, and one of them grabbed his hands and tied them behind his back. He looked around him and saw hundreds of goblins in complete battle armor with ten standards waving colorful flags in the slight twilight breeze. The sun had just gone behind the mountains and the shadows enveloped everyone in the darkness of the exiting sun.

The goblin that had spoken to him ordered that they light torches, and a handful of goblins scattered to do so. Within minutes they had large, lantern style torches lit next to every standard.

Corben saw that all the standards were different. Having been out here in goblin country for so long, he had seen many of them already, but some he did not recognize.

A horn blasted in the distance, less than a mile away. The goblins heard it as well, and all of them scattered and formed a semi circle perimeter with one opening from the south. They all waited patiently and Corben could feel their increasing nervousness with each second that went by.

Torches begin to filter through the wood line and he heard horses approaching, many horses, in fact so many that it sounded like they were just crashing through the woods. Then he saw the fist and sword standard of the Trielian Kingdom and he felt hope. He was going to live.

The Trielian soldiers exited the wood line, came to a blazing halt, and lined up ten wide in some places. The others then formed up in ranks uniformly behind the first line. Corben thought they might be analyzing their opponent and would attack shortly, but the goblins did not move or make a sound. They just stood erect and watched the Trielian warriors form up.

One warrior dismounted his horse and with a large grunt slammed his standard into the ground ten feet in front of the first row of horses. He stood there silently with his hands on his hips. A man in full combat armor and a large, elaborately decorated blue and black cloak emerged from behind the horses. He walked boldly and without hesitation up to the goblin that had spoken to Corben earlier.

Corben heard the Trielian warrior's name called out by a subordinate in the first rank and he recognized it, Azrull, as one that of one of the warriors who had been at Valewood during the Doreal Celebration.

Azrull now spoke in the goblin language. Corben could not understand a single word, but he began to worry. The tone of his speech was not aggressive, but was obviously diplomatic.

Azrull leaned down, looked at Corben and then shook his head sadly.

"Are you Corben Annesie from Valewood?" he asked.

"I am, sir," Corben stammered. He hoped with all hope that he was there to rescue him. "What is happening here?" he asked.

"Something very big. Something very big, indeed, and you are the biggest part of our success in tonight's event."

Corben looked down and his hopes began to dissipate. This did not sound to him like an answer that would come out in his favor.

Azrull stood up, faced the goblins, and spoke to them in their language once again. When he finished, they all cheered excitedly for many minutes and then began to dance and build a large fire five feet in front of Corben.

Sensing that the fire pit would be for him, he stood up, but a large goblinoid hand him pushed from behind back down to his knees and kicked his back, sending him to the ground. He tried to get up, but he felt a foot planted squarely on his back and pinning him down. Another foot landed on the back of his head and held his face down in the dirt. He could not breathe with the dirt in his nostrils and he turned his head to the side. The foot adjusted and pinned him down even harder by crushing his left ear.

"This is a momentous day for you goblins!" Azrull said, both in goblin and the common language, for the benefit of Corben. "We will from this day become a partnered force in destroying the First Human King, hence destroying the prophecy. At the same time we will eliminate the power of the two types of magic, Wrae and Kronn. Together we will band together, take control of this realm, and form a new empire that will create fear and destruction to all who oppose us!"

The goblins cheered excitedly and danced even more furiously and out of control.

"Together," Azrull continued, "we will bring back the spirit and unleash the power of Gralanxth in order to accomplish our new reign together!"

The two goblins holding Corben down lifted him up and threw him into the fire that was now fully ignited.

Corben landed face first in the flaming logs and felt his hair burn away first and then his skin bubble on his face. He struggled to stand up, but his hands were still bound behind him and he fell down again. His legs and arms now began to burn, too, and the rope binding his wrists fell away as it burned.

Now he was able to use his hands to regain his balance and stand. The pain from the fire was extreme. He heard the intense and terrifying screams, but then realized the screams were his own.

He managed to step out of the fire. His body was completely engulfed in flames, and he lay on the dirt and tried to roll out the fire, but darkness overcame him.

Soon he was at peace.

Before he faded out completely, he saw a large black ball of twisting smoke materialize into a massive goblin that stood over ten feet high, its body chiseled with massive muscles. The goblins cheered.

Their god Gralanxth had blessed them with his presence. He had arrived to help them make the goblin race the most powerful force of Wrae Kronn.

Epilogue

The old man stood up, straightened his robe, and looked at the children as they absorbed the tale he had just told them. He knew they had many questions, but he smiled with his own excitement in not revealing all that they would soon want to know.

"It is time for you to return home. It is getting late," he said.

The sun had begun to dip below the forested trees around and the cool, early evening temperature had begun to chill their bones.

"When can we come back?" one of the girls asked.

"Soon. You will know when to return, but bring more children. Soon I will be teaching you more than just tales, but once we begin that phase, we cannot have others join us. Only now is the time. Find as many as you can, and return then," he said with a warm smile.

They stood up, told the old man goodbye, and began to run back down the hill. As they jumped from boulder to boulder, he called out to them one last time.

"I will have a great tale for you when you return! Our hero will begin to find out that he will need friends like you if he is to survive."

They waved back at the old man and continued on to their dismal homes in the impoverished village below.

Acknowledgements

To my wife and best friend, Crissy, who believed in me all the way as we partnered together raising our kids. I will love you everyday as the day I first saw you on our blind date.

To Rob Carr, a fellow soldier, who edited this manuscript and gave me amazing advice and insight.

To all of my beta readers for their help in the early years. There are so many of you, dating back to the days when I worked for Dreyer's in Union City.

To the JTOC crew for our camaraderie, during those long summer days, and to the many of us who had dreams in the creative arts.

To Tom Hunt who read through the original manuscript of over 200,000 words, and gave great advice.

To my son Mitchell who makes me proud every day.

To Loganpaul Eickhoff, James Tucker, Dave Benevidez and Chris Black for their fantasy fiction advice.

To Tom Hunt again and Tom Zerull for our inspiration into fantasy through our long nights and weekends playing AD&D.

To Evan Allen for his amazing map-making skills.

To David King for turning my visual of the cover into realization.

To David Hall for helping me realize that there is a big world of story through comics and baseball.

To my mom who taught me the love of reading and then writing. I miss you mom.

To Eve Hall who encouraged my creative writing to be perfect.

To Gary Stoppenbrink who shared my love with Science Fiction and Fantasy.

To my brothers Darrell McDaniel and Gary Stoppenbrink Jr. who shared this journey with me.

Thank you to all of you.

Thank you so much for reading one of our **Fantasy** novels.
If you enjoyed our book, please check out our recommended title for your next great read!

War of the Staffs by Steve Stephenson & K.M. Tedrick

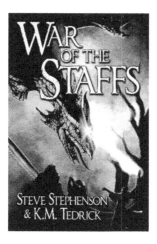

"Offers an enjoyable romp for high fantasy fans." –*KIRKUS REVIEWS*